Gatekeeper

John Beresford

ISBN: 9781091135451

For Nikki

Who dreamt of alternative futures.

CONTENTS

ACKNOWLEDGMENTS

I'm lucky to have had help crafting this work, so in time-honoured fashion, thanks are due.

To my friend and erstwhile colleague Mik Peach for the stunning cover. If you want to see more of Mik's work, head off to http://mikpeach.500px.com/composites.

To my (small) army of beta-readers: Natalie Beresford, Blythe Beresford, John Arnold, Chris Morrissey, Uzma Ali, and Graham Phythian. Each of them provided some feedback that changed the narrative in some way. From the 9,000-word critique to the handful of bullet points, from the smallest typographical slip to the suggestion that changed an entire character for the better, it was all good.

And in this edition – finally! – a proper map, courtesy of Tiffany Munro at https://feedthemultiverse.com/. Thanks Ti!

And, in the spirit of leaving the best 'til last, to Nikki, to whom this copy is dedicated. For never complaining when I shut myself away in the garret for hours on end, or ignore an attempt at conversation because I'm deep inside my head grappling with a plot element that is fighting back, or a particularly compelling descriptive phrase (not that there are many of those!) that just won't lie still.

My sincere and grateful thanks to all of the above, and to you, dear reader, for taking a chance on this story. May you be one of a multitude!

John Beresford
June, 2015

JOHN BERESFORD

Also by John Beresford:
The Berikatanyan Chronicles Series
Water Wizard
Juggler

Other Work
War of Nutrition
Well of Love
Valentine Wine.

Chapter 1

The air reeked of fear and death. Beyond the field arc, Mars hung low on the horizon, the ancient god of war fixing his single baleful red eye on the smaller conflict about to unfold below. Jann Argent's cellbike deposited him in the airena as an invisible crowd roared its support through hidden speakers, the noise rendered flat and metallic. From the opposite side of the airena a second bike entered, swerving to a stop and flinging Jann's adversary over the handlebars. The man completed a slow motion tumble to the dirt floor, reminding Jann to compensate for reduced gravity. No-one could live normally on the tiny moon of Phobos without gravometric compensators. In the airena they were dialled back to make the Tournament more "challenging".

Red dust settled around his opponent's feet. Jann recognised the scarred face of Torsten Vogler. The infamous German pharmacist, drug dealer, and creator of highly addictive infradone was on his third and final attempt at the Tournament. This bout would be tough enough, even before the added complication of half gravity.

Vogler began circling the airena. Jann compensated, keeping distance between them, his well-muscled frame poised to react to an attack move. Relying on his well-honed peripheral vision to warn him, he scoped out the weapons placed at random around the dome. Prison guards demonstrated some imagination in the choice of weaponry selected for each bout. They had a varied armoury from which to pick: antique swords or spears from a private collection; more modern pistols or rifles; or 21st century micro-crystal steel blades balanced for throwing or close combat. Recently the wardens had become even more inventive, adapting construction tools like nail guns and welders for use in the airena. Jann had even heard stories of wild animals being chained up under the dome, restricting available fighting space while increasing the Tournament's entertainment value. Such tales were likely apocryphal given the logistical difficulties of importing exotic species to a prison moon.

'Got your memory back yet Argent?' the German mocked.

There were, of course, no guilty criminals on Phobos. In common with prisons throughout the system it was filled with innocent men, most with an advantage over Jann Argent. They could remember *why* they were innocent, or enough about their real guilt to concoct a plausible story of betrayal, poor justice, or being framed.

Vogler plucked a titanium steel halberd from the sandy floor of the airena, examined it, and brandished the deadly blade in Jann's direction.

'Maybe I can give you something to remember me by!' he said, leaping across the gap between them.

Jann smiled.

'I'll never forget that ugly face,' he said.

Vogler had misjudged his jump in the reduced gravity. The livid scar on the man's cheek bulged as he realised his mistake. Twisting in mid-air he tried to swing the halberd at Jann's neck, but succeeded only in presenting the shaft of the weapon into his outstretched hands. Jann grasped the pole, pivoting into a crouch to increase the turning force the German had already instigated. Jann's manoeuvre pitched his adversary into a higher arc, arms and legs flailing for balance. He hit the dirt for a second time, bounced once and disappeared in another cloud of red dust.

Taking advantage of the camouflaging murk Jann circled, intending to surprise Vogler from the rear. The halberd's blade glinted in the pale sunlight, betraying his position. The German stepped from the red mist, a replacement weapon already in his hand and a determined set to his face.

'Too predictable Argent,' he growled, 'this bout is mine.'

A well-judged leap brought the scarred German within centimetres of Jann, landing feet first and throwing up a brume of dust. Jann blinked the grit from his eyes but Vogler twisted again, kicking low and sweeping Jann's feet out from under him. He landed hard on one shoulder, the German already on him, his short blade pressed against Jann's throat.

Jann held up both hands in a gesture of submission, instantly rendered redundant by the screaming whistle which blasted across the airena, drowning out the metallic cheering from the audience and announcing the end of the bout. The men stood, dusting themselves down and grinning, Vogler with triumph; Jann with relief.

'Well played you ugly kraut bastard,' Jann said.

'Two more rounds and I'm outta here,' Torsten replied. 'Better luck next time loony.'

'I hope so—it'll be my last try. Don't go getting yourself killed now.'

'No chance. Just be grateful it's only to the death in the final round. You'd already be toast.'

somewhere in ohio
9 Mar 2073

The crowd crammed the big top well beyond its fire limit. Once the ringmaster completed his announcement, they settled to an expectant hush. Many of them already seen the star performer—some more than once— but on this last night of the current run, anyone who could possibly find a ticket had parted with outrageous sums for one final chance to watch the mesmerising fire dance of the show's famous poi artiste.

Acolytes clad in flame red and orange costumes entered

the ring carrying two burnished copper fire buckets and a large bronze tray containing an array of torches, rings, and balls. With a flourish, the tallest assistant set light to the buckets. They whooshed into flame, the fire licking around the rims as if trying to climb out onto the sandy floor.

A tall woman in a hooded gold lurex cape stepped from the shadows, three spotlights tracking her movements. At her appearance the flames ceased their escape attempts, quietening to a more languid shimmer as the hush of the crowd solidified into absolute stillness. She shrugged off her cape, revealing a mane of flame-red hair gelled into spikes, and a well-muscled figure challenging a tight copper spandex costume studded with rubies and golden rhinestones. On her wrists a pair of matching gold bangles inset with topaz sparkled with reflections from the fire and the spotlights. A single audience member yelled a guttural encouragement, quickly shamed into silence by his neighbours in the rapt crowd. The woman strode towards the fire buckets, her glitter-covered legs scintillating in the flickering firelight.

She began her act with traditional fire-eater fare: juggling flaming torches with calm precision, spinning fiery hoops and batons, and swallowing live firebrands. As each new trick unfolded the stillness of the audience gave way to gasps and shrieks, although the performer never appeared to be in any danger from the fire. The flames did her bidding, her skill and mastery demanding total control.

After what seemed only moments, she reached the climax of her act, selecting two large poi balls from the bronze tray and dipping each into a bucket. They ignited with explosive roars, matched by expectant cheers from the crowd. She began to spin them, circling first vertically then crossing and lifting the ropes to helicopter two fiery rings above her head. With a short run she crossed the ring, bounced off a strategically placed trampette, and vaulted onto the back of a young mare which had been awaiting its rider. The mare's glossy chestnut coat shone with annular reflections of the spinning poi. Unfazed by the crackling fires, the animal waited for a gentle nudge from her mistress before setting off around the ring to more tumultuous cheers from the spectators. The cantering horse and the fire-wielding rider circled the ring, burning complex spiral patterns into the air and into the retinas of the adoring audience, now standing as one and thundering their applause as the star left through the curtains in a trail of smoke and sparks.

The woman dismounted in the yard outside the ring, where the ringmaster stood waiting for the cheering to die down before introducing the closing act.

'Nice job, Elaine,' he said. 'We're striking soon after midnight. Don't take too long in the shower.'

Amber flecks burned in Elaine Chandler's hazel eyes as she flashed the man an angry look.

'I know the goddamn schedule Miles,' she said, waving a dismissive hand in his direction. 'I'll take as long as I take.'

She strode to her trailer, still bristling from her exchange with her boss. Why were these people so fucking clueless? She threw open the door and ripped off her spandex bodysuit, careless of anyone who would see her full-figured nakedness before the door closed behind her.

'*Just let them try it on tonight,*' she thought, anger still bubbling close to the surface. '*I'll burn the fuckers!*'

Clouds of steam ballooned from her shower stall, but eventually Elaine allowed the jets to run cold. By the time she stepped out into her cramped living space her temper had boiled away. She towelled off, shivering against the cold, damp air, and dressed in a grey flannel jumpsuit. Her gaze flicked over the camper's walls, plastered with posters and flyers from her performances stretching back over the past four years. She stared at the image beside the rear window. It showed her first night, before which her life was a complete blur. She may as well have landed from Mars for all the memory she had of anything until joining

Miles Miller's Marvellous Manifestations. She had a natural ability with fire, a personality to match, and absolutely no clue who she really was. In less than two hours she would leave for another town, another week of shows, where she would smile and bow at the cheers and applause of her adoring fans and then return to this cold quiet space. A physical echo of the cold quiet space in her head where normal people kept their memories.

valley of the cataclysm
4th day of run'utamasa, 935

A thin wind eddied around broken fragments of rock that littered the valley floor. Like a memory of the powerful currents that had created the shards, it lifted small plumes of dust into the evening air where they danced and curled. Green shoots peeped from beneath the shale at intervals; hopeful reminders of the lush carpet which once covered the scene. The chill breeze gusted as a calloused foot stepped on one of the razor-sharp slivers, crushing the incipient shrub beside it and driving the point of rock into the soft skin between toes, drawing blood.

'Ach!'

The owner of the bloodied foot collapsed onto a boulder. He rubbed his toes and examined the damage, as much as was visible through the grimy lichen stains covering his feet. He pressed hard against the pain, checking that nothing remained in the wound, and sucked blood from his fingers.

The last golden thread of daylight winked out as the sun dropped below the western hill. The old man would soon have to give up his search for the day. It would be hours before either of the twin moons rose to provide enough light to search by, but with only a filthy threadbare shift to cover his bony frame, he could not remain outdoors after dark without risking hypothermia. He let out a tired grunt, slipped a dirty canvas bag back over his shoulder and took to his feet again, favouring the one recently injured.

He limped in the opposite direction from the setting sun, shuffling through the dusty shards as he went, his eyes focused on the ground in front of him. When at last hardly enough light remained for him to be able to see his feet, let alone whatever object he searched for, he stopped. With another soft grunt he bent to retrieve something at first indistinguishable from all the other detritus littering the valley floor. He wiped the booty on the frayed hem of his robe until it gleamed in the failing light. A small, sharp, irregular lump of brass. He nodded, opened up his sack and dropped the metal in.

The old hermit gazed out over the desolate valley, an almost imperceptible smile passing across his face. Another gust of wind, colder now and carrying the first drops of the malamajan, disturbed his sparse hair. With a shiver he turned back up the hillside.

mars correctional facility, phobos
12 Dec 2072

The clatter of spoons in thin aluminium bowls and a continuous throb of conversation filled the prison canteen. The air in here stank of corned beef and cabbage.

'You going to get out this time Argent?'

Brook Needham grinned. He had been Torsten Vogler's cellmate. The story of Jann's defeat in the quarters three months ago still, according to some, afforded the best chance to needle him. Vogler had made it through to the final, where Venter Milanovic had killed him in what many believed had been a grudge match. Venter's sons were both infradone addicts. He was serving life for the murder of their dealers. The opportunity to exact his revenge may have provided added incentive for the man to kill Vogler, but Jann knew he would have fared no better against the lifer. He was consequently grateful

7

for his defeat even if it meant months of piss-taking.

Jann held up a hand in front of his full mouth to indicate he could not reply to Needham's rhetorical question. Across the refectory table from Needham, Billy "Diamond Wheezer" Spears segued neatly into the older, but still far more popular topic for winding him up.

'Don't really matter, do it? He don't know where he'd end up if he did get out. Little lost boy.'

On the outside Billy was known as Diamond Geezer on account of his jewel-studded teeth. Since his arrival on Phobos one of them had been torn out to pay off a gambling debt, leaving him with an audible wheeze whenever he spoke.

Around the table, all the convicts laughed with exaggerated hilarity. Jann swallowed the last of his dinner, dropped his spoon into the bowl, and stood up.

'Gentlemen,' he said, regarding them each in turn before turning away from the table.

'Sure you can remember the way back to your cell, Argent?' Billy wheezed. The others laughed again.

'Get plennya practice loony,' Needham shouted after him, copying Torsten's epithet. 'You're gonna need it if you wanna make your last shot count.'

Jann needed no reminders that his up-coming Tournament entry was his last chance at freedom. Three strikes and you're out, that was the rule. Only on Phobos it should be three strikes and you're *in*. Permanently. Space was limited on the prison moon. The Tournament provided a rudimentary form of population control, but only in the Final. The winner got to go home. The loser went home too. In a box.

Back in his cell Jann snatched a besom from behind the door. He closed the door, checking the corridor outside through the grille out of habit. His bunkmate Jonno looked up in surprise from his dog-eared wank magazine.

'Short dinner. Food no good?'

'Food's the same as always. It's the company I didn't

like the taste of.'

Jonno slipped the magazine under his pillow and put his hands behind his head.

'Let me guess. Needham, Wheezer and their usual winnets, with all those tired old jibes about—'

'Tired jibes is all they've got. None of them have a single original thought.'

Jann rested the broom at head level between the two double bunks.

'Well you're not exactly renowned for your memory,' Jonno grinned.

'Don't you start.'

He began a series of fast chin-ups on the suspended broom handle. After the first twenty Jonno retrieved his reading material, flipping back to his page.

Three hundred chin-ups and forty-five minutes later Jann dropped from the broom, wiped his face on a sheet from the unoccupied lower bunk, and vaulted onto his own bed to catch a nap before his first shift as offender-side security detail. He knew the position would attract even more needle from certain quarters, but it was worth the hassle for the increased exercise time and snack allowances.

'Do you think it'll ever come back?'

Jonno's magazine slipped under his pillow once more.

'Give it a rest Jonno.'

'Genuine question, mate. I'm not taking the piss.'

Jann blew out a long breath.

'I dunno. I've been over and over it. There's not even a flash. Not a hint of anything before I was standing in that room.'

'With a body.'

'Of course with a body! For fuck's sake, what else am I doing here?'

'And no ID.'

'Is this supposed to help? Christ, you've heard it a hundred times. You know the story almost as well as I do, and it's *my* story!'

'Yeah, but right now it only has a middle. You can't remember how it begins, and no-one knows how it ends.'

'It ends with me banged up for murder. Of someone I never met—'

'Can't remember meeting.'

'—in a place I've never been—'

'Might never have been.'

Jann threw a pillow at Jonno's head.

'If you think making me angry will trigger a memory...'

'Sorry. Worth a try though, eh?'

'Tried it already. Tried and failed. I was mad for more or less the entire interrogation and trial. When I wasn't confused or...'

'Suicidal?'

Jann's face, already red from his exercise, turned a deeper shade.

'It was one solution,' he muttered.

'Your latest plan is only one degree better.'

'Are you saying I'm going to lose? In the Final?'

'Are you saying you won't?'

'I could say I'd be winning either way.'

'Assuming you make it to the Final.'

'I have to make it. I've started down this road now Jonno and it's the only road I have that leads out of this fucking shit hole.'

Chapter 2

Pera-Bul slipped below the horizon as the pilgrim emerged from the forest. The cold white light of the second much smaller moon, Kedu-Bul, now provided his only guidance across the boggy plain that stood between him and his destination. One last obstacle. In less than an hour Kedu-Bul too would set, plunging him into darkness and heralding the torrential malamajan, rendering an already treacherous journey almost impossible. The screech of a ghantu echoed from the dark woods as if urging him on. He hitched up his dirty loincloth, adjusted the threadbare sack hanging around his shoulders into a more comfortable position, and set off across the plain, mud oozing between his toes at each step.

The last meagre fingers of Pera-Bul's light glowed from behind the hills ahead of him, silhouetting his goal on the opposite edge of the plain: the tall castellated towers of the Court. The night was too dark, the Court too distant to tell whether the King's pennant flew, but the pilgrim did not need to see the traditional sign of occupation. There was no doubt the King awaited him. If he arrived late, it would mean his head.

*

In the large hall of the easternmost turret of the Court, the King paced around a heavy cauldron hanging from an enormous iron gimbals. Beneath the massive vessel a fire burned, the rhythmic flickering of its ruddy glow synchronised with the chants of a small group of robed figures who stood to one side, hands clasped and eyes closed.

A thin, hook-nosed man in a mustard-coloured shirt and bright lemon hose capered after the King, struggling to keep up as he circumnavigated the pot.

11

'Where is that cursed bell maker?' the King growled, his face as red as his tunic. 'And what is wrong with these mages? This fire should be white hot!'

He stopped pacing, fixing the chanters with an angry stare. Surprised by the King's sudden halt, his companion narrowly avoided colliding with him, rubbing the bump of his nose and adopting a strange lopsided grin to hide his embarrassment.

'I'm sure they will do better once the final maker arrives, sire,' said the grinning man, his voice as thin and reedy as his frame. 'We have almost all the pieces. At present the fire mages are conserving their powers until the last of the metal is added.'

The King snorted.

'Powers? I could surround the forge with candles to greater effect! I am no maker of bells, but even I can see this is nowhere near hot enough. The rim will crack at the first peal!'

A few of the fire mages shuffled their feet. One of them opened his eyes. The cadence of their chanting stuttered as an ember leapt from beneath the cauldron, barely missing the hem of the King's robe. It came to rest beside his foot, smoking.

'Your Majesty must allow the mages to concentrate.'

The shorter man's eyes bulged, his strange grin faltering.

'Their magic is weakened without their leader, and—'

'Are these all we could find?' the King asked, raising his voice and peering at the mages. 'I'm sure there were twice this number when... before...'

'All the Elements are suffering, Majesty, with no-one to lead them. Fire is maintaining better numbers than most, but these are only journeymen compared with the Witch's mastery of the flame. She left no heir, and as yet there is none to match her.'

The King turned an exasperated stare on the other.

'Will it be enough?' he asked, kicking the smouldering

ember back towards the blaze.

Before his advisor could reply a metallic clink diverted the King's attention, announcing the arrival of the last bell maker. The old man set down his sack on the granite floor and collapsed, panting, on a wooden bench inside the door. The King strode over to him, his courtier staying close behind.

'Do you have them? The last pieces?'

The bell maker rubbed his feet, his eyes glittering in his grime-covered face. He reached for his sack and opened it. The King peered in.

'Is that it? Is that all of it?'

The man nodded. Another bell maker picked up the sack, examining its contents while a third brought cheese, bread and a flagon of watered wine to refresh the exhausted artisan.

'Well?' urged the King. 'Can we finally make a start?'

The woman bowed without meeting the King's livid gaze, carried the sack over to the enormous vessel, and added the haul to the pile of metal fragments already beginning to melt from the heat of the furnace. The mages' chanting took on a more urgent rhythm to which the fire responded, glowing brighter and licking up the sides of the cauldron.

Outside the tower Kedu-Bul slipped unnoticed from the night sky as the first drops of rain began to fall. The fire raged, the brass melted, and the bell makers set to work.

somewhere in ohio
10 Mar 2073

A fire burned in a deep stone pit, just this side of white hot. Above it hung a vast iron bucket, its molten contents bubbling and steaming. She felt sweat start from her face in the extreme heat, running down her cheeks but evaporating before it could drip to the flinty granite floor.

Coruscating patterns drawn by the dancing flames bounced and jagged across the polished surface beneath her feet. The pulsating roar of the furnace almost drowned out the hushed threads of a song. It seemed familiar. Like a childhood nursery rhyme. She felt as though she should know the words, *would* know them if only she could make out the singing more clearly, but as she reached for the elusive memory another roar joined that of the flame—a thousand other voices cheering the fire on, their owners hidden in the blackness beyond the crucible.

She had to control it. The idea split her mind in half: part incredulous, mocking at the thought of controlling fire; part feeling it to be a natural desire, a thing easily accomplished with the right skill. The flames licked more fiercely at the lip of the container, threatening to overwhelm it. The noise from the unseen crowd took on a frightened edge as the molten mass surged and spat, belching up huge smoking gouts to splash against the rim, sending fiery sprites cascading out onto the floor where they sputtered and died. If she did not act soon the cauldron would surely be cleft apart. She cast around the room, searching for water, or earth, or anything she could bring to douse the fire. There was nothing. She turned to the window, thinking to find something outside she might use. Through the unglazed portal a huge animal watched her, the whites of its eyes glistening against the black night. She stepped back in horror before realising they were not eyes but two moons, riding low to the horizon in a starless indigo sky.

She moved around the cauldron, still searching for anything to put out the fire. On this side of the room the cheering voices became louder. The flinty floor had somehow become sand. Finally! Something she could use to extinguish the blaze. She scooped up two handfuls of the fine grit and turned back to the cauldron. It was too late! The vessel had already split in half! But where was the cascade of molten metal she had feared?

She dropped the sand in surprise. The furnace had gone. In its place two smaller bowls now hung from silver chains in front of her. The invisible crowd cheered again as she stepped toward the vessels. At her touch, their supports disappeared leaving her holding a flaming pot in each hand, suspended on their chains. She ran out into the darkness, still hoping to find a trough, or a river in which to douse the boiling pots.

A wall of cold night air slapped her. She sat up, without knowing she had been lying down. The chill of Elaine's trailer replaced the heat of her dream. Her breath steamed in the air, caught by a shaft of light between her thin curtains. She shivered, fighting to hold on to the memories that had seemed so familiar and real in the tableau but which had already begun to evaporate.

mars correctional facility, phobos
10 Mar 2073

The chiaroscuro of whirling bright lights dissipated, allowing Jann Argent's eyes to adapt to the relative gloom of his surroundings. He had no idea where he was. A room. Dilapidated. Faded. Old. The only illumination a strange blue glow filtering in through the worn blinds. He could make out shapes. A bed. A nightstand beside it. A bureau, with a bentwood chair. A door to another room. And one to a hallway, hanging open with its lock broken. A hostel room then? Or a small dwelling?

A peculiar smell hung in the air. Thick and sweet. Jann could not tell where it came from. He crept across the room, his eyes still not accustomed to the murk. On the other side of the bed, in front of an incongruous ornate marble fireplace, a body lay on the floor. A man, blood oozing from an open gash in his throat. A metre or so from the corpse a large knife had fallen onto the carpet, spattering the white stonework of the hearth as it fell. He knelt beside the body, felt briefly and hopelessly for a pulse, picked up the knife. He turned it over in the pale light washing from the window. The bloodstain on the blade looked black in the electric blue glare.

Three beams of incandescent white light tore through the room from the hallway. A voice barked out unrecognised words.

'Drop the weapon!'

Jann did not know what it meant. He stood up, squinting against the powerful lights.

'Drop the weapon and get on the floor! Now!'

He was bewildered. Where was this place? Why were they shouting at him? He opened his arms, trying to appear harmless.

'But... I...' he began.

'DOWN! NOW!' cried the voice. The three beams resolved themselves into silver tubes, carried by three men in dark red uniforms. Each man held what looked like a weapon in their other hand. A fourth man—the one doing all the shouting—also brandished one of the weapons, holding it with both hands and pointing it at Jann's chest. Jann dropped to the floor, letting the knife fall from his fingers.

The shouting man stepped up to Jann and jerked his hands together behind his back. 'You are obliged to answer any question put to you by a member of the MIF.' he barked. 'You have the right to a Protector. If you do not have access to a Protector one will be appointed for you. You must provide a DNA sample on request. These are the rights and obligations as determined by the Council of Mars. Do you understand?'

Jann had no idea what the man was talking about, but the last part had sounded like a question. He nodded.

'Do you understand? Answer the question!'

'I don't understand what you're saying,' he replied.

The man pulled him to his feet.

'Clear, sir!' he called. 'Sounds like he's some kind of foreign.'

A fifth man entered. In contrast to the other four, he wore a cream coloured suit. He carried no weapon, only an air of superiority and calm indifference. He checked around the small room, poked his head through the second door and walked over to the body.

'Do we know who this was?'

'Prefect Montague of District Seven,' replied the shouting man.

Cream Suit stared at Jann for several seconds before asking: 'Did you know this man? Prefect Montague?'

'I don't understand,' said Jann.

'Why did you kill him?'

'Who are you people? Where am I?'

'He was still holding the knife when we got here, sir!'

'I don't know how I got here,' Jann said. 'The man was already dead.'

'We're going to need an interpreter,' said Cream Suit. 'Anyone recognise his language?'

The others shrugged.

'The medical examiner will tell us when the Prefect died,' Cream Suit said, 'and he'll be able to tell us more about this guy too, I expect. Let's get him back to the station.'

Two of the men holstered their weapons and grabbed Jann's arms, pulling him to the door. The sudden movement woke him up. He was sweating. The dream again. With the advantage of his years of trial and imprisonment, during which he had begun to learn English, he could now understand what the men were saying in his nightmare. But he still could not work out how he had come to be standing in that room, on that day. His memory, before the swirling lights blinded him, was a complete blank.

It was working all right now though: today he would face his opponent in the Tournament Final.

*

His approach to the airena was at once familiar and

17

strange. Jann had ridden this corridor many times on a cellbike—the automated delivery vehicle used for every bout except the Final. For today, the contenders were granted the "privilege" of walking to the dome themselves. He smiled. He had walked a long road to arrive at this point, but in reality only a few dozen metres separated him from the door to his future. One way or another.

Jann paused at the entrance, surveying the scene. On the other side of the dome his opponent adopted the same cautious approach. Jann could not make out his features at this distance but he already knew it was Looper Feldsen. Feldsen's selection for the Tournament had caused some bad publicity for the prison governor. When your number came up you could choose whether or not to compete, but there was no way to exclude inmates from the draw. Looper threw the whole idea of fighting for freedom into the melting pot. No-one wanted to contemplate letting a man as handy with a garrotte as Looper loose on society again, and yet here he was.

Jann looked up. The light filtering through the field arc appeared brighter this time. Mars had circled nearer the sun. When he first arrived here almost eight years ago, Jann had read up on his new "home", discovering Mars' orbit is the second most eccentric in the solar system. With its axial tilt the planet also has a semblance of seasons. On Phobos the only noticeable difference was the increase in the sun's power.

He examined the bowl of the airena, making mental note of the positions of the usual pikes, blades and ropes as he stepped through the door onto the sandy floor. A low growl from his right drew his attention. His excellent peripheral vision had on this occasion failed him. An adult tiger, its collar fastened to a length of rusty chain, bared its teeth at him.

He took an inadvertent step back, a thrill of fear mixed with excitement tingling along his spine. The big cat pawed at the sand. It had seen Jann as soon as he moved into the airlock at the airena entrance. Now it lunged for him, straining against the chain which was shackled to a stanchion bolted to the airena wall. So the rumours had been true! Tournament organisers had saved their special treat for the Final. Unable to reach him, the tiger roared its frustration at Jann. To one side of the beast a glint of sunlight on metal caught his eye. Something half buried in the sand. It looked like a welding torch, but he could not be certain. He added it to his mental catalogue.

The hidden speakers burst into roars of approval at his entrance. At this moment the audience comprised only those watching from the penal colony. Although the Tournament was broadcast live to untold billions on Earth, enjoying stellar ratings, it would be another ten minutes or so before the Earth-side spectators saw Jann set foot in the airena. A second swell of cheers echoed across the sands in recognition of his opponent's arrival. A movement caught Jann's eye. Before he could react Looper crashed into him, sending him sprawling in the dust. His opponent ran on, a weapon in his sights. The starting siren sounded belatedly. Jann shook his head, but there was no time to bemoan the murderer's flouting of the rules. Looper had already found a spear and launched it in his direction. Jann dodged easily, the spear burying itself in the sand a metre or so behind him, but then narrowly missed having his cheek sliced off by a flying scimitar. It was clear Looper was trying to wrong-foot him with a continuous onslaught, hoping to force an opening for an early kill. He had struck lucky, finding two weapons in close proximity, and was already running for a third—a rapier. Offence would be Jann's best defence against such an attack. He retrieved the spear, sighted along it and threw it, grunting with the effort. His timing was off. The shaft sailed high over his opponent as the short, powerful man bent to retrieve the rapier. Jann could not risk facing Looper unarmed. He ran toward the airena wall, putting some distance between them while searching for anything close to hand. Looper was strong but not very fit. He needed that quick finish. If Jann could stay ahead of him and tire him out, even a little? Any slight advantage was better than none. Twenty metres away Jann spotted the handle of a throwing knife visible above the sand. Circling to avoid being trapped with Looper between him and the only nearby blade, he seized the knife, rolled, turned, and threw in one fluid movement.

'Ach! Bastard!' yelled Looper as the well sharpened steel buried itself in his thigh. He stumbled, the rapier falling from his grip. Seeking to press his advantage, Jann ran across the dirt between them, hoping to seize the sword, but Looper pulled the knife from his leg and threw it back. Having to swerve the flying weapon slowed Jann down. Both men fell on the rapier together, snapping the blade from its hilt. Looper twisted underneath Jann, flipping him over. With a chill, Jann saw his adversary had one hand on a garrotte he had concealed in his pocket. Although illegal to bring weapons into the dome, once again Feldsen had flouted the rules in favour of an easier win. Kill first, answer questions later.

In a split second his opponent wound the thin steel cord around Jann's neck, twisting it hard. The wire dug in, constricting Jann's breathing, but did not bite into his flesh. With Looper's track record in mind, Jann had come prepared. The deadly hawser tightened over a thick towel Jann had wrapped around his neck beneath his tunic before leaving his cell.

Knowing his rudimentary armour would not protect him for long, Jann summoned his strength for one swift, hard jab of his elbow into his opponent's ribs. Looper let out an agonised grunt. In the same instant Jann twisted from under him, levered himself up with his leading arm, and took off across the airena, checking behind to see whether the winded Looper would follow.

Momentarily disorientated, Jann was startled by a deafening roar. He skidded to a halt, narrowly avoiding a collision with the tiger but kicking sand into its face. The maddened beast lashed out, savage claws slicing three evenly spaced cuts into Jann's shirt. Three lines of blood welled through the shredded material. Stabbing pain throbbed from the wounds.

'Argh!' he cried, falling to the sand. Almost fainting from the burning in his chest he rolled out of the tiger's reach as it strained and jinked against its chain.

He fought down the pain. He had no weapon, but neither did his opponent. Looper was still searching for a replacement for the ruined rapier. Jann spotted the welder. It was close by, on the other side of the tiger. Jann ripped off his shirt, mopped his chest, and waved the bloodied cloth in front of the tiger's face.

'What's this?' he whispered, throwing his shirt behind the animal. While the tiger investigated the enticing smell given off by the bundle, Jann ran around to the welder, pulled it free from the sand, and thumbed the "on" switch. His meticulous preparation had paid off. His cellmate Jonno, a construction engineer before his conviction, had given Jann chapter and verse on many of the power tools he could expect to find in the airena. The welder's simple control interface glowed into life. Sitting in the sun since the dome had been prepared, it had amassed a small charge. The tool was useless as a weapon from this distance but Jann had another idea. He guessed the power level was enough for a single pulse at full burn. With luck it would be incandescent, if only for a fraction of a second.

He checked Looper again. The man limped in the direction of a hunting knife, looking the other way. With the tiger still snuffling at his bloodied shirt Jann crept to the wall. He dialled the welder to maximum and fired it against the rustiest link of the chain, melting it almost instantly. The chain fell to the sand with a dull clink.

Feeling its tether slacken the tiger rounded on Jann, a low growl rumbling deep in its throat. Jann pivoted, throwing the discharged tool in the direction of his opponent.

'Go on!' he urged.

The silver device flew gracefully under the reduced gravity, glittering in the sun. It hit the ground in a plume of red dust.

Whether attracted by the shining tool, the stronger smell of blood from the wound on Looper's thigh, or the vulnerability telegraphed by his opponent's limp, Jann would never know, but with an enormous bound the animal leapt after Looper, covering the distance between them in seconds. With another ferocious roar, the tiger brought Looper down before ripping out his throat with deadly efficiency.

Even though the beast remained absorbed with his grisly meal Jann was relieved when an armoured prison officer arrived on a cellbike to offer him a ride out of the dome. As he mounted the bike behind the guard, the speakers erupted with tumultuous applause.

new york
15 Feb 2073

Early evening sun glanced in through the gleaming window of a crowded Lower East Side bar, its reddening glow finding an echo in the pitcher of Breckenridge Ophelia that dripped rivulets of condensation onto the table between Patrick Glass and two of his colleagues.

Patrick's hands shook. This would have made scanning the letter difficult had he not already read it fifteen times. He could recite it from memory, but somehow seeing it on paper, holding it, made it simultaneously more real and more unbelievable. He took a swig from his ice cold Breckenridge, cleared his throat, and continued reading.

"While the company recognises the valuable work you have produced over the past few years, your recent presentations to our most prestigious clients have indicated a profound variance between the expectations of both the company and its clients, and the creative

direction you clearly wish to take with your designs. Regrettably this does not align with the senior management team's ambitions for the company in the foreseeable future and for reasons of these creative differences we feel it would be inappropriate to offer you partnership at this time. Furthermore we would respectfully request and urge you to keep more closely to the given brief in any future undertakings. If this is not acceptable to you, for creative or other reasons, then it may be better to consider whether your future would be more profitably pursued outside the company."

He took another sip of beer, setting the glass down and drawing an intricate pattern of interlocking circles in the cold mist on its sides with careful strokes of his index finger.

'"Not align with their ambitions"?' he said, waving the letter in the faces of the two men opposite. 'Where the fuck have they been heading for the last six years? Only in the direction I've given them. Christ there wouldn't even be a business if it wasn't for me.'

'Sucks, Pat. Really sucks,' said the man seated to Patrick's left, chugging from a bottle of Coors.

'Didn't you bag them the Boeing contract?' asked the other, nursing a pint of Crispin Original Cider.

The bar was filling fast with office workers, some taking a swift "relaxer" before the commute home, others for whom a cosy corner of the room or a comfortable stool surrounded by convivial fellow drinkers provided a more homely resting place than their living quarters. This latter group, to which Patrick Glass belonged, would be here for the long haul. He reached for the pitcher, topped up his drink, and watched the bubbles rise into the foam.

'Boeing,' he nodded. 'Microsoft, Procter & Gamble, Oracle Corporation, FrakkerJakk, SpaceX. I've lost count of the number of balls I've kept in the air for those bastards. Name a significant company we've done business with over the last six years. I either won it, or led the creative team. Sometimes both. Last year I was the only one winning anything.'

'So, what? Do they think you're burned out or something?' Coors asked.

'Nah,' said Crispin. 'They know you're still the shiz. When was your last win? A month ago? Six weeks?'

'About six weeks, yeah,' agreed Patrick still watching the bubbles in his glass, his head cocked to one side. He dropped the letter back on the table and locked his fingers together in front of him.

Through his beer a distorted refraction of the bar's only TV displayed what appeared to be an enormous metal dolphin floating beside a tall concrete tower. A news bulletin broadcast progress on the assembly of a Prism ship to replace the doomed Endurance which had exploded some years earlier.

'Exactly,' Crispin continued, his gaze flicking between Patrick and the bulletin. 'All this "creative differences" is just a crock of horse shit.'

'So what's your theory if it ain't burnout or lack of creative credibility?' asked Corrs. 'Cos this ain't the first time our buddy here has been passed over, you know?'

'No?'

Patrick sighed, running both hands through his thinning steel-grey hair and rubbing his brows with the heels of his thumbs.

'No. More like the third, or is it fourth? Story of my life. People say life's a balancing act but mine's all roundabout and no swing. Beginning to feel like the whole thing ain't worth it.'

'What? You gonna move on?' asked Crispin.

'Move on, move out, ship out, I dunno. But I've got to do something. I'm not sticking around juggling problems for this bunch of clowns for another six years, making them millions while I sweat it out until one or two a.m. to come up with yet more examples of design genius that are "in the wrong creative direction". If they think they're headed up shit creek then let's see how well they do without my paddle!'

mars correctional facility, phobos
10 Mar 2073

The call to attend a meeting in the prison governor's office had not been long in coming. Whether to avoid any possibility of retribution from Looper Feldsen's cronies— even a psychopathic murderer collects a few friends during a life sentence—or simply because the procedure for dealing with Tournament winners was well practised, Jann Argent did not care. In a little while he would be free. Off this rock for good. He could say goodbye to the artificial gravity, the grey dinners, and the even greyer inmates. He would not miss any of it. He barely had time to shower after the cellbike left him at the gate to his cell block before one of the guards said the governor would see him immediately.

So the sun was still up, shining pale through the polarised glass when he took a seat in the governor's anteroom and waited for the assistant—a privileged inmate by the name of Tench—to inform the governor of his arrival. The governor's suite provided a stunning view over the prison complex. The electric blue dome of the airena swelled upward below the window, an almost perfect mirror of the red crescent of Mars hanging in the sky above. Jann had not seen it so clearly in all his time on the prison moon. Tench's hand on his arm interrupted his appreciation of the scene. Jann stepped into the inner sanctum.

'Argent. Congratulations. A most inventive victory.'

'Thank you sir.'

'Come in, don't be shy. Take a seat.'

Jann sat in the only vacant chair. Two metres of matt finish mahogany separated him from the governor.

'Have you heard of Perse?'

Jann frowned, trying to place the name and wondering why they were discussing other inmates.

'Ng? You mean Percy Ng?' he ventured.

The governor threw a brochure onto the table between them, its cover depicting an artist's impression of a rural idyll that could have been anywhere on Earth except for the sky. It had two moons.

'No, Perse. With an "S".'

"*New challenges in the first off-world colony*" ran the strap line on the glossy cover as the magazine slid to a halt on the tabletop, facing Jann. "*Be who you always wanted to be!*" added a splash bubble.

'Never heard of it, sir.'

Jann made no move to pick up the brochure.

'I'm sure you'll appreciate that we can't simply have convicts wandering around in society,' the governor continued. 'I mean, it might be alright if we were talking about a forger, or an embezzler, or someone who we could say was too old to be a danger.'

Jann had already made more than four from the two sets of two he was being shown.

'What are you saying, governor?' he asked. 'That there's no release after all? That winning the Tournament just gets me a better class of prison?'

'Oh Perse isn't a prison!' the governor exclaimed, smiling. The man's smile stopped at his mouth. The rest of his face remained grim. Closed. As unfathomable as Jann's own unreachable memories.

'No, not at all! It's a new start. A fresh challenge.'

'Somewhere to put me out of the way.'

'We prefer to call it a mutually beneficial solution. We lose an inmate, with the positive publicity and the increase in morale that goes along with seeing someone win the Tournament and leave the prison moon. You get—'

'Out. I get out. But I don't get to go home.'

'Well in your case Argent, it's a moot point isn't it? Since you claim to have no idea where home is.'

'How long do I have to stay there? On Perse.'

The governor leant forward in his chair, pushing the magazine closer to Jann.

'You'll find everything you need to know in—'

'How long?'

'It's... a one-way trip.' the governor admitted, avoiding Jann's gaze. He held up a hand to forestall Jann's protest. 'You're all in the same boat—or should I say on the same Prism ship—you and the other pioneers. Perse is a long way from Earth, but it's the closest we've found to an Earthlike planet and it's not as if you'll have to break new ground. Two ships are already in transit. They'll arrive several years before yours.'

'Will they—?'

'No-one will know you're an ex-con,' the governor reassured him. 'We've set you up with all the necessary paperwork. Ten percent of the colonists are sourced through a public lottery. Your number came up.'

Jann frowned at a sudden off-the-wall thought.

'You'd have sent Feldsen out there if he'd won? A goddamn psycho flying out to the stars? Not exactly the fresh start most of them would've been expecting!'

The governor pursed his lips.

'Well there is research that suggests psychopaths thrive in frontier conditions. But I believe in Feldsen's case we may have had to find an... alternative... solution. Anyway that point too is moot Argent, since you are our winner. Congratulations again! Tench has all your paperwork ready. You leave right away.'

Chapter 3

Feeble yellow light crept through a reinforced glass cover, past the bodies of countless long-dead flies. Claire Yamani shuddered as she walked underneath it. In front of her, a dingy corridor dissolved into gloom. There was barely enough illumination to make out the numbers on the apartment doors. If the hallway had more than one light fitting the bulbs must be as dead as the flies. Her mother set down a basket of emergency provisions while she fumbled in her pocket to check the key fob for the fifth time, breath steaming in the chill air.

'It's one-oh-four Mum,' Claire said.

Claire's mum had been suffering severe short-term memory problems. A side effect of sleep deprivation.

The cold, shabby hallway didn't worry Claire. The apartment itself would be better. She'd seen plenty of places that looked bad from the outside. With a bit of love and attention on the inside, any of them could be transformed into little palaces. Good example? Their old place. From the street it pretended to be run down, even for the area. Where they lived hadn't been a slum, but it wasn't overly affluent either. Even with his important job in the city her father couldn't have afforded that. Not in Toronto. And now...

Her mind veered away from the memory.

So even though they had to move "slightly downmarket" as her mother put it, to something not much better than social housing, they could still put up their drapes, arrange their throws and scatter their cushions to make the place almost as rich and opulent as a Bedouin tent. Like a smaller copy of home.

'It must be the next one,' her mother said, peering at the number on the nearest door.

She picked up her basket and walked on, the wheels of her suitcase clicking across the tiled floor. Claire followed.

The door to their new apartment swung open with a high pitched squeak. Claire stepped back, wrinkling her nose in disgust at the smell.

'Ugh!' she said, her heart sinking.

The mix of old grease, wet dog, and shit made her gag. It would take more than a few cushions to make this place feel like home. She walked behind her mother into the living area. An ancient smartscreen with a crack on one edge had been bolted to the wall opposite a worn, coffee-stained sofa. Under the small window a plastic garden table with four chairs served as a dining suite. Through a door to the right of the screen, the kitchen owned up to being the main source of the appalling stench, its crazed tiles thickly spattered with splashes of brown and yellow grease.

Her mother set down her basket on the table.

'Why don't you take your case to your room and unpack?'

She offered Claire a weak smile.

'I'll see if I can clean this mess up a bit.'

Opposite the kitchen a short corridor led off the living room. Claire tried the switch but these bulbs were blown too. She opened doors to admit more light as she walked: bathroom; toilet (ugh! *That* door could stay closed for now); bedroom; another bedroom. This second bedroom proved larger than the first, so Claire backtracked to the smaller room, set her suitcase on the bed, and stared at the blank walls. Maybe she could put up some posters to hide the worst of the cracks. Clean the window. She reached into the outside pocket of her case and retrieved a wind chime, the only one of her collection she'd managed to keep. She opened the window to let in some air, hanging the chime on the catch where it could respond to any breeze.

The bed, a simple steel framed single with a thin mattress, reminded her of old movies she used to watch with her Dad. Ones where the hero had been wrongfully imprisoned. He'd spend most of his time lying on just such a bed, chewing on a toothpick or smoking a roll-up. She sat down beside her suitcase, bouncing on the mattress to test it for comfort. Needed some decent bedding to pad it out a bit. It wouldn't be so bad. Not *so* bad. She had to make the most of it anyway. Bad or not, this was her life now. Her Mum would need help acclimatising to it.

Claire returned to the living room, expecting to find Mum already busy cleaning the place up to her standards. Instead the older woman sat on the threadbare sofa, her head in her hands, rocking. Claire put a hand on her mother's shoulder.

'Mum?'

'Why did he have to go and get himself killed?' her mother shouted through her tears. 'Stupid, stupid man!'

'Let me make you a coffee?' Claire suggested, pulling a jar out of the basket.

'I need something a bit stronger than coffee!'

'We don't have anything.'

'Of course we don't have anything! We can't *afford* anything! I'll probably never have another glass of Chablis as long as I live!'

She broke down in sobs again.

'So, will a coffee do for now?' Claire asked, trying to change the subject.

Her mother coughed a teary laugh. She smiled up at Claire, wiping her face on the back of her hand.

'I suppose so. We don't have any milk.'

'I'll get some. I saw a shop in the square.'

Claire waited on the landing listening to the click and whine of the elevator machinery, but although she could hear voices, and the occasional metallic banging from below, the lift showed no sign of ever reaching their floor. She decided the stairs would be quicker. Three youths hung out on the first half-landing, each holding a can of strong lager. As she rounded the corner they spread out across the staircase, blocking her descent. A cracked plastic inhaler sat on the tiled windowsill, loaded with an infradone cartridge. Claire recognised the distinctive logo from a public information film. Two spent cartridges had been discarded on the landing floor.

'New girl,' said one, staring at Claire through blown pupils.

'Watcha got for me, blondie?' asked the second, leering.

'Pay no attention to these low-lives, baby,' said the third. 'They have no idea how to treat a lady. What's your name sugar?'

'Claire. Claire Yamani.'

They all laughed, a forced unnatural sound containing no mirth.

'Yamani!' said One.

'Show us Yamani,' said Two.

Claire smiled nervously, tried to squeeze past the nearest of them.

'Yo, he means it,' said Three reaching into his pocket. 'Come on. Show. Us. Ya. Mani.'

palace of kertonia
1st day of run'bakamasa, 935

The sound of a conductor's baton tapping on a gold filigree music stand bounced around the throne room. No ornate drapes hung at the windows, no rich tapestries decorated the walls. The room's cold austerity offered nothing to stop the sound being reflected and amplified by the black marble floor, pillars, and vaulted ceiling until it resounded like the march of a hundred peg-legged soldiers. As the echoes died, a matching hush crept over a small choir. Their attention focused on the holder of the baton: a strange figure with piercing dark blue eyes regarding them from deep sockets set in a waxen face, surmounted by an unruly shock of dyed purple hair, its grey roots beginning to show at the crown.

31

The conductor gave a curt nod to a string quartet who sat in an alcove to one side of the hall. They played a short introduction before he raised his baton to signal a section of the choir to begin. The group sang in three-part harmony, a light and airy ditty which soon banished the gloomy pall that had hung over the singers only moments before. They exchanged smiles with the players as they warmed to their music, which swelled to fill the arches, booming around the black columns as if seeking to drive out the last remnants of cheerlessness from the dismal surroundings.

At the Northern end of the room a carved black marble throne rose from the floor, the rock itself appearing to have flowed upwards in obeisance to offer a resting place for someone of ultimate power and dominion. Beside the throne a large bird with sable-dark plumage and piercing cobalt blue eyes, perched on an onyx stand. A silver chain tethered one leg.

Seated on her throne, the Queen wore an expression as dark as the stone. After only a few more bars she jumped to her feet, her night-black dress cascading around her ankles giving her the appearance of floating above the ground.

'Stop!'

The choir choked to a halt. The purple-haired conductor faced the Queen, his right shoulder twitching into a one-sided shrug.

'Majesty?'

'What is this?'

'It is the recital for the memorial—'

'We know why we are here! We are asking if you are expecting us to say the blessing over this child's ditty?'

'I... er... that is...' stuttered the conductor.

'To hold the power of the ceremony,' the Queen went on, 'the music itself must be an anthem of power! Surely I do not have to explain this to you, of all people?'

'No, Majesty, of course not, but as you know we do not

have access to the original—'

'The lullabies? We would not dare to use them again in any case!' the Queen snapped. 'The power of those refrains is far too great a risk. This is a memorial service only, not a repeat of the Car'alam. For pity's sake we thought we could trust you with this. Must we take care of every little detail ourselves?'

'No, Majesty. Not at all. Forgive me but, if it please your Majesty I thought simply that, as the original ceremony used lullabies then it would be in keeping to carry forward the child-like theme. This nursery rhyme—'

'Is far too jolly!' the Queen interrupted, flicking her long black hair and straightening her back in a futile attempt to stand taller than the musician. 'This is a sombre occasion. We are honouring lost souls, absent friends. We must be reverential, not convivial!'

She retook her throne, sitting erect with shoulders back, her hands curled over the ornate carved arms. Facing the choir she tossed her long black hair off her pale face once again before closing her eyes and taking a long, deep breath. In a sonorous, powerful voice, the Queen began to intone a solemn chant, its notes resonating with the glossy stonework of the hall, its dark meaning matching the blackness of the marble. As the Queen warmed to her song the choir took an involuntary step back, clustering together. The conductor coughed. The Queen stopped. She opened her eyes, appearing momentarily disoriented.

'With respect, Majesty,' the conductor began.

The Queen raised an eyebrow, but said nothing. The conductor cleared his throat again.

'With respect, that is more usually recognised as a funeral march.'

The Queen regarded him without speaking until he could no longer hold her gaze.

'And do you not believe,' she replied at length, 'those we lost *deserve* a funeral?'

cape canaveral, florida
27 Apr 2073

Outside the massive Armstrong spaceport, an award winning design by the 21st century's most prestigious public works architect, the Valiant hovered at anchor. Its gravnull field shimmered electric blue in the early morning sun. In the distance, surrounded by a complicated gantry that reminded Jann Argent of a pile of jack straws, a second Prism ship could be seen under construction. Cerulean sky peeked through the three dimensional jigsaw of its partially completed hull.

With a barely audible click Jann's remote controlled wrist tag fell open. He handed it covertly to one of his escorts.

'Don't get no funny ideas about hoofin' it, Argent,' said the other. 'Ain't no way out of this compound that we're not guardin'.'

Jann gave the man a look but refrained from making a smart reply. The first guard pocketed Jann's tag before handing over a small backpack.

'Good luck to you Argent,' he said. 'Wouldn't fancy it myself, but I hopes you goes on alright.'

'Thanks,' Jann replied.

He looked at the bag, hesitating.

'Don't worry, it's all there,' said the second guard. 'More'n our job's worth to go stealing your trinkets. Prob'ly not real gold anyways.'

Jann shouldered the pack, turned on his heel and headed off towards the nearest entrance, where two armed military police checked his credentials.

'Lottery?' one asked.

Jann nodded.

'Check your luggage at desk "L".'

Inside the impressive departure hall several hundred people waited to be processed before joining the Valiant's passenger complement, the queues managed by the ever-present goons. The brochure Jann had first seen on the prison governor's desk, which he had read from cover to cover a dozen times on the journey from Phobos, was short on detail of the colonisation program and long on marketing. All it really told him was that, of the Earth-like worlds so far discovered, Perse was the best prospect for mankind's fledgling attempt at life off planet.

A smartscreen mounted close to the entrance confirmed the guard's instruction for lottery winners to check in at desk L. He joined the long queue, which moved at a good pace. There were several manned workstations under the "L" sign. Keeping one eye open for the next available agent, he scanned the departure hall more carefully. Passengers who had already completed check-in congregated around the perimeter of the hall, apparently grouped by family, friendship, ethnicity, or similar taste in clothing. A constant train of maglev floats carried stacks of aluminium flight cases across the concourse in the direction of the Valiant; a reminder that this was still more of a military base than a passenger terminal.

Along the middle of the hall a row of substantial steel pillars held up the roof of the building, many of them fitted with smartscreens. Fingers of sunlight and reflections from the mirrored sheen of the Valiant's gravnull field filtered in through enormous smoked windows. Beside the nearest pillar, illuminated from two sides by the unusual light, a raggle-taggle bunch of travellers had assembled. A woman and an older man sat on a low bench while a girl and a tall, middle-aged man stood nearby reading the smartscreen. Unlike the other groups Jann had seen, they did not appear to have anything in common. They were not engaged in conversation, hardly even looked at each other, yet they gave the impression of belonging together. The girl, a plain, willowy youngster with long ash-blonde hair who appeared to be about fourteen years old, noticed him staring at the group. She smiled and waved. He smiled back and returned her wave, embarrassed to have been caught watching them.

When he had completed the brief check-in process, Jann walked over to the group.

'Hi, I'm Jann Argent. Is this where we wait?'

The girl offered him her hand. A surprisingly grown-up gesture for one so young.

'Claire Yamani. This is my mother Nyna. I don't think it matters where we wait, but you're welcome to join us.'

Jann smiled at the girl's precociousness. The middle-aged man reflected his ironic expression, also offering his hand.

'Patrick Glass. I'm another of Claire's recruits. We're a small but select bunch.'

'Lucky bunch too,' Claire added. 'We're all Lottery winners.'

She fixed Jann with a stare, her eyes as clear blue as the sky shining through the patchwork hull outside the departure hall.

'How about you?'

Jann hesitated, reluctant to start the first of his new friendships on a lie but realising he had little choice.

'Yep,' he replied, not meeting Claire's gaze. 'My number came up sure enough.'

court of istania
1st day of run'bakamasa, 935

The setting sun painted the sandstone walls of the Court a deep, warm red. They glinted as if in competition with the polished red marble of the Court's interior, dimly visible inside the great wooden doors through which the King marched. His long, flame-red hair flew out behind him in a physical echo of the velvet drapes fluttering at the open windows. As he passed each casement his flying locks caught the dying rays of sunlight and flashed to match his temper.

'Is it done?' he demanded. 'Hmm?'

In the courtyard a temporary gantry had been erected to hold the great bells, now recast from the shards recovered from the valley two full days' ride to the south-east. A small group of bell makers waited on one side of the framework. Their leader stood talking with a short, thin man in a citrine-coloured tunic and hose, a chequered tricorn hat pulled onto his head at a jaunty angle. The King's sudden appearance cut short their conversation.

The Jester pirouetted across the courtyard, bowing low before the King.

'We have just this moment finished sire,' he said, with a wide grin.

'This is not the time for cutting capers man!' exclaimed the King. 'Let's hear them!'

'Of course, Majesty. Immediately.'

He gestured to the chief bell maker, who hefted a long, leather-headed mallet and shuffled over to the bells, avoiding the King's eye. Weighing the unwieldy mallet, he struck the nearest bell. It rang with a pure note. The clarity of the sound did nothing to ease the tension in the bell maker's face as he turned to the middle bell. It too rang out, a little higher than the first. The man hesitated, at last catching the eye of the King who flicked his fingers to indicate he should continue.

At the third tone, which should have been lower than either of the others, the reason for the bell maker's discomfiture became apparent. Its flat, discordant sound caused the King's hands to fly to his ears. He let out a strangled cry of rage.

'What innominate sound is this that assails my ears? The work of incompetent fools?'

The bell maker prostrated himself on the stone flagged floor of the courtyard.

'A thousand pardons, sire. The feebleness of the furnace proved insufficient for a proper casting. This is the best we could do.'

The King's horrified expression gave way to a look of resigned indignation. At length, his shoulders drooped.

'There is neither time nor wherewithal to repeat the casting,' he sighed. 'It will have to do, though it will indeed be a poor tribute to those lost. Is the transport ready?'

'It is sire,' the Jester replied stepping forward and grinning once more. 'It but awaits your command.'

The King strode back through the heavy wooden doors, muttering 'yes, yes, we have no time to waste.'

The nearest bell maker helped his leader up off the stone floor. The group made ready to transfer the bells to a waiting cart. A squall sprang up, sucking red velvet drapes out from the still open door of the Court and setting the bells rocking on the makeshift gantry. The rig, only ever intended to serve as a temporary hanging for the bells, was not engineered to withstand any shearing forces. Before the bell makers could react the swinging bells had set up a simple harmonic vibration throughout the rough structure. Its joints creaked and moaned.

'Quickly!' the Jester shouted to the makers, 'we must secure the bells!'

'It's too late!' cried one, jumping aside to avoid the largest bell which came crashing down as the gantry gave way, hitting the stone flags with a loud 'bong!' A fist-sized chip of brass flew from the lip of the bell, slicing open the cheek of the bell maker. Moments later the middle bell fell onto the first with a clang, rolled for a short distance, and came to rest against the rear wheels of the waiting cart. Dust from the courtyard blew onto the bell, delineating a large crack running from shoulder to lip. The only undamaged bell—the one which had rung flat—hung drunkenly from the splintered gantry, still swaying in the wind.

cape canaveral, florida
27 Apr 2073

The sing-song chime of a public announcement echoed around the departure hall. A hush fell over the crowds as people stopped what they were doing to listen.

'Promotional videos will shortly be running in several small theatres across the spaceport. Any colonists wishing to learn more about the colonisation program, the forthcoming journey, or what to expect on arrival at Perse, please follow the directions on the display screens to your nearest theatre location.'

Grateful for the opportunity to fill in the considerable blanks left by his single source of information on his impending new life, Jann was surprised to discover most of the others in his motley group were also keen to tag along.

The older man, who had not spoken since introducing himself as Terry Spate, remained similarly reticent on the subject of the film. Jann suspected an interesting story lurked behind the man's gentle gaze, if he could ever prise it from him. Patrick agreed to come along purely to avoid breaking the group up.

'I don't suppose I'll learn anything new,' he said, 'but the seats might be a bit more comfortable than this bench. Anyway I've only just met you guys. If I take off now we may not find each other again until we're on Perse.'

The words "on Perse" sent an unexpected thrill along Jann's spine.

'We never really expected to win the Lottery,' Claire said, 'so we didn't bother finding out much about the program. The chance to get away from where we were...'

She let the sentence hang as they took their seats. The lecture theatre was quite small and had filled quickly. As soon as the doors closed, the screen in front of them lit up with the opening titles of the video. With a backdrop of images from the James Webb Space Telescope and footage from the departure of the first two Prism ships, a well-known Network News presenter described the program from the initial discovery of Perse to the tragic accident that had befallen the doomed Endurance.

'Perse is an Earth-like planet ninety-seven light years distant. It's not the first habitable planet to be discovered but is favoured over closer candidates since it's likely to have a more temperate climate and has a relatively stable tectonic structure. It was dubbed "Perse" because its star appears in the constellation Perseus. Due to the length of the journey, colonisation is being treated as a one-off, one-way affair. On arrival there will be no way of returning messages, information, or passengers to Earth. The original colonisation program included four ships to be launched at six month intervals. The first two of these—Endeavour and Intrepid—departed for the new world nine years ago. The tragic and catastrophic failure of the third launch, resulting in the loss of everyone on board, then disrupted the program. Over twelve hundred passengers and crew were killed when the Prism drive on the Endurance malfunctioned, after which further launches were halted until a thorough investigation had been undertaken.

The good news for you folks is that the cause of the malfunction has been found and corrected on the fourth ship, your very own Valiant. A replacement for the Endurance, which will be named Dauntless, has already been commissioned and construction is nearing completion in the adjacent space dock, as you will have seen on your arrival.

While we do of course mourn the loss of those many lives, and offer our sincere condolences to their families and friends, many of you registered on the Valiant will owe your places indirectly to that accident. The disaster badly affected the popularity of our colonisation program and the Valiant has only recently reached its full passenger complement, following the introduction of Lottery places on the two remaining ships, which are open to anyone.

Rest assured that the Valiant is fully functional and perfectly safe, and waits only for its precious human cargo before engaging the renewed marvel of the Prism drive to leap away from the solar system at near-light speed.'

The video wound up with a description of the

mechanics of cryosleep which, Jann noticed, caused Claire to squirm in her seat; waking procedures; the overall journey time; and a very brief explanation of why the ships were unable to return once their outward journey was complete. Artists' sylvan impressions of life on the new world of Perse, similar to those in Jann's brochure, accompanied the final few minutes of the presenter's script. The video flashed up a scrolling message to warn viewers that these images remained unverified. Even if there had been a way of transmitting actual photographs back from Perse, the first ship had presently completed only nine years of its journey. It would not arrive at the new planet for ninety more.

As the lights came back up the audience began to make its way back out into the concourse. Jann caught up with Claire, intrigued by what she had begun to say earlier.

'Sounds like life was bad in... wherever it is you want to get away from?'

'It wasn't great,' she said.

'I guess not,' Jann said, 'if it's a more attractive option to freeze yourself in cryogenic suspension for a hundred years and fly off into the black unknown. Want to talk about it?'

Chapter 4

'We had to move soon after my father died,' Claire began, her attention focused on the glowing hull of the Valiant outside.

'Oh! I'm so sorry—' Jann said.

She held up her hand.

'Don't be.'

She risked a glance at Jann but had to look away again quickly.

'It's been almost three years.'

'Did he—?'

'He was mugged. The news media made a big thing of it at the time. We didn't have much street crime where we lived back then. At least, not killings. Dad had some high-up job working with the government. I never really knew what. I was only eleven when it happened. Mum didn't talk about his work. Anyway it turned out he hadn't been there long enough to qualify for much pension, so we had to move. The new place—well, the *first* new place—was... not good. I was... I was attacked the day we moved in. They took my—'

She stared at the polished steel floor of the concourse, composing herself.

'— my zip-phone, and some cash. I wasn't bothered about the money—I didn't carry much—but the zipper was a birthday present. The last thing...'

Claire's throat closed up. Her shoulders began to shake. Jann put his arm around her. She leaned in to the hug. It felt good. His shirt had an unusual smell. Not unpleasant, but Claire didn't recognise it. She looked up, trying to locate her mother, but her eyes had filled with tears and she couldn't see her.

'Sorry, Claire,' Jann said. 'I didn't mean to stir it all up.

You don't have to—'

'Honestly, it's fine. I'll be OK,' she said, wiping her face on the sleeve of her jacket and tossing back her ash-blonde hair.

'Anyway,' she continued, clearing her throat, 'I managed to make it back inside the apartment—oh! I just realised! Mum never did get her coffee that day! Sorry, where was I? Yes, when I opened the door and Mum saw me all upset and dishevelled she made up her mind we had to move away from that place as soon as possible. She applied to a housing association. They put us on a list but even so we had to wait nearly six months.'

She sniffed again. Patrick caught up with them and offered her a clean, white handkerchief, embroidered with the letters *PG* inside an unusual pattern of circles.

'Thanks,' she said, smiling.

She wiped her eyes and blew her nose.

'We didn't go out much after that.'

'So your new apartment was an improvement?' Jann asked. 'When you eventually moved?'

Claire laughed.

'No! It was the same. Another dump in a different neighbourhood. We should've known. Well, Mum should. I was still only just thirteen, going with the flow. We tried a few more times...' she thought back, counting off the moves. 'Four more to be exact. It never got any better. Worse really. A new bunch of wasters hanging about in the stair wells, substitutes for the crappy furniture and nasty smells, but mainly the same. So after the fifth move, Mum decided the Lottery was our only way out. If we hadn't won I think we might have emigrated.'

Jann snorted.

'Bit of a difference between a few thousand kilometres across an ocean and—what was it?—ninety-something light years to a totally different planet.'

Claire handed the handkerchief back to Patrick with a small smile she hoped was apologetic.

'Ninety-seven,' she said. 'I suppose it depends how you look at things. We're going to be asleep during the journey to Perse so to us it will be quicker. Easier than spending days on a boat, getting sea sick.'

'I read the odds of winning the Lottery,' Patrick said, taking back his handkerchief and folding it carefully. 'It's not something you can plan your whole life on.'

Claire fixed him with a piercing stare.

'I knew we'd win,' she said. 'Mum needed a back-up plan but I never gave it much thought. Perse was always going to be home.'

Her mother rejoined the group. She gave Claire a reproving look.

'I hope you haven't been boring everyone with silly stories about life in the slums,' she remarked.

Claire huffed with indignation.

'Really mother,' she said, waving an arm at the small group, 'does anyone *look* bored?'

cape canaveral, florida
27 Apr 2073

Jann Argent had not seen Nyna Yamani properly before now. She was sitting down when he first joined the group, and took the row behind him in the lecture theatre. Claire had clearly inherited her striking ash-blonde hair from the stunning and statuesque woman, and was also developing a similar forthright and uncompromising attitude.

'Perhaps they're just being polite,' the older woman said, a slight smile playing across her lips. Reflections off the Valiant's forcefields shining through her long pale hair from behind gave her the appearance of wearing a halo.

'In any case,' she continued, 'some things are better left private.'

She stepped away from the group but if she intended Claire to follow, the girl either missed the implied directive or chose to ignore it. Her mother took a seat on a nearby bench, facing in the opposite direction from the group. She looked uncomfortable, but Claire picked up the thread of her story again, interrupting Jann's thoughts. He smiled at her typical teenage rebellion.

'She's probably worried about the trip,' Claire said, glancing over at her mother. 'The idea of travelling at near light speed makes her nervous.'

'Maybe she doesn't like strangers,' Jann said.

'Understandable if you've had a series of bad experiences in the slums,' Patrick agreed.

'Well I like you,' Claire beamed, 'and she's usually happy to trust my judgement.'

Jann examined his boarding card.

'Will we be sleeping together?' he asked. The information video had explained the layout of the cryogenic pods—they were arranged in capsules, each containing nine pods—but not how places were allocated.

Claire gave Jann a mischievous look but did not reply.

He blushed.

'No... I... er... sharing a capsule I meant.'

Patrick came to his rescue.

'Unlikely,' he said. 'We all checked in at different times. I think they use a simple "first come, first served" allocation method for the pods. Unless you're family.'

'You said your father hadn't worked long enough for a decent pension,' Jann said, switching to a safer topic. 'What did he do before he took on the government job?'

'Something else my Mother doesn't talk about,' Claire said. 'And I'd be too young to remember much if he had said anything.

'Which I don't think he did,' she added.

Her pensive expression made Claire even more unremarkable to look at but Jann had already learned there was more to this girl than her plain looks suggested.

'I haven't really thought about it until now,' Claire mused, 'but they never discussed the past. And we didn't have a single photograph of Mum or Dad until they moved in to Gresham Place.'

'Gresham Place?'

'That's where I grew up,' Claire explained. 'Where we lived before Dad... was killed.'

'Claire!'

Nyna Yamani watched them from her bench, an angry expression clouding her face.

'Can I have a word with you please?'

'Sorry,' Claire said to the others. 'I'll be right back.'

Puzzled by her mother's edginess and apparent mistrust, Jann turned to Patrick.

'So what makes you want to up sticks and head off into the wild black yonder?'

'It's a leap of faith,' Patrick replied. 'But in a way, I'm running away from something too. Just like Claire.'

offices of siddy, lamplugh & sears
16 Feb 2073

A standard issue black and white plastic sign on the door read "ABRAHAM SIDDY—SENIOR PARTNER'. Patrick knocked.

'Come.'

Patrick's boss sat at a modern oak desk, his attention focused on his computer monitor. The company had a "non-confrontational policy" on office layouts so the desk sat across one corner of the room, the chair on the inside. This afforded its occupant an impressive view of the city, and Patrick a not-so-impressive view of what filled the screen. Siddy was engaged in a video call, one corner of his display showing the output from a transcript program recording the session.

'Take a seat Paddy. I'm nearly done here.'

Patrick bristled at the epithet. A shortening of his name he had always hated. Siddy knew of Patrick's dislike. He also knew that Patrick knew he knew. Opposite the desk a low table with four leather chairs provided an informal meeting area. Patrick threw his crumpled, beer-stained letter onto the table and sat down. After a few minutes his boss wound up the call. He picked up the letter.

'Is this what you wanted to talk about?'

'That's part of it, yeah.'

'Look, Paddy—'

'Patrick.'

'OK, Patrick. Lots of people don't make partner right away.'

'After six years? Name me one person who brought in as much business as me, didn't make the grade, and is still with the company.'

'Ah, well,' said Siddy, regarding him with a cool expression. 'Maybe you've answered your own question. Opportunity is where you find it Pad— Patrick. If it's not working out...'

'Are you trying to get rid of me?'

'Of course not! Your work is right up there with the best.'

'It IS the best.'

'Yeah, yeah, OK. Some of it is. But you spend too much time on private projects. And you won't stick to a brief. I've told you over and over. When a client has a firm idea, they don't want chrome plating if they've asked for maroon flock.'

'So you want creative designers who aren't allowed to be creative?'

'Within the fucking remit Patrick! You know the drill: the customer is always right.'

'Look Abe, you know as well as I do—half the time the clients have no idea. They only think they do. If we let them stick to what they know, all their collateral would end up the same. If ad agencies had worked like that forty years ago we'd still be watching bouncing paint balls and dancing automobiles! It's up to us to show them new ideas. Lead them out of their comfort zone.'

'Yeah, well, maybe in some companies. Here, we like to give people what they want. Like I said in the letter, if that don't sit well with you...'

He let the sentence hang. The air between the two men seemed to solidify. Patrick stood up.

'OK, I'll make it easy for you.'

He reached into his back pocket and pulled out an envelope, folded and creased as if it had been there for days. He threw it down onto the table in front of his boss.

'My resignation. I'll work the standard notice.'

'Please. Don't do me any favours. If you want to leave right away—'

'Fine! I'll clear my desk. Be out of here today.'

*

'And that was that,' Patrick said, shielding his eyes from the setting sun.

'Did you know you'd won the Lottery at the time?' asked Jann, 'Or did you have another plan?'

Patrick hesitated.

'I... didn't win the Lottery. I thought it would be easier to fit in if I didn't let on how I got my place on the Valiant.'

Jann looked puzzled.

'Sorry, I don't understand. I've been... out of the loop... as far as the colony program goes. If you're not picked and you don't win a place, how—?'

'I bought my ticket,' Patrick admitted.

Jann's eyes widened.

'Jeez! I didn't even know you could do that.'

'Let's just say it's not widely publicised. And it's not cheap. But six years of decent share options... Those shares did OK on the back of lucrative contracts *I* won for those pricks. Once I'd cashed it all in and sold my house, my car, I just about had enough.'

The sun finally dipped behind the nearest building. Patrick lowered his hand.

'Besides, we won't be needing dollars where we're

going,' he added.

'That's a massive investment,' Jann said.

'It's only money.'

'I meant your time. All that effort. Six years.'

'It wasn't that hard a decision in the end. I never felt like I belonged there. That's why I chose this Perse trip. When I thought about it, I realised I've never really fitted in anywhere.'

'You have family?'

Patrick interlocked the fingers of his hands, turned them over and examined his palms.

'Not any more,' he said at length. 'I only have the vaguest memories of my father. He never visited unless he'd been able to scrape together some maintenance to try and impress my ma. Never stayed for long. Once I started school I didn't see him again. I don't know what happened to him.'

'Friends?'

'Not really. I was the typical shy, arty kid. You could probably tell the tale yourself. Bullied, never interested in socially acceptable stuff like sports, hung around with the only other art nerd in school. Fast-forward to my career, same story. Square peg, round hole. They kept me on because I was damned good at my job, but I was always passed over in favour of lesser talents who were better at the glad-handing and beers after work. I used to dream about being able to turn back time, start again. I can do that on Perse. Good as. Get away from all those past mistakes.'

Patrick fell silent, staring out at the crackling blue of Valiant's gravnull field, memories crowding in on him. After a while, Terry left the group, returning a few moments later carrying a plastic beaker of water.

'Guess it's my turn to tell a story,' he said slowly.

valley of the cataclysm
21st day of run'bakamasa, 935

A significantly smaller crowd attended the first memorial than had witnessed the original ceremony. The day was still, not even a light breeze disturbing the dust that had accumulated in the intervening years. The Valley of the Cataclysm as it had come to be known—Lembaca Ana—had not seen such a throng in all that time. The few pennants hanging from the ceremonial spears of the Queen's platoon or the King's honour guard dangled unmoving in the pellucid air of a warm afternoon. Among the handful of nobles who had elected to join the reduced entourage, none could have articulated what they expected to see. If asked they would perhaps mutter about "honouring the lost"; "paying tribute to the brave"; or "exalting the memory of the Elementals". Superficially they wanted to be able to say they had been there at the first memorial. Secretly they wondered whether anything magical would transpire. They did not want to miss out.

The Piper appeared more relaxed on this occasion. The music his Queen had insisted upon was much simpler, for one thing. Years ago it had been an integral part of the power the ceremony had conjured. He had been the sole focus for that part. Now the music merely provided a backdrop. The small choir, note perfect in practice, had become accustomed to singing in the presence of the Queen, who declared from the very beginning she would perform the chant. Normally she would have been open to the Piper's advice. Actively seek it out, even. He could legitimately claim to be her most trusted advisor. On this matter though, she was adamant. In spite of his misgivings, the Queen would sing.

On the floor of the Valley, children from the guild schools took the positions of the four Elementals at the corners of the granite quadrangle. Hand-picked by their tutors as the most promising young acolytes in each discipline, they had yet to attain a level of mastery equivalent to journeymen. They could not even dream of Elemental status. Mages were born to such power. It passed down through particular families and could not be learned after even a lifetime of study. Rarely, but frequently enough to allow young mages to hope, an Elemental arose from a new bloodline. But for today's memorial, where no demonstration of power was either sought or expected, the acolytes sufficed. Each bore a similar expression of awe and wonder at the role allocated to them.

At the northernmost end of the Valley the bell tower had been rebuilt. The newly cast replacement bells, albeit damaged or deficient, hung in preparation for their first peal. Three bell ringers stood ready, ropes held in their experienced hands. The Piper took up his pipes. Having received almost imperceptible nods from both the Queen standing nearby and the King, who had taken up his original position on the eastern hill sat upon his kudo, the Piper began to play the funereal music which the Queen had chosen.

The choir waited for their cue, upon which they began to sing while the Queen stood rigidly erect, her hands clasped in front of her, eyes closed, until the introduction had finished and the music invited her to begin.

Her words rang out across the sleepy Valley, the bells picking up the beat of the chant. Their peal established a dissonant but strangely hypnotic rhythm with its single flat note and two brassy, strident voices from the pair of cracked bells.

No spheres of Elemental power appeared before the children, no raging vortex formed, but when the time came for the bells to ring in unison, all the onlookers gave a low gasp of surprise. The sound of the chime billowed visibly through the air, expanding outward from the bell tower like ripples in a pool.

The Queen's eyes flew open at the crowd's reaction.

Seeing the strange tide of atmospheric distortion surging over her head towards the centre of the quadrangle, she stepped back. Her chanting faltered, as did the singing of the choir. Whether caused by the interruption in the music, or the ripples reaching the vortex point directly above the locus of the granite floor, no-one could tell, but at that precise moment the waves died away, breaking up like aerial foam on invisible shingles. An eerie silence fell across the Valley of the Cataclysm. Onlookers exchanged nervous glances, a few cleared their throats. No-one spoke. They waited, not really knowing what they waited for. Would there be another sign, or a portent? Would the vortex reopen, spitting back the missing Elementals? When it became apparent that nothing further would happen, the crowd began to disperse, keen to make their departure before night fell in the strange place.

somewhere in west virginia
11 Apr 2073

In her dream, Elaine found herself back in the ring. But this was a lucid dream: Elaine watched her own performance from a seat in the audience, but simultaneously inhabited herself. Once again she held a pair of fire pois, their flames licking up around her wrists. She felt no pain. The fires would not harm her; they were hers to command. She began to spin them. Before long her arms were encircled with continuous hoops of flame, the pois no longer visible as separate entities. They had become subsumed in the glow of her fiery bracelets. Living, flaming extensions of the topaz-studded bangles she always wore.

A bell sounded in the distance, tugging at her memory. Insistent. She recognised the sound, yet the detail remained out of reach, indistinct. She turned her attention back to the fires, willing them to swell and roar. She knew, without understanding where the knowledge came from, that the fire would always obey her. She could command it to do anything with a thought, or a gesture, or a song. Its power was immense.

She forced it to accelerate. As its speed increased, the faint tolling of the bell sped up too, striving to match the fire. Faster and faster it rang out until the individual chimes could no longer be distinguished. The sound became a continuous trilling, coming closer as the power of the fire built until the heat burned into her face and the smoke swirling around her head made her choke and cough.

She emerged from the dream hardly able to breathe. The inside of her trailer was ablaze, thick billows of greasy black smoke surrounded her. Through the wall, the clattering of a fire alarm's bell was joined almost immediately by the rising and falling of a fire engine's siren approaching. She crawled, coughing and retching, to the sink, soaked a towel with water and wrapped it around her face.

The door burst inwards, kicked by the reinforced boot of a fire fighter wearing full breathing apparatus. He clambered through the plumes of smoke, put his arms around Elaine, and dragged her through the splintered fragments of door into the cool clean air of the trailer park.

'Take it easy ma'am. You're OK. We'll get you some oxygen.'

Another fire fighter fastened a mask over her face. She felt a cold blast of oxygen and sucked in a deep breath, coughing out the deadly fumes.

'You OK?' asked the fire fighter. 'Feeling better?'

Elaine nodded, unable to speak. The oxygen had now brought her fully awake. Though her eyes were wide open, her gaze was directed inward, to the memory of her dream. Rather than fading, it had burned through her mind dispelling the amnesia of the last four years and awakening her to her true identity. With perfect clarity and chilling certainty she recalled her previous life in all its glorious detail. She knew now that she did not belong here. What had rendered her speechless was not the wealth of rekindled memories of her old home, but the frightening realisation that she had no idea where it was, or how she could return.

Chapter 5

Terry Spate took a sip from his water, smiling at the young man who had so adroitly extracted their stories from the blonde girl and the graphic designer. On the short side of medium height and with an athletic, well-muscled frame, Jann Argent reminded him of a much younger version of himself, except for his silver hair and the cable chain around his neck. Terry had never been one for jewellery.

He felt some empathy for the Yamani girl too, trying to escape from something but also looking forward to the challenges of a new world, just as he was. As far as he could tell, all he had in common with the burned-out artist was his age.

'This isn't like me at all,' he began. 'I'm a private man these days. Prefer my own company. I guess this... Perse thing is a bit overwhelming. Makes me realise I don't want to be alone for once. On the trip, I mean.'

He ran stubby fingers through his thick brown hair, pausing to scratch his head.

'Suppose that sounds a little crazy, what with all these hundreds of folk we'll be sharing the ride with.'

'A man can still feel alone, when he's surrounded by strangers,' Argent said.

He stared past Terry, his pale blue eyes unfocused, flicking constantly from left to right. Argent's seat on the bench commanded a clear view of both sides of the spaceport's assembly area. Terry smiled, the deep lines of his craggy face remembering the pattern of it.

'Yes! Exactly young man. That's the root of it. But... well... we may not have known each other very long, this little group, but somehow you're already like family.'

Argent's gaze hardened, his eyes resembling shards chipped from the frozen north Atlantic, staring at Terry just long enough for him to start to feel uncomfortable. Then the man's features broke into a smile, his eyes thawing once more and resuming their restless scanning of the hall.

'Yeah. Funny that, isn't it?'

'So I thought, seeing as how we're all telling our stories...'

'Passes the time,' Glass agreed, 'if you're up for it. No pressure.'

'My whole life has been "no pressure",' said Terry.

He thought for a moment.

'At least, until recently.'

He took another sip of water, trying to order his slow thoughts into a coherent tale.

'I'm an outdoors man. Always have been. Worked on the land for the last thirty years or more. In fact if you were to ask me, I literally couldn't remember a time when I did anything else.'

Argent fixed Terry once again with that intense, discomfiting icy stare.

'*Literally* couldn't remember?' he asked.

Terry's shoulders twitched. He felt his face colouring up.

'I had a fall when I was younger,' Terry admitted. 'While I was out in the woods. Guess I must have been climbing a tree or something. Woke up flat on my back not knowing where I was. But like I said it's more'n thirty years ago. Ancient history. I've not let it stop me doing what I always loved—cultivating the land. With the trees, and plants, and flowers. Out there under the sky, rain or shine. It's in my nature, see? Never wanted to do anything else. Built myself quite a reputation too, over those years.

'I started simple. Maintenance jobs and lawn work and such. Later on I moved up to small gardens. It's always come natural to me, working the soil. Those gardens! They were really something. Pretty as a picture. Word spreads quick when your customers are happy. Wasn't long before the business grew into more than I knew what to do with. Like I said, I'm a private man. Didn't sit too well with me when things began to get out of hand. Fame and notoriety, well, they're just not for me. So I moved. Started over.

'Kept going like that for a while, but reputation has a way of catching up with you.'

He took another sip of water as Argent nodded.

'Yeah. It can stick like shit,' he said.

'Or sugar,' countered Terry. 'Too sweet's as bad as too smelly. Anyway a few months ago I got the call. New owners at Harcourt Manor. Said they were looking to re-landscape the entire place in a more traditional style. They'd heard of me. Heard people making me out to be the Capability Brown of the 21st century. Would I be interested?'

'And were you?'

'Are you kidding? One of the most well-known estates in North America? Just about the nearest thing we have to the stately homes of England. At my time of life—I'm fifty-eight in case you were wondering—folk always do wonder on account of me still having all the colour in my hair—anyway at my time of life it would have been my crowning achievement. The pinnacle of my career.

'So for once I put my desire for anonymity and an easy ride to one side. Went over to the manor to scope the job out. I started to picture how it could look as soon as I walked up the driveway. Sketched out a few of my thoughts for the owners.'

'And they liked it?' asked Glass.

'Loved it. Wanted me to start right away. Money no object. They trusted me from the off. Said they were going to let me "realise my vision" and they'd be happy just to see the finished article.'

'Wow. Impressive.'

'Well, it would have been. But it's not finished.'

'How come?'

'I walked away. Literally.'

*

Light but persistent rain had kept up all morning. It dripped from Terry's cap onto the shaft of his spade as he dug deep into the soft brown earth. Beside him, on the tarmac driveway, a barrow load of evergreen trees—young kurrajong—stood waiting to be planted. Stretching ahead of him towards the perfect symmetry of the manor house, a length of green twine marked the planting line. Behind him a regiment of poplars guarded the first half of the avenue, ready for inspection.

The sun, invisible above heavy, iron-grey clouds, had almost reached its zenith as Terry removed the last spadeful of dirt from the hole. He selected another sapling. Beads of sweat stood out on his face, indistinguishable from raindrops. He heeled the tree into the ground, levelling the sodden loam around it with the toe of his boot. Wiping his brow on his shirtsleeve he took a step back to check the verticals, pausing for a moment to admire the work so far completed.

Satisfied, he retrieved his spade and moved the barrow to the next planting mark. Between the line of trees and the edge of the tarmac, a deep imprint of his boot had flattened a tiny young campanula, breaking its stem and grinding its only three flowers into the mud. The sight of the broken bloom immobilised Terry. Conflicting emotions welled up in his chest. Shame that the little flower had been spoiled as a direct result of his hubris, sadness at the defiling of its beauty, anger at the waste. The rampion took on a symbolic meaning for him, a crystallisation of how the power of a man can cause destruction even in the very act of creation. He had devoted his life to the nurture of all growing things, to the lore of soil and the beauty of nature. The trees already planted, standing in their perfect rank behind him, were only the latest to give testimony to his decades of work, love, and care. And yet now they also seemed to stand in judgement, like mourners beside a freshly dug grave. One careless footfall taking life from one of the rarest and most precious of his wards.

He shook his head, wiping more rainsweat from his brow. It had been an accident. It was just a flower. No need to build it up to be an icon of his clumsiness. And yet something else about the broken bloom called to Terry. Its three bell-like buds lying in crushed disarray on the stamped earth appeared like a physical echo of an image long forgotten. A faint memory, hiding behind a door in his mind that had remained closed and locked for most of his life. A door now standing ajar. The smallest chink of light blazing through it as if summer lay beyond and it was he locked on this side of the wall, in permanent greyness where the rain never stopped.

He shuddered. As he fought to unearth the long-lost memory, digging it out of his mind in the same way he might excavate the tap root of an invasive weed, he realised this was not how things were supposed to be. He was wasting his talents here. He should be a maker, not a destroyer. A gentle man who had held the power of life in his spade-like hands, one who had sown that life and nurtured it, watered it and fed it and protected it from harm. If he could destroy it so easily, so carelessly, what purpose did he serve here really?

A low rumble of thunder rolled across the leaden clouds above him. He threw his spade into the barrow, turned on his heel, and marched down the driveway, away from the manor house.

*

'That was the last I saw of it,' Terry concluded. 'I never went back. Only spoke to the owners one more time. I don't know how long it took them to realise I'd gone but they caught up with me through my messaging service. I couldn't make them understand. They kept saying it was just one flower. Asking me to carry on. Finish the job. But I knew I couldn't. I didn't belong there any more.'

'Lucky you won the Lottery then,' Argent ventured.

'Unless you had another getaway plan?'

Terry looked surprised.

'Oh, I didn't have to rely on the Lottery for my place on the Valiant,' he said, smiling. 'Horticulture is one of the most sought after skills for life on the new frontier. Someone has to be able to tame the local vegetation! We're taking a crap load of seeds with us but there's no guarantee any of 'em will grow in whatever passes for soil out there. We may need to adapt to new crops—cereals, fruit, vegetables. They were desperate for people who had the experience to tell the difference between a plant and a weed. No, I won my place on my own merit.'

hills above the valley of the cataclysm
21st day of run'bakamasa, 935

The blood-red rays of the setting sun gave an eerie orange hue to the Jester's costume as he gambolled and tumbled along beside the King's kudo, his face fixed in a mirthless rictus grin beneath his tricorn hat, upon which the bells tinkled. In contrast, the King's mouth had set in a bad-tempered grimace. He would have counted himself among those who did not know what to expect from the memorial ceremony, but even so he could not hide his disappointment. He kept a tight grip on the reins of his rust-red stallion Anak'Adah to prevent the animal from shying at each new variant of cavorting the Jester performed.

'Do you have to do that?'

'It is my job, sire, to keep the entourage entertained on the long and weary journey back from the tedious and pointless ceremonial they have recently witnessed.'

'No need to rub it in.'

'And a hard task it is too,' the Jester continued, as if the King had not spoken, 'since the debacle proved every bit as unprepossessing and monotonous as I had predicted.'

'Yes, yes, alright,' the King said. 'I get the message. You

were right.'

The Jester paused for a moment in thought, and then ran to catch up with the King, capering even more enthusiastically as he burst into improvised song:

'The Blood King is a mighty sire
His shield and sword run red
His arm is strong, his one desire
To see his rivals dead,' he sang

'Steady on,' said the King.

But the Jester had been caught up with his Muse. He continued:

'And yet he sped to yonder dell
Wherefrom the mages fled
To listen to a remade bell
And venerate the dead

His enemy did give a chant
Upon the granite bed
The echo of her music scant
To summon up the dead

For all the nobles gathered round
As I had often said
Both saw no sight nor heard no sound
Of dear departed dead.'

'Enough!' shouted the King, causing Anak'Adah to rear up in surprise.

The King settled his steed back into a trot.

'Mount up, Jester! Let us have no more capering for today. The nobles can find such entertainment as they may from contemplating the view.'

The King's entourage entered the band of mist that habitually gathered at the extreme edge of the Valley. It formed both a meteorological and a psychological barrier, beyond which life would return to normal, leaving the Valley of the Cataclysm behind physically and emotionally. The fog had become so common in this place it was now considered to be the entrance to the Valley.

No-one spoke as they negotiated the murky path, kudai picking their way along the dirt road with unerring instinct until at length they emerged into daylight once more. On this side of the mist the sun appeared to burn more brightly, lifting the general mood of the troupe.

'My liege should never have agreed to the Black Queen leading the choir.' said the Jester, moving his kudo to ride alongside the King.

'I don't see how I could have stopped her, short of going to war about it. It was only supposed to be a memorial, not a rerun.'

'War would be preferable, in my mind, to this endless petty bickering and skirmishing. The people are tired of it, majesty. They seek leadership. Stability. There can be no true prosperity when rogue elements from the Palace mount guerrilla attacks on our borders.'

'Perhaps I should organise a summit?'

'Talking is not the answer sire! We have already wasted too much time and too much wind on summits, agreements and treaties. They all lie in shreds, trampled into the grass by the hooves of the Queen's cavalry!'

'Does it always have to come back to war?' the King asked.

'It always has in the past, sire,' the Jester pointed out. 'Your royal highness might ponder upon why that is. History has many lessons, if only we take the time to learn them.'

'I was only a boy when my father died, as you know, but I can remember him saying there would be no peace on Berikatanya until one or other of the great houses gained overall ascendancy. An outright win followed by imposition of strong rule was his answer to centuries of turmoil.'

'He was a wise man, Majesty,' said the Jester, taking a six-stringed celapi from his saddle bag and starting to pluck out a tune for his earlier verse. 'A wise man.'

cape canaveral, florida
27 Apr 2073

As Terry concluded his story, Jann reflected that the older man had thought about the future in much greater depth than any of the others. They were all running away from something. In contrast Terry was running—walking, Jann corrected himself in view of the man's age and build—towards an idea of a new beginning. The next chapter of his life. He wanted to ask about Terry's expectations for life on Perse when a commotion at the nearest departure desk caught his attention.

An athletic looking young woman with red hair gelled into spikes, the taut lines of her well-muscled figure and full breasts broadcast by a snugly fitting vermilion jumpsuit, engaged in a heated argument with the clerk at the desk. Jann could not quite hear his side of the exchange, but the man's expression and body language telegraphed a struggle to maintain the required professional courtesy. He had no such difficulty hearing the woman.

'Yes, I know I'm late, but you have to let me on,' she said, slamming a hand down on the desk in front of her. 'My people are already there.'

Jann moved closer to the desk, where he could listen to both sides of the conversation.

'Your relatives were on one of the earlier ships?' the clerk asked.

'They will be going out of their minds wondering where I am,' the woman continued, ignoring the question. 'I should be back there now.'

'I'm sorry you were unable to travel with them,' the clerk replied, tapping at his keyboard and frowning at the screen, 'but giving you a place now would mean another passenger being bumped to the Dauntless.'

'Yes? And?' said the woman, throwing up her hands.

'That ship doesn't leave for a full year,' said the clerk. 'I really don't think I'll be able to find anyone prepared to give up their ticket and wait for a year!'

While Jann had been absorbed with the exchange, Patrick had moved unnoticed to stand behind him. The older man stepped around Jann and walked towards the desk. Jann took hold of his arm.

'What are you doing?'

'She can have my place if it's that important to her,' Patrick said. 'I'm not in any hurry. I can wait a year.'

'Are you crazy? You just quit your job and sold your house and car. Where are you going to live for a year? What are you going to live *on*?'

Patrick hesitated, looking from Jann to the woman and back. He shook off Jann's hand and took another step towards the desk.

'This is supposed to be the start of you taking care of yourself first Patrick!' Jann insisted, hurrying after him. 'You can't put your life on hold for a total stranger!'

'...you *please* just ask?' the woman was saying. Amber flecks in her deep hazel eyes flashed as she fought to control her temper, giving the clerk an imploring look. 'I have to get to Perse as soon as possible.'

The woman pronounced "Perse" with an unusual inflection. It sounded to Jann as if she had said Berse instead. The agent looked again at his screen, and back to the woman, frowning. Finally he locked the screen with a sigh.

'OK. Let me see what I can do,' he said, 'I'll have to speak with my supervisor.'

The woman leaned back on the desk, turning to face the concourse and catching sight of Jann and Patrick, now only a few metres away. She stared at Jann, holding up a hand to shield her eyes against the low sun. An unmistakable look of recognition passed across her face before she turned back to the desk to await the clerk's return.

The now familiar melodic chime sounded again through the departure hall, followed by an announcement informing passengers that boarding would commence in fifteen minutes.

cape canaveral, florida
27 Apr 2073

'See you on the other side!' Patrick called as the tera-lift doors closed, cutting off his cheery farewell wave and whisking Jann Argent up to the next level.

His fellow traveller had been right. With the exception of Claire and her mother, none of the small group shared a cryo capsule. They had queued together for the huge elevators that carried fifty people in each compartment up through the maze of gantry work to the embarkation level almost a thousand metres above the departure hall, but once they entered the interior airlock and felt the distant thrum of the idling Wormwood engines vibrating the deck beneath their feet, they had each taken a different direction.

Jann turned left out of the tera-lift, following the signs to his capsule group as the video presentation had explained. Before watching the clip he had expected the embarkation process to be similar to his experience on the journey from Mars, but back then he had been travelling on a commercial passenger craft. On colony ships the passengers were left to take care of themselves as much as possible. Personalised ID cards restricted access to secure areas of the ship, while remaining sections enjoyed a much more relaxed regime. Colonists could come and go as they pleased, although there was no time to explore before departure. Jann felt the throb of the engines increasing in pace as they powered up to leave the mooring gantry and head out of the atmosphere.

In his capsule, two of the cryogenic pods were already occupied. Three other men had undressed down to their underwear prior to entering their pods, the polycarbonate hatches standing open to reveal softly lit padded interiors. Jann thumbed the OPEN button on his own pod and chose one of the four remaining free lockers for his clothes. He hesitated for a moment before taking the chain and its pendant from around his neck and folding it into his shirt.

A smartscreen on the wall of the capsule showed the curve of the Earth dropping away below them as the Valiant rose through the layers of atmosphere. The vibration of the engines quickening to a low hum gave the only other indication their journey had begun.

Jann's weight on the reclined seat of his pod activated small robot arms. They moved over his body, attaching sensors at strategic places. As the clear plastic hatch lowered, a small puff of aerosol anaesthetic released inside the pod. Once unconscious, the robots would insert the cryogenic liquid dispensers into his veins to begin the process of preserving his body for the one hundred year journey. The next planetary crescent he saw on the smartscreen would belong to Perse.

The last thing Jann heard as he drifted off to sleep was the whine of the Wormwood "Prism" drive, increasing beyond hearing to supersonic pitch as it started to push the ship out of the solar system.

Chapter 6

Claire stood in the clearing, her heart pounding as if she'd run a sprint race. A bead of nervous sweat trickled down her face. She dashed it away with her free hand.

Pera-Bul—the alpha moon—was setting. Soon only Kedu-Bul, a hundred times dimmer, would remain. A feeble source of light, barely bright enough to see by, but which through countless years of tradition had illuminated the Hunt.

She took small comfort that only the best were chosen. The Hunters meant "the best sport". Those who would prolong the chase. Provide the most thrills. Take unexpected chances, death-defying risks, maybe even escape capture altogether.

Claire had a few tricks up her sleeve. In the days before the contest she'd spoken to no-one, trusted no-one with her ideas. Instead, she concentrated on her training, exercising mind and body so both would work in total harmony. When it came to the moment her fate was decided, she may have only fractions of a second in which to decide on a course and execute it. She needed to be at the top of her game, and she was.

In the last few minutes of alpha light, she breathed deep, trying to calm her racing heart. She rubbed at her tethered wrist where the leather cuff chafed, focusing her thoughts on her chosen exit from the clearing. She didn't look towards it, or even deliberately away from it. Any observer would see no clue to her intentions.

Once released she would have half an hour's lead on the Pack, and another fifteen minutes before the Hunt proper set out from the Court. She discounted those last minutes. Not much of a bonus when the Pack were on your heels. Berikatanyan dogs were bred for enhanced sight and smell; their long muscular legs gave them frightening speed over clear ground. Claire did not intend to allow them such an easy advantage. Where she planned to flee, the Pack would be hard pushed to follow.

Pera-Bul edged closer to the horizon. In the surrounding forest the night creatures stirred. One more danger for Claire to factor into her escape. At best, a few of them could be said to be benign. Even these would give the unwary a nasty nip, although they only retaliated if attacked first. In the worst cases the smallest bite could be fatal, as many of the smaller animals carried racun glands. The deadly poison was used to tip the arrows, spears, and hand blades of the Hunt who, beside their toxic weapons, also possessed determination, intellect and intent. But in front of her, the forest presented an equivalent menace. Its denizens—the true hunters—brought animal blood lust, strength, instinct and blistering reaction times to the party.

As if these didn't present enough of a threat, Claire also faced danger from the vegetation. Over millennia the forest had evolved its own defences to the animal life that tried to make a living within it. She'd schooled herself well in the almost endless list of vines, shrubs, leaves and spines she must avoid to survive the Hunt.

Unremarked by the animal and vegetable threats surrounding her, the forest canopy extinguished the last fingers of light from Pera-Bul. With a soundless flash of cold white flame conjured by an unseen Fire mage, the leather cuff burned away from her wrist. The Hunt was on!

Claire raced through the dark wood, her feet barely touching the soft earth. She avoided breaking a single twig underfoot, dodged right and left, ducked and weaved to ensure not even the slightest bend or sway of a branch or leaf would betray her passage. Beneath the dense canopy, the darkness just this side of total, her night-adapted pupils swelled to take in every scintilla of reflection. So far there'd been no sign of the Pack. She still had a little time until the Hunt began their bloodthirsty quest.

Ahead of Claire the forest trail forked. To the right, the track continued unimpeded, the dirt packed solid by the animals and traders that used it, the vegetation well cleared. A good choice. She would leave no trace. But for almost three hundred metres in that direction there was no natural cover or deviation in the path. She could be spotted from far behind.

She neared the fork. Had to decide. The left-hand route, even closer to total darkness and heavily overgrown, required extreme care. Any damage would betray her entry but once through, after only a few metres, she'd be invisible to passing hunters. And—she shook the leather bladder at her hip—she had just enough scent mask remaining to give her a chance of eluding the Pack.

She stopped at the fork. Stepping over the first fronds of bracken she ripped the flask from her belt and squirted its contents behind her, checking as best she could in the crepuscular coppice that she left no tracks. After a dozen metres, unwilling to burn more time covering her entry to the dark path, she turned away from the main trail and set off at a run through the thickening undergrowth.

Fifty metres further into the bushes Claire began to regret her choice. Too late now to turn around—the Pack would certainly be passing the fork at any moment—the dense vegetation had slowed her progress to a crawl. Worse, she could no longer make out the path. Each gap between trees looked as though it might be a way forward, but each was blocked with bramble, or sickmoss, or trapweed. Claire stopped, trying to quieten her breathing. She considered her options.

The pounding of her heart diminished. Faint music played beyond the trees to her left, borne on a light breeze blowing between the two largest trunks. She turned toward it, the space resolving itself into a clear track. Amazed she had not seen it before and determined now to discover the source of the unexpected melody she pushed on along the new passage. The strain became louder with every step. It seemed somehow familiar to her. Others had spoken of how music called to them, but until now Claire had not experienced it for herself. She felt almost impelled down the path. She had neither the desire nor the ability to turn aside or find another direction. Her plan had been to veer and jig during her flight, to be completely unpredictable, but all concerns over being caught evaporated from her newly calm mind as she sought out the origin of the refrain.

The wood remained as pitch dark as when she first stepped onto this numinous route, yet her feet found their own way, stepping over obstacles concealed beneath the ground cover, avoiding trip hazards and pot holes. She travelled almost as quickly through this section of the forest as she had on the open path. After another few metres she glimpsed a flash of bright white between the low-hanging branches. The music, much louder now, filled her mind. Her heart pounded. She rounded the trunk of an enormous, ancient oak and stepped into a clearing. Several more venerable oaks surrounded the space, but within the glade nothing grew, the forest floor carpeted instead with bracken and leaf litter. The sweet woody smell of the decaying leaves drifted up as she walked over them. In the centre, on a low outcrop of rock, sat an old man in long robes. Facing away from Claire, his face obscured by a floppy white hat, he played an unusual pair of bifurcated Pan pipes bound with a purple ribbon. He glanced round as she entered the glade.

'Father!'

Albert Yamani ceased playing. Released from the spell of the music, Claire slumped to the ground, the soft carpet of fallen leaves breaking her fall. She hadn't realised she was so tired, but now the music had stopped a terrible fatigue overwhelmed her. Her father knelt beside her.

'The effect will soon pass,' he reassured her. His voice had an unusual melodic quality, a faint reminder of the beautiful strain he had been playing.

'Come,' he continued, 'sit.'

Claire struggled to her feet. 'The Hunt. I have to—'

'They will not find you here,' Albert replied.

'How—?'

'This part of the forest is hidden from them. I used the power of the music to summon you.'

The strange pipes hung from her father's belt, the purple ribbon fluttering in the gentle air currents still sighing through the dell.

'I didn't know you could play.'

'These aren't mine,' he said, 'but yes. Music is much more important than you realise. We can all play.'

'We?'

He held up his hand.

'You are on a journey, Claire. Things will become clearer once you reach your destination.'

'I don't know where I'm heading,' Claire said, looking around the clearing, 'but I can't stay here.'

She couldn't believe they were somehow protected from the Pack. From the Hunt.

'I must find my way out, without being caught.'

'You have many advantages over those who would seek to do you harm,' her father said.

He reached inside his robes.

'I have something here to help you decide which path to choose.'

He opened his hand. A fine silver chain unravelled from between his fingers bearing a heavy pendant which dangled above the forest floor. In the dim light Claire couldn't make it out.

'What—?'

The old man wound the chain around his hand. The pendant spun slowly. She could see it more clearly now. A pair of golden faces, looking in opposite directions, held in a small circular frame of polished elder wood. The faces, sitting above a single neck, formed the shape of an ancient tree. Their expressions were identical; neither smiling nor sad. Claire stepped closer so her father could slip the chain over her head.

'Trust your instincts and your judgement,' he said. 'You will know which way the wind is blowing.'

The gentle breeze that had continued to blow since she first heard the music freshened at that instant, plucking at her long blonde hair and throwing it across her face.

'But—' Claire began, fingering the hair from in front of her eyes and looking up.

She stood alone in the clearing. Her father was gone. Through the gloom, back in the direction from which she had entered, several dogs barked. She shivered. Time to leave. She looked around the glade, intending to select the best exit. All of the spaces between the ancient oaks offered potential paths, but her father's words echoed in her mind. She followed the wind.

The darkness closed in again as Claire left the clearing, as black as before and yet somehow not. By some trick of nature the canopy had thinned above the path she chose. She must have spent longer there than she thought. There were still several hours until dawn, but the first glowing hint of early morning light had begun to define the line of the horizon. Behind her, the baying of the Pack was muted. Either they'd taken a wrong turn, or her more certain feet carried her away from them faster.

Without any warning she emerged from the forest onto a cliff top. Below her the river Mizar cut its meandering groove through the valley, from this height a gossamer thin silver thread of life picked out by the ghostly moonlight. At first glance she thought she'd reached a dead end. She could see no way to cross the gorge. Moving along the rocky edge she noticed a line of darker black against the pale inky sky. A ropeweed strand hung down from the branches of an enormous ancient yalloak tree directly in front of her. It was a perilous leap, but Claire knew she could make it.

She retraced her steps into the shrubs at the forest

entrance, took a deep breath, and ran as fast as she could to the edge. She judged her pace and the length of her stride perfectly, taking off from the lip of the escarpment and catching the ropeweed with both hands. Securing her feet in the weed's knotted tendrils she swung out across the gorge. Her swing didn't have enough momentum to make the crossing at the first attempt, but she rocked the strand backwards and forwards until she felt it would go no higher, leaping free at the opposite vertex.

The landing knocked the breath from her lungs but she rolled through it and continued running. This territory was unknown, but the Hunt could never cross the gorge at that point. She'd gained at least two hours on her pursuers. Even so, she didn't rest. On this side of the river short grass covered the high ground, cropped by the local population of herbivores. In an hour or so the sun would crest the horizon. She needed to make cover before then.

Soon Claire reached the bank of the river. It looped back around the bluff, picking up speed as it fell toward the sea. The beta moon hung above the cliffs, the sky around it a uniform clear black. She cooled her feet in the rushing water, sparkling silver in the moonlight. As it ran over the rocks the river burbled, almost as if it spoke to her. She cocked her head and listened to the sound. 'Ikuti saya,' it said. 'Ikuti saya.' Like her father's music, the language sounded familiar. Although she didn't understand the words, the river seemed to say "follow me".

Maybe what her father had said about the wind blowing could equally apply to the water flowing? She set off along the riverbank, keeping pace with the stream as it raced around the rocks. Before long the flow entered the deep gorge she'd swung across earlier. The river made a wide sweeping bend to the left. Captured by the sheer rock faces on either side, the sound of the racing water was louder here. As Claire rounded the curve she caught sight of a small coracle, moored at the water's edge. There was no sign of its owner, but her need was greater. Whoever had left the craft here wasn't at risk of death from the pursuing Pack. She stepped in and cast off. Instantly the current caught the boat and set it spinning wildly. Claire grabbed hold of the gunwale in time to stop herself being thrown into the water.

Before seasickness had chance to kick in, the coracle settled into midstream and stopped turning. She watched the umbral bank zip past. Surely the Hunt would never find her now? With no scent trail and so much distance between them?

The river's roar became much louder as the small craft rounded another bend. Claire's eyes widened. Only a few hundred metres ahead the water pitched over a fall. In the dark it was impossible to tell how far the raging waters dropped. She lay down, wedging herself against the sides, hanging on as tightly as she could while the boat heaved and tossed in the increasingly agitated waves. With a sickening lurch the vessel flew out over the falls into the blackness. Her stomach flipped as she fell into the abyss. The impact with the water below jarred Claire's teeth in her head and pitched her out into the freezing cold river which churned and bubbled, thundering in her ears. The fierce current dragged her under and bore her along, fighting to hold her breath against the buffeting undertow.

On the point of sucking in a lungful of icy water, Claire's flailing arms hit the release button in the side of her cryopod. The capsule lights flickered into life. The booming noise of the river resolved into an alarm siren blaring outside her pod.

capsule e17
12 Jun 2170

Claire swam up towards full consciousness, coughing and spluttering. The dream tugged at her, trying to drag her back down, but the alarm demanded her attention. Confused by the light and air when moments before she'd been drowning in the dark, it took a few seconds for her to notice the pod's clear polycarbonate hatch hadn't opened. She could hardly breathe. There was something wrong with the atmosphere. She hit the release button again, harder this time, still with no effect. Where were the medical staff? The video presentation had said passengers coming out of extended cryosleep would have crew around to help reorienting.

She hammered at the hatch with her fist, but even as she did Claire knew no-one would come to her aid. There must have been a catastrophic malfunction. If she didn't find a way out of this pod soon she would suffocate. Panic strapped her chest, making it even harder to breathe. No time to indulge her fear—she had to think! That briefing film had given no information about the cryogenic process or its equipment beyond those few details needed to start the sequence and what to expect on waking. Claire already felt nauseous, a known factor after long periods of freezing. She did not want to contemplate throwing up inside the pod. Its hatch was only designed as an atmosphere seal, not a physical barrier. It didn't look very substantial.

Claire drew up her legs, placing both feet against the hatch. She gave a tentative push. Nothing happened. Beginning to pass out, she put all her strength into one last desperate kick. The intermittent hooting blare of the siren became deafening as the seal released. The hatch lifted. Claire gasped, sucking in lungfuls of air between sobbing coughs. She crawled out of her pod and collapsed on the steel floor of the capsule.

*

Shivering, Claire slowly regained consciousness. Her mind still fogged with the after-effects of cryosleep, she had no way of telling how long she'd been lying on the floor. Her breath steamed in the air. Beads of condensation covered all the metal surfaces inside the capsule. Why was it so cold here, outside the pod? Her gaze swept the other eight units. Status lights on each glowed an angry red. On the wall above the last unit, rivulets of molten metal had congealed. A frozen testament to the failure of the control and monitoring system. The alarm siren had silenced itself while she was unconscious, replaced by a flashing amber light above the capsule's main control panel. Claire forced her sluggish, aching limbs to stand her up so she could read the display.

CAPSULE ID: E17
OPEN PODS: 1
SEALED PODS: 8
VIABLE: 0

More detailed metrics from each of the units followed the headline status, but Claire didn't get as far as them. She stared at the last line of the summary status. Viable zero? She ran to the nearest pod, wiped its hatch clear with her vest. The face of the woman inside was not that of someone suspended in cryogenically induced torpor. Her open eyes stared, their smooth surface covered in a layer of fine frost. Her mouth hung loosely in a surprised O, lips also frosted and blue. Her skin had an unnatural grey pallor. The woman was dead.

Afraid to acknowledge the truth of the control panel's grim statistics, Claire moved to her mother's pod. She was dead too. They were all dead. All but her. Somehow, her dream had saved her from the complete failure of every cryopod in this capsule. That explained the uncomfortable chill. She wasn't supposed to be awake. No-one was. The ship must still be in transit to Perse.

Claire ripped open her locker, dressing quickly. Mother! A sob rose in her throat. She bit down on the rising emotions threatening to overwhelm her. She couldn't think about them now. She had to warm up. Had to find out where the ship was.

She retraced her steps to the lift that had brought her to this level who knew how many years before. Automated lights reacted to her presence, illuminating the corridors at her approach. She hoped the heating worked the same way. Right now she could still see her breath in the gelid air.

At the lift doors a com panel showed her how to reach the nearest restaurant area for this section. She knew from the briefing video that the control areas of the ship would be out of bounds. They were restricted to crew and engineers, requiring a coded pass, but the restaurant should have an information display. There were several such areas in each section, designed to provide hot meals for the passengers and crew once they'd woken for the final few days of flight, in time to overcome the cryo-induced tiredness before making planet fall on Perse.

The restaurant opened off the main corridor, with seating for one hundred colonists, view ports along the opposite wall and a servery to the left. She walked in, waiting for the lights to react to her presence. Sure enough as they flickered into life the air vents began to hum too. Before long the air coming from them warmed up. Claire began to feel a little more comfortable.

She could see nothing through the view ports, which meant the ship was definitely still in transit. Near light speed, super-fast hydrogen atoms flying through the vessel posed a radiation risk to passengers. To counteract this a plasma field surrounded the Valiant, preventing anything from impacting the ship but also stopping anyone looking out. Normally the entire passenger and crew complement were asleep while the ship travelled at maximum velocity, but for Claire the active plasma shield meant her only view through the restaurant windows was a uniform fuzzy grey.

Opposite the servery four desks had been set aside as a working space, each with a com terminal. Claire fired one up, navigating to a status screen. She rocked back on her chair when the flight time scrolled up.

JOURNEY TIME REMAINING: 4.11.21_ 15:15:32

The seconds counted down as Claire stared at the numbers, stupefied. Almost five years of the trip remained.

pennatanah bay
16th day of ter'utamasa, 965

Felice Waters gazed up at the faded banner, its ragged edges flapping in the wind blowing in off the white-flecked ocean behind her. She could not remember exactly how long it had been since the sunlight bleached the legend to nothing, but anyone arriving now—assuming another ship ever did arrive—would be unable to tell the banner had once offered a "WELCOME TO PERSE".

She cracked a wry smile. It needed replacing anyway. The fabric was too short for "WELCOME TO BERIKATANYA", which the majority of Earthers now used when referring to their adopted planet. It had seemed the height of arrogance to continue calling it Perse once they discovered a civilisation already living here, who naturally had another name for their home world.

All was quiet in what passed for an arrivals hall as she completed her routine inspection. All was always quiet. The ramshackle structure, intended to be a temporary affair, had been cobbled together from various prefabricated units brought on the Endeavour. The only part of the construction that could legitimately claim to have been engineered was the mooring stanchion, its foundations sunk deep into the coastal bedrock to provide a solid anchor point for debarkation.

The buildings here had been extended once the Endeavour's crew discovered arrival would involve a more convoluted process than had been envisaged, but they had not seen a passenger since dealing with the last of those from the Intrepid. The third ship, Endurance, had been expected six months after the Intrepid. Felice had completed her preparations in plenty of time, her sense of duty and attention to detail a hangover from her years working homicide for the NYPD, but the Endurance never came. Now more than eight years overdue, Felice could only tick the boxes in her self-imposed inspection schedule and wait. With no means of communicating either with ships in transit or with Earth, ninety-seven light years distant, she recognised the pointlessness of wondering why Endurance was late or if it—or indeed Valiant, the fourth and last ship—would ever arrive. She simply had no way of knowing. Felice intended to be ready though, if and when they did turn up.

Her colony records made no secret of her previous career so the captain of the Endeavour had suggested she head up a small security force on the planet to handle any local policing that may be required. The Earthers soon discovered the Berikatanyans had their own ways of dealing with crime. In any case there had been no misdemeanours worthy of the name. Those Earthers who aligned themselves with one of the two local political factions accepted the jurisdiction of their adopted peers. In the small group who elected to stay on the coast and carve out a life independent from the indigenous population, barring a few drunken brawls there was hardly any crime here either.

With no criminals to lock up and no arriving colonists to induct, Felice had a pretty quiet life. Until the day she received an unusual request. A rider from the Blood King's realm of Istania arrived to ask if she would help investigate a strange occurrence involving one of the Intrepid passengers. The message was very brief. As far as Felice's limited Istanian could discern, it seemed to be saying the man had his hand stuck in a rock.

She had a mental image of someone messing about in a rocky area, perhaps panning for gold in a stream, or hunting for seafood delicacies in a rock pool, who had become wedged between rocks and been unable to pull free. She could not understand why such a situation required the services of a detective. Surely anyone could help the poor guy extricate himself?

Figuring it would at least give her an excuse to spend time away from doing nothing very much in her "office" in the arrivals hall, she rode off to Istania. The day had been fine and warm and she made good progress along the simple dirt roads criss-crossing the coastal lands. She had no difficulty locating the place at which the incident had occurred. A small crowd had gathered to see the spectacle of the Earther with his stuck hand. Two of the onlookers were stationed close to the road to watch for Felice's arrival. They waved as she crested the nearest mound.

Whatever ideas Felice may have had about the possible cause of the problem flew from her mind at her first sight of his predicament. Nothing could have prepared her for what she encountered. Sweating profusely and with an agonised look of profound panic on his face, the man knelt at the side of the road with his hand stuck in a rock, exactly as the message had said. Literally stuck inside the rock.

valiant flight deck
11 May 2175

Claire Yamani sat engrossed in an advanced training package on dimensional engineering and the principles of the Prism drive when the Valiant's automatics begin to flicker into life. She looked up from her smartpad to scan the readouts on the wall of the flight deck, reaching for a salted peanut from the dish resting on the arm of her chair. Almost the last of her meagre supply.

With five years of journey time to kill, she had quickly established that the food supplies and washroom facilities showed every sign of being good for her enforced five-year incarceration. The rudimentary cabins provided little in the way of comfort or indulgence, but Claire had long since abandoned any expectations of luxury in her life. Once she'd confirmed she would be able to feed herself and stay warm for the rest of the journey, Claire opened up the mental box in which she had shut all thoughts of her mother, and allowed herself to grieve properly.

It hadn't taken her long to work out she would die of boredom if she had to rely on only the passenger areas to entertain her. Nothing was designed for long-term life support, let alone the maintenance of a teenager's mental health for an extended solitary confinement. She exhausted the supply of colonists' primers in the small library within a week and few other opportunities for intellectual stimulation presented themselves. So with an expectation of success born from nothing more than youthful enthusiasm, a willingness to study a subject in unusual depth, and a very long time in which to do it, she'd set out to hack the ship. Her short-term goal—the information in the central computer—had taken five weeks.

With the perspective of almost five years, the memories of her initial attempts felt like the efforts of a juvenile delinquent, but they gave her access to the onboard data systems, the extensive engineering, medical and technical libraries, ship status outputs and passenger details. The years Claire would normally have spent finishing high school and college, possibly even starting on a post-graduate course, she'd instead immersed herself as a full-time student of the knowledge available on board.

That took care of her mental fitness. Physical well-being posed a different problem. After working out how to recode her personal ID, she gained entry to the crew sections of the ship and sought out more comfortable quarters. Since the vessel's design only allowed for minimal living facilities during the few days before arrival, even these were still fairly Spartan. The Valiant provided no gym equipment or other such luxuries. Instead, she developed a series of simple callisthenics along with half a dozen jogging routes through the ship to help keep her in physical shape.

The one thing she lacked had been company. With systems and automatics now humming into life all around her, that was about to change. Flight deck panels confirmed, as her early investigations suggested, the captain and senior crew would be awakened first. Nine of them occupied the capsule nearest the bridge with another three in an adjacent capsule which they shared with VIP passengers. Claire didn't want to alarm any of them by waiting beside their pods while they came round from a hundred years of suspension. She knew they'd be making their way to the flight deck soon enough.

Her wait proved shorter than expected.

'What are you doing here?' a stern, commanding voice enquired.

'It's a long story,' Claire replied, standing to introduce herself and shake the captain's hand.

The Valiant was still three weeks out from Perse. Once Claire had related the highlights of her tale to the captain and his officers they adopted her as a kind of amusing and highly intelligent mascot, but the crew were fully occupied with their pre-arrival duties and check lists so outside of meal times, and the few short periods of downtime the officers enjoyed, she still found herself left mostly alone. The rest of the passengers, including her erstwhile companions, wouldn't start the post-cryogenic recovery until the Valiant had reached a position only three days from planet fall.

common room 'c'; deck 8
2 Jun 2175

'So you must be a bloody genius by now after five years' continuous study!' Jann Argent said between mouthfuls. No-one had told him how ravenous he would be once the cryo-induced nausea had passed. He helped himself to a second portion of steak and ale pie from the servery, returning to their table with a wide smile. He gave Claire an appraising glance before taking another mouthful of pie. Her plain features were now tempered with a new self-assurance, giving her a poise that the fifteen-year-old version had lacked.

'I wouldn't have recognised you,' he continued, 'but I guess you're five years older than the last time I saw you. Which is weird, because it was only yesterday.'

'Feels like five long and lonely years to me,' Claire said. 'I'm glad it's over.'

'And I'm so sorry about your mother,' he added. 'Never got to know her very well. Seemed like a feisty lady. I think we could have been friends... eventually.'

'Thanks. I did all my grieving a long time ago,' Claire said, staring out through the nearest view port.

Jann followed her gaze. The blue crescent of Perse could be seen now they had dropped from near-light speed to allow the navigator to make the adjustments for their orbit insertion trajectory.

'But she would have loved to see this,' Claire added.

The ship's intercom chimed. The Captain's voice, flattened by the tiny speakers, announced the ship would soon begin its entry into the atmosphere. All passengers were instructed to strap themselves in.

'It's a safety precaution,' Claire said once the intercom had clicked off. 'All the available telemetry indicates the weather on Perse is very mild.'

'It's going to take me a while to get used to you knowing so much about everything,' Jann said.

'She's a regular walking encyclopaedia.'

Jann twisted against his newly-fastened seat restraint at the sound of the familiar voice. It belonged to the woman they had seen arguing at the check-in desk immediately before boarding.

'Hi,' he said. 'So they let you on after all.'

The woman raised an eyebrow.

'Looks that way,' she replied.

After a moment she smiled and extended her hand. Large topaz stones set into the gold bangle that circled her wrist glowed with inner fire.

'Elaine Chandler.'

Her hand was warm and dry, in contrast to Jann's

which to his embarrassment had become distinctly clammy.

'Jann Argent. And this is Claire Yamani.'

'Hello Elaine.'

'Yes, I know who you are. The whole ship knows your name by now. Pleased to meet you young lady.'

Elaine introduced herself to Patrick and Terry before strapping into a chair opposite Jann. The cafeteria-cum-assembly room, one of fifteen throughout the ship, soon filled. A total silence fell over all of the one hundred passengers as they became mesmerised by the approaching jewel of Perse which now occupied the entire view port. A display screen beside the nearest port ran an animated loop showing how the Valiant would drop through the atmosphere to anchor at a landing pylon with its gravnull field still engaged. The pylon should have been erected by the crew of the first ship to arrive. There had been no plans to build a more sophisticated passenger terminal such as they had left on Earth. With only four ships expected to make the journey it would not have been worth investing the manpower in such a structure. Disembarkation would be a much simpler process, in keeping with the new "frontier" lifestyle they had all been told to expect.

The animation interleaved with a 3D map indicating Valiant's progress on its landing trajectory, together with some telemetry giving land and wind speeds and external ambient temperature—still showing the large negative number associated with being in space.

'Beautiful, isn't it?' Claire said as they came near enough to make out details of the coastline in between pillows of white cloud.

From this height the sea resembled a solid slab of aquamarine glass, calm and unmoving.

'Like Earth, with a different pattern of continents,' Patrick said.

'According to the blurb it's significantly younger than

Earth, as planets go,' Terry said. 'Around a billion years younger.'

'How can they tell?' asked Jann.

'Beats me,' Terry admitted, 'but it's right here in the book.'

'Didn't you learn all about it Claire?' Elaine asked, raising an eyebrow in what Jann had begun to recognise as a trademark expression. Claire reddened.

'Well, not... *all* about it,' she said. 'But they don't work out the planet's age independently. It's based on an assessment of the age of the star. Planetary systems form at around the same time as their sun, near enough.'

'Told you,' Elaine laughed. 'Walking encyclopaedia.'

'So how do they tell how old the star is?' asked Jann, ignoring Elaine's outburst.

'It's part observation and part where the star fits in the model of similar suns,' Claire said. 'I don't think it's an exact science—more a best guess.'

'But unlikely to be out by a billion years,' Terry said. 'That's like a factor of twenty-five percent. Wouldn't be a very good model if it was as wrong as that.'

While they had been talking, Valiant had descended several hundred kilometres and entered the atmosphere. An electric blue glow suffused the view port as the navigator shut down the interstellar Prism drive and switched to gravnull fields. With the outside temperature climbing through zero, the ship continued to fall, slowing and heading along the coast towards the anchor. The indicated land speed showed a reading of 20,000 kph, dropping rapidly. After another few minutes, the white structure of the anchor point could be seen on the coast, with half a dozen squat box-like buildings beside it.

'Wheeee!' shouted Claire. 'It's so pretty!'

A sudden and unexpected gust of wind caught the ship, turning its nose away from the mooring mast. Lighter blue forks of electrical energy skittered across the view port. The ship's engines thrummed through the hull as pilot and navigator tried to counter the force of the wind, but it soon became clear they would overshoot.

'He's going to have to go around again,' Jann said.

The freshening wind began to whip white plumes off the waves below them. Claire twisted in her seat to watch the foam.

'This is much more exciting than I expected,' she said, her eyes sparkling.

A low warning buzzer started up, soon accompanied by a further message from the captain over the intercom.

'We're experiencing some atmospheric disturbance—' he began.

'Can't he just call it wind?' Terry asked with a wry smile.

'—and a minor problem with the gravnull field,' the Captain continued. We'll have to abandon this approach and make another attempt. Please remain seated and strapped in, we'll have you down in no time.'

The man's voice carried more stress than his words revealed, but Jann said nothing to the others. Through the view port the sea looked much choppier than it had been only moments ago, as the force of the wind increased still further. Spray flew across the surface of the water and dripped down the stanchions of the anchor mast, now approaching even faster than before.

The alarm buzzer became a klaxon as the faint blue glow in the view port disappeared altogether. The ship heeled to one side and collided with the mast, a metallic groan reverberating through the cafeteria matched by a dull grinding tremor transmitted along the spine of Jann's chair. He gripped the arms, his seat belt digging into his waist and ribs. The others hung on too as the ship listed, engines straining to reinstate their gravnull field and maintain the artificial interior gravity against the natural pull of Perse below them.

Claire let out another yelp, whether of fear or excitement Jann could not tell, as the Captain came over the intercom once more.

'Crew to emergency stations. Secure all decks and brace for impact. Passengers please remain calm. Stay in your seats. We've experienced a total failure of our drive system and have sustained a destructive collision with the anchor mast. We have to ditch. Further instructions will be given shortly. Do not panic.'

'Don't panic?' yelled Patrick. 'We're going into the sea!'

'Do we even have lifebelts?' asked Terry.

'I think the crew are a bit busy right now Terry,' Jann said, watching the foaming surface of the ocean approaching rapidly through the view port.

'We'd better brace ourselves like the Captain said,' added Claire. 'Without gravnull this ship has no brakes!'

A wall of foaming water loomed in the view port before Valiant hit the sea, throwing Jann against his harness and knocking the breath from his lungs with a whoosh. Claire's terrified screams faded from his mind as he blacked out.

Chapter 7

Jann came to almost immediately. He released his seat belt and checked the others over for any visible signs of injury. As far as he could tell they had suffered nothing more serious than scratches and bruises. The view ports showed a submarine tableau outside the ship, bright sunlight filtering through the surface of the ocean a few metres above. A radiant blue fish swam past. Their section of the Valiant was obviously submerged. From the little he knew of the ship's layout that meant the main hall was also probably underwater, including the primary doors. The Captain's last message had mentioned securing all decks, so the access doors and hatchways would have closed automatically. Even if they could override the doors to the forward sections they risked flooding the cabin. They needed another way out.

Close by, Claire stared at the view port.

'We're in the sea?'

'Looks like it,' Jann replied.

She unsnapped her belt.

'We still have time to escape,' she said, jumping to her feet. 'The ship will float for hours unless there's a hull breach. Are you OK?'

'I'm fine. How are we going to get out?'

'Need a terminal to find the nearest emergency exit,' said Patrick, who had also come round. He shook Terry's shoulder, trying to wake him.

'There aren't any working ones left in here,' said Claire, glancing at the four com terminals against the far wall. The workstations had not survived the high magnitude impact.

'But there should be one nearby,' she added. 'There was a time I thought this ship was well designed. How could they have left out something as simple as emergency floor lighting? Every commercial passenger plane has that!'

Most of the hundred passengers still occupied their seats. Some were unconscious, others stared through the view port, trying to comprehend the watery scene. In the corridor outside the common room, shouts were being exchanged along with sounds of a scuffle.

'What's that?' asked Terry, waking with a start and looking towards the doorway.

There were signs of panic beginning to build now that some of the seated colonists had realised the ship was sinking. Jann stood up and called for attention.

'Everyone stay calm!' he yelled, holding up his hands for quiet. 'Parts of the ship are submerged but we have plenty of time to evacuate. We can't use the main doors—they're underwater. Does anyone know where the nearest emergency exit is?'

Some of those causing the disturbance in the corridor had gathered around the doorway to listen to him. One of them shouted down the passageway.

'Nazeem? Nazeem! Don't open the door! You'll flood us out. Didn't you see another way out earlier?'

The man relayed his friend's inaudible reply. The closest exit was a couple of hundred metres away, back towards the stern of the ship.

'He's right,' said Patrick, who had found a terminal behind the servery and brought up a schematic of their level. 'Turn right along this corridor. It's about fifty metres down the third passage on the left.'

Jann hurried to the doorway with Elaine close behind. As he rounded the bulkhead he could see a man he assumed to be Nazeem still trying to operate the door release. The automatic had disengaged, its indicator blinking red. Nazeem hit the manual override repeatedly with the palm of his hand.

'Come on! Come on you bastard! We've gotta get out of here.'

'Nazeem!' shouted Jann. 'Not that way! You'll flood the

whole compartment.'

Nazeem hesitated, eyeing Jann hesitantly. His uncertainty was quickly overwhelmed by the man's blind panic.

'Got to get out!' he repeated.

He smashed a nearby fire cabinet, snatching an axe from inside and laying open his arm on the broken glass. Before he could attempt to jemmy the door open with the blade Jann reached him and wrested the tool from Nazeem's grasp.

'You'll drown us all if you go that way,' Elaine said over Jann's shoulder.

She spoke calmly but Jann saw a smouldering determination in her eyes. Somehow her words pierced the crazed man's panic. He became calmer.

'We have to use the emergency exit,' she said.

'She's right Naz,' shouted the friend who had relayed his earlier message. 'We can't get out that way.'

Water had begun lapping around their ankles. Further up the corridor, which now angled upwards, small rivulets leaked from under doors and ran across the steel plates of the deck. An intercom crackled into life.

'This is the Captain. All passengers must leave the ship immediately through the nearest emergency exit. Do not, repeat do not attempt to access the main doors. Avoid the forward assembly areas and levels B through D. Do not attempt access to engine rooms or crew quarters. Do not collect any belongings. Do not open any internal doors with red indicator lights. I repeat, leave the ship immediately.'

Those areas meant the crew quarters, engineering section and flight deck must already be submerged and sealed. The captain and crew had no way out. If anyone in there opened an escape hatch the ship would sink even faster. While the Captain had been speaking the water had risen almost to their knees.

'I'm going to find the hatch,' Jann shouted over to

Patrick.

He beckoned to Elaine.

'Help him release everyone from their seats,' he said, 'and then follow me.'

The water level was still rising fast. At this rate it would flood the entire common room within minutes. There must be a hull breach somewhere.

Jann found the emergency airlock, skim-read the instructions posted beside it, and armed the door release. He shielded his face and threw the switch. The explosive bolts detonated, throwing the outer door clear. A thin stream of water ran in, cascading down the corridor and tripping sensors on the inner hatch. A steel shutter began to slide closed.

Jann braced himself inside the opening, his feet wedged on the bulkhead, his back pressed against the closing door.

'Patrick!' he yelled, beckoning the nearest passengers through the hatch. 'Elaine! Come on! There's not much time!'

Only a few metres away, Patrick shepherded the rest of the colonists who were now having to hold on to rails and stanchions to make progress against the strong inflow. In front of him, Claire's gaze fixed on the hatch, her expression determined as she waded through the rushing water. A gust of wind blew in from the outside, whipping her hair across her eyes. Jann reached for her hand, steadying her as she clambered out. With a groan of buckling metal the ship leaned further over, increasing the flow of seawater and steepening the incline of the corridor. Several of the passengers screamed. Behind Patrick, one of them lost his footing and tumbled back, hitting the rising surface of the floodwater with a loud splash.

'Hang on!' yelled Patrick to the others, holding on to the man in front of him until Jann could grab his hand.

One by one the bedraggled and frightened travellers crawled to the outer hull and launched themselves into the foaming waters. By the time Elaine reached the exit the wind had become a howling gale, plucking handfuls of water from the tops of the waves and hurling them against the faces of those emerging from the downed Valiant. The cafeteria had flooded. A few at the rear of the group started to panic—shouting and screaming while they trod water. Those at the front fought to scramble on to the cramped space in the few metres of corridor left above the rising flood. Jann remained braced across the inside of the hatch, Patrick behind him, each helping the terrified colonists to climb through to safety.

Somehow Jann's contorted face and straining muscles, the Herculean effort he expended to prevent the door from closing on them and removing their last chance of escape, communicated itself to the rest of the group. Their panic abated. Nobody wanted to be the one to make Jann slip, or release the door. That fear overrode the hysteria, allowing an almost orderly exit. Jann's stoicism, coupled with Patrick's alacrity and determination to stay until the last, most vulnerable passenger had been dragged from the corridor behind him and pushed through the hatch, saved one hundred lives.

'Is that everyone?'

'Just you and me.'

'You go then. If I move this damn door will go.'

'Sure?'

'Stop wasting time. I'll be right with you.'

They hit the ocean together with a splash.

pennatanah landing point
2 Jun 2175

The smell of damp clothing hung over the bedraggled crowd like a reminder of a bad mood. Those who arrived first were already wrapped in towels, or robes, or sheets. The unlucky majority reached land after the supply of such luxuries had been exhausted. They sat shivering in their waterlogged underwear, huddled in small groups around portable heaters and contributing to the odiferous humidity.

Jann Argent thought the scene reminiscent of the images of flood plain refugees he had seen on the vidcasts he watched back in pokey. He scoped out the exits in his habitual way, then glanced at the new friends he had first met a hundred years ago. He could not share tales of prison cell TV shows with them.

Very little conversation punctuated the thick atmosphere of the immigration centre. Most people stared sightlessly into middle distance, the shock of their recent experience plain on pallid faces and in red-rimmed eyes. All the sobbing had ceased, at least. They had all seen enough salt water and wanted to avoid contributing more. Their tears had long since dried up, even though the tracks were still evident on many faces.

A small group of Perse immigration officers did the rounds with cups of water, hot drinks and sandwiches. The belated and catastrophic arrival of the Valiant had caught them unawares. Once the ship had dropped out of light speed and established radio contact, those on planet had only three days' notice of their approach, but even the best preparations would have been no match for the disastrous crash-landing. The officials were still playing catch up, trying to alleviate some of the worst after-effects while assembling as much information as they could about the survivors. Jann took a sandwich. The local bread had an unusual blue tint and a hint of mace in its flavour, but it took the edge off his hunger.

At one end of the assembly hall an athletically-built woman with cropped black hair stepped onto a small podium. She tapped the foam windshield on a microphone protruding from the lectern.

'Could I have your attention, please,' she said, jerking back in surprise when her first words boomed out across the room and began to howl through the speakers.

'My name is Felice Waters. I am the senior immigration

controller here. As you can see, we were not very well prepared for your arrival, for which I apologise. Fact is, we were expecting the Endurance. She's nine years overdue. Your ship wasn't supposed to be here until after her. So what are you all doing here, that's what I'd like to know?'

A few polite chuckles did little to relieve the exhausted tension in the air.

'Anyway, even if we'd been ready for you we weren't equipped to cope with the crash. Valiant managed to transmit the passenger records to us before... before we lost contact with the crew, and we've been checking you off against those as quickly as we can.

'We should be done in the next hour or so, and there are more supplies of dry clothing on the way so please bear with us. We'll try and make you as comfortable as possible. Normally there would have been a welcome presentation, but that's been put back until tomorrow to allow you all time to dry off, have a meal and gather your wits.'

The woman paused, consulting a page of hand-written notes.

'It's important I mention one thing right away,' she went on. 'Some of you may already have heard rumours about this so ahead of tomorrow's briefing I wanted to give you the shortened version before hearsay has a chance to start circulating. You'll all have seen the marketing video about how life would be once you arrived here. The reality is a little different from what you were expecting. Turned out this planet is not uninhabited.'

She paused again to allow a ripple of surprise to subside.

'The Earther population has had to fit in with the social structure already in place. A society we landed in the middle of when we came here nine years ago. Near as we can tell it's been going for several hundred years. Anyway like I said, more of that tomorrow when you'll be honoured by a visit from one of our local dignitaries.'

pennatanah landing point
2 Jun 2175

A few hours later the last of the arrivees—Jann had almost stopped thinking of them as refugees—had been provided with warm dry clothing. Some of Waters' colleagues fired up a portable range and a queue formed for what promised to be a basic meal. At least it would be hot.

'Smells good.'

Jann wheeled to find Elaine occupying the place behind him in the line.

'You stalking me?' he asked, only half joking.

'Yep.'

'Thought so. Do you mind if I swallow my dinner before you slit my throat?'

She raised an eyebrow.

'Do I look the throat-slitting type?'

'You can never tell.'

'Well, a girl likes to have some mystery, but whether or not I would despatch some of the more odious low-lives I've encountered in my past, I don't think I'd be very popular if I did away with the hero of the hour.'

Jann felt his face redden but said nothing.

'Come on! Don't be modest. There's a hundred people who wouldn't be in this queue if you hadn't burst into action out there.'

'Right place, right time. I've always been good with doors.'

'Holding them open? Your mother teach you those old-fashioned manners?'

Jann stared at the makeshift servery in front of him.

'I don't remember.'

He shrugged, then noticed Elaine regarding him with the same stunned look of recognition she had flashed in the departure hall a hundred years ago.

'What?'

She looked away.

'Nothing.'

'No, come on. That's the second time you've stared at me like that. Like you know me, or know something about me. What is it?'

Elaine checked the queue behind them. Ahead only three or four people remained before they would be served.

'I can't talk about it here. I'm not sure I should talk about it at all.'

She sighed.

'There again if I leave it long enough I probably won't need to say anything.'

'You're not making any sense,' Jann said.

He reached the front of the queue. The rudimentary servery comprised a series of four metal bowls sitting in a trough of water, heated from below with a small log fire. The first two contained a choice of mains—a meat stew cooked with small yellow sultana-like fruits and accompanied by pea-sized blue vegetables; and a vegetarian option made mainly from larger blue vegetables cut into strips. Both were being served with a similarly binary selection of staples. In the third bowl a steaming pink mashed root vegetable gave off an interesting smell redolent of nutmeg. The last bowl contained the only thing Jann recognised: plain boiled rice. Supplies the first two ships must have brought with them, unless the early settlers had found somewhere it would grow.

He opted for meat stew with rosy-coloured mash. Elaine chose the vegetable dish with rice.

'You veggie then?'

'Not always, but I'm not sure what's gone into that stew.'

Jann regarded his steaming plate with new suspicion.

'Looks a bit like beef.'

'Yeah, well, I don't think there are any cows on B— Perse.'

'Must be some kind of edible local animal. The blurb said livestock can't survive cryosleep, so whatever it is it ain't real beef.'

'Exactly. Could be anything. Shall we eat al fresco? I think we have time.'

'Time?'

'Before it starts raining.'

They collected cutlery and carried their meals outside. The weather had become calmer now, only a light breeze ruffling the spikes of Elaine's flame-red hair. They chose a grassy mound with a good all-round view where they could eat in comfort and watch the swell. The raisin-like yellow fruits in his stew tasted of cinnamon, giving it a Moroccan edge. He devoured it all, surprised how hungry he was.

Breakers crashed against the pebbles on the nearby shore, trying to wear down their resistance to a quieter life in the cold depths beneath the churning foam. The thought of the darkness and coldness of the deep brought Jann a pang of guilt for the lives he had not been able to save. Across the bay, the bow of the Valiant stood out of the waves glistening wetly in the light from a single bright moon riding low in the sky.

'I wasn't joking about it being a brave thing you did,' Elaine said. 'Most people would have looked after themselves. Only.'

Once again Jann did not reply. He felt nothing like a hero.

'You might need that brave streak again after tomorrow,' Elaine went on, finishing her last mouthful of rice.

'Sounds like you know what's coming,' Jann replied. 'You heard rumours?'

'Call it insider information.'

'Rumours.'

'No. It's more than that. Why don't you remember your mother?' she asked, changing the subject.

'I don't remember anything before I... before eight

years ago.'

'*Eight* years?' Elaine asked, fixing Jann with a piercing stare.

'Yeah. What's so unusual about that? I guess I had some kind of episode—brain fart or whatever. When I came to I was standing in a room I'd never been in, with a man I'd never seen.' Jann stopped himself from revealing the man had been dead. Something about Elaine tempted him to share the whole truth with her, but circumspection had been one of the many lessons his years on the prison moon had taught him.

'And it's never come back, your memory?'

'I keep hoping,' Jann admitted, 'but so far, no. The odd inexplicable dream. Corridors. Doorways. Falling. That kind of thing.'

A few fat spots of rain splashed onto Jann's empty plate.

'Eight years is a long time to have amnesia,' Elaine said, standing up and taking the plate from him.

'Yeah, well, I've learned to live with it. Live for the moment, isn't that what shrinks and life coaches always say? Well the moment is all I have.'

pennatanah landing point
3 Jun 2175

The next day an excited buzz flew around the processing hall. According to rumour the promised "visiting dignitary" would be a Queen. Jann had eight years of antipathy towards authority figures. He determined in advance not to let home-grown royalty impress him. Elaine's reaction proved more puzzling. She seemed positively disappointed. They shared a cold breakfast before taking their seats in the assembly hall.

'Something bugging you this morning?' he had asked as he wiped up the last of his mushroom ketchup with a nub-end of crusty roll. The local sauce had been a revelation. A small consolation for having to drink his coffee black. He soon discovered dairy animals did not yet exist on this new world. He would have taken creamer had it been on offer. Unfortunately replacement supplies were sitting on the bottom of the bay in the drowned Valiant.

'I really wanted to see the other one,' she muttered.

When pressed she had refused to elaborate, telling Jann he would find out soon enough. They had not exchanged more than half a dozen words since. Now the presentation was about to begin, Elaine had disappeared.

Silence rippled across the hall as the promised Queen entered, marching past the few ranks of seats. She wore a full length black dress, intricately embroidered with glistening ebony thread which reflected the light like polished jet. It swayed and rustled as she walked up the central aisle. Her long glossy black hair, held away from her face by a circlet of polished stone set in the centre with a black diamond, fell down her back like an ebony cataract in full flood. Her smooth skin was deathly pale, as if she had caught too many rays of silver moonlight instead of being tanned by the sun. Only a slight greying of her hair at the temples gave any hint of her age.

The short figure of a man Jann took to be one of the Queen's advisors maintained a respectful distance behind his queen. His face too had a waxen appearance although in his case its lack of colour was accentuated by the contrast with his hair, dyed a loud shade of purple.

The Queen mounted the few steps to the small stage at the front of the hall to be greeted by a man in full dress uniform. Claire had pointed him out to Jann earlier. Commodore Brian Oduya, captain of the Endeavour, most senior officer of the fleet left alive and notional leader of the Earther colony on planet. The Queen maintained a regal bearing while she stood behind the Commodore waiting to be introduced. Jann thought her an imposing, charismatic figure, but the slight smile that creased her lips made her seem more approachable than he had expected.

Clearly someone who demanded respect, yet skilfully avoided appearing aloof or domineering.

Commodore Oduya stepped to the front of the podium.

'We are indeed honoured this morning to have a very important guest. She has graciously agreed to make a special trip to be with us after yesterday's tragic incident to deliver her message in person—an honour we have not previously enjoyed. But rather than listening to me, I'm sure you would all prefer to hear from the Queen herself, so without further ado I am delighted to introduce her Majesty the Queen of Kertonia.'

He clasped hands with the Queen, a tradition she was clearly unfamiliar with, before stepping aside. The Queen moved to the centre of the podium, her long dress giving the appearance of floating. Inclining her head in the Commodore's direction, she began her address.

'Thank you Commodore, and may I bid all the newcomers welcome to Berikatanya.'

She paused as a murmur of surprise together with the occasional muttered "told you so" rose through the gathering. Once everyone had settled back to polite silence, the Queen continued.

'As I am sure some of you have already heard, that is what we call our world. We do not recognise the name Perse. Having never seen our sun in your... constellations, it means nothing to us. We are sure you will soon adjust to the correct name of your new home.

'In some ways, you are fortunate your arrival has been delayed so long. If you had arrived according to your original plan, you would have found things not so... straightforward. The first colonists to reach our fair Berikatanya expected to have the planet to themselves. For us, before that first ship came, we had not even conceived of life on other worlds. We had barely begun to learn about the planets circling our own sun, let alone those at such unimaginable distances as your own.

'So these two groups of surprised people were at first quite suspicious of each other. One might even say hostile to each other's presence here. Fortunately for you—for all of us—we were able to negotiate a way forward. It became clear you Batu'n...'

The Queen stopped, two small circles of colour darkening her cheeks. Her pale green eyes scanned the audience. She drew herself up to her full height before continuing.

'Forgive us. In our language your planet is known as Ketiga Batu, so you will sometimes hear yourselves referred to as Batu'n. It is not an insult, but only a term that comes more easily to us than "Earthers". Anyway it was clear your people could not return. Your ships, though undoubtedly impressive feats of engineering, are designed to make one journey only. We would never have insisted on condemning you to the cold space between worlds for a second time, even if you could have found an alternative destination.'

Jann began to wonder how these simple folk, who at first sight had no technological sophistication to speak of, could possibly have "insisted" on the humans leaving if the crew and passengers of the Endeavour had been intent on staying, but he could not let his thoughts distract him for long as the Queen was coming to the interesting part: what would happen to them next.

'... begin an integration program for those who wanted to join in more closely with Berikatanyan society—either with my own people or across the plain in Istania—where we would welcome you into our lives and find roles for you to match your skills. There are many areas of study in which the Batu'n are more advanced than ourselves, and yet as we understand it many of you came seeking a slower, more rural pace of life. That is exactly what we can offer you, in exchange for hard work and a commitment to honour our allegiances and principles.

'Of course we also accept some of you will not wish to

become integrated. This is understandable. There are several smaller colonies that remain separate from Berikatanyan rule. They are engaged in land clearance projects, the study of our local animals and plants, and other such activities. Your people will be able to explain all this in greater detail. Over the next two or three days they will ask you to decide where you would prefer to be placed.

'My small entourage will stay here at Pennatanah so we may escort those of you who elect to join me at Palace. For those travelling to Court to join the King, we are unable to provide any assistance, or to predict what the King will do for you. It may be necessary for some of your own people to journey here from Istania to fetch you.

'I would encourage you to consider carefully which path you will take to your futures on our world, as once you have made a decision there is no possibility you will be able to change your mind.'

The subtext of the Queen's words was lost on Jann, although he was acutely aware of one. Her speech concluded with another welcome after which the meeting turned over to Felice who explained the logistics of where people could find more information and how to register their decisions. The assembly then broke up, most of the Valiant passengers filing out of the hall, chattering and laughing with excitement as they discussed their options, each beginning to form their independent conclusions about the future.

Elaine—who appeared beside him soon after the Queen's party had left—was still determined to sign for the King's Court. This seemed the best option to Jann too, at first, even though he had been looking on it as "the opposition" since listening to the Queen's speech. But her address reminded him of something about Elaine Chandler that had been nagging at him for some time. When the Queen introduced herself and welcomed the newcomers to her world—the world of Berikatanya—it had immediately connected in Jann's mind with the strange way Elaine always sounded as though she was calling the planet Berse, instead of Perse. Almost as if she knew its real name, even before they arrived here.

pennatanah landing point
3 Jun 2175

Terry Spate waited for the excited crush around the chalkboards to dissipate. They had been set up to allow the new colonists to divide themselves between the Berikatanyan factions and the Earther colonies. Roles and locations were mapped out in a series of grids, one for each of the main groups. Some of the positions had limited capacity but Terry did not expect his preference to be oversubscribed. A last small group of chattering young women signed up for a new life in the Queen's lands. Terry stepped forward, eyes still fixed on the boards. He was rolling a piece of chalk around his fingers when he heard a voice he recognised.

'You'll have to move faster than that to nab the plum spots,' said the Yamani girl.

He had seen her around the hall, but not caught up with her in person until now. He beamed her a gentle smile.

'I don't move fast these days,' he said, choosing his words deliberately.

He offered her the chalk.

'Not sure as I ever did, truth be told.'

'So have you blown your chances?' she asked airily, ignoring the proffered chalk and scanning the board.

'Doesn't look like it.'

'Must be your lucky day.'

'I like to make my own luck young lady,' Terry rumbled. 'Then I've only myself to blame if it goes pear-shaped.'

'I think I've decided to go along with that Queen. She

103

seems like a decent sort. Not that I have any experience of royal types. Didn't see many of those where I've been living. I do have vague memories of the government wallahs my dad used to hang around with though. I think I'll be OK with Palace protocol.'

Terry shot her a rueful glance.

'I think it's you who's left it too late,' he said. 'Those ladies have taken the last three places at the Palace.'

'You're kidding!' the girl squealed, stepping forward and looking from board to board until she found the right column.

'Damn it all!'

'Did you have a second choice?'

'No.'

She collapsed onto a nearby chair, shoulders slumped. Terry took the seat next to her.

'I hadn't really thought it through very well,' she admitted. 'Part of me shied away from involving myself right away in an alien community. It felt a bit weird. That's Sensible Me talking. Wanting to take more time to adjust to the rural pace before jumping in with both feet. Impetuous Me had already been caught up with the romance and glamour of the Palace. Or the idea of it. I mean, where else would someone like me be able to hang out with a queen?'

'I can see how it would be attractive. To you I mean. Much more glamorous than what I'll be doing.'

The young woman looked mortified.

'God, I'm so wrapped up in me I never asked what you wanted to do. Where are you going?'

'I've signed up—was about to sign up—for one of the forestry clearance details. It's a good match for my skills. Not that there'll be much in the way of posh gardening for a while yet, but it'll keep me outdoors. I like being out in the open. It'll be nice to breathe some fresh air now I've left that pod behind. Doesn't look like the people here have made much progress with their agriculture in the past nine years. Far as I can tell anyways. I guess that's mainly for want of skilled plantsmen and the fact most Earthers have been mesmerised by ...'

He caught himself but it was too late. A toss of her fine pale hair and flashing eyes made it all too plain she knew where he had been leading.

'... the idea of court life,' she said, finishing his sentence. 'The glamour and glitz, far removed from the real world.'

'Yes, well I don't suppose the reality is all that glamorous or glitzy, not on such a technologically challenged planet, but most of them won't realise until it's too late.'

An awkward silence fell between the two, punctuated only by the sound of heavy rain on the roof.

'Wouldn't surprise me if there's some argy-bargy going on with that King and Queen neither,' Terry added at length. 'It might be uncomfortable to find yourself too caught up in one side or the other until you know exactly how the land lies.'

They sat in silence for a few minutes. Terry moved to make his mark on the chalkboard when the girl snatched the chalk from his hand, strode over to the nearest one, and wrote her name on the "Earther" list.

'I'm coming with you,' she declared. 'Keep you out of mischief.'

pennatanah landing point
4 Jun 2175

Jann stood between two boards looking first at one and then the other. And then back to the first. The left hand board, headed 'Court', held considerably fewer names than the right, which bore the legend 'Palace'. This latter, the home of the Queen, no longer had any free spaces for women although there were still a handful of jobs available for men. Jann figured the Queen's charismatic presentation had swayed many more people in her direction and had also been responsible for a general antipathy towards the King. He understood those feelings. He would have admitted being drawn to the enigmatic and beautiful Queen. On the other hand (he looked back at the Court board) he had never been one to follow the crowd. The thought of being part of a smaller, and therefore more select, group appealed to him.

'Jann Argent?'

The voice disturbing his bilateral quandary belonged to the immigration officer—Felice something.

'Yes?'

'Would you come with me for a moment, please?'

She did not wait for his reply, but walked off to the back of the hall, down a short corridor to an unmarked door which she opened to allow him to precede her into her office. It was smaller and less well-appointed than the last office he had been in, and without an impressive picture window giving a breathtaking view of Mars, but Jann felt there were other parallels with his last interview. He shivered. What was this all about?

'Have a seat.'

'What's this about?' he asked, voicing his thoughts.

Felice flipped open a folder lying on her desk.

'Your passenger entry,' she said, placing her right hand flat over his photograph. 'Your *secure* passenger entry.'

The chill along Jann's spine tingled anew. Beneath his shirt, his pendant felt cold against his chest. The governor had told him his encrypted travel record, available to the authorities, would not conceal his past. This woman must have read about his time on Phobos, his story of memory lapses, his work with the security detail. She knew almost as much about him as he did. He glanced from the officer to his records and back, unable to speak.

'Don't worry, I'm not about to share it with anyone. As far as I'm concerned you've done your time. You won the right to a second chance in that Tournament. Normally I'd be keeping a close watch on someone like you, but I've read all this...'

She tidied the pages of his record and closed the folder.

'...and it seems to me the conviction was dodgy in the first place.'

The folder disappeared into the bottom draw of the woman's filing cabinet.

'But beyond the lack of any real evidence against you, I've also seen first-hand how you handle yourself when you're up against it.'

Her reference to Jann's heroic actions after the downing of the Valiant made him relax a little.

'Says you were a security man.'

'If that's what it says. I might have told them I was a door man. They must have assumed I worked security. Got me on the cell-side detail though, so I'm not complaining.'

'Ever do any detective work?'

'I was a convict, not a cop.'

'Pity.'

'So if you're not going to cuff me and send me to whatever passes for hard labour on this planet, what is this about?'

'I could use a little assistance from someone who can see both sides of a story,' she said. 'Probably better if I don't explain too much. It wouldn't help if you started off thinking I'm crazy. Besides, it'll be easier to show you than tell you.'

Jann blew out the breath he had been holding.

'All sounds very vague. Can you give me anything? I mean, I don't mind helping you out if it's something I can do, but I might have had plans of my own, you know?'

'Far as I could tell your plans didn't extend much beyond not staying here. I watched you for quite some time, trying to decided where to put your mark. It was never going to be the Colony, was it?'

'No,' Jann admitted. Little point in hiding what she had

already seen.

'I couldn't decide whether the Court or the Palace is the better bet.'

'Well, if you want to help me out we'll be heading for the Blood King's Court.'

'The *Blood* King? Never heard him called that before.'

'We try to avoid mentioning it in advance. Gives people the wrong idea. But that's his official title among the locals.

'Anyway it's his land where the... where my little problem is. My latest little problem. There's been a few recently, but I can fill you in on some of the background on the way.'

She stared at Jann, as if trying to decide how far she could trust him. He wondered what could be so crazy about this "problem" of hers. He also wondered why someone would be known as the Blood King.

'Just because we're heading out that way doesn't mean you'd necessarily be signed up with the King,' Felice continued. 'We can leave it open for now. Say you're with me. Give you more time to come to a firm decision.'

Jann leaned forward. He found the chance to scope out the Blood King's realm without having committed himself in advance very tempting.

'OK. When do we leave?'

'You're almost the last to make a mark on the boards. Everyone else leaves tomorrow. We'll tag along with them, provided you're packed and ready.'

Back in the hall, Jann sought out Patrick. He stood talking with Elaine.

'Made your mind up yet?' he asked as Jann walked up.

'Kind of. I'm leaving for Court in the morning.'

Patrick beamed.

'Excellent! We'll all be travelling together.'

Elaine punched him on the arm.

'We'll make a courtier of you yet, hero!' she crowed.

'You're both going to the King too?'

'Oh yes,' said Elaine, her eyes narrowing. 'I wouldn't

dream of going anywhere else.'

Chapter 8

'I expected flyers,' Jann said.

They had left the coast around mid-morning to make the journey to the Blood King's Court. A tenacious mist still clung to the ground in patches, obscuring their path. Fortunately local weather conditions did not faze the animals they were riding—Berikatanya's equivalent to horses. Similar in most respects, the local mounts were a little taller on average, with no mane and faces more reminiscent of llamas. Despite these differences all the Earthers still referred to them as horses. As far as Jann could remember, he had never ridden before. He was managing to stay in the saddle without too much trouble, but struggled to keep up with Felice.

'Can't spare them for a regular job like this,' she replied over her shoulder.

No representatives had been sent from the Court to escort them. Felice, making the trip anyway on account of her most recent request for investigation of unusual occurrences, had been adopted as de facto leader of the group for the duration of their journey.

'They're not in very good shape after nine years,' she went on. 'We'd already lost two of the four we started out with. The new pair that came with you on the Valiant are sitting at the bottom of Pennatanah Bay, along with all the spares and replacement power packs. But in any case, the locals don't like them.'

'Don't like them?' said Jann, a little breathless. 'You mean such an overt display of technological superiority intimidates them?'

Felice barked a laugh but did not reply right away. Ahead, the short trail of Berikatanyan horses picked their way between boulders as they began to climb the slight incline into the foothills of the mountain range separating the Blood King's lands from those of the Black Queen. A handful of riders still looked uncomfortable in their saddles but most had settled in to the rhythm of the animals' stride well enough, the present slow pace of the march allowing those with no riding experience to overcome their nerves.

'It's not really about who's superior and who isn't,' Felice replied at length. 'It's more important we carry on doing everything we can to fit in here. We use the flyers when we have to, or in emergencies. Ferrying newcomers to their new homes doesn't count.'

'So if I fall off...'

Felice laughed.

'Maybe if you severed your femoral artery or something.'

'You use them often then, the flyers?'

'A few times.'

'Not many arteries severed here I guess.'

'Mainly to transport supplies to places that are hard to reach. Once or twice we've had to protect ourselves from incursions.'

'Incursions? Really? So things aren't always as easy-going as the Queen made out?'

'Most of the Berikatanyans are fine with us being here. Or at least, too scared of their lords and masters to resist our presence openly.'

'But not all of them.'

'A few small groups tested our mettle early on. Once they discovered we're more than capable of looking after ourselves they pretty much left us alone. They're kept busy enough with the local unrest now anyway.'

'There's unrest?'

'Something else we thought we should keep quiet about in case it put people off. Basically there's an ongoing feud between Palace and Court that kicks off every now and then. Skirmishes, the odd border dispute. They've had full-blown wars in the past but it's been a few years since there was a major battle. Although tensions have lately been picking up rapidly. Wouldn't be surprised if there's another fight looming.'

'How long has it been going on?'

'Couple of hundred years, near as we've been able to find out.'

Jann reined his mount to a halt.

'Two hundred years? And you didn't think it was worth mentioning?'

Felice did not stop, or reply. Jann heeled his horse to a trot until they were riding abreast once more.

'Nearer three hundred probably,' she said. 'We have to fit in. It's unrealistic to expect there not to be a few problems. We've been here nine years and the trouble has never escalated beyond an occasional raid in small areas of disputed territory. It hasn't involved any Earthers. Pointless frightening anyone from the Valiant. Scaring them off from enjoying what will most likely be a happy and productive collaboration with one or other of the Houses.'

'Still think you should have at least told us,' Jann said, 'especially if it's getting worse. It's not right, letting people make up their minds without knowing the full facts.'

They rode on for some time, not speaking. Jann chewed on the irony that you could travel almost a hundred light-years and still not escape human duplicity. After a while, Felice changed the subject.

'So you're not a murderer then?'

'No, but I must have looked like one.'

'Standing at the scene, covered in blood, mutilated corpse on the floor, no other witnesses.'

'That's about the size of it.'

'No other suspects either.'

'Apparently not.'

'And you with no memory of who you were, where you were, how you got there, or who he was.'

'You've committed all this to your own memory? You must fancy me.'

She laughed again.

'Don't flatter yourself. I'm a career girl. But I'll say this much—you don't sound like any of the murderers I've ever known.'

'How many is that?'

'Enough.'

'Encouraging.'

The travellers reached the top of the incline. Where the ground levelled out, the vegetation began to change. Scrubby coastal plants gave way to lush green grasses and shrubs. Small groups of blue-skinned grazing animals wandered the plain, paying them no attention. In the distance Jann could make out a few copses of broad-leaved trees.

Now that the three carts carrying the handful of colonists unable to ride had reached level ground, the company increased its pace. Elaine, who had stayed back to ensure the wagons negotiated the hill successfully, spurred her horse into a position close behind Jann and Felice.

'Ever get your memory back?' Felice asked him.

'I have snatches occasionally. And weird dreams. But mainly it's all still a blank.'

'Any headaches?'

'No. Why?'

'Amnesia is sometimes associated with headaches or migraines.'

'Not in my case. Does it give you bad dreams?'

'Depends. I guess the dreams could be your subconscious trying to break through. Do they have a pattern?'

Jann considered the question for a moment. The nightmares had really bothered him back on Phobos. Their frequency and intensity gave him many sleepless nights, bordering on a phobia of going to sleep altogether. Since his arrival on Berikatanya they had not troubled him. Now he thought about it, even the memory of them had faded.

'Doorways, mostly. And falling.'

They approached the first of the copses, a small clump of trees which had grown up beside a shallow pool. A brightly coloured bird took off from one of the trees with a raucous cry, startling a few of the leading horses.

'Falling is a very common dream,' said Felice. 'To your death, off a cliff...? What kind of falling?'

'Not sure really. Just through the air I think. Or through the dark. I could never see where I would land.'

'Usually it means you feel you've lost control of your life.'

She checked over her shoulder. Close behind them a startled horse had unseated one of the riders. Elaine had dropped back to help the man back into the saddle.

'Which I guess in your case would have been true. When you were on Phobos,' Felice continued. 'Big time. What about the doors?'

'They were usually open. I could see through to the other side but I could never reach it. Never step through. Like I'd been nailed to the spot.'

'It's all connected in one way or another,' she said, turning back in her saddle to face him.

'Open doors represent new opportunities. Closed ones are about chances you can't take, or changes you can't make. The fact the door was open, yet you couldn't walk through it suggests you're subconsciously aware of an opportunity or a change, but in your waking life you're being prevented from moving forward. Paralysis is another representation of the same thing. It highlights a situation in your life where you feel pressured but you can't take action. All of this can be explained by your imprisonment for something you don't remember doing. Something totally out of character.'

They rode past the copse. The trees grew more densely than had been apparent from a distance, hiding most of the pool from view. The bird with the iridescent plumage had returned, perching in one of the nearest branches. Felice watched the woods as they moved along the rough stony path.

'You're pretty clued up for an immigration officer,' Jann said.

'Dreams are a sideline. They've always fascinated me. I used to work homicide back on Earth. Came here to set up the local police outfit. Or that was my idea. Turned out there wasn't much policing required, so I opted for immigration. Then there wasn't much of that needed either, so I guess you could say I'm a bit of a square peg in a round hole.'

'Didn't fancy the Court, or the Palace?'

'I'm not much of a joiner. I wanted a rural idyll, not a medieval feudal system. It's easy to find yourself sucked in.'

They rode on for some time, Jann lost in his thoughts. The implications of the tensions between a high-tech interloper and two home-grown feudal—and feuding—structures were only beginning to become clear to him. A shout from the rearmost cart snatched his attention back to the present. He turned his horse, already behind Felice who had spurred her mount back along the line. One of the carts was under attack!

A small group of raiders, scruffily dressed in worn leathers with black scarves tied around their faces, had concealed themselves in the copse. They had caught up with the last cart as it passed hoping to surprise the occupants and subdue them before they could raise the alarm. The driver lay on the grass, what looked like the shaft of an arrow protruding from his shoulder. The remaining colonists defended the wagon as best they could using whatever came to hand—frying pans and kitchen knives mainly. One of the marauders had climbed onto the bench seat and taken hold of the reins, trying to turn the cart.

Even as Jann rode up the efforts of the raiders were clearly doomed. They had failed to maintain their stealth and were outnumbered by the rest of the group. Felice had drawn a pistol. She gesticulated with it as she rode down one of the raiders.

'Perga darsan!' she yelled, aiming at the man's head.

He turned and ran for the safety of the copse. As Felice wheeled her horse to take a bead on the second bandit, the one on the cart started screaming. His tunic had burst into flames and set fire to his beard.

The burning raider leapt to the grass, rolling frantically around to extinguish himself. His comrades did not wait to see if he succeeded, but followed the first at a run back toward the copse.

Sat unmoving on her horse in the middle of the trail, Elaine burst into laughter. Felice holstered her weapon.

'You think this is funny?'

Elaine flashed the immigration officer an angry look, her eyes smouldering. With a toss of her spiky red hair she steered her horse around. The animal reared up, showing the whites of its eyes before setting off back up the trail at a gallop.

'We're not going to finish them off?' Jann asked, watching the now smoking raider limp away after the rest of his group.

Felice turned her horse back along the path.

'What for? They know we're on our guard. They won't try again. We're moving too fast now for them to catch us, and if we wanted to "finish them off" as you so delicately put it, we'd have to follow them into the trees, where they'd have the advantage.

'No, we'll press on. It'll be dark soon enough. We can make camp once we've passed the last copse.'

As Felice had predicted, there were no repeats of the first attack. In a few hours they reached the spot she had identified as a good place to stop for the night: a wide sweep of flat grass beside the river which afforded a clear view for several hundred metres in every direction; a source of fresh water; and some scrubby bushes they could use to make a fire.

After they had eaten, the group divided along lines of friendships struck up in the departure hall, forged in the aftermath of the crash, and tempered with their choice of the Blood King's Court. Small gatherings sat around communal tents or beside the fire. Jann, Elaine and Patrick walked down to the river where they found a large flat-topped rock on which to sit with their feet dangling in the slow-moving waters. After a short time, Felice joined them.

'You were very evasive about your little problem before we left. How about you fill me in on this mystery we're supposed to be solving? Something about magic?'

Elaine shifted her position on the rock, turning to face Felice, her expression unreadable in the congealing dusk.

'It took me a while before I finally admitted there could be only one explanation for some of the things I've seen,' she began, 'but in the end I did admit it. There is magic here.'

Patrick lifted his feet out of the water and dried them on the bottoms of his trousers.

'Sounds a bit far-fetched,' he murmured, 'but you don't strike me as the type for wild fancy. You don't really fit the pattern.'

'It wasn't my first guess.'

'But you've explored all the possibilities?' Jann asked.

'When you work in homicide, it's never long before someone mentions the fundamental principle of the world's most famous detective. When you have eliminated the impossible, whatever remains, however improbable, must be the truth.'

'Sherlock Holmes,' said Patrick.

'In one.'

'I don't remember Holmes ever falling back on magic as an answer to any of his conundrums,' Patrick said, drying between his toes, 'but assuming you're right, what kind of magic is it?'

'Varies. What I've heard about is not much more than parlour tricks really. Lighting candles, blowing them out. Opening and closing doors. That kind of thing.'

'Have you seen any of it for yourself?'

'Yes. Well, maybe. It's always hard to be sure. Remember how that marauder's tunic caught on fire earlier today?'

'I assumed one of our lot had put a match to him or something,' Jann said.

'Hardly the kind of defence you'd come up with in a crisis is it?' Felice laughed. 'Striking a match? No, but it's a good example of what I mean. Fire is involved in quite a lot of the tales I've heard, and sometimes there's no logical explanation of how it starts, or what it does.'

'Nothing dangerous enough to be a threat in this ongoing feud you told me about though?'

Elaine snorted, flashing Jann a disdainful look. She appeared to be on the verge of making a sarcastic remark, but thought better of it.

'Whatever magic is around right now, there are hints it was much more powerful at one time,' Felice continued, 'especially in the hands of certain individuals. But the locals are reluctant to talk about why they don't do more with what little magic they have left.'

'Certain individuals,' Elaine echoed. It was more of a statement than a question.

'What's this about a feud?' asked Patrick, who had moved to sit on the inner edge of the rock and had been giving Felice his full attention for some time.

'We normally leave it up to whichever faction you join to put their side of the story,' Felice began.

'Faction? Makes it sound like a guerrilla war.'

'Well it is. In a way. It's certainly more political than religious. For all their faults the Berikatanyans seem to have avoided any kind of religion. Their beliefs—as far as

I've discovered—are a kind of rural humanism.'

'Like the Celts.' Patrick said.

'More or less, but without the druidic element. They don't worship nature, but they do understand the ebb and flow of the seasons, and they respect the environment.'

'Sounds more like some of the North American tribes then,' Patrick offered.

'Yes. They're the closest parallel I could think of too,' Felice agreed.

'Anyway for whatever reason, the forces allied to the King and Queen, and their ancestors, have been sparring for somewhere around three hundred years. Sometimes there are periods of calm—like now. It's been relatively quiet since we arrived. Not sure how much of that is our influence. Maybe they're taking stock. Waiting for us to show our hand, or come down on one side or the other. But from what I've been told it won't be very long until things kick off again. Some border dispute or argument over water rights will flare up. Before you know it there'll be all-out war.'

'Jeez.' Jann scratched his head. 'So much for the rural idyll.'

'That's why we're careful to play an even hand with each side. We haven't shared our tech with any of them— not that we brought a lot with us. A few small arms to keep the peace and the odd flyer. We weren't expecting to have to pick sides between two flaky local tribes. As you know from your briefings the whole intention of the colony program was to build, grow, or invent everything we would need once we landed. The machines and tools we do have are only meant to facilitate that principle. To see us through the first decade or so while we find our feet.'

'So what will it mean, us deciding to throw our lot in with the King?' Patrick asked. 'Are we expected to join his army, or something?'

Jann shook his head.

'I'm no conscript,' he said. 'There's always two sides to an argument, and rarely one side entirely in the right. I'd need to know a lot more about the situation before I'd fight for anyone.'

Felice did not appear to have a ready answer for Patrick. After a while he jumped down from the rock, dusting off the legs of his jeans.

'That's enough to think about for one night,' he said. 'I'm going to try to get some sleep. Night.'

'Good night,' said Felice.

Elaine followed Patrick without a word.

campsite
5 Jun 2175

Night had fallen while the small group were talking. Both moons shone down on the camp, their light shattering into flickering motes on the river as it ran over submerged boulders, throwing deep shadows around the rock on which Jann and Felice sat. The chittering of an anonymous creature echoed in the nearby copse, answered by a throaty hoot from the opposite riverbank. Jann stared at the moons, seeing them together for the first time since arriving on Berikatanya.

'Weird,' he said at length.

'What's weird?'

'There are two moons. Like on Mars. But I never saw Mars' moons from the planet.'

'No. You lived on one of them.'

'Yeah, but even in transit to Phobos, and before I left to come here, I never had chance to see it in the Martian sky at the same time as Deimos.'

'Why is that weird?'

'What's weird is that I recognise them. They seem familiar. How can that be, if I've never seen them before?'

'I don't know. You think it might be a suppressed memory? Something to do with your amnesia?'

'Maybe. I just know I've seen them before. And that's not all.'

Felice waited while Jann gathered his thoughts.

'These horses. Or whatever they're called here.'

'Kudai.'

'Right. There were no horses on Phobos. The only thing I rode was a cellbike, maybe a dozen times. So how come I know how to do it?'

'Some people are naturals.'

'No, it's more than that. It's like an echo of a muscle memory. It felt strange at first but within a mile or so I didn't have to think about it. Starting, stopping, speeding up, slowing down. I almost know what the horse—the kudai—is thinking.'

'Kudo. Singular.'

'You learn the language here then? I heard you shout something at that raider earlier.'

'It's Istanian. We're in Istania now. The land of the Blood King. They use a different dialect in the Black Queen's country, but if you know one, you can understand the other.'

'The Queen spoke pretty good English yesterday.'

'Most of the nobility do. It's almost like a badge of honour. And they've had nine years to practice.'

'So have you.'

'True. It's not all that hard once you master the basics.'

'So they all speak English? The Berikatanyans?'

'Varies. Around the main towns it's quite common. Less so in more rural areas. But don't worry. You've already made a start. You know what a kudo is.'

He laughed.

'Yeah. And back on the subject of... kudai... the kind of connection with an animal we were talking about only comes with practice. Takes years.'

'So you were a rider in your former life. Nothing strange about that.'

'A rider on a home world with two moons.'

'OK, yeah. I admit that is peculiar. Mars is the only inhabited planet we know that has two moons. Was, until we came here.'

Jann stared again at the night sky. The smaller moon rode close to the horizon, a few minutes away from setting. It was getting late.

'Maybe you dreamt it?' Felice suggested.

'It feels more real.'

'Dreams do. Sometimes.'

'Yeah, I know. But you can usually tell afterwards. I mean, they seem real while you're dreaming them but when you wake up it's obvious it was a dream.'

'I don't have an answer for you Jann. Like I said, dreams are just a hobby of mine. I'm not pretending to know anything about how they might stray into reality.'

'Or open a doorway to the future.'

'Huh?'

'I had the notion it may be a prediction rather than a memory. If somehow I knew I'd see two moons once I came here.'

'That's a little "woo woo" for me. Maybe things will become clearer once we arrive at Court.'

'You think?'

'One way or another. The more time passes the more chance there is some memory will return. There may be other familiar things at Court that will give you clues you'll eventually be able to piece together.

'I suggest you turn in,' she added, easing herself off the rock. 'It'll be raining soon.'

'You're the second person to predict that.'

'Really? Well, it's not hard. It rains most nights here. That's why the locals call it malamajan. Translates as "night rain".'

forest clearance project
5 jun 2175

Terry Spate stretched, listening for any creaks or pops from his aging frame that had not been there the day before. Satisfied he was in good enough shape for his first day's work he lifted the flap of his tent and stepped out into the early morning sunlight.

The camp was a simple affair—a few canvas tents surrounding a dammed brook with a fire pit nearby. Terry breathed deeply, savouring the loamy tang of the forest air, and released his breath with a broad smile. He already felt more at peace here than he could ever remember. For the first time in his life, he had a feeling of being in the right place—of coming home—that he could neither explain nor understand. A gentle breeze, apparently a constant feature of Berikatanyan weather, stirred the tops of the surrounding trees. The rustling sounds, combined with the soft song of the river as it ran over the dam, disturbed long-buried memories he still could not quite grasp. They had a childlike quality inexplicable in view of his lack of recall, yet utterly distinct. He refused to let it bother him. He had had a lifetime of coping with his memory loss. Being on a new planet was no excuse to abandon his usual approach to the problem. If his memories came back then all well and good. If they did not, he was no worse off. A source of fresh water, a fire for cooking, and a forest-load of clean air—what more could a man want?

He bent, sinking his hands into the soft black earth of the forest floor. It felt cool. As it ran between his fingers the rich compost released a cocktail of memory-stirring smells. The feel of it sent a warm shiver through him. The grains and clumps of soil trickled off his hands and back to the ground, their moisture catching the rays of the early sun and glistening as if they contained pure gold.

'Morning!'

Claire Yamani stepped out of her own tent, setting off

the wind chime she had hung from the door pole. Its three clear notes tinkled a merry tune. The breeze caught it, playing its music with natural flair. Claire smiled and rubbed her eyes, squinting at Terry against the low sun.

'Sleep alright?'

'Fine,' he said. 'I've always enjoyed nights under canvas. Did a fair amount of camping when I first started working the land. Couldn't afford anything else. How 'bout you?'

'Bit firmer than I'm used to,' she replied, massaging one hip with her hand. Her smile widened. 'But I'll survive.'

The smell of fried breakfast reached them from the camp fire. They walked over to join the rest of the group. Progress on the forest clearance project had been slow up to now. They only had a small team—Terry and Claire brought their number to eight—and they only used hand tools. That did not matter to Terry. He had been using spades, forks and machetes for as long as he could remember. On their arrival at camp last night Claire had expressed some puzzlement at the lack of power tools. David Garcia, the team leader, explained the colonists avoided them on principle. Sources of power were uncertain and usually in inconvenient places. More importantly, anything operating without a visible source of energy spooked the locals. The Earthers had concluded it would be easier to rub along with their three Berikatanyan team members if they stuck to manual labour, even if the work took ten times longer.

'I didn't expect to find any local people doing this work,' Claire said around a mouthful of breakfast sausage. 'I thought it was exclusively a human—an Earther project,' she corrected herself.

'I asked David about that last night after you turned in,' Terry said. 'Apparently the Queen decided an exchange of labour, rather than her simply having Earthers coming to the Palace all the time, would help to integrate our two peoples.'

'Is that what we're doing? Integrating?'

Terry thought for a moment.

'Well, we're the interlopers aren't we?' he replied.

'Although,' he added, regarding the clearing with a big smile, 'this place already feels like home to me. I've always loved the great outdoors. It's perfect here.'

Claire smiled at him. A light, fresh breeze played around the fire pit, picking up wisps of smoke from the glowing embers and making them dance in the air.

'Yes. It's lovely. You'd hardly know we weren't on Earth.'

After breakfast Garcia called the group to order, spearing a sheet containing the week's assignments to a handy twig near to the camp. The sheet was headed "*14 Ter'Tanamasa*". A brief glance was enough to show Terry that each member of Garcia's team had a heavy week ahead. He and Claire had been allocated a new section at the north of the existing clearing. Pattana, one of the three Berikatanyans on the team, led them over to the right spot.

'Come. I show you,' he said in halting English.

Terry picked his way across the open space, following Pattana and Claire.

'What is "Tanamasa"?' he asked the young man.

'It group of remalan,' Pattana replied. 'Um... months.'

'Like a season?' asked Claire.

'Yes. Season. This now is Ter'Tanamasa. Next be Run'Tanamasa. Year is past halfway.'

Where trees had been felled and undergrowth cleared the ground was still uneven, a mess of stumps remaining to be dug out, muddy puddles where rainwater had collected in new depressions, and leaf litter. A low, throaty growl echoed from the forest to Terry's left.

'What's that?' he asked Pattana.

'Kuclar', the Berikatanyan replied. 'Um... big cat. Very shy. Not bother us.'

At the edge of the clearing the forest encroached with dark mystery, cutting off the light and replacing it with a mote-filled brown smudge of half-revealed corridors and woody halls, each bordered by tall trunks and criss-crossed with low hanging branches.

Ahead of him Claire stopped, peering into the gloom. She leaned forward, resting her hand on the trunk of the nearest tree for balance. She gasped in surprise as a sudden gust of wind blew out from the forest, catching her hair and whipping it across her cheeks.

'You alright?' Terry called. 'Is it the big cat?'

'No, it...'

She turned to face him, pulling at the strands of hair. The churning wind died away, replaced once again by the light breeze that had played with their camp fire earlier.

'Never mind,' Claire said, blushing to the roots of her hair.

'You look like you've had a shock,' he said.

'Two, actually,' Claire said, fixing him with a frightened stare.

ketakaya forest
6 jun 2175

'You didn't tell me much last night about this mystery we're trying to solve,' Jann said, addressing Felice's back as she rode ahead of him on a narrow section of the trail.

After a simple meal they had struck camp around mid-morning to complete the two day journey to Court. Her assertion had proved correct: there had been no repeat of the marauders' attack overnight. Now, an hour in to the day's travelling, there was still no sign of trouble as they made their slow way along the edge of a dense forest.

The day was again sunny, but at breakfast Felice had warned everyone to dress warmly against the chill they would find in the deepest parts of the woodland. Ahead of Jann on the scrubby trail that followed the tree line, Felice set as brisk a pace as possible allowing for the slower carts. When the path widened again she tugged at her traces, slowing her mount until Jann caught up and they could ride side by side.

'Beyond telling me there's magic involved,' he added. 'Want to fill in some of the blanks?'

'Now's as good a time as any,' Felice agreed, 'but I'll have to give you a bit of background first. Stuff I've pieced together from many separate conversations over the years. Some of the locals are more willing to talk about it than others. It helps if I can get them alone. If there's more than one or two they clam up tighter than an airlock in a hard vacuum.'

'How long has this been going on?'

'I'll come to that.

'I'm not being deliberately vague,' she added in reaction to Jann's exasperated grunt, 'it's just that things have changed recently and you need to understand why the change is significant.'

'Fine. Tell it your own way.'

'I don't know where the magic comes from, or what it used to be capable of, but I know it takes one of four main forms. Don't laugh, because these sound quite mythical. They are Earth, Air—'

'—Fire and Water?'

She nodded.

'Exactly.'

'Find any cauldrons? Broomsticks?'

'OK you're not laughing but you're still not taking it seriously.'

'Well excuse me. I travelled here at almost the speed of light for a hundred years in a ship that's about as advanced as anything we've ever built. Now you're telling me it brought me to Camelot?'

'Do you want me to tell you what I know, or not?'

'Sorry. I'll shut up.'

'Good. So you've recognised them as the traditional Elements from old Earth. Each has a small number of people who can make their Element do their bidding. The locals call them suhiri, which translates roughly as mages. And each has—had—a leader, known as an Elemental.'

'Had?'

'That's right. Some time ago, I haven't been able to find out exactly when, they suffered some kind of disaster. A magical "oops".'

'What kind of oops?'

'The big kind. All the Elementals disappeared.'

'That's magic!'

'The suhiri didn't think so. The Elementals weren't just leaders. They were the ones who harnessed and channelled the power of the Elements, effectively granting increased power to the suhiri. Without them, the mages were weaker. So much weaker, most of them could no longer work their magic at all. Even the most adept were reduced to simple parlour tricks.'

Felice reined her horse to a stop. They had reached the entrance to the woodland path. She waited for the nearest riders to catch up with them. Elaine rode at the head of the leading group.

'Each of you wait here until the person behind you catches up,' she announced. 'Once you've passed the message on, you can follow us through the forest and leave the next rider to give directions. That way no-one will miss the turning.'

'What about the carts?' Elaine asked.

'The path widens out after the first few trees. It's a tricky turn but the road soon becomes easier.'

Felice held back until she could be sure her message was being passed on. Jann, Elaine and two others followed her into the wooded gloom of Ketakaya forest. The woodland echoed with the calls of a dozen different animals, but they all kept well away from the riders.

'Parlour tricks?' Jann prompted, once they had reached the widened part of the path and could ride together again.

'The one we're going to investigate is a good example. There's a local fire mage who has only been able to produce a small flame since the Elementals disappeared. He was in the habit of lighting his domestic fire with it. A few days ago his neighbours found him standing outside the smouldering ruin of his home looking more than a little confused. Somehow, while he'd been setting his fire in his usual way, his magic regained its full force and burned his house down.'

'So what made it suddenly... er... flare up?' Jann asked with a smirk.

'Still not taking this seriously, are you?'

'I can't. Not really. Too much like the pap fiction I used to read.'

Felice grimaced.

'It's all there was on Phobos!'

'Well it's up to you what you believe. If what the locals say is true then you might have chance to see for yourself before long.'

'Oh?'

'They could only offer one explanation for the fire mage's sudden surge of power. That the Fire Witch had returned.'

Jann whistled.

'Fire Witch, eh? I take it she's the Elemental in charge of burning.'

'That's right.'

'Anyone seen her?'

'No.'

'I guess your fire mage was lucky he didn't burn to death along with his house.'

'Ah. Well that's the real reason we're here. I'm not usually involved with the locals' problems. If it had only been about returning powers...

'I might be interested as an onlooker but it's not my job to find out whether the Fire Witch is at the heart of it, or where she may have been hiding herself.'

'So...?'

'The lucky mage didn't burn because the fire was put

out. That's why they called me in. It was doused by an Earther.'

'Good for him.'

'Her.'

'Lucky she had a bucket to hand.'

'She didn't put him out with a bucket. She used water magic.'

Jann stopped his horse.

'What?'

'When I said I'd been called in to investigate, I meant to look into why Earth people have started to display magical abilities. Some of them, at least.'

'She just conjured the water up?'

'That's what we're trying to find out.'

'This isn't the first example,' Felice added. 'Far from it. I've had a guy with his hand buried in a rock—actually inside the stone, you know, not stuck in a crevice. That was the hardest one. Mostly it's been small things. This is the biggest since we arrived.'

The trees, which had been thinning out for some time, now gave way to open grassland as the lead riders in the group emerged from Ketakaya. Across the plain, visible above the gentle rise of the land, the Blood King's pennant fluttered atop the Court flagpole.

southern blood plain
same day

The sun had barely crossed its zenith as the company made its way over the plain. When they crested the low mound that had all but hidden any hint of their destination, the Court came fully into view. The deep red sandstone towers caught the bright sunlight and sparkled at the riders, a shimmering contrast to the deep ochre of the forest into which the Court nestled. A faint heat haze rippled the air between them as the warmth of the day settled into afternoon.

Now they were in sight of the Court, Felice rode ahead to make sure they were expected, leaving Jann and Elaine to look after the rest of the travellers. They waited at the edge of the forest until they could see Patrick bringing up the rear, confirming the whole group had traversed the gloomy woodland path. Once through the woods no-one could fail to notice the obvious way marker of the flapping pennant. Elaine had been impatient to follow Felice but Jann insisted they stick together, the unprovoked attack of the previous afternoon still fresh in his mind.

Now they rode in silence, Jann lost in convoluted considerations of everything Felice had told him, ignoring Elaine's occasional attempts at conversation.

'Something's bugging you,' she said.

'Mmm?'

'You haven't said a word since Felice took off. And you've got a face on you like a thunderhead.'

'Sorry.'

'So what is it? Where did you go?'

'All this magic stuff has thrown me a bit of a curve,' Jann admitted. 'It's the last thing I expected.'

'New planet. New rules. Once you settle in here I'd be willing to bet you could get used to anything.'

'You're remarkably laid back about it. But you didn't hear the things I heard.'

'I heard enough. I was riding right behind you the whole time.'

'Fire Witch? Sounds like a character from an opera. Sounds scary.'

'Scary? No. She might be a bit on the fiery side, but I expect she's a pussy cat underneath.'

'Right. Like you'd know.'

Elaine hesitated, shifting in her saddle. She looked straight at Jann, appearing to make up her mind about something.

'I—'

As she spoke a loud whooping noise came from behind

131

them to the right, from another part of the forest. The curve of the plain hid the source of the sound, but it sent a chill all the way down to Jann's shoes.

'It's an attack!' he yelled, wheeling his mount around and checking both sides of the track for bandits. The commotion unsettled the other animals in the train. They shied this way and that, flaring their nostrils and showing the whites of their eyes as the riders fought to keep them headed in the direction of the Court. Jann stood up in his saddle, shouting to the rest of the group.

'Head for the Court—quick as you can!'

Halfway through his barked instruction the first of the attacking riders appeared over the mound, quickly followed by three more. Similar in appearance to the first attackers this latest crop also wore long black scarves wrapped around their heads to hide their faces, but these were mounted on sleek black kudai. Between the swathes of cloth their eyes burned with a fierce hatred. Jann did not stop to find out how many more would appear. Wheeling around again he gave his steed its head. Thankful to be allowed to flee the approaching noise, the animal leapt in the direction of the Court, still looking incongruously tranquil in the vale below.

The grass steamed in the sun creating a low blanket of mist that swirled and churned as the flying hooves of their mounts kicked through it. Jann looked across the plain, calculating who was likely to be safe and who at risk. Some of the fastest riders were already approaching the Court. The three wagons were also making good progress although their tailgates bristled with arrows and the passengers were being jostled about as the fixed wheels bounced over the uneven ground. One of them nursed a shoulder wound but the rest appeared to be unharmed. He could not see Elaine or Patrick anywhere.

An arrow shot past Jann, clipping his arm and tearing the cloth of his shirt. It embedded itself in the turf a hundred metres in front of him and burst into flame. The grass was alight in places, each separate patch of fire joining with its neighbours to create a blazing carpet. Too close to run around, Jann's horse vaulted over the burning sward. He glanced behind, fearful the carts would catch, but their iron-shod wheels rolled across harmlessly, the carts themselves travelling too fast to be affected. As the last of them crossed the line of burning grass the flames swelled and grew taller until they formed a wall of fire through which most of their pursuers were unable to pass. Four of the closest riders had made it across the line before the blaze peaked and were closing on the rearmost wagon.

Where had the fire come from?

'Jann!'

Elaine's shout reached him over the roar of the flames. She sat on her horse at the crest of the mound, the spikes of her red hair silhouetted against the clear blue sky, her hands held aloft in a strange gesture. Her topaz-studded bangles blazed with an incandescent orange-red glow that suffused her hands as if she were juggling fireballs. As he watched a bolt of fire flew from her left hand, striking the back of the lead marauder as he caught up with the last wagon. The powerful charge passed right through the man. He dropped from his horse, bounced twice, and lay still in a smoking heap.

'Hurry! The fire won't stop them for long!'

His mind a whirl of confusion and fear, Jann spurred his horse after the others as another attacker fell burning to the ground. The remaining two reined their kudai around and headed back towards the forest. Ahead of him the enormous red wooden gates of the Court opened to receive the first of the riders. With the immediate danger from the marauders passed, Jann dropped back, waiting until all three wagons had reached the safety of the barbican.

Raising his hand against the glare of the sun he looked across the plain. Elaine rode calmly—almost majestically—

over the blackened grass. Parts still flamed, elsewhere the stubble smouldered, but some eldritch power kept her animal's hooves from harm.

Still stunned by Elaine's sudden and unexpected display of power, Jann realised he did not want to speak with her. He tugged at the reins, riding through the Court gates to join the others. The Fire Witch was no longer merely a whispered legend, or a character from an opera, but he had been right about one thing. She was frightening.

Chapter 9

The fourth day of the forest clearance detail had, once again, dawned fine and dry with a light, freshening breeze. Terry marvelled at how civilised the weather patterns were on this planet. It hardly ever rained during daylight hours. But for all the lack of rain, there was never any let up in the wind. From the gentle gusts of today to the occasional howling storm such as the one that heralded the Valiant's demise, the air on Berikatanya was always moving. It helped the task along though. It would have been sweaty work without the zephyr.

Claire proved both a pleasant and a diligent working companion. Terry was glad she had opted to come with him. They had developed a close friendship in the short time they had spent together. He knew she had lost her father several years before leaving Earth and suspected she looked on him as an ersatz replacement, but he could live with that. Having never had children of his own he had some small reservoir of fatherly affection to spread around. Claire was welcome to it. The warm affinity he felt for her had not blinded him to the fact she was not always an open book. She met certain topics with a frosty stare or selective deafness. Among these subjects, a question he had often asked, and to which he remained determined to find an answer. He needed to catch Claire off-guard. To approach the subject from a direction that did not scare her into further silence.

They had taken a break from the hard logging, which was almost complete in the area where they presently worked.

'That is last of big trunks,' their Berikatanyan co-worker Pattana said as he joined the rest of the crew sitting on a large log at the edge of the clearing.

'If we were working this project on Earth we'd be ready for the rotivator about now,' Terry observed. 'Only we don't have one.'

'Rotivator?' asked Claire.

'Shame you never worked with me back then young lady,' Terry smiled. 'I could have introduced you to my collection of professional powered gardening tools. A rotivator is a motor-driven hoe—or a set of hoes I should say—all mounted on a rotating armature. It rips up the soil a treat.'

'We do it by self,' said Pattana. 'Believe if machine does work of man, take something away from man.'

'Fruity snack?' called Pattana's close friend Umtanesh, who enjoyed a somewhat better command of English.

He threw a shining red fruit in Claire's direction.

She caught it in both hands and bit into the crisp flesh.

'Lucky catch,' said Pattana. 'Stop it flying back.'

Terry laughed.

'Flying back?' Claire mumbled around her mouthful.

'When these guys told me what they call this fruit,' he said, 'I had to explain why I found it so funny. You're eating a bumerang.'

Claire giggled, wiping the juice off her chin.

'It's delicious. Thanks Umtan. I'll make sure to catch any others you throw my way.'

The Berikatanyan fruit, with a shape similar to an apple, was a prized delicacy in both Palace and Court according to their native team mates. They grew everywhere in this area. Quite a bit sweeter than any apple Terry had ever tasted, bumerang flesh had a flavour and texture closer to a mango, but its skin was thinner and also edible.

'Where's mine?' Terry asked with a wide smile.

Another bumerang flew through the air, catching him by surprise and almost knocking him off the log.

'So do you want me to make a start on the manual rotivating?' asked Claire, finishing up her fruit.

'If I answer your question,' said Terry, looking her in

the eye, 'will you answer one of mine?'

Claire gave him a wary look.

'Depends what it is,' she replied, standing up and flicking a few small pieces of bumerang skin from her jeans.

'You know what it is,' Terry whispered. 'I've asked you often enough.'

She sighed.

'You're not going to let this drop are you?'

Terry did not say anything. The silence hung in the breeze for a few seconds, disturbed only by the gentle buzzing of the local insect life and the rustling of the treetops. Claire frowned.

'Alright! But it doesn't make any sense. It's almost... embarrassing.'

'Tell me anyway.'

She sat back down on the log. The other team members left them to resume work in the clearing, carrying away the last of the logs and fetching the hand tools they would use to complete the clearance. Claire watched them for a little while longer before fixing her gaze on the edge of the clear ground, where she had first admitted to feeling the shock.

'See that glade there, just beyond the tree line?'

'The one where it happened?'

'Yes. When I first caught sight of it, I couldn't believe it. I had a dream—back on the Valiant. It saved my life, really. Woke me up in time to evacuate my pod before I suffocated.'

'I don't understand.'

'In the dream, I met my Dad. We were in the woods. In a glade. In that glade.'

'What... the one... that one over there? It looks like the one in your dream?'

'Not just looks like it. It *is* the one in my dream. It's identical. The trees, the light, even the motes of dust in the air. It's the glade from my dream.'

'How...?'

'I don't know. I don't believe in prescience or any of that mumbo-jumbo, but I can't explain it any other way.'

'No wonder you looked so surprised.'

'That wasn't all. That's not what made me cry out.'

Terry finished up his bumerang, throwing the stone into a patch of clear ground as the locals had taught him. He waited for Claire to continue.

'Have you noticed anything about the wood here?'

'It's pretty hard to cut down,' Terry joked.

She laughed.

'Yes, it is. I've got the blisters to prove it. But the wood. The trees, I mean, before we fell them. They're electric. Some of them. Some of the time.'

'Electric?'

'It gave me a shock the first time I touched one. I reached out to steady myself when I peered into the forest. When I put my hand on the tree, I got a shock.'

'Are you sure it wasn't just the jolt of recognition when you saw the glade?'

'No. It was much more than that. Like static, but it went right through me.'

'Were you OK?'

'It didn't hurt, if that's what you mean. It was more exciting than frightening. Maybe I should have called it a thrill not a shock. It didn't make me want to pull my hand away.

'Quite the opposite, actually,' she added. 'I felt more alive. Like I had tuned in to something. Something fundamentally natural and powerful. It made me feel connected.'

Terry thought about how he had felt when he first touched and smelled the earth here in the woods. He looked at Claire. Her eyes sparkled with excitement at the memory.

'Are you two doing any work today?' Garcia called from the centre of the clearing.

'Sorry! Yes,' Terry replied, getting to his feet.

'I don't understand any of this,' he said, helping Claire up, 'but I believe you. It's not crazy. I've not had any electric shocks, but I know what you mean about feeling connected.

'I wouldn't mention it to anyone else,' he added. 'Not right now. Let's keep it to ourselves.'

'Fine with me,' she said, smiling.

She touched his arm.

'Glad I told you though. I don't feel quite so stupid.'

Break over, Terry set to with the Berikatanyan equivalent of a spade. It had surprised him how similar all the local tools were to those he used back on Earth, but on reflection he realised it was not so surprising after all. Form followed function, so if you needed something for digging, or hoeing, or loosening compacted sod filled with roots, that "something" was likely to look pretty much like a spade, a hoe, or a fork. He had taken the spade, leaving the fork for Claire, who was working an area still thickly knotted with roots.

They had not been at it for long before the ubiquitous wind started to pick up. Claire's shouts of exasperation as she encountered ever more tangled tubers were matched by increasingly powerful blasts of wind, as if whatever weather gods the locals believed in shared her frustration at her inability to extract the tenacious vegetable matter from the soil.

Small eddies of air picked up the piles of leaves and twigs left over from the felled trees and blew them about the clearing. Terry heeled his spade into the earth and stopped what he was doing. Claire had hold of a large root with both hands. She strained to pull it out. She had already dug along as much of its length as she could reach with the fork.

'Gah!' she cried, losing her grip and falling backwards into the mud.

The wind picked up a small branch and flung it at

Terry. He sidestepped.

'Need any help?'

She flashed him an angry look.

'I've got it. This sodding thing hasn't seen the best of me yet!'

She scrambled to her feet and dug the fork into the ground with renewed vigour. The branches of the surrounding trees rustled their encouragement in the wind. Terry retrieved his jacket, which had been in danger of blowing away. He pulled it on, fastening it against the chilly gusts.

Garcia walked over to him, one hand raised to shield his eyes from the flying dust.

'If this gets any worse we're gonna have to call it a day,' he shouted over the noise of the trees and whipping wind.

'Come. Out. Damn you!' yelled Claire, wrapping the root around both arms, digging in her heels, and leaning backwards. One of the smaller tents at the camp side of the clearing ripped free of its moorings. It flew over the trees, disappearing quickly from sight.

'That's it!' bellowed Garcia, 'if we don't tie everything down we're not going to have anywhere to sleep tonight!'

He stomped off in the direction of the camp. Terry called out to Claire.

'We're going to ride out the storm at camp! Leave that for now!'

'No!' Claire grunted through gritted teeth. 'I've almost got it.'

'You'll be caught in the storm!' Terry warned. But even as he said it, he could see the wind had formed a vortex around the clearing, with Claire at its centre. She was unaffected by the weather.

'Nnnnnnnnnnagh!' Claire grunted again, giving one last mighty tug on the root. It came free with a wet ripping noise, depositing her once more on her arse but this time with the offending root still held firmly in both hands.

'YES!' she shouted, her face lit with a huge grin.

Almost as quickly as it started, the wind dropped. A bird called from a nearby tree, echoing Claire's exultation. Over at camp, Terry could see the three Berikatanyans staring at her with awed expressions.

the blood king's court
15th day of ter'tanamasa, 965

Jann reined his horse to a standstill, the gates closing behind him. Barely organised chaos reigned in the Blood King's courtyard. Archers ran to their positions on the battlements to protect the Court in the event of any further attack. White-robed men and women helped the wounded down off their mounts and out of the carts, ushering them from the hubbub to a place where their injuries could be tended. Ostlers calmed the animals, leading them away to stables. Whoever they were, whatever they were doing, everyone kept a respectful distance from Elaine. She sat still, astride her steed, recovering her breath and her composure. The enormous wooden gates swung shut with a muted thud and guardsmen shot iron bolts as thick as a man's arms into their keeps. A familiar voice called out through the melee.

'You?'

It was Felice. She strode towards Elaine across the courtyard. Jann dismounted to join her.

'You're the Fire Witch?'

Elaine regarded Felice with a disdainful look.

'I don't understand,' Jann said. 'How can you be the Fire Witch? You're from Earth.'

'No. I'm not from Earth,' Elaine corrected him. 'I was *on* Earth. I'm from here. I was never meant to leave. Leaving was a mistake. An... accident.'

She shook her head, running a hand through her flame-red hair and eyeing a young man in an elaborate uniform who strode towards them.

'It's a long story. And it looks like it's going to have to

wait for another time.'

The majority of their group—those not wounded—were being corralled by a small contingent of Court guards. The man in the distinctive uniform, clearly someone of senior rank despite his youth, halted in front of Felice and gave a curt bow.

'Miss Waters. Is whole group here?' he asked, his English hesitant and heavily accented. 'Is anyone not belong?'

He glared at Elaine as if expecting Felice to denounce her as a marauder.

'It is, Tepak,' Felice replied. She glanced around the small group of Earthers.

'And no, there are no strangers.'

'Very well. Must make haste. King demands meet with you immediate. This not normal way, but very strange happenings make him stop other meets. Follow me please.'

Despite his rudimentary grasp of English, it was not a question.

'Good,' said Elaine. 'I wanted a word with him anyway.'

The officer did not acknowledge Elaine's comment but led the way into the main keep. His men made sure no-one remained behind.

'Tepak?' Patrick asked as they followed him into the building.

Felice thought for a moment.

'Probably closest to army captain in Earth terms,' she said.

After the heat of the day, the air inside the keep felt cool. Flaming wall sconces relieved the hard shadows cast by the bright afternoon sun, releasing a heady incense that battled with the scents of potpourri filling richly decorated ceramic dishes, and of the fresh flowers spilling from ornate gilt vases standing atop towering pillars of red marble. Their footsteps echoed from the matching polished floors as they hurried past busts of previous kings and heavy tapestries depicting historical victories. Jann soon lost his bearings in the corridors. On reaching a long antechamber, the guard captain stopped and held up his hands. At the other end of the room two costumed soldiers holding long ceremonial axes stood guard beside a pair of tall whitewood doors.

'Wait here,' their escort instructed.

With silent efficiency the guards who had followed took up positions at all the exits from the antechamber. Their captain disappeared through the white doors, closing them behind him.

Most of the group took seats on long wooden benches arranged along both walls. Jann, Felice, and Elaine remained standing in the middle of the room.

'Can you give me the abridged version? Of your story?' Jann asked.

'I'm not sure that would be such a good idea,' Elaine replied, her gaze remaining fixed on the whitewood doors, her expression grim.

'Why's that?' Jann pressed. 'Does it have anything to do with you recognising me at the spaceport? And at the landing site?'

Elaine raised an eyebrow. She stared Jann in the face. Amber flecks in her eyes reflected the flickering flames from the wall sconces.

'This again?' she asked.

'Don't play games. I saw the look on your face the first time you noticed me. You needed a hydraulic jack to lift your jaw up off the floor.'

'You'll have to believe it's not a good idea for me to explain,' she said. 'You have blanks in your memory. I had blanks in my memory. Mine came back.'

'So mine will? Why don't you help it along?'

'I might not be helping. Besides, there are parts of it I still don't understand. I'd only been on Earth four years when I remembered who I am. You'd been locked up on Phobos for what did you say? Ten years?'

143

'I didn't mention Phobos.'

Elaine reddened.

'I might have overheard that part.'

'You didn't hear very well then. It was eight years, not ten.'

'Whatever. I was right—the times don't match.'

'What times? What are you saying?'

'Too much already, is what I've said.'

'And what triggered the return of your memory?'

'I heard the bell ringing. A dreadful racket. Sounded like it was cracked.'

Felice looked shocked.

'The ceremonial bell? But that hasn't been rung for thirty years. You boarded the Valiant long before it rang. You were in cryosleep.'

'No, I wasn't on the Valiant. Although I was asleep. In my trailer. Back when I worked the circus. I heard it in my dream. It woke me up. Saved my life, actually, but that's another story.'

'This is crazy,' Felice said, shaking her head. 'Even if the timing matched up, there's no way you could have heard a bell—*the* bell—ringing here. It's ninety-seven light years away. Sound can't cross the vacuum of space but if it was possible, it would still be travelling.'

'I don't believe it's as crazy as you think,' Elaine retorted. 'If I—we—can be translated across such a vast distance in an instant, why not the ringing of a bell?'

Felice looked puzzled for a moment. In an uncanny echo of their conversation, a bell tolled in a nearby tower.

'The tech guys were talking about something like this shortly after we first landed,' she said. 'The boffins on Earth had been experimenting with instantaneous transmission of messages based on... quantum entanglement I think they called it.

'It was still only in the lab back then, but they hoped to develop it into an interplanetary messaging system.'

'There you go then,' Elaine said, her eyes flashing. 'It

must be at least possible.'

'Maybe, but they still had no way of sending sound waves, let alone people,' Felice replied. 'And from what the Endeavour techs said, the whole scheme relies on having a set of paired particles at either end of the transmission—so you have to start off with them in the same place and then move one. Or both. That couldn't work to send a one-way message.'

Elaine frowned.

'But I was here to begin with,' she said. 'And so is the bell. I was the one who moved, and without going into too much detail the way I moved was... well... out of the ordinary.'

The two women stared at each other.

'That story you mentioned earlier. The one locals are reluctant to tell. It's my story. I was there. So it must have at least been possible for me to be "entangled" or whatever you call it with something here on Berikatanya. Something that meant I could hear the bell when it rang.'

Jann had barely been able to follow the conversation, and from the look on his face neither had Patrick, but Felice's expression turned to shocked recognition.

'I can't explain it,' she said, 'but I do remember a really bizarre thing about this quantum business. The boffins reckoned once you had a pair of entangled particles, whatever you did to one would be reflected in the other, but instantaneously, wherever those particles are in the universe. If that's true, then it might explain how you could hear a bell even though the actual sound would still take years to reach you. Even if, in fact, it hadn't even rung at the time you heard it. As long as it would ring, eventually.'

'Whoa!' Patrick said, holding up his hands. 'That is seriously weird.'

Before he could say any more, the whitewood doors opened. The captain emerged from the throne room, accompanied by a shorter man dressed all in yellow, carrying an iron-shod staff. The short man rapped on the marble floor to attract the attention of everyone in the group.

'The King will see you now,' he said, with an incongruous and lopsided grin.

forest clearance project
19th day of ter'tanamasa, 965

There being no repeat of the dangerous winds they experienced earlier in the day, Terry and the rest of the gang worked until dusk began to creep out from under the forest canopy, sucking the light from the open ground they had cleared. Once the last of the large roots were removed, the going became much easier. The whole crew had relaxed into the easy rhythm of turning and sifting the rich, red soil to extract the few remaining shards and scraps of woody material along with some of the larger rocks. With Terry's guidance, they made sure to retain some smaller pebbles for good drainage. Once he could no longer see the contents of his sieve clearly, Terry stuck his spade in the ground, hung the sieve from the handle, stood and stretched, feeling the bones of his spine crackle.

'Aaah!' he sighed. 'I think two or three more days will see it done, but that's more than enough for today. We've made good progress.'

Claire propped her own spade against his.

'I'm ready for a bowl of that stew,' she said, matching Terry's stretch.

The smallest of their Berikatanyan comrades had appointed himself head chef of the simple camp. He had been struggling to keep up with the rest of them in the clearance work, but had an eye for local herbs. He had produced some extremely tasty stews and broths for everyone.

'Although I really will have to shower first,' Claire added, pulling strands of ash-blonde hair away from the sweat on her face. 'I stink.'

'After you then,' Terry said. 'You're quicker than me. I wouldn't want to stand between you and a bowl of steaming Rebusang.'

They set off back to camp, a much easier walk now the majority of the ground clearance work in this section had been completed.

'You're getting pretty good at the local language,' Claire said, smiling at Terry.

He walked on for a few minutes, considering her statement.

'Thanks,' he replied at length. 'Surprised myself actually. I was never good with languages. Always embarrassed to try. I don't like to think about this, but when I was younger the local kids tormented me real bad. We must have immigrated from somewhere. Took me a long time to get the hang of English.'

'Where were your parents from?'

'I don't know. I have no recollection of them at all. It must have happened before the accident, but even after I woke up I still couldn't understand a word anyone said.'

'Maybe it's part of your amnesia?' Claire said.

'Maybe.'

They entered the camp. All the Berikatanyan workers were already there. Nembaka, the chef, stood over a steaming pot with his two friends seated close to the fire. None of them were eating. Their conversation ceased as Terry and Claire appeared. Claire veered off to pick up a change of clothes and a towel. As she approached her tent a freak gust of wind—a memory of the earlier gales—blew from the direction of the clearing and lifted the entrance flap.

A surprised murmur rose in unison from the three Berikatanyans.

'Sakti Udara,' the nearest of them muttered.

Terry collected his own towel and a fresh shirt and waited for Claire to shower. She returned the favour so they could dine together. With the day's dirt and grime rinsed from his hair and skin, and clean clothes on his back, Terry felt ready to sample Nembaka's delicacy of the day. Its wonderful aroma had been teasing at his guts since they returned from the clearing.

As they walked over to the fire pit the Berikatanyans stood as one. Each of them bowed to Claire. She laughed.

'What's all this about guys?'

They did not respond, but Nembaka made haste to serve Claire first, handing her a steaming bowl full of rich stew but taking care to avoid eye contact with her. The others refused to sit down, or serve anyone else, until Claire had made herself comfortable on a patch of grass and begun her dinner.

Terry joined her once his bowl had been filled. The tendrils of aromatic steam curling upwards from the contents carried hints of spices as yet untried along with fresh notes reminiscent of coriander and lemon grass while underneath these he could detect an undercurrent, a bass note, of strongly flavoured meat redolent of venison.

'How is it?' he asked, taking a seat on the ground next to Claire.

'D'licious,' she replied past the remains of her mouthful.

'As good as it smells then,' said Terry, lifting a spoonful to his nose.

'Mmm.'

Pattana approached, standing at a respectful distance until they had both noticed his presence, then taking a single step forward.

'Excuse me, Sakti,' he began. He dropped to his knees, holding out his hands and staring at the grass.

'If it please, I make this for you.'

In his shaking hands he held a small wooden implement which as far as Terry could see in the reflections from the distant firelight was carved from the very stuff they had been felling for the past three days. The locals called it kaytam, the Earthers referred to it as blackwood. If it was as hard to work as it had been to cut down, the gift represented many hours' skilful whittling and polishing.

Claire set her bowl down on the grass and took the object from Pattana's hands. It resembled a spoon, but with one edge fashioned into two prongs, like half a fork. Terry remembered seeing something similar on Earth. Back there it had been called a spork. Claire twisted the shaft. The handle slid out from the head of the spoon to reveal a gleaming blade made of what looked like slate. Unlike slate, this stone had been polished until it gleamed and glinted, dancing in harmony with the flames of the campfire.

'It is more...' Pattana struggled for the right word, '...suitable for Sakti eat with sunyok than Batu'n eaters,' he explained.

Claire held up the smooth sharp blade. The low, slow growl of a kuclar reverberated from the deep forest, filling the pregnant silence.

'This is a sunyok?' Claire asked.

Pattana nodded.

'What is "Sakti"?' she asked, her voice barely louder than a whisper.

'You are Sakti Udara. She who commands the wind.'

Claire laughed.

'Commands the wind? What, you mean my tent flap? That was only a coincidence.'

'It much more than that, great one. You summoned storm today. Morning time.'

'I did not! I got mad at a root! The wind was blowing anyway.'

'And when great ship appeared,' Pattana continued, paying no attention to her denials.

'What? You think I caused the Valiant to crash land?'

Claire stood up, catching the bowl of stew with her foot and sending the contents flying over the grass.

Pattana cringed, prostrating himself on the ground.

'Pattana offend you!' he wailed.

'Get up! You haven't offended me!' Claire insisted, reaching for the man. He shrank from her outstretched hand.

'Not punish me!' he cried. 'Mean no harm. Only want bring gift.'

Terry watched a volley of emotions chasing each other across Claire's face. He had no idea what was going on either, but the man was clearly terrified.

'Claire won't hurt you,' he said, grasping Pattana's arm and helping him to his feet. 'But she doesn't understand this "Sakti" business. Nor do I for that matter.'

'Long time it been since person have such power over air,' Pattana murmured, swallowing repeatedly. 'You must be Sakti Udara. No other can do this.'

'But I haven't done anything!' Claire insisted. 'It's all just a coincidence.

'Besides,' she went on, turning the sunyok around in her hands and speaking almost to herself, 'how could I be your Sakti Udara? I'd spent my whole life on Earth until a few days ago.'

the blood king's court
15th day of ter'tanamasa, 965

Behind the tepak and his strangely-attired companion the massive whitewood doors completed their swing, coming noiselessly to rest against the marble walls of the Blood King's throne room. Fires burned in burnished copper bowls set atop carved columns of the same red-hued stone, intricately patterned with veins of white and both paler and darker shades of red.

A crooked smile creased the face of the yellow-garbed man as the group took in the majesty of the room. Jann assumed he must be the court Jester, despite his lack of a tricorn hat. Grasping his staff with both hands the small man performed a complicated handstand-cum-backflip manoeuvre using the staff for support before running up the hall, twirling the rod and shouting: 'They're here, Majesty! They're here!'

Before the first of them had set foot in the hall the Jester had taken up a position to the King's left, where he stood whispering into the monarch's ear.

Jann glanced around. Elaine had been standing at his side moments earlier but had now dropped back, behind another group of Earthers who were sidling in, trying to remain in the shadows and not make themselves the target for any wrath that might be forthcoming from the royal person. He hurried to keep up with Felice, who was approaching the King.

'That's right, enter!' the King intoned, his voice appearing to rise from somewhere beneath the solid throne on which he sat, deep, gravelly and utterly serious.

'Come forward, let us see you all,' he added, beckoning to the group who had been hugging the wall. They shuffled into the centre of the hall, still trying to avoid the mote-filled beams of light that struck diagonally through the air from each of seven windows high up on the western side of the chamber.

'We have had some fiery jinks this afternoon,' the King continued, pitching his voice to carry the length of the hall.

'Such power as we have not seen for many years.'

It was impossible to discern the King's height while he remained seated, but even in repose he had a regal bearing. A mass of dense red beard obscured most of his face, joining up seamlessly with the equally thick red hair covering his head and rendering precarious the perch of his crown. Both beard and hair were flecked with grey. He was dressed in rich robes of red, orange and gold, patterned in a way oddly recognisable to Jann though he could swear he had never seen its like before. The King's left hand rested on a short rod of polished marble, a kind of ceremonial mace, balanced on a purpose made stand.

His right hand, with which he gestured at the crowd at regular intervals, rested when not waving or pointing on the arm of the carved marble throne.

The Jester continued to whisper in the King's right ear. Jann marvelled the monarch could keep a train of thought going long enough to say anything. Unless of course he simply parroted what the yellow dwarf suggested. Indeed the King had now stopped speaking. With his head cocked to one side the Jester had once more stolen his attention.

The final few members of the colonists' group crossed the boundary between antechamber and throne room. The captain of the guard gave an abrupt hand signal to two of his men. The whitewood doors swung shut, the only clue to their movement a slight change in the acoustics of the hall.

Several of the group started to fidget, clearly uneasy at what might happen next. Felice stepped forward.

'If it please your Majesty—' she began, but the King flashed her a warning glance, holding up a finger of his right hand while he continued to listen to the Jester.

'Big balls, Waters,' Jann murmured. 'I'm impressed.'

'We believe it is one among your group who is responsible for the fire which defeated the black rebel attack,' the King said, his deep-set eyes flicking from face to face. 'How this came to be, we do not understand, but we would speak with her wherever she is.'

It did not escape Jann's notice that the King already knew the gender of the fire starter. Perhaps not so surprising, since there appeared to be a general assumption it had been the Fire Witch. He resisted the impulse to turn towards Elaine. She was attempting to stay out of sight, but others in the group had seen her performance and were already looking in her direction.

She stepped out from behind the small group, staring at the King.

The King grasped his mace. He rose slowly to his feet, his eyes narrowing as he recognised Elaine.

'You!' he exclaimed.

After a beat, Elaine crossed her arms, her golden bangles flashing with reflected torchlight.

'Me,' she said, flicking hair out of her eyes with a toss of her head.

'But... you're dead. You were killed.'

'Apparently not sire,' Elaine replied, curtseying low with a flourish.

'How is this possible?'

She raised an eyebrow.

'You were there.'

'The others?' the King asked, walking forward until he stood on the edge of the dais on which his throne rested.

Elaine shrugged, spreading her hands in the air.

'There's possibly one more. Maybe two.'

She glanced at Jann before turning her attention back to the King.

'We should speak in private,' she said.

'Indeed we should,' the King agreed, nodding.

He raised his arms in an expansive gesture encompassing the whole group.

'My new friends,' he declared, 'it seems I must curtail our brief encounter. A small banquet has been prepared for you in the main dining hall, and quarters in which you may cleanse yourselves of the dust and grime of your journey. Tomorrow we will begin the task of integrating you into your new life here in Istania, but for now please relax. Enjoy the feast. We will join you later.'

At a signal the whitewood doors swung open again and the Earthers began to file out under the direction of the guard captain and his men. The King retook his seat on the throne. He rested his bearded chin on one hand and continued to stare at Elaine.

'Do you want me to stay?' Jann asked her.

She bristled for a moment before flashing him a small smile.

'Don't worry about me. I can handle the King. Go and

wash. Eat. I won't be long here.'

Felice was already leaving the hall. With one final backward glance at Elaine as she walked towards the King, Jann followed her out of the throne room.

the blood king's court
15th day of ter'tanamasa, 965

The Jester did not cease his continuous narrative into the King's ear as Elaine neared the throne. She paused while still a few metres away, glaring at the short yellow-garbed man for several moments.

'We should speak in private sire,' she repeated, without inflection.

The King held up his hand to silence the Jester, who scowled at Elaine before smiling a crooked smile and leaping from the platform. He gambolled and tumbled down the hall, calling:

'Wait for me! I shall escort you to your quarters and entertain you with jokes and japes until dinner!'

Elaine waited while the whitewood doors swung closed. Once certain she and the King were alone, she rounded on him, striding up the stairs of the dais until she stood level with the throne.

'Your ridiculous ceremony has cost me four years of my life on a Baka-forsaken damp green squib of a world where they think magic is only conjuring tricks and sleight of hand!' she seethed.

'After all I have done for you. All my ancestors have done for yours. Years of loyal service going back generations. Elementals through the ages as far back as Tuakara, through famine and war, arguments and treaties. For what? To be banished in the blink of an eye. Washed up in nowhere land with no memory of who I am or what I am capable of, and no way to exercise my power even if I had remembered it was mine. The portal ceremony was a disastrous farce.'

The King's face reddened with indignation but his eyes betrayed his fear of her.

'You agreed to take part!' he said.

'As did we all!' she shouted. 'Little did we know we would all be plucked from the seat of our power and cast through the cosmos.'

'You said there might be others?' the King asked, his manner reeking of appeasement.

Elaine sat down on the top step with an exasperated sigh.

'There are signs,' she said. 'But it is very confusing.'

'How so?'

'I am certain the man who calls himself Jann Argent came through the portal with me,' she replied.

'You know him?'

Elaine stopped. It may not be in her best interest to reveal the extent of her knowledge to the King.

'I thought I may have recognised him, yes, but there is a discrepancy with the timing. I spent four years on Earth. He tells me he had been there for eight.'

'Everyone who was lost fell through the portal at the same instant,' said the King. 'How is it possible for you to arrive at the portal's end at different times?'

'Not quite the same instant,' Elaine corrected him. The memories of her previous interactions with the King, of which there must have been many, had not fully returned, but she would not kowtow to him in any case. Her earlier expression of Fire power gave her an unassailable advantage and a warm feeling of ultimate security.

'The Juggler disappeared first, as I recall, with Albert close behind.'

'Yes, yes, very well,' the King agreed, 'but there were mere seconds between you all.'

'Seconds here,' Elaine said, 'but no-one understands enough about the vortex to say whether time could be distorted within it, or by how much. That could easily explain our different arrival times.'

'I—' began the King.

'But I fell last,' Elaine went on, ignoring him. 'If my memory is accurate then the man Argent must have traversed an instant before me. Others, those who fell first, could have appeared on Earth many years earlier than I. Some may even have died there.'

'There have been indications the Air Mage has also returned,' the King said.

'But if my supposition is correct, Albert would be a very old man indeed,' Elaine said. 'And what of Petani and Lautan? What became of Earth and Water?'

'I know not. But it is a puzzle how you and this Argent came to find your way back here.'

'A lucky happenstance in his case,' Elaine explained, 'his memories have not yet begun to return, although they surely will the longer he spends on Berikatanya. You would do well to keep him under close scrutiny.'

'I shall find him a job in the Court,' the King agreed.

'For myself, the bell summoned me back. It awoke my slumbering memory. With some determination and a good deal of argument I was able to secure passage on the Valiant.'

'The bell?'

'The ceremonial bell. One of those that rung during the portal ceremony.'

'But that's impossible!' the King exclaimed. 'The bells were destroyed. We had to remake them, but even so it has been years since they were last rung, at the memorial service.'

'That Batu'n immigration officer—Felice Waters—told me it had been thirty years. The noise of their ringing would still be travelling to Ketiga Batu, even if it were possible for sound to traverse the vacuum of space.'

'Yes. We had plans to repeat the memorial every year, but they came to nought. There no enthusiasm for raking up the past. The first time was a sombre affair and with regret we let the idea drop. But that still doesn't explain how you were able to hear it.'

'There are theories,' Elaine snapped.

She did not want to waste time explaining the little she had heard of quantum entanglement to the King even if she could.

'Maybe I had a connection to it somehow, who knows? But I am here now, and you owe me.'

Chapter 10

Planting day dawned damp and misty at the forest clearance camp after the overnight rains. Terry Spate had risen early, keen to make a start with the seeds and young plants now the days of hard graft preparing the soil were done. The rich loam lay hidden beneath a thin blanket of wispy fog that curled and boiled under the influence of the weak morning sun, but which would soon burn off once the day turned another hour or so. Terry topped up his bowl from the pan as Claire emerged from her tent.

'Morning!'

'Morning. Ready to cut some drills?'

'I will be when I get my shit together and grab a bite of breakfast,' Claire replied, casting around at the side of her tent for the tools she had left drying the night before. She picked up her hoe, checking its blade.

Umtanesh strode up to the campfire.

'No time for eating mistress,' he said. 'You must come with me.'

Across the camp at the end of the dirt track Terry saw a black-garbed rider sat astride a horse, its coat steaming in the morning chill. The man held the traces of a second, riderless mount which shook its head as he watched, the hot breath pluming from its nostrils adding to the blanket of fog in the clearing.

'What? Why?' Claire asked, also staring at the rider.

Terry stood up, his breakfast bowl falling unnoticed to the ground.

'What's all this about?' he asked Umtanesh.

'Sakti is summoned,' replied the man. 'Come.'

Umtanesh walked off towards the mysterious horseman.

'Wait. Summoned? Who by?' Claire called after him.

158

'The Queen hears of your powers,' Umtanesh said without turning back. 'She asks you attend Black Palace for meet with her.'

Claire screwed up her face. Terry could see the prospect of being whisked away from the familiarity of the camp to the great unknown of the Black Queen's Palace did not appeal to her. Tendrils of mist curled around her feet as if the clearing itself tried to hold on to her.

'You'd better go,' he said. 'She's the big cheese in these parts. A refusal may be seen as an insult. Besides, I doubt this "Sakti" business will go away until you've at least spoken with the Queen. Maybe you can convince her it's all a mistake.'

Claire's gaze flicked from the rider to Terry and back, fear plain on her face.

'Which it is,' she murmured.

'I've never ridden a horse,' she added, handing her hoe to him and starting across camp.

As she neared the black rider, he dismounted and bowed.

'Sakti,' he said. 'Allow me to adjust the saddle for you.'

He looked Claire up and down, assessing the length of her legs. Turning to the second steed, he checked the tightness of the girth and shortened the stirrups. Satisfied, he bowed again to Claire.

'Pembwana is ready for you mistress.'

'Pembwana?'

'That is her name. The Queen chose for you herself. It is a great honour.'

'Just hope I don't end up on my ass instead of my horse,' Claire joked, stepping up to the animal who snickered and nodded her head as if appreciating the humour.

She turned to Terry, eyes wide.

'I don't...'

He smiled and gestured with the hoe.

'Go on. You'll be fine. This guy will look after you. I

expect the Queen will bury him if he lets any harm come to you.'

Claire placed a foot in the stirrup and swung herself up into the saddle at the first attempt. The horse stood still while she mounted, but turned with Claire as she wheeled around to flash Terry a beaming smile.

'I did it!' she squealed.

'Sakti, it is a full day's hard ride to the Palace,' the rider said. 'We must leave.'

'Go,' said Terry.

Claire took hold of the reins. Pembwana tossed her head, turning at the slightest signal from her new mistress. The Queen's horseman set off at a fast trot in the direction of the rising sun, his ebon cloak billowing out behind him. Claire followed, riding the black mare as if she had been in the saddle all her life.

Terry watched as the two riders left the camp, disappearing around a bend in the track a few minutes later. His young friend did not look back, but a stiff breeze stirred the trees, lifting columns of mist from the forest floor and blowing them away across the clearing.

the blood king's court
15th day of ter'tanamasa, 965

The whitewood doors swung shut behind Jann Argent, cutting off Elaine from his sight. Still trying to process the latest revelation about her, he hoped her audience with the King would satisfy her high expectations. At the last moment before the doors closed, the Jester came tumbling through, almost knocking Jann off his feet.

'Come, come!' he cried, 'Follow me! To the quad! To the quad!'

'Full of himself, isn't he?' Patrick said. 'Telling us all to follow him while he's stood at the back.'

Jann smiled, but the lemony gyrator had soon made his way to the front, where he was forced to slow his pace or risk leaving everyone behind.

After another interminable series of confusing turns and corridors they emerged into a paved assembly area set in an open air space surrounded on all four sides by the Court walls. Jann soon lost any sense of the complex layout of the building.

The afternoon sun cast lengthening shadows from the western wall, throwing the back of the quad into semi-darkness compared to the brightness of the side from which they entered, where the light glinted and sparked from the crystalline stonework of the Court. Felice hurried over to consult with the Jester and the guard captain, who stood together in the middle of the quad waiting for the group to file out. Once the Earthers had all assembled, the Jester addressed them in a surprisingly rich, loud voice.

'Your colleague,' he began, with a nod towards Felice, 'has given us a brief outline of your skills and interests. There is some scope for matching these with the available positions, but as you will appreciate life here is somewhat simpler and more prosaic than many of you will be used to. We cannot guarantee to find you a position which will make best use of what you already know.

'Your quartering depends to some extent on the role you are chosen for in the King's service,' he continued, pacing up and down in front of them. 'A few of you may have to spend some time thinking about alternative roles you would be prepared to fill.

'What are you good at? What did you do on Ketiga Batu? Do you wish to pursue similar employment here, assuming it exists, or would you prefer to try something new?'

'I wonder if the King needs a new emblem for his flags?' Patrick mused.

'I expect I'll be slipping off with Felice once we're done here,' Jann replied. 'She still has the watery riddle to investigate.'

A guard entered the quadrangle at a run, stopped in

front of the Jester and muttered a few hasty words in Istanian.

'Excuse me,' the Jester said, 'think about what I have said.'

He walked with the guard to the shadowed side of the quad where they engaged in animated conversation.

Jann strolled over to Felice.

'Ketiga Batu?'

'It's their name for Earth,' she explained. 'I'm sure the Queen mentioned it in her address.'

'Ah, yeah. I remember. When do we check out your mystery?'

'I think events might have overtaken us in that respect,' Felice said, looking towards the Jester and the guard.

They were still talking, both staring back at Jann. A moment later the Jester shrugged and returned to them.

'The King has need of additional guards,' the Jester said as he stepped squinting into the sunlight. 'Do you have any experience of security work?'

Jann exchanged the briefest of glances with Felice. He suppressed a smile.

'Yes,' he replied, 'some.'

'Very good,' said the Jester. 'You will come with us.'

the blood king's throne room
15th day of ter'tanamasa, 965

Smoky orange fingers of late afternoon sun stroked the marble dais of the throne room. The King had not moved since the Fire Witch withdrew to her chambers. He languished on the cold stone, his chin resting on one hand, his eyes unfocused, gazing across the room but not seeing. The sound of uneven footfall disturbed the silence. The King looked up.

'Did you find him?'

'Yes sire.'

'Capital,' said the King, his face breaking into a broad

smile.

'It is strange. I expected to recognise him.'

'It has been many years.'

'Not for him. Eight, did the Witch say?'

'She did.'

'And yet the Witch remains unchanged. Whatever fate befell Petani at the portal's end, they must have been eight hard years. He is much leaner than I remember. And more serious.'

'Where have we placed him?'

'In your guard, sire, where he will be attached to the Court. Available at any time should you wish to question him further, or allocate tasks that will allow us to see what powers he retains. What memories will resurface.'

'The portal had effects far beyond those we expected.'

'Indeed it did sire. But with the Witch returned, can fortune have smiled on your House a second time and brought back the Earth Elemental also?'

'There is no guarantee that all will find their way back. The Witch implied it was mere chance Argent found passage from Ketiga Batu. He has no memory of life here. The Gardener may as well be dead.'

'But imagine if he can be brought back to life, sire! His memories may yet be rekindled. With both of your Elementals returned and no sign of either of those loyal to the Queen, a victory would be assured.

'Should we decide to prosecute our advantage,' he added, grinning.

'It is doubtful we could persuade either of our mages to side with us in the absence of the other powers,' the King sighed. 'You know what they're like. It's all about "balance in the Elements" and fairness. They would not engage in an uneven conflict.'

'Then perhaps we should think about re-engineering the portal, sire,' said the Jester, stepping closer to the King.

'With some small changes a repeat of the memorial ceremony could reopen the vortex. It may be possible to

render the Elementals' departure somewhat more...
permanent?'

The King snorted.

'And how do you suppose we could persuade them to
take part?' he asked, his face reddening. 'The first time
almost killed them all. Cast them an unimaginable distance
through the cosmos. Even those who managed to return
have done so with the utmost good fortune. They would
not risk such a venture again.'

'No, indeed sire,' the Jester agreed, bowing. 'It would
take careful planning. A good story. A compelling reason
to repeat the attempt. Assurances that we now understand
the magic well enough this time around to avoid...
mishaps.'

The King did not reply immediately. He sat unmoving
on his throne as if he had become one with the marble.
Cold, hard, and passionless. He gave out a heavy sigh.

'Well, you are better versed in such matters than I,' he
said. 'If you believe you can concoct a credible tale, then
go ahead. Mayhap the Elementals' time is at an end. Would
we be better served investing our energies in the fortunes
of normal men? Especially when they bring technological
wonders to rival that which we call magic.'

the blood king's court
15th day of ter'tanamasa, 965

The last feeble red rays of late evening sun cast long
shadows on the refectory table at which Jann Argent sat, a
simple but wholesome repast of bread, cheese and pickled
local vegetables half-eaten in front of him. He chewed on
the grainy Berikatanyan loaf, watching a kitchen maid
setting candlesticks on the tables in readiness for the final
meal of the day.

'Want some company?'

He looked up, shielding his eyes from the low sun.
Elaine stood a little way away, a plate of cold cuts in one

hand.

'You could toast some bread for me,' he replied.

'Don't get smart, or I might toast you,' she said, taking a seat beside him.

'Sorry. Still trying to wrap my head around you being a real witch.'

'*The* real witch, if you don't mind. You do know I'm an Elemental?'

'Apparently. I saw the Element for myself. How does that work then?'

'You could say it's an accident of birth. Elementals are always the most powerful mages of their time, but there's more to it. Just being a good mage isn't enough. We come from very few bloodlines. One, in my case.'

'You mean all the Fire Witches there have ever been came from your family?'

'And Wizards. It's not gender specific. But yes, before me they were all ancestors of mine. And if the family doesn't produce a mage of extraordinary power at any time, then there won't be an Elemental until one is born, or grows into his or her power. Very occasionally an Elemental arises from somewhere else, but it's been centuries since that last happened.'

'For Fire?'

'Water.'

'Ah. So you're pure.'

Elaine pulled a hunk of bread off his loaf, spreading it with a rich red chutney.

'In respect of my bloodline, certainly,' she grinned. 'The inherited traits that confer great power can occur naturally at random, but those who possess them usually seek to strengthen their gifts through choosing appropriate mates.'

She chewed her bread, watching him. Jann reached for the last of his cheese.

'You don't strike me as the mating type,' he said, biting into the soft yellow curd, savouring its unusual salty flavour.

He had wondered how close to a cow or a goat the Berikatanyan animal would be whose milk had produced it, before remembering there were none. This particular cheese was made from nuts. Elaine filled a glass with water from a tall jug in the middle of the table.

'It's true, Elementals tend to be solitary figures. The great power we are capable of sometimes leads to a certainly... overbearing... temperament. In some individuals.

'You mean you're hot-headed,' Jann smiled.

'People are frightened of our capacity for harm,' she said, ignoring his cheap shot, 'even though most of our efforts are for good. Any display of "witchcraft" scares off most of those who could be friends, let alone potential partners. It's not really surprising the pool of Elementals is so small.

'And on top of that, wielding such great power requires some sacrifices. Meditation, study of the lore, long periods of practice. Doesn't leave much room for socialising.'

'It's tough at the top.'

They continued to eat in silence until the sun dipped below the Court walls. The kitchen maid returned to light the candles up and down the refectory.

'So it must have been easy for you to work the fire back at the circus?' Jann asked, wiping up the last of his pickle with a crust of bread.

'I didn't have any power on Earth,' Elaine replied. 'It began to return as soon as we landed here, but I still haven't regained full use of the Fire.'

She looked at him closely again. Jann knew she was thinking about his memory. About when, or whether, it would come back. So many aspects of this planet were familiar to him, but the majority of it remained out of reach, shut behind doors in his mind that so far had refused to open.

Elaine drained her glass.

'Do you fancy something a little stronger than water?' she asked.

He gave her a quizzical look.

'I have wine in my quarters.'

'You have wine? In your quarters?'

'I do.'

*

Elaine occupied a suite of rooms far more opulent than his own, Jann admitted as soon as they had settled themselves on her deep-filled sofa. She poured them each a glass of tawny yellow wine, its flavour faintly reminiscent of cloudberries.

'I can usually see both sides of a debate,' Jann said, savouring a second mouthful of the rich, sweet wine, 'so I suppose I should allow that the Fire Witch of Berikatanya deserves a bit more plush than a lowly court guard.'

'You are more than just a guard,' Elaine said. 'Your memory has been much more badly affected than mine.'

Jann gave the conundrum a moment's reflection.

'I wonder if it has anything to do with how far back we were each thrown.'

Elaine choked on her drink.

'You remember being "thrown"?' she asked, wide eyed.

'No. But I can infer it from what you've told me so far.'

He swirled the wine around in his glass, watching the syrupy rivulets run back into the bowl.

'And from what I've heard you say when you thought I wasn't listening.'

'I wish I could tell you more, but I just... have this feeling it's important for you to recover the memories at your own pace.'

'There are things that already feel right,' he said, setting his glass on a low table and turning to face Elaine.

'Such as?'

'Having two moons in the sky for one thing. And the smells are so natural here, it feels like coming home. At the same time "home" is a bit of an unknown place. As if your

167

parents have moved while you were out and when you come back, it's to a different house. It still smells of Mum & Dad and the dog, but you don't know where anything is.

'And this wine,' he added, picking up his glass again and inhaling the bouquet. 'What is it?'

'Buwangah. It's made from cloud fruit. They're similar to the grapes they have on Earth, but rounder and orange. They grow on very high ground, just below the snowline. The skin carries a unique form of sugar that gives the wine extra sweetness.'

'The King seemed pleased to see you,' Jann said, changing the subject.

'He's glad to believe me on his side again.'

'Again?'

'The Elementals long ago recognised their power could win or lose battles. That's a big responsibility. It's not always clear which side is "right" in any dispute. Political influence waxes and wanes. There's nothing like democracy here, but still if we had aligned ourselves exclusively with one of the noble houses, the other would not have been able to stand.'

'Was it necessary to pick a side?'

'Maybe not, but the establishment—two houses as benign dictators of their own realms—is better than many alternatives. The Elementals didn't consider it part of their role to determine which house should be in the ascendant.'

'So what did you do?'

'It wasn't us. Not the current leaders of the Elements. At least, not the ones who led when the vortex was created. Our ancestors made a pact to ensure there would always be balance between the Elements. We call it Te'banga. Fire and Water chose opposing sides. Earth and Air also took different Houses.'

'So you ended up with the King.'

'Yes, along with Petani.'

Jann stopped swirling his glass and gave her a quizzical look.

'It's the Elemental name for the wielder of the Earth power.'

'And the other two—Air and Water—'

'—aligned with the Black Queen,' Elaine nodded.

'And that arrangement gave balance. Te'banga.'

'Yes.' She shrugged. 'As near as we could achieve.'

'I still don't understand why you had to pick a side,' Jann leaned forward. 'It would have been equally "balanced" if you'd all agreed to stay out of it altogether.'

'Maybe. But such an agreement would always have risked one of us being persuaded to take a side. Despite our powers we are all— Ha! I was going to say "all human". I lived on Ketiga Batu too long. We are all Su'matra. The King and Queen are both very rich, powerful and persuasive. If one of us had been tempted to join in, the others would have had to get involved too, to maintain Te'banga. We decided it would be more successful to divide ourselves as we did.

'Besides,' she added, taking a sip from her wine and unconsciously matching Jann's swirling of the amber liquid in her glass, 'there are advantages to being a favoured member of Court.'

'Tell me about it,' said Jann with a rueful smile.

He looked across the room at Elaine's enormous double bed, comparing it with his lonely cot in a distant part of the Court.

'I wish I had some special powers.'

Elaine lifted one eyebrow.

'How do you know you don't?' she teased, pouring him some more wine. 'Weren't you going with the Waters woman to investigate strange manifestations? If other Batu'n can demonstrate power, even in a small way, why not you?'

'I can find out more about myself here at Court,' he replied, taking the refilled glass. 'And if I was capable of wielding any of these powers I think I'd know.'

'You might. There are other kinds of power, besides

the Elements,' she said, leaning back on the sofa with her hands behind her head. She stretched, before giving a sudden gasp of pain.

'I'm not used to such fast riding,' she said, frowning and rubbing her thigh.

A silence fell between them. Through the window of Elaine's chamber the first of the two moons rose over the nearby forest, a featureless silver orb in a clear black sky.

Jann drained his wine glass.

'I should go,' he said.

forest clearance project
20th day of ter'tanamasa, 965

Terry Spate stood at the edge of the clearing for several minutes after Claire spurred her horse out of the forest. He stared along the track, shielding his eyes from the glare, Claire's hoe still held in his other hand. Once he was certain he would not catch another glimpse of the riders, he wiped his brow, looking back across the cleared open space. The breeze had died away for once, allowing the heat of the day to begin to make its presence felt.

Most of the rest of the group had not yet breakfasted so Terry took the chance to check on his garden. Years of creating tranquil oases of colour had made it almost a psychological imperative for him wherever he went. In one small spot behind his tent he had been busy planting, constructing a miniature replica of his last home; enough to give him something to do in the downtime between the hard graft of logging and tilling. To satisfy his innate desire for creation.

The unfamiliar plants of Berikatanya had responded well to his care. The garden thrived. Where the local flora beside the trails and in hedgerows were not yet carrying their first buds, in Terry's plot they were almost ready to burst into full bloom, their heads heavy with the promise of colour to come. A tingle of expectation ran through him, a palpable excitement and anticipation. He had no idea what hues his blooms would display, yet he was certain the overall effect would be stunning in both its variety and its coherence. He had found the rich loam beside the clearing even easier to work than in the heavily wooded areas. He had hardly any need for tools. What clumps of soil there were fell apart in his hands, the dark brown earth glinting with tiny golden specks as its moisture reflected the sunlight.

It energised him, working with the soil. He often felt compelled to drive his hands deep into the earth, the cool damp compost parting to allow him to sink up to his elbows, bringing up large spade-like handfuls that he would let run through his fingers. In the early morning, the chestnut peaty smell assailed his nostrils, blowing any last traces of sleepiness from his mind and giving an inchoate clarity to the day. If he found time to work in his garden in the evening, the green fresh fragrances of the plants and the feel of the earth in his hands would strip the tired aches from his bones, the cramps from his muscles, and the incipient fatigue from his eyes.

He felt more at home here than at any time in his life. Closer to the land, more in tune with the flowers, herbs and cereals. Even after his long years of toil on Earth, his keenness to meet the new demands and challenges this young world presented was undiminished.

At the edge of his plot, a young kinchu sat watching him, its rabbit-like face twitching as it caught his scent. He smiled.

'Help yourself,' he murmured.

'You ready, Terry?' the group leader David Garcia called from beside the firepit, wiping the last of his breakfast from around his mouth.

'Whenever you are!' Terry replied.

He selected a few hand tools from the bag inside his tent, rested the hoe over his shoulder, and set off across the clearing to join the others in the long day's work of planting.

the blood king's court
17th day of ter'tanamasa, 965

The dull click of Jann Argent's footfalls echoed in every direction in the dusty catacombs of the Blood King's Court. Everywhere he looked another corridor offered a possible route through the maze of heavy stonework, or a doorless chamber opened up, lined with ancient leather-bound tomes or rolls of yellowing parchment. He had been sent for a guard's uniform, and had already spent almost an hour searching for the Keeper of the Cloth or whatever the man was called. He would have gone back to the beginning and started again, only by now he did not know where "the beginning" was either.

He was starting to envy Patrick who, once Jann had been assigned to the King's guard, decided to get away from Court for a while, take some time to explore the rest of Istania, and discover what opportunities there might be for someone with his talents. Right now, being outside in the fresh air seemed a much more attractive option.

Jann's flickering torch cast cavorting shadows on the web-covered walls, conjuring thoughts of tortured demons or heavily chained prisoners tormented by both their crimes and their jailors. Around yet another corner, he found a chamber markedly different from those he had encountered so far. The opening was entirely enclosed with a framework of iron bars stretching between the stone pillars. In the centre of the arch a heavy gate stood ajar, its padlock hanging loose on the hasp. Behind the ironwork, which had flaked and rusted with age, several oaken shelves held many dozens of scrolls. By the light from his guttering torch Jann could see the nearest of them were ornately illuminated in various colours.

He swung the gate open. The hinges complained with an eerie high-pitched moan that resurrected his mental images of tortured demons. He stepped through into the chamber, set his torch in a wall sconce, and pulled out one of the scrolls.

'What are you doing there?'

Startled, Jann dropped the scroll.

'Careful with that!' the gruff voice cried, its owner moving into the light of Jann's torch. An enormous bunch of keys hanging from the man's waist jangled as he moved.

'Sorry,' Jann said, reaching for the scroll.

'Leave it! Leave it!' cried the man, pushing past Jann to retrieve the yellowed parchment. He dusted it off reverently.

'Do you know how old these are? Who are you anyway? And what are you doing here?'

'My name is Jann Argent. I was trying—'

'Aha! So you're Argent. I've been expecting you. Took your time, didn't you?'

'I got lost.'

'I can see that! You won't find any guards uniforms in here!'

'How did you—?'

'I'm the Keeper of the Keys. Least, that's my proper title. We keep all the uniforms down here too—they last longer out of the light—so some wags have started calling me the Keeper of the Cloth. I suppose it amuses their pea brains.'

'That's who they told me to come and find.'

'Yes, very funny. I expect they thought it would rile me up and I'd give you a hard time. But that's nothing like the stick I would have given you if you'd damaged my scroll!'

The old man pushed the ancient parchment back onto the shelves, slotting it into the exact place Jann had pulled it from without a moment's hesitation.

'What is all this stuff?' Jann asked.

The Keeper of the Keys glared at him. One of his eyes was milked by a cataract but both fixed on him with a baleful stare.

'This "stuff" as you so eloquently describe it is the history and lore of the Blood King and his line stretching back over a thousand years. You wouldn't normally have been able to get in, only I've been doing some research. Must've left it open. My memory...'

'You really shouldn't be in here now,' he added, tutting and ushering Jann out of the chamber.

'Come along,' he growled, 'out of here. I must lock up. Don't want any other precious artefacts casting to the dusty floor, do we?'

Jann retrieved his torch.

'Careful with that!' the Keeper hissed, reaching for Jann's arm.

'I don't allow fire in here!' he said. 'Far too dangerous! Come on, out with you! And keep your damn flame away from my parchments!'

Taking care to leave a good distance between the torch and the dangerously over-stacked shelves in an effort to appease the old man and win back some semblance of credibility, Jann stepped over the threshold. The surprisingly nimble Keeper followed on his heels. The rusty iron gate clanged shut behind them. Selecting the right key from his ring without looking, the old man secured the padlock, tugged at it to make sure it was fastened, and turned to peer at Jann once again. In the flickering light from the torch, his milky eye seemed to move over Jann's face as if searching for recognition.

'Some of that old lore would give you nightmares,' he said, chuckling almost to himself. 'Stay out of there in future, if you know what's good for you!'

He set off down the tunnel without waiting for Jann. The cold darkness of the catacombs enveloped him within seconds.

'Come on,' he called from the dark, bringing Jann to his senses. 'Do you want this uniform or don't you?'

Jann hurried to catch up with the Keeper. After several minutes walk through the tunnels and innumerable turns that left Jann with no idea of his way back to the scroll room, let alone how to exit from the maze, they arrived at a polished wooden door standing ajar. Warmth emanated from the room together with the faintly herbal smell of an exotic tea.

'Come along young Argent,' said the Keeper, his tone much friendlier now his precious scrolls were safe and he had returned to the heart of his demesne. 'Make yourself comfortable.'

This was clearly the Keeper's study. Possibly even his living quarters. Across the room two other doors, closed for the moment, may have concealed a bedroom and a bathroom. Jann presumed the old man would eat in the refectory along with all the other Court staff and visitors. A fire burned in a black metal grate, before which stood two stuffed armchairs—one considerably more worn than the other—and a small sofa. Against the far wall a desk had almost disappeared under an enormous pile of more scrolls, parchments, and leather-bound books. Above the desk Jann was astonished to see eleven other rings of keys, each as large as the one the Keeper carried on his belt. A twelfth hook, the space on the wall beneath it displaying a smudged circular stain, indicated where this last ring belonged.

The Keeper opened the double doors of a cavernous closet. Inside uniforms of different hues, ranks and sizes hung in ordered lines. He looked Jann up and down for a second or two before selecting a guardsman's uniform.

'Here, try this.'

Jann took the heavy suit, which appeared to be made from the Berikatanyan equivalent of wool but felt much stronger and heavier. It had been dyed a deep red. He glanced around for somewhere to change.

'Come on, come on!' the Keeper urged, 'don't be shy. I don't have all day.'

Jann removed his jeans and donned the heavy uniform. Almost at once his arms and legs began to itch.

'Don't worry about the itching,' the old man grinned, his prescience catching Jann off guard. 'Everyone suffers at first. It will soon pass.'

'How so?'

'Am I a physician?' the Keeper asked, flapping his hand in dismissal of the question. 'It just will, you'll see. How's the fit?'

Jann moved around a little. The suit was stiff from disuse, but otherwise fitted well.

'It's fine.'

'Good. At least my last good eye is still working.'

The Keeper returned to his desk while Jann changed back into his regular clothes.

'So I can take this?' Jann enquired, curling the heavily embroidered jacket over the hanger.

The Keeper remained absorbed in the open scroll laying on his desk atop a disordered pile of paperwork.

'Excuse me?' Jann said.

'Hmm? Yes, yes of course. Take it. It's what you came for isn't it?'

'What is that?' Jann asked, peering over the old man's shoulder. 'Music?'

The lines on the parchment were criss-crossed with small bubbles drawn on top of various geometrical shapes.

'Music?' the Keeper said, rounding on Jann and fixing him with his one good eye. 'Music? This is much more than music.'

'Oh?'

'These are the songs of power.'

Jann regarded the man. His tone had softened from his previous gruffness. It was almost reverential.

'Songs of power? I thought all the magic here came from the Elements?'

'It begins with the Elements, young man, but there is much more to it than that. Those who control the Elements are powerful in their own right, but there is power in music too. It can enhance the Elements, or it can oppose them. And certain songs—the songs of power such as this—can bring the Elements together to enable such magic as makes the world tremble. The Universe, even.'

'Why is this one so special.'

'This is a Lullaby,' said the Keeper, whispering the epithet as though it were holy and running his hand over the edge of the ancient parchment.

Jann could not suppress a laugh. The bark of it echoed out into the catacombs. The Keeper rounded on him.

'You mock the sacred texts of the Lullabies?'

'I'm sorry, no,' Jann said, recovering his composure. 'The only power I ever heard of a lullaby having is the power to put children to sleep.'

The Keeper relaxed a little. He gave a wry smile.

'Indeed,' he said, 'in recent times these songs have been sung to children. They were not always known as the Lullabies. Since the passing of the Elementals their power is much diminished, but the people still remember them. Still teach them to their young ones.

'There are three, in total,' the Keeper went on, indicating two other scrolls rolled up on his desk. 'It is most likely there were more, but these are the only ones to have survived from the time of the Great Mages.'

'How old are they?' Jann asked, keen to make further reparation for his earlier outburst.

'Their provenance has passed beyond memory,' the Keeper replied, 'as has the language in which they were first written. The words are kept alive through the singing but there is no-one left who knows the tongue, or understands it.

'But if you had been here,' the old man whispered, his eyes becoming misty from the long-buried memory, 'when the songs were last sung in the presence of the Elementals. Well, the power was immense. So overwhelming, indeed, that it caused their ultimate fall and brought about the end of high magic in Berikatanya.'

JOHN BERESFORD

Chapter 11

the palace of the black queen
20th day of ter'tanamasa, 965

Still riding hard behind her black-robed companion, Claire
Yamani rounded the northernmost tip of the mountains he
called Tubelak'Dun. She was rewarded with her first sight
of the Black Queen's Palace. The view sent a tingle of
excited anticipation through her. They'd been travelling at
a fair clip for most of the day, stopping only to water the
horses and later for a hasty bite of lunch when he'd rather
stiffly introduced himself as Negel, a hodak of the Queen's
honour guard. As soon as they'd eaten, Negel insisted they
needed to push on if they were to make the Palace before
nightfall. Since then he'd set a harder pace, but to Claire's
surprise her riding skills proved up to the task. Now the
late evening sun limned the gleaming towers of obsidian
and black granite with a fiery glow, lighting the Queen's
flag flying above the high central tower an incandescent
orange, the colour mirrored in the smaller pennants which
decorated the other, shorter turrets. It looked like a dark,
secretive version of a Disney fairy castle.

Ostlers and other Palace staff met them in the huge
courtyard as they entered the gates. Word of Claire's
imminent arrival had clearly spread. She heard several
muttered "Sakti Udara"'s as she reined Pembwana to a halt.
She dismounted as Negel snapped to attention.

'Majesty!'

The Black Queen glided toward them through an
imposing pair of blackwood doors. She crossed the
polished jet-black flagstones edging the courtyard,
regarding Claire with an unreadable expression before
addressing the rider.

'You made good time, Hodak Negel.'

'As you instructed milady.'

'Make sure the kudai are well looked after.'

The Queen turned on her heel.

'Follow me!' she said, retracing her steps across the courtyard.

Everyone else had already busied themselves with their tasks. The Queen's instruction had been intended for Claire alone. She hurried from the glow of evening into the relative gloom of the Black Palace.

Several servants worked to light lamps, torches, and candles against the coming night. A soft glow began to illuminate the halls as Claire caught up with the Queen, maintaining a respectful distance behind her. Yellow torchlight bounced off polished surfaces everywhere. The Black Palace was well named. It appeared to be constructed almost exclusively from black materials. Obsidian columns, black granite walls, burnished jet floors in staterooms giving way to dark slate in common areas.

Claire followed the Queen through another massive pair of blackwood doors into an enormous hallway from which a double staircase led up to a galleried landing. Directly opposite them a magnificent archway beneath the first rise of stairs let onto the Queen's throne room, her glistening black throne visible at the far end.

Portraits covered the walls of the hall and stairways. Claire gave them each a cursory glance as she hurried to keep up with the Queen. Halfway across the imposing hallway she came to an abrupt halt, letting out an involuntary gasp of shock. The Queen wheeled around in surprise.

'What ever is the matter my dear?' she asked, her tone sharp but her expression showing some concern. 'Are you in pain?'

Claire pointed at the left-hand staircase.

'Th-that portrait. The man there with the light coloured hair and the blue tunic. Near the top.'

The Queen followed Claire's gaze and smiled.

'Yes?'

'Who is he?'

'He was a very dear friend of mine. He and his wife were taken from us before their time. Sadly missed these fifty years or more. A very powerful and influential man.'

'Taken from you? He died here?'

'Not exactly. It's a long story. But in his time he became one of my most trusted allies and principal advisors. He was an Elemental. The last Air Mage of Berikatanya.'

Claire's eyes widened as she processed the words, her attention flicking back and forth between the Queen and the portrait. She swallowed down a knot in her throat that threatened to choke her.

'It's my father,' she said.

the palace of the black queen
22nd day of ter'tanamasa, 965

Claire sat wrapped in the largest, fluffiest towel she'd ever seen, perched on the edge of the largest, softest bed she'd ever seen in what was almost certainly the largest, most sumptuous bedroom she'd ever seen. Her head whirled with the memories of all that had happened since she arrived at the Palace, mixed up with thoughts of what was still to come.

The Queen had been engaged in an important meeting with her senior advisors and military experts, discussing defensive strategies in light of increasing tension with the Blood King's forces. She had interrupted this high-powered gathering to welcome Claire to the Palace. Once Claire's heritage was revealed, the Queen gave instructions for the summit to be postponed indefinitely.

'I must admit I suspected—hoped even—it might be true, my dear,' the Queen had said while Claire stared open-mouthed at the enormous portrait of her father. 'All the reports of the atmospheric disturbances we have received since your arrival suggested a link, but of course no-one could explain it. A Batu'n girl—forgive me my dear, but that is how we saw you at first—with the powers of an Elemental? Why, it's unheard of! There have been tales of some Batu'n demonstrating rudimentary magic, almost accidentally in most cases, but none have shown the level of mastery of an Elemental.

'Until now that is,' she had added. 'Come, I must see you safely to your room before I make some changes to tonight's banquet.'

So saying, the Queen had brought her here. Her room. A room of her own, in a Palace. She shook her head, her ash-blonde hair, still wet from the bath, flicking droplets of water across the room. One landed on the sky-blue dress hanging beside the bed, absorbed into the cloth in an expanding dark stain. Claire gave a little cry, rushing over to dab at the damp patch with a dry corner of towel. This dress had, the Queen told her, belonged to Claire's grandmother. Air Mage before her father and one of the most powerful Elementals there had ever been.

'She was a great loss,' the Queen said, her hand resting on the dress before hanging it up beside Claire's bed. 'Your father stepped into the role while still a young man. He would probably have equalled his mother in his mastery of the Air, but when the Vortex took all our Elementals, that vast potential of his was lost to our people—ours and the Blood King's. The whole of Berikatanya suffered.

'You must tell me of him, later,' the Queen continued, smiling at Claire, 'and of your childhood.'

Until that moment she'd seemed distant and aloof. Cold, even. But her seldom seen smile, friendly and open, did a little to dispel Claire's disquiet at the thought of what would be expected of her.

'It seems inconceivable your parents never told you of your heritage,' the Queen mused.

'I suppose they decided there was no point,' Claire said. 'We had no magic on Earth. Father couldn't use his power. If he'd tried to tell me I'd have thought it was a fairy story, like the ones he used to tell me at bedtime.'

'Well, we can talk about it later,' the Queen had said, walking to the door. 'For now, you should bathe. Wash away all the dust of your long ride. I shall send a maidservant to dress you, and one of the courtiers will attend to explain about tonight's festivities.'

Another shiver ran through Claire. Whether a chill from the damp towel, or the prospect of being guest of honour at the Queen's feast, she was unsure. The thick glass in her bedroom window rattled. The wind had risen again outside, gusting against the walls of the Palace. Through the distortion of the loose pane she could make out the Queen's standard, flapping in the high wind. Was this her doing? She had no idea. No clue how she might have started the storm, no notion of how to stop it if she had. It just happened. She sat back on the bed and towelled her hair dry, trying to calm her nerves to see if that had any influence on the wind, which had now begun to howl round the tower.

There was a knock.

'Come in,' she called.

A young girl with a startled expression put her head around the door.

'If it please your ladyship, I come help get dressed.'

Claire burst out laughing at the unexpected deference.

'Come in, and please don't call me "your ladyship". I'm no more a lady than you are.'

The girl's demeanour became even more alarmed, so that Claire thought her eyebrows might disappear entirely under her hairline.

'My name is Claire,' she went on, 'or if you must you can call me Miss Yamani.'

'Very good. Miss Yamani,' said the girl, apparently comfortable with the less familiar form of address. 'You are ready for dressing?'

'I'm quite sure I can manage to dress myself, thank you,' Claire said, not wishing to hurt the girl's feelings. 'But you could find something to dry my hair.'

The maidservant looked puzzled for a moment before leaving, returning a moment later with another towel. She retrieved a gilt brush from the nightstand. Once Claire had donned her family heirloom dress, the girl brushed the tangles from Claire's hair, alternating towel and brush until her ash-blonde locks were almost dry.

'Have I upset Miss?' the girl asked, stepping back from her task.

Claire frowned.

'Not at all. What makes you think that?'

'Miss make me work hard drying hair. Could have done by self. With powers.'

Claire blushed, but before she could own up to her woeful lack of control over her "powers" there came a second knock at the door. As if summoned by some unseen signal from her dry hair, the promised courtier arrived to escort Claire to the dining hall.

A hush fell as she appeared on the balcony above the hall. Her knees almost buckled at the sight. A cursory glance at the ranks of tables below her suggested around two hundred people had gathered for what the Queen had called a "hastily organised ceremonial dinner" to celebrate the return of one of her Elementals.

'If we'd only had more time, my dear, we could have done it properly. As it is, I'm afraid I've run the court staff ragged to try and drum up as many of the Princips as possible but I must apologise. It will be a sad little affair compared with how it might have been.'

The Queen's words echoed through Claire's mind, making her dizzy at the thought of "how it might have been".

'Everyone is so pleased, my dear, I can't tell you. To have one of our Elementals returned to us, particularly in these difficult times. Well, it gives us all such reassurance.'

'But... I don't have the first clue how to be an Elemental,' Claire had insisted.

'You mustn't worry about that young lady,' the Queen had countered in her most dismissive tone. 'You have the power by virtue of your birth. That's the main thing. It will be a simple matter to learn how to use it. You'll see. For balance to be restored is of utmost importance. Especially in light of the rumours coming out of Red House.'

'Rumours?'

'We hear the Fire Witch has returned.'

The Queen had gone on to explain the four Elements, with special emphasis on Air and Fire.

Claire and her escort reached the head of the stairs but now, having bowed low, the courtier withdrew. Clearly he wasn't invited to dinner. Claire would have to negotiate the staircase on her own. The sound of pipe music drifted up to meet her. A haunting tune at once strange and recognisable. Claire sought out its source. On a small dais behind the top table in the dining hall, a short purple-clad figure stood playing an unusual set of bifurcated pipes. The instrument was bound with a purple ribbon that fluttered in a current of air, its movement tugging at Claire's memory. With a gasp Claire recognised it. She stumbled, clutching the banister. They were the pipes from her dream!

A murmur from the assembly below reminded her where she was. They were waiting for her. Recovering her composure, she stepped onto the central landing. At once everyone in the hall rose to their feet, taking their lead from the Queen, and began an eerie ululation. The Berikatanyan equivalent of applause was strangely affecting. Combined with the evocative music of the piper, it made the hairs on the back of Claire's neck rise. She kept her gaze focused on the Queen, who indicated with a nod her place at the top table. With great relief Claire reached her seat, curtseyed to the Queen hoping it was an appropriate gesture, and stood awaiting another clue as to what would happen next.

The Queen smiled.

'Well done, my dear. You look exquisite.'

She picked up a large silver sunyok, its handle chased with a pattern that matched the ring she wore and which Claire noticed for the first time. It was set with an enormous black opal that glimmered in the candlelight. The Queen gave a single sharp rap with the sunyok, and sat down. Claire took her seat beside the Queen. The rest of the hall followed suit with a rustling of expensive garments and a low murmur of inaudible comments.

'Your dress fits perfectly,' the Queen said. 'You must have exactly the same figure as your grandmother.'

'I guess,' Claire replied.

'Let us hope you take after her in other respects.'

The first course arrived. Claire noticed a blue theme to the dishes. An arrangement of salad leaves in various shades of blue sat around a small turquoise fish. It was impossible to tell whether the colour derived from the cooking or a natural feature of the fish itself. She forked a small piece free from the centre of the dish and tasted it tentatively. The flesh was firm without being chewy and had a strong but pleasant seafood flavour. As she ate, the sauce released flavours of cinnamon and blueberry.

'This is delicious!' she exclaimed, smiling at the Queen.

'It was a favourite of your father's,' the Queen said, returning the smile. 'I'm so glad you like it. It's Barawa fish. There isn't really an equivalent word in your language. At least, not one I have learned so far.'

'Everyone speaks very good English here,' Claire observed.

'Not everyone,' the Queen corrected her, 'but all the heads of state and most of the nobles, along with any Palace staff who are likely to come into contact with the Batu'n, took up the challenge as soon as we began the integration program. There are only two native languages on Berikatanya, and they are really dialects of the same language, so it was an interesting intellectual exercise to learn a new tongue. Most of us at court treat it as a badge of honour. A way we can demonstrate our superior intellect on a daily basis.'

'It's as if you'd been using it your whole life, your Majesty,' Claire said.

The Queen beamed. 'Why thank you my dear. Most gracious.'

'Have any huma... Earth... Batu'n learned Berikatanyan?'

'Well my dear, as I said there are two languages. To be strict, neither of them is called Berikatanyan. Here at the Palace, and throughout my realm, we speak Kertonian. In the kingdom of the Blood King they use Istanian. But to answer your question, a few Batu'n have picked up a phrase here or there, perhaps a little more if they choose to work away from the Palace where English is not so widespread.'

'I'd like to learn,' Claire said, taking a forkful of darker blue leaves that tasted of pepper. 'It would be like returning the favour. It doesn't seem right you should learn our language when you were here first. We're the interlopers.'

'Your attitude does you credit my dear,' the Queen said. 'Your father would be very proud. But of course you are more of a restored native than an interloper. In any case, interlopers or not, we don't look down upon the Batu'n. They bring new ideas and methods to our society. They are an influence for good. Some of our people have made small beginnings learning Batugan technology, so for that reason alone it is good to use the correct terminology. But if you're serious I will ensure Kertonian lessons are added to your curriculum at the Academy.'

'Academy?'

'The Elementary Academy. They tutor all our mages and Elementals there. We have made arrangements for you to study under our most experienced mages in the Air guild. You need to gain control of your powers my dear, before you blow us all away!'

Claire flashed the Queen a horrified look. The older woman burst into a peal of tinkling laughter.

'I am joking Claire dear,' she said as soon as she stopped laughing.

'But there is a serious message underneath my attempt at humour,' the Queen went on. 'There are perilous times ahead. I will have great need of my Air Mage very soon. You must learn everything you can. I'm sure you will soon outpace the Master Mage, but he is all I can offer. That, and access to your father's scrolls and lore books so you may study at your own pace once you have mastered the basics.'

Her hand hidden by the ornate filigreed table cloth, Claire gripped the edge of her seat to restrain her rising panic. The Queen's expectations, and her assertion that Claire would soon surpass a native Air master, filled her with dread. She could barely control her own emotions, let alone this new power she supposedly had. Determined to put on a brave face, she finished the last of her Barawa fish before a butler swooped in and whisked the plate away.

'When do I start?' she asked, smiling for the Queen's benefit.

'Tomorrow,' said the Queen. 'No time to waste.'

the blood king's court
12th day of run'tanamasa, 965

Daylight never reached the catacombs of the Blood King's Court. Even the uppermost levels were more than ten metres below ground, buried beneath the basements and sub-basements that provided quarters for the Court staff, and storage for the provisions to feed dozens of nobles, courtiers and visitors. Jann Argent had no idea of the eventual depths plumbed by the deepest of the mazes of corridors. It had been hard enough to learn the area he was assigned to patrol.

Though they remained unlit by the sun, still there

seemed somehow to be less light in the cellars during the night than in the day. Maybe it was a psychological thing, but as Jann sat at his watch station between his regular rounds, he could not help thinking the darkness encroached further into the alcoves at this time of night, making the shadows sharper and blacker.

His post, positioned next to an iron gateway, afforded a view in both directions up and down the long corridor that formed the main spine of this section. From here, with his acute peripheral vision, he could keep an eye on all the entrances to the area of his watch and, owing to the peculiar acoustics of the chambers, could hear anything happening in any part of the tunnels within his patrol. He soon fell into the traditional modus operandi of watchmen of all ages and dynasties. He skipped every other patrol round, settling deeper into the comfortable chair the Keeper of the Keys had lent him and perusing a small selection of parchments from the Keeper's extensive collection.

After their initial awkward encounter, the old man had adopted Jann. He had few visitors, secreted as he was in the bowels of the Court, and despite his outward gruff demeanour he took an interest in Jann's education. Their first discussion of the songs of power—especially the Lullabies—had led to a lengthy debate about the time of the Vortex, when the Elementals had been lost. Something in the Keeper's description of the events had chimed with Jann, reawakening his resolve to learn more of the cataclysmic event that could hold the key to his memory loss. His keen curiosity persuaded the Keeper to ferret out half a dozen parchments from the dusty piles on his own desk, along with a couple of others from a high shelf at the very back of his study. These now decorated Jann's workstation. He had been learning to read Istanian in preparation for studying the transcripts of the magical ceremony at which the Vortex appeared. Those two most ancient scrolls were the sole remaining record of the event.

Tonight Jann felt his language skills had improved enough for him to make a decent attempt at understanding them. In another tantalising hint of his unremembered life, he found Istanian had come easily to him despite its unusual structure. His mind absorbed the vocabulary as fast as the sands of the airena back on Phobos soaked up the spilled blood of the combatants.

With the Keeper's words in mind, he moved his candle to the edge of his small desk before unrolling the first of the two parchments. Satisfied that he would not incur the old man's wrath for bringing his beloved artefacts too close to a naked flame, Jann bent to his task.

"A single note, almost painful in its purity, silenced the crowds lining east and west sides of the Valley. A breeze teased the pennants of the assembled nobles on both summits, catching the heavy official robes of the Piper and rippling them against his legs. His hair— newly dyed a shocking purple for the ceremony—blew across his sallow brow in an unruly manner. Beneath his untamed locks a slight frown revealed the depths of his concentration as he added second and third notes, followed by a simple melody played on the other half of his bifurcated instrument. Behind him, a small choir took up the tune, humming at first and later, as the music increased in complexity, chanting softly in words unfamiliar to the throng.

On the Valley floor the Elementals stood at their appointed corners on the granite quadrangle. Each dressed in their ceremonial robes, the colours—red, blue, black, and white—were as rich and vibrant as the Piper. The first bell chimed from the alabaster tower set at the northernmost end of the Valley, beyond which the Lumsegar ocean was visible in the distance; waves churning brown with stirred sand. At the sound of the bell, the supreme Suhiri closed their eyes and raised their hands towards the centre of the square, palms upward. As the music and singing continued to swell, filling the Valley with sound, their immense powers congealed into swirling spheres of coloured mist which floated above their upturned hands, each torturing the main hue of its holder's robes into myriad tones; a jumble of polychromatic threads and eddies.

On the eastern hill the regal figure of the Blood King sat erect on his rust-red kudo Anak'Adah. Now the Elementals had begun summoning their magic the King leaned forward in eager anticipation, his gesture echoed by his entourage. At the movement, Anak'Adah twitched his head against the traces, snickering nervously. The King laid a hand on his neck and murmured words of quietude.

The piper began a second melody where before he had only been playing a single refrain. With a more urgent tempo, his left hand flew over the notes while his right continued with the original. The choir split into even halves, those moving to stand on the piper's left taking up the new tune and matching its tempo with a different song; those on the right maintaining the first. A second bell began to toll from the tower, keeping the beat of the new chant.

A fifth figure entered the quadrangle. Dressed in a harlequin costume combining the four hues of the others, he walked to the centre of the granite block and raised his arms. The crowd murmured their recognition of the Pattern Juggler as the colours in the Elementals' balls of mist deepened and the globes began to gleam. Beads of sweat stood out on the brows of the robed figures but they remained otherwise unaffected, standing motionless and erect with their eyes still shut.

Sweat appeared too on the face of the Piper, who now began to introduce another refrain to his music. Scarcely seeming to draw breath, his nimble fingers almost blurring with the speed of his playing, he maintained both the slow original and the faster second tunes while weaving a third melody, its tempo somewhere in between the two, in the interstices. The choir picked up this third song, two singers separating from each group and joining to form a third distinctive chant standing behind the piper.

As the last of the three bells began to chime in time with this final melody, an expectant ripple passed over the watching crowd. On the western hill the young Black Queen sat on her ebony kudo Pembrang at the head of her own assembly. Dressed in black so that she appeared almost to be one with the animal, she too remained deathly still. Whether hers was a less nervous beast than its counterpart on the opposite crest, or simply under the control of a more able rider, Pembrang stood unreacting to the scene unfolding below, his breath steaming in counterpoint to the slowest of the three rhythms. The only movement to be seen on the western ridge, the ends of the Queen's long black hair flicked and fluttered in the occasional breeze, the rest held in place by a polished obsidian circlet on her head.

Below her in the Valley, the balls of Elemental power now glowed with bright intensity. The harlequin figure gestured at the white globe which began to spin faster, becoming a thready vortex of paler air that spiralled up above the Valley floor, gaining in speed and height until it circled the quadrangle. As it settled into position he reached out towards the black sphere which emitted a thin glistening thread of power. The fell thread appeared to suck light from everything, following the path of the vortex and beginning to thrum. Separate from the sound of the music, which still filled the Valley, and yet somehow connected with it, the subsonic vibrations carved a circular scar in the granite floor, releasing fine chips of stone which were sucked up to circle the Valley inside the vortex."

Jann set the parchment down on his desk, rubbing at his eyes with both hands. The distant chime of the tower bell reminded him that he had already missed two rounds. It was slow work reading the scrolls, even with the aid of a huge Istanian dictionary the Keeper had lent him. He knew he ought to patrol the corridors at least once more before his shift ended, but the second scroll begged for his attention.

His upholstered chair creaked as he shifted position, checking up and down the corridor. He replaced his candle, now burnt almost to the holder, before unrolling the second instalment of the portal story.

"Unremarked by the crowd in the face of this mesmeric performance, the Gatekeeper took his place on the northern edge of the quadrangle between the blue and white clad figures of the Elementals. His ruby cape swirled as he walked to the appointed spot, the Janus amulet swinging against his chest, catching the light on its ancient golden faces. Behind him the tower bells continued their tripartite chimes while the choir and the piper redoubled their efforts to be heard above the noise of the wind.

The arc of pulverised granite circled over the heads of the six players, its tail joining its head to form a single band. The harlequin-costumed Juggler, his hands now above his head guiding the stone circle, stared at the holder of the red ball. Immediately a tongue of incandescent fire licked out from the ball, caressing the granite dust. The dust began to glow, then to melt, until in a few moments a spinning river of magma topped the quadrangle, sparks showering onto the still solid granite floor as the wind whipped and howled, goading the molten rock to still greater heat.

Those nearest the quadrangle shuffled backwards in awe, their hair whipping across faces and eyes, their clothes pulled this way and that. The black-clad Queen and, opposite her, the King with his dark red robes given an even bloodier look under the ring of fire overhead, regarded the scene with sombre expressions. The Juggler glanced at the Gatekeeper, who gave a cursory nod. At this the Juggler's concentration switched to the final robed figure, his blue ball now the only remaining light under the fiery circle. A jet of pure cerulean water shot upwards, quenching the magma. With a crack like hot glass falling into a frigid lake, the sky above the quadrangle ripped along the arc of fire, seeming to fall in on itself to reveal a black, fathomless void.

Steam from the quenched magma drowned out the gasps of the onlookers. The hot gouts momentarily span around the circle before disappearing, sucked into the newly-opened pit. Outside the ring of darkness the air continued to circle, while the hole itself remained still, featureless, a silent well in the middle of a whirling cacophony of madness.

With an expression of utter surprise, the Pattern Juggler was plucked from the centre of the quadrangle. He plunged upward into the void, followed by the Air Mage and the Earth Elemental. The Water Wizard appeared to melt into the rock, liquefying in an eye blink and running through tiny fissures between the stones. But the liquid too was at the mercy of the pull of the black well. It slowed, stopped, and began to run back towards the centre. The bell tower groaned under the influence of the blackness. In front of it the Gatekeeper and the Fire Witch lofted almost together into the air as the building cracked. With an ear-rending screech of tortured masonry the whole edifice came crashing to the ground, crushing several of the audience and releasing its bells to shatter into pieces on the hard granite.

Onlookers' hands flew to their ears, agonised by a subsonic pop as the vortex snapped shut. The wind dropped. Black and red riders regarded each other across the silent Valley. The stunned throng remained still, some shaking their heads, others simply staring unbelievingly at the restored sky until the last rays of sunlight died on the horizon and the night pulled its dark shroud over the scene."

Jann stared at the page. The description of the harlequin figure at the centre of the quadrangle intrigued him, but it was the second of the non-Elemental participants who tugged at his memory. His index finger traced the text to the mention of the Janus amulet. He reached under his tunic, drawing out the pendant he had been reunited with at the spaceport, which he had been wearing when he came to his senses in the Prefect's grisly chamber. It spun in the candlelight, its paired golden faces staring in opposite directions with identical expressions resembling, in the flickering gloom of the crypt, an ancient tree. The walls of the catacombs seemed to close in on him, the dark tunnels stretching away in both directions like a doorway to the past, and to the future. He stared, unseeing, down the corridor in the direction of the past. With a soundless mental snap he stood under the clear black sky of Lembaca Ana—the Valley of the Cataclysm. His head ached as the shard of memory pierced his mind. He could smell rain in the air, hear the wind summoned by the Air Mage. On the hillsides the Black Queen and the Blood King sat facing each other, each surrounded by their armies. Observers thronged the Valley floor, standing at first silent and then gasping as one when the Elementals began to draw on their powers.

As suddenly as the memory began, it was over. Jann sat once more at his workstation in the subterranean corridors of the catacombs. His candle guttered on his desk in a sudden breeze from an opened door which closed with a loud clang behind the guard who had come to relieve his watch.

'Morning Argent!' he called, in thickly accented English.

Jann replaced the amulet under his shirt.

'Paga Hamarti!' he replied, eager to show off his rudimentary Istanian to Hamarti, his watch leader. He tidied away the parchments into a drawer, locked it, and pocketed the key. Turning back to Hamarti, Jann rubbed his eyes once again.

'Never been so glad to finish a shift,' he said as the man approached the watch station. 'I'm for my bed.'

tunnels of the blood lake
12th day of run'tanamasa, 965

Beyond the ancient walls that marked the end of the maze of catacombs in which Jann Argent had worked his lonely shift, lay a subterranean lake. The ex-convict remained unaware of its existence. Known only to the original builders of the Court, even those as old as the Keeper had no memory of it. Its waters lapped at the stonework as they had done for centuries, the currents and eddies too weak to erode the edifice with any speed. Yet the water had time on its side. No matter how slow the task, it would be accomplished eventually.

On the other side of the lake, beyond a small sandy shore on which the slow ripples broke and which thus protected the construction, stood another dark wall into which was set a heavy black iron door. Forged with a process long ago lost to the present-day artisans, the remarkable purity of the iron ensured it remained unaffected by damp or rust even though it had guarded the empty shore for more than a thousand years.

Behind the door, along dark corridors and tunnels that had not seen torchlight or felt a footfall for almost as long as the door had stood closed, a steep stone staircase led up to a heavy wooden trapdoor set into the floor of a large meeting room. The room, itself accessed by another flight of worn sandstone stairs, was lit by several torches burning in wall sconces. In the centre of the room sat a substantial oak table long enough to seat two dozen in comfort. Notched and polished from years of use, the table top reflected the flickering light of the torches onto the faces of the three men who occupied the room, one at the head, one to his right, and one to his left.

Head took a long draught from a tall flagon of beer before smashing the vessel down onto the table. He glared at the other two in turn. A foamy slop from his half-empty mug glistened and flashed as the small bubbles burst.

'So she's back, the Witch?' he growled.

'From what we've heard, it is almost certain,' said Left, dabbing at the foam and drawing arcane patterns on the table top with a beery finger.

'How is that possible?' asked Right. 'They all fell into the Vortex, just as we planned. There should have been no way back.'

'To be entirely accurate,' Left said, watching his artwork drying and disappearing from the wood in front of him, 'we didn't know whether there would be a way back or not. We had no way of divining where the Vortex would take them. We only assumed it would be away from here.'

'Far enough away that they could never come back,' Head said, taking another swig of beer. 'So much for that idea.'

'Have any of the others returned?'

'Not as far as we know,' said Left.

'But we cannot be certain!' Right said. 'If one can come back, the others may also.'

'This is intolerable!' yelled Head, smashing his tankard back onto the table once more. 'We can not endure another battle with Elementals in control!'

'But what can we do?' Right asked, running his hands through his hair. 'The Witch will be at the King's right hand once battle commences. There is no way to put a wedge between them in such a short time.'

'Then we must kill her,' said Head. 'Now, while there is still time. Before she comes fully back into her power.'

'It is true, if the reports are to be believed, she has yet to retain her full mastery. Even so, she is a dangerous adversary.'

Footsteps on the stairway disturbed the meeting. All three turned to see who entered. A pair of bright purple boots appeared on the stairs, followed by legs in darker violet hose.

'We have a problem,' said the owner of the boots, completing his descent and taking a seat at the opposite end of the table.

'We know Mungo,' said Head. 'We were just discussing a solution.'

'You were debating doing away with one of the Elementals,' Mungo said. 'The problem I am talking about is that you have more than one to deal with.'

Left and Right whipped around, their eyes wide.

'You have seen another?' asked Left.

'Which is it?' asked Right.

The older man grunted.

'Stop winding these two up. Tell us what you've seen.'

Mungo leaned back in his chair, which creaked in protest.

'The Air Mage is at the Palace,' he said.

'So the old man survived too,' said Right.

'Not the Air Mage we knew. I have yet to learn what happened to him. I'm talking about his daughter.'

'His daughter?'

'How do you know she's the daughter of the Air Mage?' asked Left.

'Don't tell me you haven't noticed all the wind we've been having lately!'

'That's hardly the work of an Elemental.'

'She had no idea she *was* an Elemental before she came

here!' Mungo insisted. 'And she has no control over her power as yet. It comes and goes with her mood.'

'Perfect time to finish her off as well then,' said Head draining his flagon. 'Before she learns.'

Chapter 12

Late morning sun glinted off the ranks of swords, spears, and armour of the King's infantry. They waited on the Istanian side of the enormous rolling plain that straddled the border between the two estates. It afforded no hills, rises or covering vegetation to present either side with a tactical advantage. Across the incipient battlefield the Queen's army, in their uniforms of matt black, with little metal ornamentation or protection, reflected none of the sun's rays. They stood in a single mass like a giant ink stain on an impossibly large page of green parchment.

When he looked back over the short time he had been at the Blood King's Court, Jann Argent found it hard to understand how quickly the tensions between the two camps—Court and Palace—had escalated. He remembered his conversation with Felice Waters shortly after arriving at Berikatanya about the years of turmoil. He could never have expected that within a few months, the political posturing and arguing would bring the factions to the point of actual warfare, or that he would be taking an active part in it. Gazing across the chosen battlefield brought the reality of the situation home to him. The massed forces of the Black Queen's army confronted the substantially greater numbers of the Blood King's troops, who were also better equipped with both armament and armour.

During his two months in the King's service Jann had first risen to command his own watch, and soon been promoted a second time. The swiftness of the promotion surprised him, but since it conferred a place in the King's honour guard he was not complaining. The Blood Watch were hand-picked guardsmen. Usually able enough with sword or bow, they were not only chosen for their skills with weapons. They were tasked with the protection of the royal personage and as such they were selected more for their unswerving loyalty to the King. Jann had always maintained he was no conscript and would take no part in a battle, but had soon realised the wisdom of keeping his principles to himself. Such talk risked making his life at Court very uncomfortable. In a society where anything less than total obeisance to the monarch was utterly incomprehensible, his circumspection had been interpreted as quiet devotion to the King's cause. Ironically, this had led him to a role away from front-line fighting.

The image before him reminded Jann of his time in the catacombs, reading from ancient parchments in between security patrols of the dark, echoing chambers and corridors. The accounts of the vortex were still fresh in his mind. Now, wearing the crimson dress uniform of a seba-tepak of the Blood Watch, he sat on his chosen kudo, Perak, watching the two forces. Waiting for battle to commence, he compared the scene in front of him to that described in those dusty scrolls. A more peaceful time when the two Houses had come together to take part in the fated ceremony of Car'Alam.

As always, he could see both sides of the arguments that brought the King and Queen to this point. In truth, to Jann's mind, all of their disagreements could have been resolved with diplomacy. Yet the Court advisors had seemed determined to avoid reaching a resolution through debate, despite the best efforts of the Palace. They whipped up the passions and ancient hatreds until it appeared battle was the only way to determine who was in the right; who in the wrong. Even at this late hour Jann could see the Jester, his traditional yellow vestments hidden beneath a heavy woollen coat, leaning over in his saddle to mutter some venomous words of encouragement in the King's ear. Jann did not trust the man, despite his genial grin and his manically foolish capering.

The men of the King's Kudai sat on their steeds

awaiting a signal from the commander. Their mounts remained silent, for the most part, with the occasional snicker of impatience for the forthcoming ride across the plain. A gentle breeze picked up, carrying the distinctive dusty smell of the animals to Jann's nostrils. A few of them tossed their heads. The wind had brought other scents to their more sensitive noses, disturbing their calm.

A murmur rippled through the infantry. Swords and shields flashed in the sunlight as if signalling readiness for battle. The men swayed from foot to foot, or shared a tension releasing joke with their comrades in arms. The King, seated on Anak'Adah at the top of a ridge on the Istanian edge of the plain, shielded his eyes from the reflections and assessed the Queen's forces while still being harangued by the Jester.

The wind increased in speed, blowing leaves and small twigs across the sward. Without warning a stronger gust picked up a helmet left lying on the grass, flinging it at the head of a nearby infantryman, who fortunately was protected from the first injury of the battle by dint of wearing his own.

The suddenness of the wind aroused Jann's suspicions. He peered over the plain to the opposite rise. Through the haze he recognised the figure of a young girl in a pale blue dress, her long blonde hair flying in the wind, her hands clamped to her temples.

Claire.

Jann ducked as a small rock flew past him and buried itself in the side of the mound near to where one of the King's other guards sat. The man leapt to his feet.

'What was that? Has the battle started?'

Jann laughed mirthlessly.

'There has been no signal, but I think the Queen is tired of waiting. And she appears to have help.'

per tantaran, kertonian side
24th day of sen'tanamasa, 965

Claire Yamani stood beside the Black Queen on the Southern Ridge overlooking the battle plain of Per Tantaran. The Blood King's forces faced them, surrounding the larger Northern Ridge. An involuntary shiver passed through her at the sight of the formidable army, their swords and spears flashing under the morning sun.

'I'm not ready,' she said.

The Queen shot her an impatient glance before her features softened.

'You will be fine my dear,' she said. 'Your tutors are full of praise for your progress.'

'But it's only been two months!' Claire wailed. 'I haven't even completed my first year—how can I fight a battle? I'm not a warrior! I'm not even a proper Mage!'

'You are an Elemental!' the Queen snapped, her irritation rising to the surface once again. 'And what's more, you are your father's daughter. Air has been in the service of Kertonia for centuries. You must do your best. That is all any of us can do.

'Look at our pitiful forces, compared to theirs,' the Queen went on. 'The King has outsmarted us. Clearly Istania has been mustering in secret for many months. Without the power of the Air, we have no hope. Would you have my people slaughtered before your very eyes?'

'No of course not, your Majesty,' Claire replied. 'If there were anything I could do I would do it—'

'Then *do* it,' the Queen insisted, cutting off Claire's objections. 'Whatever it is you *can* do, you *must* do. And do it now, while they are still deciding how they will press the battle to their own advantage.'

Claire closed her eyes, trying to shut out the muted buzz of conversation from the surrounding infantry, the snickering of kudai clearly audible across the plain even at this distance, and the rising nausea in her stomach. She searched deep inside her own mind for the calm nexus her tutor had taught her about, the well-spring of the power she'd not known was there until scant months earlier.

With a warm glow of excitement she felt the power begin to grow. She clamped down on the thrill. Too much emotion would render it uncontrollable. She could do more damage to the Queen's forces than she wreaked against the King's unless she remained fully in control. Her energy built, and the breeze picked up in answer to the Elemental call. She felt the wind blowing around her, stirring her hair into a fluttering halo. She reached out to it with her mind and sent it flying across the plain, urging it to increase in strength and speed until it could lift small objects, then larger ones. She opened her eyes, the better to direct the stream of moving air.

A boulder rose from the ground. It flew towards a group of four riders and buried itself in the earth only centimetres from the head of one sat on the grass. The rider next to him struggled to hold his mount steady as it shied. He wheeled the kudo around to stare across the plain. Even at this distance she recognised him. It was Jann Argent.

Claire's control faltered at the sight of her friend. Her power stuttered. She'd never expected to see Jann in the opposing forces even though she knew he'd opted to join the Blood King's Court. He watched her, his expression indecipherable from so far away.

'What's wrong, Claire?' the Queen asked, the tension in her voice and her use of Claire's given name clear signs of her disquiet. 'Don't stop!' she cried. 'Command the air to our purpose! Now! Before we lose the advantage!'

But Claire had already lost the moment. The sight of Jann, but more importantly the realisation that her actions could result in his death, had torn her from the core of her power. Above all this, the few lessons she'd sat through at the Academy had impressed on her the importance of balance in Elemental magic. It went against everything she'd been taught, everything she understood about the natural forces, for her to be the only Elemental engaged in the battle.

'It is all balance, point and counterpoint,' Claire's tutor Pac Sau'dib had said. 'Fire and Water, Earth and Air, each a complement of the other, each a part of a greater whole. This we call the Te'banga.'

How could there be balance if there were no other Mages present? Two of the four were lost, but Fire was rumoured to have returned to Berikatanya in the unlikely form of Elaine Chandler. Claire shielded her eyes from the sun, searching the far ridges and mounds of the plain. She could find no sign of Elaine in the King's entourage. She could do no more with Air in the absence of Fire.

'I'm sorry, your Majesty,' she murmured. 'I have failed you.'

With one last powerful gust, the wind blew itself out. As if taking their signal from this, the King's forces began a charge across the plain, shouting and ululating as they came. A phalanx of infantry surged forward from the centre while separate charges circled East and West to present an attack on three fronts. Another cold shiver ran down Claire's back as she watched the Queen's outmatched infantry run to face them. The physical battle commenced.

Swords and shields flashed as the first sounds of combat reached the Queen's rise, soon joined by the sickly metallic smell of fresh blood. Claire turned away, the sights of punctured bodies and severed limbs too much for her. Within minutes the Queen's forces were overwhelmed, her men outnumbered many times over. The battle would not last long. In a confused melee of emotion Claire knew she should do something to stop the slaughter.

'Please Claire!' the Queen called, her voice hoarse with despair tinged with anger. 'We are being eviscerated!'

With her back to the battle in an effort to calm and

order her thoughts, Claire reached again for her power. Her earlier trepidation at the lack of balance, an intellectual debate more suited to the classroom than the battlefield, no longer held her back. She had to act. The only question was: could she do *anything*?

As the still unsettling feeling of Air power welled up once more, she turned back to face the field and raised her hands again to her head. Her palms felt hot with Elemental energy as she sent a gale across the plain, bowling over all in its path. She watched the progress of her wind, remembering Jann's presence and trying to steer it away from where he had stood. She glanced over to the opposite rise to confirm he was out of harm's way. A second figure moved from behind the King's kudo to stand at Jann's side, a shock of spiky red hair visible under the fierce sun. Elaine. The Fire Witch had come to join the fight. Now balance was indeed restored. The last intellectual shackle binding Claire's power fell away. She unleashed the full force of her mind.

per tantaran, istanian side
24th day of sen'tanamasa, 965

Elaine Chandler laid a casual hand on Jann's leg.

'So, the Air Mage has returned, and it's our little friend Claire,' she said, watching his face.

When his expression remained unchanged, she removed her hand and stood regarding the battle for a moment.

'I wasn't going to involve myself,' she added. 'Not after what that bearded cretin did to us.'

That provoked the reaction she had been waiting for. Jann looked down on her.

'Not involve yourself? I thought you were the secret weapon?'

She laughed, squinting up at him as he sat on his mount.

'Maybe I am, but when I believed I was the only Elemental to survive the portal, it would have gone against every principle I hold sacred to take part in a war. The King's forces are already in the ascendant. With my help the other side would stand absolutely no chance.'

'Isn't that the idea of war? To win?'

'But not at all costs.'

She looked out again over the battlefield. The wind conjured by the new Air Mage had slowed the rout, aided by the various objects that were being flung about with surprising accuracy.

'For Elementals, the principle is more important than the end result.'

Jann snorted.

'Those with power always talk that kind of bollocks. It's easy to have principles when you're invincible.'

Elaine rounded on him, the amber flecks in her eyes telegraphing the sudden flames of her anger.

'Actually it's not that easy to stand by while your friends and loved ones face danger, knowing you could help but determined to work on the side of fairness!

'But this is not the time to debate the finer points of Elemental philosophy. Shut up and let me concentrate!'

Elaine accessed her core with practised ease, conjuring her powers instantly. Within seconds she was directing coruscating blasts of fire at the Black Queen's forces, some so strong they melted the swords of a few of the King's men who happened to be standing too close.

Elaine could see the appearance of her fire had caught Claire's attention. The young and inexperienced Air Mage was trying to retaliate, to bring her biting winds to bear against the Witch. But the effect was not what she intended. Elaine grinned, exulting, as she felt the force of the wind enhance her flames rather than extinguishing them. The fire burned white hot as it seared across the gap between them, leaving eddies of superheated air in its wake. More of the King's men, caught in the crossfire, began to ride or run from the plain, their armour smoking. Two or three spears burst into flames, their shafts reduced quickly to ash.

'Have a care, Bakara!' cried the King. 'Whose side are you on?'

The Queen's infantry began to retreat in blind panic, crashing into each other and climbing over the bodies of the dead and wounded as they sought shelter from the streaming jets of fire that continued to pour from the space in front of Elaine's outstretched hands. The facets of the topaz gemstones set into her golden bangles gleamed and flashed in the fire, encircling Elaine's wrists with blazing hoops. The King's victory seemed assured. Nothing could stand against Elaine's augmented power.

With a subsonic whine of gravnull engines, two Batugan flyers appeared from the direction of Pennatanah, skimming low over the plain. The Elemental forces ceased as suddenly as they had begun, as if a universal switch had been thrown, rendering both Air and Fire power impotent.

Elaine and Claire staggered in unison as their powers were stripped away. They stared at each other, stunned, unable to explain the cessation of energy. The flyers banked, glinting in the sun, their engines pulsating. Elaine caught sight of Felice Waters at the controls of the lead craft, her black hair suffused with cobalt reflections from the crackling blue halo that limned the sleek silver machines.

Each flyer came to rest facing one army, hovering menacingly between the foes. With a click and whine of oiled gears, a pair of chromed barrels emerged from beneath each cockpit and took aim at the warriors. Behind Jann and Elaine, the Blood King let out a strangled cry of rage.

tunnels of the blood lake
26th day of sen'tanamasa, 965

Despite burning brightly in their sconces, the flickering torches could not dispel the black mood in the stone walled meeting room. The air seemed thicker than usual with the smell of stale beer. The torchlight cast deeper shadows around the scratches and scars on the heavy wooden table, rendering its appearance even more battered and worn than normal.

The gathering enjoyed a better attendance than in recent times, a fact that did nothing to improve the already foul odour of the room. All twenty chairs were occupied and more had been brought in from other chambers. Even so some attendees were forced to stand, most choosing a position close to the racked beer barrels along the back wall. One of those who had been drawing himself a flagon of ale gave out a snort of disgust.

'The Old Tommy's finished!' he said.

'Never mind the Old Tommy!' replied the stern faced man at the head of the table. 'We have more important things to discuss than the contents of your tankard!'

'Or your guts,' added the man to his left, sneering.

A ripple of laughter spread through the room, which died almost as quickly as it started when Head pushed his chair back and stood up, planting both his enormous fists on the table with a grunt.

'Enough!' he growled. 'Some of us have just witnessed the greatest Elemental defeat in the history of Berikatanya! If any of you think this is a matter for jest, you may as well leave now. We need a serious discussion. There are things here beyond explaining. It will require all our wits to determine how we should proceed in light of this new conundrum.'

A murmur of assent greeted Head's words before the meeting fell silent, each occupied with his own thoughts or unwilling to voice them. At length an older man, standing by the wall at the opposite end of the table, cleared his throat. All eyes turned to him.

'Perhaps,' he began, rubbing at his rheumy eyes, 'perhaps not entirely beyond explaining.'

The assembly waited for him to continue. He stepped away from the wall into a circle of torchlight.

'What I mean is—agreed, this is the most significant example we've had of it, but there have been others. Smaller, perhaps, but similar in effect.'

'Other what?' asked Head, leaning further over the table. 'Similar to what?'

The older man shrank back towards the wall again, but recovered his courage after a moment. He continued in a stronger voice.

'Other examples of Batugan technology quelling Elemental magic,' he said. 'Years ago, when they first came, they flew around more often in those silver machines. I live next door to a fire mage. He was always complaining he couldn't set a fire in his grate when those contraptions were in the air.'

'Hey, that's right,' said another man, seated at the table in front of the first. 'I didn't make the connection before now, but I have a friend who's a water mage. He swore his garden irrigation used to dry up back then. It was never obvious the flyers were to blame, but he's had no problems since the Batu'n stopped using them.'

'This is nonsense,' called a deep voice from the stairs as a pair of purple boots came into view.

'Must you always be late to these meetings Mungo?' asked Head. 'Now of all days, with this latest development to debate.'

'Late, but not too late to quash this rubbish I hope,' the Piper said, touching the shoulder of a seated man and taking his place at the table.

'Begging your pardon kemasara,' said the older man, 'but it's not nonsense. I seen it with me own eyes.'

'Then how do you explain,' the Piper asked, turning to

the man, 'how the new Air Mage was able to conjure up a storm so powerful, it blew the newest of their space ships out of the air not three months ago?

'If the Batugan technology is so inimical to Elemental forces, surely she would have been prevented—even unknowing as she was of her own power—from exhibiting any magical abilities at all, let alone such a force as to down an entire space ship?'

The room erupted, everyone talking at once. Several people sided with the old man, while others had been swayed by the Piper's argument. The shouting continued until Head banged his tankard on the table.

'Silence!' he roared. 'This is a debate not a wrestling chamber!'

'I watched that ship the day of the crash,' said the man without his Old Tommy. 'It were different somehow from they other flyers.'

'How so?' asked Head.

'They flyers have a blue light crackling all round 'em,' the man explained. 'Didn't see nothing like that with the big ships. Least, not this 'un. I don't know how they make 'em fly, but it must be different, else they'd have that blue light too.'

The Piper rubbed his chin.

'That's a very interesting observation,' he muttered. 'Perhaps I was mistaken. There may after all be a connection between their technological power and the quenching of the Fire Witch's flames. I do know this,' he added, looking around the room to make sure his point would be understood.

'I have spoken with the Air Mage. She says there is no magic on Ketiga Batu. The Batugan home planet is completely devoid of anyone we would regard as a mage. Mayhap it is their technology prevents them from conjuring the power of the Elements.'

the blood king's throne room
28th day of sen'tanamasa, 965

The Blood King sat on his red marble throne, one hand curled around the ornate mace of state, the other gripping the carved arm of the stone cold seat. The knuckles on both hands showed white through his skin. A heavier than usual cloudburst lashed the throne room windows as the malamajan reached its nightly peak.

'Gah! So close! We were so close! The Witch had them. How can we have lost such an advantage so quickly?'

His ubiquitous companion, his usual yellow garb appearing a dull ochre under the candlelight, hopped from foot to foot in a pale imitation of his habitual mirthful gambolling. For once, he did not smile.

'Majesty, there are rumours that the Batu'n—'

'Rumours! I am the King! I do not deal in rumours, half-truths or superstitions! Tell me what happened!'

The Jester paled.

'No-one knows for certain, your Majesty.'

'Pah!'

'But,' the Jester went on, summoning his courage, 'a handful of your subjects have observed... coincidences... involving the appearance of the Batugan flying machines. They suggest a connection between the machines' energy source and a suppression of Elemental power.'

'Suppression of Elemental power?' the King growled. 'What nonsense is this? Elemental power cannot be suppressed! It is infinite!'

The Jester held up his hands.

'Indeed Sire, it is certainly true there was never any hint the Elements were vulnerable before the arrival of the Batu'n.'

The King's knuckles turned a paler shade of white at the Jester's words, but he said nothing.

'And since the Elementals were snatched from us, there have been no displays of magical power such as we saw

211

yesterday that could make clear the connection of which I speak.'

The King continued to glare at the Jester without speaking.

'But there have been lesser examples. Too many for it to be a true coincidence. And now we may have seen the final proof. The battle was all but won—'

'Don't I know it!'

'—until the silver flyers appeared. There can be no other explanation.'

'Then what are we to do?' asked the King, rising from his throne. 'If the Witch's power is quelled, how shall we prosecute our plans?'

The Jester shrugged.

'The Queen's mages are similarly hobbled, sire,' he said. 'The mysterious effects of the Batugan technologies quell all Elements, not Fire alone. And our forces remain superior to hers.'

'Not for long,' said the King. 'Not now she has seen the extent of our armies. We have tipped our hand. She will muster help, mark my word.'

The Jester sat on the top step of the marble dais and removed his tri-corn hat.

'There may be a way to ensure that magic never bothers us again your Majesty.'

'How so?'

'The vortex may yet prove to be the solution.'

The King's face reddened, his barely-suppressed rage rising to the surface again.

'The Vortex? Nerka jugu! Not this again! How in hell's name can the Vortex help us? It is a spent charge.'

'Not necessarily Sire. Our first attempt removed the Elementals for sixty years. Hardly a small thing. During their absence has your power not grown? Your influence exceeded even your expectations.'

'And yet still we cannot win a battle,' the King muttered, falling back onto his throne.

'As I understand it Sire, it is most unlikely the... unfortunate few... who may be captured in the event of a re-opening of the Vortex would be able to find their way back a second time. It is a remarkable coincidence that they managed it once, but in any case we have learned the Batu'n colonisation program is very short-lived. Only one other ship is expected, a ship that must already be in transit.'

The Jester stared at the King, judging his mood.

'Better yet,' he said, leaning forward, 'our scholars believe it may be possible to create a two-way Vortex. If we can achieve that, then perhaps an even greater influx of Batugan technology could be undertaken. They brought very little with them, seeking a rural life. We may be able to persuade them of the benefits of bringing more of their wonderful machines through a re-opened portal. It would make their lives so much easier, while at the same time quenching the mages for ever.'

The King sat back, his ire still plain on his face.

'*Our scholars believe,*' he mocked. '*Perhaps we could persuade them.*'

He shook his head.

'It hardly seems like a firm plan for victory to me. But in any case, it is all moot. The Vortex cannot be opened unless all four Elementals are present, not to mention the Juggler and Gatekeeper. Even if we could convince the Witch and the Queen's Air Mage to participate, we are two Elementals short. Having been on the receiving end of a fraction of her wrath concerning the last attempt at the Ceremony, I can say without fear of contradiction the Witch will never take part in a repeat event.'

The Jester's trademark grin reappeared, his eyes glinting.

'If what your scholars tell me is true, sire, that may not be such an insurmountable problem after all.'

213

Chapter 13

Patrick Glass sat alone in his chamber, idly plucking a celapi borrowed from one of the Court musicians. He had thought to compose a song celebrating the return of the Elementals, but everything he tried led to a dead end. Several sheets of half-written music lay scattered on his desk, most of them covered in complex doodles of nested circles drawn while he had been waiting for inspiration.

His room, although much less well appointed than Elaine's, or even Jann's, was not Spartan. As yet he had no role in the Court, so could hardly complain. He had a comfortable bed, a wardrobe for his sparse collection of clothing and other belongings, a small table, a grate in which a cheery log fire burned, and a pair of ancient but still serviceable armchairs. A portrait of the Blood King hung over the mantle, eyeing Patrick with a stern look as if to remind him of the benefactor to whom he owed such luxury as the chamber afforded.

His intention for the song had been a stirring reminiscence of the unexpected reappearance, first of the Fire Witch and then the Air Mage, but his fingers kept returning to a minor key with a much more subdued melody than the one he sought. Nevertheless as he continued to play, words formed unbidden in his mind and he began to sing:

> Long red hair and an angry stare,
> What can I do for you?
> I got tunes to spare, I can draw with flair
> But what can I do for you?
> Could there be a job for this Earther boy?
> Left his home on the Perse convoy
> Tell me sire and I'll jump for joy
> What can I do for you?

A knock at the door disturbed his embryonic muse.

'Come in,' he called.

Jann Argent's head poked into the room, his face flushed with exertion.

'It is you!' he exclaimed. 'Someone told me you were back! You could have let me know.'

'I had no idea where to find you,' Patrick replied, 'or if you'd be on duty. Now that you're an honour guard and all.'

'How long have you been here?'

'Since yesterday.'

'And?'

'If you mean did I uncover any clues or explanations, then no. I'm sure I came close a few times. Several people gave me funny looks, some said I looked familiar, but in the end it all led to nothing. Most simply ignored me. Even those who thought they saw a resemblance to someone they might have known weren't prepared to talk about it or say who it was I reminded them of.'

'Ah well, it was worth a try. So what are you going to do now you're back?'

Patrick shrugged.

'Dunno. Don't fancy your job much.'

'You could do worse.'

'I wouldn't have believed that even before the war broke out.'

'Hardly a war was it? One battle? Even that went off like a damp squib.'

'Yeah, literally from what I heard,' said Patrick, laughing. 'The fireworks were well and truly doused.'

Jann nodded.

'It's rattled a few cages that has. Whispers in corridors and sideways looks. Mutterings of how the Batu'n are demons in disguise and it goes against the laws of nature to be able to stop the Elementals so easily.'

'Maybe I should write a ballad about that instead.'

'Was that you playing before I arrived?' Jann asked.

'My first attempt at something new. I haven't made much progress with it.'

'I don't think the King would appreciate a song about—'

'What's that?' said the King, appearing at the still open door. 'What would I not like a song about? I like all kinds of songs.'

'Forgive me your Majesty. Patrick was saying—'

'I was trying to compose a ballad to celebrate the return of the Elementals sire,' Patrick interrupted.

'Capital idea!' the King said, 'why would I not like a song about that, Argent?'

'I... er... that is, no reason sire.'

'I wanted to talk to you about music anyway,' the King went on. 'I've been discussing with the Jester the possibility of holding another ceremony.'

'Ceremony?'

'Yes. We tried it before a few years ago without much success, but with your help I think we could make a better fist of it this time round.'

'If I can be of service in any way sire, I'm glad to help. I have yet to—'

'Yes, yes, quite so,' the King said, 'need to find you something to do, and with your musical bent this would be ideal.'

'Actually I'm more of an artist your Majesty.'

The King squinted at Patrick, then clapped him on the shoulder.

'You are? You are! An artist! Capital, capital. Just the job. Even better than being musical, I should say, for the role we have in mind.'

'What role is that sire?'

'Well in part it involves conducting the orchestra, but there's more to it than that. I'll leave it to the Jester to explain the details. Now that we know you're happy to take it on we can start coaching you. Some time with my court musicians at Parapekotik and you'll soon pick it up, bright young man such as yourself. Capital.'

The King left as hurriedly as he had appeared. Patrick was wondering what Court role called for both musical and artistic talents when the monarch's head popped around the door once more.

'I knew there was something else,' he said. 'This concerns you Argent.'

elementary academy
1st day of far'sanamasa, 965

'I hope you all completed your practical exercises with drafts and flurries,' declared the begowned and bearded old mage as he paced up and down between the rows of polished hardwood desks.

Claire Yamani sat in the third row. The oldest student in the class by some margin—most of her classmates were children, a few as young as eight or nine—she'd started the class quite a long way behind the rest in terms of learning, although the practical work came more easily to her.

'Today I want to leave the various different types of wind on one side,' their master went on, 'and concentrate on how we might achieve finer control over the air.'

Already something of a special case on account of her age and heritage, Claire had tried to avoid standing out in more mundane ways, like declining the tutor's offer of a seat in the front row.

The master, one of the most powerful mages of the Air guild outside of the Elemental class, continued speaking of how air could be controlled at the finest level of detail. Claire found her attention wandering. She already knew what the old man would say almost before he said it. The recent battle occupied her thoughts. She'd heard no explanation of why her magic failed, nothing that could relieve the oppressive weight of shame and responsibility that the war had been lost because of her own failure. Thankfully no accounts of that day had yet reached the student body at the Elementary Academy but she knew it was only a matter of time.

Her frustration building, she stretched out with her mind and extinguished the candle burning at the corner of the master's desk. At that precise moment, the door of the classroom burst open to admit the agitated headmistress.

'Pac Sau'dib! Pac Sau'dib! You have a visitor!'

Before her tutor could gather his thoughts, the head was followed into the room by the Black Queen herself. The class gave a collective and rather loud intake of breath, jumping to their feet. Claire offered up a silent prayer of thanks that the flurry of activity had disguised her petulant blowing out of the candle.

'Do forgive the intrusion, Pac Sau'dib,' said the Queen breezily, 'but I must have a word with one of your students.'

She turned to Claire.

'Come, my dear, walk with me. There are important matters we need to discuss.'

Claire glanced around the room. Every one of her classmates stared round-eyed at the Queen. None of them moved, or looked in her direction. They didn't even appear to be breathing.

'Yes of course your Majesty,' she replied. 'Please excuse me Pac Sau'dib.'

The old wizard had not regained enough composure to reply before the Queen whisked Claire out of the classroom, which burst into a cacophony of questions as the door closed behind them.

In the corridor the Queen took Claire's arm, dropping her voice to a whisper.

'Is there anywhere we might have a private conversation my dear?' she asked. 'What we have to say is not for the ears of students. Or masters, for that matter.'

Claire found an empty room further along the passage. The Queen wasted no time in bringing her up to date with the latest theories on Earther technology and its impact on the Elements.

'So you see my dear, it had absolutely nothing to do with you. It is hard enough that you must complete your studies in order to achieve total mastery over your powers, when I would far rather have you at the Palace, but I simply could not bear the thought of you worrying, or thinking you had somehow failed me.'

'I'm so honoured you came to tell me yourself your Majesty,' said Claire, blushing to the roots of her ash-blonde hair. 'You could have sent a messenger.'

'Don't be silly dear,' said the Queen, smiling. 'You're my Air Mage. Or at least, you will be soon. One of my most trusted allies and counsellors. I had to come. It was far too important a message to entrust to anyone else. You have enough to worry about, with learning and practising until your skills match your heritage, without thinking you're not up to the task.'

'Whatever the task, Claire is more than capable of executing it,' Sau'dib said, pushing the classroom door open.

'My sincere apologies for eavesdropping, highness...'

The old tutor bowed low, his eyes never leaving Claire's face.

'...but I was concerned our young Elemental might be in some sort of trouble. I am keen to defend her reputation if required.'

'No apology necessary,' the Queen smiled. 'Your diligence and attentiveness to one of the students does you credit.'

'She is not merely a student,' the master said, wrapping his robes around him. 'Though she may be embarrassed to hear it, I don't mind telling your Majesty she may well be the most powerful Elemental I have ever encountered.'

Claire felt her face flush once again. The Queen also reddened a little.

'Did you ever meet her father?' she asked.

'Indeed I did ma'am. In fact I dormed with him when

we were students. He was a fine friend, and a formidable Elemental.'

'So how would you assess his daughter in comparison?' the Queen asked.

'Well, I may be wrong of course,' Sau'dib hesitated, 'it is still early days, but I remain convinced Claire will exceed her father by some considerable margin.'

The Queen beamed.

'It will be good to have an Air Mage at the Palace once again, especially if young Claire is as adept as you suggest Sau'dib. How long do you think her training will take?'

'We would normally expect full Elemental instruction to be a matter of years,' the old mage said, scratching his beard. 'In this case, well, the results speak for themselves. Claire has only been here at the Academy for a little over two months. She is already in Year Three of the top stream. If she continues to apply herself so diligently to her practical work she will complete the course within the year.'

the blood king's court
29th day of sen'tanamasa, 965

'If I may be of service,' Jann said as the King stepped back into Patrick's chamber, 'your Majesty has only to ask.'

'Mmm. Yes. Very good. We need someone to go on a quest.'

'A quest, sire?'

'Well, inasmuch as you will be seeking something, although perhaps not as dangerous as the more traditional quests undertaken on behalf of royalty,' the King replied, with characteristic vagueness.

Jann had often seen the nasty side of the King's unpredictable temper, but he was not about to commit himself without more detail.

'And where might I be going to undertake this quest, sire, if I may be so bold as to ask?'

'Um... where?' said the King, peering through the window. 'Ah, yes, where. We call it the Valley of the Cataclysm.'

Patrick's eyes widened.

'That sounds more dangerous than your Majesty led me to believe,' said Jann, clutching at his shirt with one hand.

The King stared at Jann for a long moment.

'The name refers to the only occasion on which there was any hazard in all the eternities the Valley has stood,' he said, his face reddening. 'And that was many years ago.'

'What will I be seeking?'

'If we are to hold a repeat ceremony, then the music required is more than a simple choir under the guidance of Mister Glass,' said the King. 'We must have a functioning set of bells.

'In tune,' he added, 'which they most certainly were not at the last attempt. Whether or not that explains our lack of success no-one is prepared to admit, but we should like to avoid any doubt.

'It may of course have been the casting process at fault. Baka knows we had enough trouble with it. Since the Fire Witch is now returned that should no longer be an issue. However, the other problem concerned the amount of brass used. I still believe there must be fragments of the originals we never found.'

'Originals, sire?'

'Yes. The bells were shattered during the cataclysm that gave the Valley its name. There is a man who still lives there. I tasked him with finding all the pieces. He assured me he had, but as I say...'

'You have your doubts.'

The King regarded Jann with a vacant expression.

'I do, yes,' he said after a pause. 'So we would like you to seek out the pilgrim. Ask him whether he has found any more bell since last we spoke. Ask him if he looked everywhere. You might even consider searching the Valley yourself.'

'Search the Valley? For fragments of bell?'

'Well? What did you expect man? It's a quest! You have to search for something!'

Patrick stood, setting the borrowed celapi down beside his chair.

'If it please your Majesty, it appears my duties as choirmaster cannot begin until we have solved the mystery of the bells. In which case I should like to accompany Jann Argent on his quest.'

The King's eyes narrowed.

'Accompany him? Why would you choose to undertake such a journey without being asked?'

'Is it an arduous trek to the Valley then sire?' asked Jann.

'It is two days' ride from here,' the King said, 'but the Valley lies on the other side of Tubelak'Dun—the Western mountains. Not an easy trip at this time of year. Not without its hazards, no.'

'Unlike Argent here,' said Patrick, picking up the threads of his question. 'or Terry Spate with whom we also travelled, I do not have any blanks in my memory. Even so sire, I have always had the feeling I am meant to be here.'

He shook his head, his mouth crooking into a rueful smile. 'But as yet I have been unable to learn why. On my travels I met and spoke with several people who mentioned the Valley of the Cataclysm. I have no evidence, but a very strong suspicion that the secret I seek may be found in the Valley. By your leave sire, I will make the journey with Argent and assist him with his quest.'

The King looked from one to the other, stroking his grey-streaked beard.

'Very well!' he declared at length. 'If that is your wish, I will not gainsay you. Make the journey. I hope you do not come to regret your choice. It is not an easy trip,' the King repeated, 'not an easy trip at all. You will see.'

valley of the cataclysm
quest day 5

The journey proved even more arduous than the King had promised. It took them five days rather than two, during the worst of which they lost one of their pack animals to a rock fall while climbing up the precipitous and slippery trail leading over Tubelak'Dun. Eventually the path began to track downwards again, suggesting they had left the worst behind them.

Shortly after cresting the ridge, the decline became steeper. The Valley of the Cataclysm stretched out below them like a verdant lost land of promise. At the start of the slope the Valley appeared to be shrouded in a shimmering light, which Jann thought at first was a trick of the air currents. The warmer air, rising up from the Valley floor, must hit the colder layers of the mountain tops, creating a ripple effect in the atmosphere. But as they entered the region of distortion he realised it was not caused by any movement of the air. It was a property of the air itself.

'Look at these weird ripples in the air,' he said, bringing his kudo to a stop.

'Yeah, I noticed them a while ago,' said Patrick, halting his own mount, Jarapera, beside Jann's. 'It's just unusual atmospherics.'

'No. That's what I thought when we crested that ridge, but now that we're in it... Don't you see? It's like the air is thicker somehow.'

Patrick shrugged.

'Dunno then.'

He turned Jarapera back down the path.

'Looks like it stops a bit further on anyway.'

'Let's just get through it then,' Jann said.

Beyond the disturbance a carpet of green covered the Valley, the burgeoning growth well in advance of the seasonal winter chill that still gripped the mountains and which they had left behind in Istania.

'Look at this!' exclaimed Patrick. 'How can the Valley be so green at this time of year?'

Jann cast his eyes down the hillside and away across the Valley floor. Even at the tops of the hills on the far side of the gorge young plants flourished.

'I'm not sure,' he said. 'Maybe the Valley is protected from the weather in some way?'

'That would only hold the winter back a bit though,' Patrick continued, guiding Jarapera down the arduous path, slippery with loose stones and shale. 'As far as I can see this is all new growth. Like Spring has come early. Perhaps being closer to the coast gives it some kind of Gulf Stream effect?'

'I don't know what that is,' said Jann, 'and I don't remember enough about Berikatanyan seasons to know whether it's peculiar or not.'

They continued down the trail, the air becoming warmer with every step, and picked up the bank of a river. After filling their water skins and allowing the kudai a drink they followed the river for two or three kilometres further.

Almost an hour later they came upon a rocky outcrop that furnished a clear view over the lower valley. The path wound down past the side of the bluff. A ramshackle stone cottage stood atop the rock, its roof gaping with holes in several places, its worn and faded wooden door hanging open on a single hinge.

'This look like a pilgrim's shack to you?' asked Jann.

'If I'd had to guess, this is exactly what I would have described,' Patrick said grinning. 'Looks deserted.'

'Hello?' called Jann. 'Hello there? Anyone home?'

Only the buzzing of an insect and the far away hooting of a bird disturbed the silence.

'And answer came there none,' Patrick muttered.

'Well there's no point going on a search for one guy in this entire valley,' said Jann, 'quest or no quest. If I don't get off this kudo soon I won't sit down again for a week.'

They dismounted. The gloomy interior of the pilgrim's shack proved as badly in need of repair as the outside, but still offered no sign of the occupant. Jann rekindled a fire in the shallow pit carved in the rock in front of the building. They squatted beside the blaze to await the return of the pilgrim, unsure how to proceed, but confident at least that the man would have to come home sooner or later, no matter how poor the accommodation.

Chapter 14

Terry Spate straightened up from his toil. The shadows were already beginning to encroach on the edge of the clearing as the day turned languidly into afternoon. He had been hoeing a neat row of duntang. The local equivalent of a potato could be boiled or mashed in a similar way, and he had resigned himself to the fact that it was now the only alternative since his beloved King Edwards seed potatoes had failed to survive a hundred years in cold storage.

He stretched his back into a more normal shape, leaned on his hoe and surveyed the clearing, smiling. If she could see it now, Claire would not recognise it. Between the untrammelled forest to East and West, several acres of tilled soil, divided into plots with narrow chalkstone paths or small hedgerows replanted to encourage the local bug life, bore a variety of young crops. Indigenous vegetables such as the duntang he had been weeding, and its close relative the dunela, along with Berikatanyan equivalents of beets, parsnips, and carrots, grew side-by-side with local grains, their very large ears just beginning to swell into maturity. There were more familiar plants too, whose seeds Terry brought with him on the Valiant and which had fared better than the King Edwards. Celeriac, onions, peas and courgette all seemed to be thriving in the Berikatanyan soil, although the carrots were not holding their own beside the native versions.

His plot was enclosed by a rude picket fence, scant protection from the local kuclar who frequently ventured out from the forest, in the hope of catching a bird feasting on Terry's crops or the insect life they attracted. A ghantu bird perched on the fence now, watching him. Known for its ear-splitting screech, the bird was quiet for the moment, blinking its large eyes and waiting for any juicy morsel that

Terry's industrious tending of the plants would uncover.

In his trademark style, the land was not altogether devoted to produce. Such flowering plants as he had been able to find growing wild relieved the paths and beds at regular intervals, along with gardenias, chrysanthemums, daisies and marigolds from his personal stash. He had planted bulbs too, but they would not put in an appearance until next year.

His pride and joy was a rambling rose positioned beside a lych-gate erected at the notional entrance to the plot. It had grown to the top of the gate and flowered within the space of a few months, greatly exceeding his expectations.

'Hey Terry!' called Pattana, 'fancy a cold one?'

Terry accepted the Berikatanyan's offer with a laugh, remarking on the improvement in his English during the short time Terry had worked with him. It would be a glass of pressed jambala juice chilled down only as far as the nearest stream could take it, rather than the ice-cold brewski he still thought of whenever he heard the term "cold one." Such delights, along with refrigerators, were very definitely a thing of the past, but he had no regrets. Being surrounded on four sides by the fruits of his nine-month labours saw to that.

'There you go,' said Pattana, handing over a glass of the dusky orange liquid.

Terry took half of it in a single draught.

'Thanks, I was ready for that.'

'So I see.'

Pattana looked out over the ranks of beds and hedges.

'I can not believe what you have achieved here Terry, in such short time.'

'Well I didn't do it all on my own,' Terry grinned. 'You had a hand in it too. You and Umtanesh and Nembaka.

'And Claire,' he added after a moment's reflection.

'Yes, but we all say... none of us see anything grow so fast! You have magic touch.'

A deep tingle ran the length of Terry's spine in

response to Pattana's words. It often crossed his mind while working the soil that being here did feel magical. As if all his prayers had been answered, even though he had never consciously said any. Like the universe recognised a need in him and brought him to the only place where it could be sated.

'Well, I've not done anything unusual, far as I know,' Terry laughed. 'Just doin' what I've always done. Somehow, it works better here.'

He downed the second half of his drink and handed the glass back to Pattana.

'You hear about Claire?' the man asked.

'What about her?'

News of Claire's confirmation as the daughter of the lost Air Mage and the inheritor of the Elemental power had reached the plantation some months earlier. Such stories did not come around too often. They spread from place to place along the trails criss-crossing the countryside like the flame from a torch applied to a trail of Istanian Fire Brandy, but it had been many weeks since any further word of her exploits had escaped from the Black Queen's Palace.

'That battle we expected? It not go too well. She was involved. Faced off against the Fire Witch. Shame, really.'

Terry's face clouded over. A distant clap of summer thunder rolled around the clearing even though the sun shone in a cloudless sky.

'She's not...?'

'No, no. She not hurt. Except for pride. I guess that took a beating. But nothing physical.'

'Bloody turf wars!' Terry said, the anger plain in his face. 'I thought I had left all that behind when I came here. So what happened?'

'Hard to make sense from so little news. Seem Witch arrived late to the party. Soon started winning though. Then Batu'n turned up in they flyers and it all over.'

'All over? Who won?'

'No-one. It all just stopped. Don't know why.'

'And Claire wasn't hurt?'

Pattana shrugged.

'Not far as I know.'

Terry stabbed his hoe into the ground, his knuckles white on the handle.

'As far as you know? Damn it! Are you sure, or not?'

'Steady Terry,' said Pattana, taking a step back. 'She Air Mage now. I know little, only. But no news of her being injured any way. Someone... famous... like that? If she hurt then word get out.'

'And what the hell was she thinking of, getting involved in the first place?' Terry asked, plunging on with his rant before Pattana had time to offer an opinion.

'She's barely out of nappies for God's sake! Too young for that kind of thing even if she'd been training for it since birth, let alone being locked up in that damned magic school for less than a season. It's ridiculous!'

He swung the hoe through the air. The blade caught the nearby duntang, slicing through the stems of half a dozen of the young plants and leaving a visible gap in their previously regimented ranks.

On the path, where the hoe had left a mark, the fine chalk gravel dribbled into a crack that opened up in the dry soil beneath.

'Terry!' exclaimed Pattana. 'Your plants!'

Terry froze in the middle of preparing another swing. He stared at the short Berikatanyan, blinking back tears. Turning his back on Pattana, his shoulders racked with deep sobs, he let the tool drop from his grasp and shuffled off towards his tent.

valley of the cataclysm
quest day 5

'He's not coming is he?'

The day, despite the spring-like appearance of the

Valley, had taken on a decidedly chilly edge now that the sun had all but disappeared behind the crest of the western mountains. The fire Jann and Patrick had kept stoked since their arrival did little to assuage the creeping cold. Jann sat where he could watch both the Valley and the trail along which they had ridden earlier. He chewed on a mouthful of their rations and considered Patrick's question.

'There's always a chance this place is permanently deserted,' he said.

A slight gust of wind moved the door, which creaked on its last remaining hinge. The dilapidated structure offered no security. It was hard to imagine anyone living in such a desolate place.

'In which case,' Jann went on, 'waiting is pointless.'

'On the other hand,' he said, as usual pondering the dilemma from both sides, 'if he does still live here, there's an equally good chance he'll be back before nightfall.'

'There's no way to prove either of those hypotheses,' said Patrick, drawing a complex pattern of interlocking circles in the dust with a stick, 'but we need some sort of plan.'

Jann gazed westwards.

'Looks like we have an hour of daylight left,' he said. 'Maybe two.'

He stood up and dusted himself down.

'You're right,' he said. 'We can't sit here for the rest of the night. Let's take a look further down the Valley. There may be other signs of habitation closer to the river.'

'Beats staying here waiting for dark,' agreed Patrick.

They stacked the fire with some fresh logs, intending to return to the shack before nightfall, and set off towards the river. After only a short distance a man came in sight, approaching them from lower down the slope. A brace of hares hung across his shoulders and a skinful of water, slung from his waist, bounced against his bony legs as he walked. He was dressed in a filthy loincloth and walked the rock-strewn path with bare feet, bent forward as if the weight of his catch was almost too much to bear. His gaze fixed on the ground directly in front of him, even at this distance they could hear him muttering to himself as he trudged his painful way back to his hovel.

'Berse'mah kelin! Tapitu lebaik datidak sema.'

'Hello there!' Jann called out in his halting Istanian.

The man stopped. He stared up the slope, shielding his eyes from the last spears of sunlight poking over the hilltop behind Jann.

'Who's there?' the old man asked in a querulous tone. 'What do you mean coming into my Valley?'

The question surprised Jann. He had not expected the man to claim ownership of the land on which they stood. He decided against challenging the point. His Istanian was not good enough for him to be certain he had understood correctly, and in any case he did not want to begin their acquaintance on a confrontational note.

'We seek The Pilgrim,' he said. 'The King sent us.'

'The King indeed,' the man said, starting back up the path once more and beginning to breathe heavily at the effort of speaking while climbing. 'Many a year it is since I had the pleasure of his company, or anyone in his employ.'

The old man emphasised "pleasure" as if the King's company was a torture more frightful than being stretched on a rack.

'Wait there,' he continued. 'I cannot see you properly from down here. What is your name? You, and your friend there?'

'I am Jann Argent,' Jann replied, 'recently arrived on a Prism ship from Earth and lately promoted to the Blood Watch.'

He looked at Patrick.

'What?'

'He wants you to introduce yourself.'

'My Istanian is worse than yours!'

'At least make the effort. We need him to trust us.'

Patrick glared at him. He called down to the old man.

'My name Patrick Glass,' he called, enunciating each word. 'I too from Earth but have no job.'

'Your words are strange,' puffed the old man. 'Prism ship? Earth? I know nothing of these things! Are you sorcerers?'

'Indeed we are not sir,' Jann said, 'but your question is timely since the Fire Witch and the Air Mage are also newly returned to Berikatanya.'

The man stopped for a second time and took an involuntary step backward as if struck on the chest, almost losing his balance.

'The Witch has returned?' he exclaimed. 'How is that possible? I saw her disappear with my own eyes. Down there,' he added, turning and waving a bony hand at the valley below. 'Years ago. More years than I can count.'

'So you are the Pilgrim whom we seek,' Jann said.

'I do not bestow that title upon myself,' the old man replied, 'but yes, there are some who call me such. A ridiculous epithet it is to be sure, for I do not engage in any pilgrimage to speak of. I bide my time here, in the Valley, in case any of the Disappeared should return.'

He completed his slow climb up the path until he could stand at the same level as the two travellers, seeing them clearly for the first time. His dark eyes glittered beneath wild brows as he searched Jann's features. After a moment the Pilgrim's eyes widened and he took another involuntary step backward.

'Gatekeeper?' he whispered. 'Can it really be you?'

He reached a wizened hand to touch Jann's face, turning it so the feeble light of the late evening sun would give him a clearer profile.

'It is you! Gatekeeper! I knew you'd come. If I only waited long enough. And it has been many years. Tana be praised!'

Jann did not know what to make of the old man's words. And yet... and yet... the title of "Gatekeeper" seemed to nestle in his mind like a jigsaw piece. His hand strayed to his tunic, feeling the outline of his amulet. The old man turned his attention to Patrick.

'You have a familiar aspect too, young man, but I cannot place it. You have not been here before, but still you remind me of someone. Someone from the days of the cataclysm.

'Come!' he announced, setting off once more up the trail in the direction of his shack. 'I am forgetting my manners. Long has it been since I had guests to entertain, but we shall dine on rabbit stew and talk of the vortex and all that came after.'

Less than an hour later the three men sat around the Pilgrim's fire pit, savouring the occasional scents of local herbs that bubbled up from the dented iron pot hanging over the flames. The old man proved both surprisingly resourceful and remarkably well equipped, at least as far as kitchen utensils and cooking aids were concerned.

Beyond the glow from the hot ash, the evening coalesced into inky black. Peda-Bul and Kedu-Bul had each cleared the crest of the surrounding hills by the time they wiped the last of the stew from their bowls. They sat back against the wall of the shack, still warm from the heat of the day, and listened to the Pilgrim's tale, the deep lines of his face taking on the appearance of craters in the soft firelight.

His account of the cataclysm closely followed the story Jann had already gleaned from the parchments during his long night shifts in the catacombs. He found his attention wandering from a combination of prior knowledge, a full stomach, and the monotonous drone of the old man's voice. Patrick, who had learned only snatches of the tale from Jann during their mountain passage, listened intently to the Pilgrim's words, nudging Jann whenever his head began to nod, or when he needed help with the language.

When the narrative reached the point where the Gatekeeper made his appearance on the Valley floor, Jann's incipient torpor fled. Now wide awake, he leaned forward to catch every nuance of the saga.

'You trained long for the position of Gatekeeper,' the Pilgrim said, his piercing, deep-set eyes fixed on Jann's face. 'Strange it is that you remember nothing of it, but then the vortex was a prodigious manifestation of Elemental power and little understood. I tried to warn them. It should not surprise me there were unforeseen side effects.'

The old man stared into the fire for several minutes, gathering his thoughts, before continuing.

'Your role is not, of itself, a magical one. By which I mean you are unable to conjure the Elements with your own abilities. Yet you have the capacity to see in two directions at once. When you stand on a threshold, you are aware of everything on both sides. You can see the way. Start and Finish. Source and Destination. When all is revealed, you were the one to control the Vortex, though it was not you who created it.

'That task fell to another. He it was who knitted together the four powers to open the door between worlds. A dangerous manoeuvre. It took great skill and courage. The ability to see a pattern in the forces—a universal design, if you will—and cause them to coalesce in exactly the right order and quantity. Yes, the construction of the vortex was one of almost infinite complexity...'

The old man's voice tailed off, his eyes clouding with memory. An ember deep in the fire popped, sending a gout of glowing ash out of the pit. The man jumped at the sound, looking at Jann and Patrick in turn as if trying to remember who they were.

'So I controlled the portal,' Jann prompted, his mind reaching out towards the long-buried memories but simultaneously shying away from the prospect.

'Yes,' the Pilgrim nodded, picking up the threads of his story once more.

'It was your doing that the portal led to... where did you

say you had arrived from? Earth? But do not carry the burden of blame for the outcome of that day,' the old man added, throwing a fresh log on the fire.

Another plume of glowing ash, disturbed by the log, spiralled upwards in the eddies of hot air. Jann watched it, the pattern mirroring a spiral image in his brain. The wood crackled as it started to burn. In that instant present and past came together in Jann's mind. The chains binding his memories fell away and he was there. There and here at the same time. Staring at the fire and staring at the blackness of the void, feeling the power coursing through him, sensing his mind directing the portal.

'If not me,' he said, turning to the man with eyes suddenly blinded with tears, 'then who?'

The Pilgrim regarded him for a moment. He reached into the folds of his filthy loin cloth and retrieved a handful of small glittering yellow fragments which he tossed onto the ground in front of them.

'It was an accident,' he said.

'Is that brass?' asked Patrick.

'Shards of the cracked brass bells,' the old man said, nodding. 'I still find them occasionally, when I'm hunting, or fishing. Some wash down the river. I know not where from. I no longer go searching. I wait for them to come to me. I am older now. Older and wiser.

'And weaker,' he added ruefully.

'So many years have passed. It was a cataclysmic shock, the shattering of the bells. Pieces flew everywhere. I doubt we will ever find them all.'

'The King believes they have all been found,' Jann lied, testing the Pilgrim's insight.

The old man snorted.

'The King believes what he wants to believe. And disregards all evidence to the contrary.'

'Except when it stares him in the face,' said Patrick.

'Or the ears,' added Jann. 'He knew the bells weren't right, after they had been made again.'

'But not why.'

'Here is why,' said the old man, waving his leathery hands at the shining brass fragments. 'I have more inside. Not a lot. But enough.'

'We should take them with us,' said Jann, looking at Patrick.

The Pilgrim leapt to his feet, snatching up the shards of metal.

'No! You must not!'

The other two men stood too, but made no move to retrieve the pieces from the old man.

'Why not?' asked Jann. 'It is what we came for.'

'Do you not yet understand, Gatekeeper?' the old man cried. 'Such a powerful spell relies on all particulars being in place. Not just the Elements of power, or the control of yourself and the Pattern Juggler, but also the music. The bells and the lullabies are at the heart of it, just as much as the other pieces. Without them the King cannot open the portal again. And without these pieces,' he added, closing his fist around the glittering fragments and shaking it at the two men, 'there can be no bells!'

elementary academy
16th day of ter'utamasa, 966

A hubbub of excited chatter filled the senior classroom. Outside the windows the day was dark; the sky heavy with rare day-time storm clouds which threatened, but hadn't yet begun, to drop their watery burden on the Elementary Academy.

'Pay attention class,' said the berobed mage who stood on a short podium at the front of the room. 'Today's lesson, as I believe I mentioned last time, will move on to the first Elemental level.'

The students settled down as the old master began to speak. Kanasa Benko, a spotty teenager seated to Claire's left, elbowed her in the ribs.

'You'll be good at this then. Air Mage,' she laughed.

Two girls in front of her and one behind cackled along with Kanasa, jeering at Claire and pulling faces.

Claire ignored them. With the advantage of several months' experience at the school she knew rising to their bait would only make matters worse. She'd been suffering these taunts since her involvement in the abortive war and her subsequent visit from the Queen. Word had soon spread of the events of battle day. Her classmates chose to interpret what happened as abject failure on Claire's part. Once she moved up to the senior class they began to refer to her as "Air Mage" in a disparaging tone, as if it were obvious to anyone with a brain that Claire was the furthest thing imaginable from a real Elemental. She kept her head down and let her improving magic skills speak for themselves. Skills in which her confidence and her abilities had grown as quickly as the master mage predicted.

'Quiet there!' the tutor shouted, looking over the rims of his glasses at the giggling girls. 'This topic is hard enough with full concentration. You will never grasp it if you treat it lightly.'

Suitably rebuked the girls settled down, but not before Kanasa treated Claire to another sharp dig with her elbow.

'Now then,' the master continued, 'in a moment I shall ask each of you to attempt the power pulse challenge I set last time. It is a really difficult aspect of Air-related magic, one few of you adepts will be able to handle with any force or accuracy. As I have already explained, success is not expected for everyone, but the endeavour is important as it will determine your path through the rest of your time here at the Academy. Those of you who succeed will progress to the na Elemental stream, as this is the first spell at that level.

'The power pulse—also known as Kema'katan—is commonly used for either defence or attack, depending on the strength and direction of the billow you create. Since we are indoors, not involved in a great battle, I shall ask you to make an attempt at blowing over these bricks.'

The master moved to the side of the classroom and removed a black sheet which had been covering a dusty pile of red bricks, arranged to form a short section of wall about a metre high.

'You are all at a junior level, so I will also allow an incantation for those who still require verbal assistance when summoning their power. Now, who would like to go first?'

Several hands shot up, including Kanasa Benko, who seemed keen on showing Claire she wasn't the only one with a mastery of the higher magical arts.

'Yes, Kanasa, since you were so vocal earlier why don't you see what you can do?'

The girl smirked at Claire before sashaying to the front of the class. A hushed silence fell over the room as she took position a couple of metres from the pile of masonry and centred herself. The other students appeared to be willing her on. Claire regarded her with mild disinterest as she raised both hands and thrust them in the direction of the flimsy wall.

'Kema'katan!' she cried, her voice breaking.

A small puff of brick dust blew out from the back of the middle row. The wall rocked a little, but remained otherwise undisturbed.

A mocking snort from the rear of the class brought a black scowl to Kanasa's reddening face. She glanced at the old mage and at Claire before retaking her seat with a flounce.

'Never mind Kanasa,' the master said, 'as I said there is no shame in not managing this. It is Elemental stuff. Fewer than one percent of my students have ever been able to achieve sufficient control for an attacking pulse. Now, who's next?'

Several of the hands previously raised remained in their owners' laps. The old mage turned towards Claire.

'Miss Yamani? How about you?'

Claire gave the master a composed look. Without the slightest glance at the rest of the class she moved into position. Standing on the opposite side of the room from the bricks, much further away than her unsuccessful predecessor, she turned to face the pile. She reached down inside herself to the core of her power. It glowed in response to her request. She felt her entire body suffused with it until it she thought she must be incandescent on the outside too. The syllables of the incantation echoed in her mind, shaping the pulse, determining its force and direction, but she knew she wouldn't need to speak them. She stretched out her right hand, palm facing the wall, and released her power with a flick of her wrist.

The short wall exploded backwards, fragments of brick rattling against the windows, shattering several. A thick brume of dust obscured one half of the classroom.

Some of her classmates screamed, those in the front row of desks scrambling back away from the bricks, ducking to avoid flying debris and shielding their eyes from the dust. Outside, the threatened rain began to fall, clattering on the remaining windows and soaking any student sitting near a broken pane. As the air cleared a puddle could be seen forming where the bricks had stood. Rain drove in through the hole Claire had blown in the outer wall of the classroom.

the blood king's court
quest day 12

By the time Jann Argent returned with Patrick Glass to the Blood King's Court, night had fallen. The cycle of the moons meant they would not rise until just before dawn. The sky was as black as Jann's mood. The memories unlocked during their conversation with the Pilgrim were still hazy, and the clarity of his mind was further stirred into muddy eddies by their second encounter with the strange shimmering distortion barrier at the entrance to the Valley of the Cataclysm. The difference between the seaward side and the rest of Istania was even more remarked on their egress from the Valley. They had left burgeoning spring behind and entered the last days of autumn, green young shoots giving way to wizened late fruit, the last dried leaves still hanging on until the next winds, bare branches wherever they looked.

'How can this be?' Patrick had asked as their mounts stepped through the shimmering mist and whinnied, their surprise and trepidation matching that of their riders. 'We arrived at the Valley in winter. Now it looks like autumn. Surely an entire year can't have passed in the few days we spent with the Pilgrim?'

'Beats me,' Jann had replied, thoughts still occupied with his revelations and experiences back in the Valley. 'Maybe there's some blight here or something?'

But his reflections on the portal and its effects on Patrick and himself had gradually coalesced with what they had seen of the Valley and its surroundings. A theory suggested itself to Jann.

'The portal had a kind of time dilation effect,' he had told Patrick. 'Elaine said she'd only been on Earth four years. I was in prison for eight. So I must have been thrown back twice as far as her. Who knows how far the others were sent? Claire's mother and father for instance. She was around fifteen when she boarded the Valiant and she'd been born on Earth. Her parents must have travelled further back in time than either of us.'

'How does that all affect the seasons here, now? The vortex closed over fifty years ago, Berikatanyan time.'

'I don't know exactly,' Jann said. 'But if such a powerful force can affect time on one side of the hole, it may have had a similar effect on the other side. This side. Maybe there's a timeslip in the Valley or something? Localised to the area under the influence of the vortex.'

Jann's strange theory stopped the conversation. They rode on for the rest of the journey wrapped in their travelling coats and their thoughts, until on the last day the sun sank below the hills just as the Court towers appeared over the horizon.

When they dismounted in the outer barbican Jann became aware of a low, almost subliminal throbbing noise he had never noticed before they left. No, not throbbing. More like grinding. The sound of something heavy sliding over rough stone.

'What's that?' Jann asked.

'What's what?'

'Don't you hear it? That noise?'

'All I can hear is Jarapera panting,' said Patrick, handing his reins to an ostler and adjusting his tunic.

Jann shook his head. The scraping was clearly audible, although he had no idea what could be causing it. Elaine rushed out into the open courtyard and embraced him.

'I thought you were never coming back!' she said, stepping away and looking him up and down. She turned to Patrick.

'Did you find him? Did you learn anything?'

'I'll say we did,' Jann replied before Patrick could react. 'Let's just say I understand why you were so pissed with the King. I have a rather large bone of my own to pick with him.'

Elaine's eyes widened, her hand flying to her mouth.

'He's waiting to see you already,' she said. 'The tower guards saw you approaching. He's in the throne room.'

Thin wisps of oily black smoke curled up from the torches lining the cold stone corridor outside the throne room. Jann hesitated for a moment, steadying his resolve, before nodding to the guardsman to open the door. The King rose at his approach, a wide smile on his face.

'Argent!' he called. 'I hear you found the Pilgrim?'

News travelled faster inside the Court buildings than anywhere else on the planet. Only the ostler had overheard the exchange between Elaine and the travellers, scant minutes earlier.

'We did sire,' said Jann, 'and what he told us has helped restore my memories.'

'Capital!' the King exclaimed, smiling even more broadly. 'So are your powers fully returned also?'

'Powers, Majesty?'

'The Power of the Earth. Are you not the Gardener, as I have long hoped?'

'The Gardener?'

'The Earth Elemental, man! Petani!'

'Indeed not sire,' Jann said, momentarily nonplussed at the unexpected turn in the conversation. 'The Pilgrim's recollections revealed me to be the Gatekeeper. My own memories of the ceremony, now partially returned to me, confirm this. Although I must confess the lore of the Gatekeeper is still very much a mystery.'

'But that is of no use to me!' the King spat, collapsing onto his marble throne. 'If my second Elemental had been restored we would certainly have had mastery over the Blacks. Her with one Mage missing and one still wet behind the ears. What use is a Gatekeeper with no gate?'

'The Pilgrim seemed to think—' Patrick began. A glare from Jann silenced him.

'That feeble minded old fool! I am surprised he still retains the capacity to think!' the King growled, not noticing Patrick's discomfort.

'Had I proved to be the Earth Elemental, I do not believe I would have the stomach for such work again,' Jann said.

He held the King's gaze, unflinching.

The King's eyes narrowed. 'Indeed?' he said. 'And why is that?'

'It was dangerous magic that created the portal,' Jann said, 'at least, as far as I now understand it. The spell backfired. Several of us were cast unimaginable distances in both space and time. As one of those directly affected, I would be reluctant to risk a repeat of that event.'

'Even though it was your King's wish?' the King asked,

his voice barely audible over the guttering of the torches.

Jann continued to stare at the King until the silence grew uncomfortable.

'I think what Jann means—' Patrick began.

Jann held up his hand.

'What Jann means,' he said, enunciating each word with care, 'is that, King's wish or not, I would not be a party to a reproduction of the ceremony. Either as the Gardener, or as the Gatekeeper.'

The King's face reddened as he rose to his feet, all trace of his earlier smile replaced with a dark scowl.

'Perhaps the days of magic are numbered after all,' he said, his knuckles blanching on the handle of his mace. 'Before the portal, we had not encountered the people of Earth, with their flying vehicles and technologies that surpass our wildest fantasies—and even our most powerful magic! Perhaps we now have no need of the old ways.'

Chapter 15

The massive white door closed behind them with a bone jarring thud. The bare stone corridor seemed cold in comparison with the throne room, or was it simply that they were no longer confronting the King's temper?

'I need to speak to Elaine,' Jann snapped. 'You should come.'

He strode off in the direction of her chambers without waiting for Patrick's reaction.

The opulence of Elaine's quarters struck Jann anew when she opened the door. The contrast between this and the sparse living conditions they had endured during their visit to the Valley made the velvet drapes, overstuffed sofas and wide, comfortable bed seem almost deliberately extravagant.

'How was his majesty?' Elaine enquired with a soft smile and a raised eyebrow.

Jann flashed her an angry look. Her smile evaporated.

'Oh. That bad.'

'He thought I was an Elemental.'

She barked a laugh, covering her mouth with a hand.

'Sorry. He really has no clue, does he?'

'Can't say I did before I saw the Valley,' Jann replied.

'Let's not fall out among ourselves,' Patrick said, pouring a glass of wine from Elaine's well-stocked bureau. 'Drink?'

'It would help,' Jann said. 'Sorry. I've still not taken it all in.'

Elaine laid a hand on his arm.

'Save it. We'll find a way to get even with the King. Tell me how much you remember.'

Jann, with occasional input from Patrick, related the story of their journey. When he came to the part where they had entered the Valley and seen the shimmering curtain of ripples in the air, he explained his time dilation theory.

'Before we go any further,' Jann said, draining his glass and holding it out to Patrick for a refill, 'how long were we gone?'

Elaine looked at him quizzically.

'How long? You must... it's been nine months since you set out to find the Pilgrim.'

Patrick spat wine across the room.

'Nine months?' He looked aghast at Jann. 'I know what you said, but—'

Jann ran a hand through his hair.

'Hell's bells. Nine months? Really? I mean, you're sure?'

'Of course I'm sure! You left here on the third day of Sen'Tanamasa and today's the twenty-second of Ter'Bakamasa. It's actually closer to ten months. Why, how long did you think you were gone?'

'It took us five days to ride to the Valley,' Patrick said.

'And we were there almost three days,' Jann added. 'It was easier coming back, so call it twelve days for the round trip.'

Elaine stared at him. She set her wine glass on a table.

'Looks like your theory was right,' she said. 'Not counting the riding time there and back, how long exactly were you behind the curtain?'

Jann did a quick mental calculation.

'Near as I can say, about seventy hours.'

Elaine's brow furrowed with concentration while she counted on her fingers.

'Time in the Valley is running something like a hundred times slower than out here.'

'Explains how the Pilgrim is still alive,' said Patrick. 'According to the scrolls and what the King told us, he should be well over a hundred years old.'

'The King must know about this,' Jann exclaimed. 'He wouldn't have sent us to search for a man who should have been dead for decades.'

'And the Jester,' said Elaine. 'While you were gone I spent most of my time trying to re-establish the Fire Guild, but I still had a lot of time to myself. Once the battle was over the King didn't bother me much. But the Jester sought me out. Him and the King are thick as thieves and a bit misogynistic I can tell you. Don't be fooled by that rictus grin he keeps pasted on his face and all that cavorting. He's about as funny as the pox. One night he pulled me into an alcove and more or less told me he would find a way to sort me out once and for all. Pretty sure the King doesn't see *that* side of him. I'd be happy to see his royal highness get what's coming to him, but the Jester is even more dangerous than me, and that's saying something!'

'Wheels within wheels,' Patrick said, taking a seat in a huge armchair facing the others. 'We can't draw any conclusions without more detail. Can we get back to where everyone fits in the story? It's OK for you two. Elaine's known who she is since before we left Earth, and you've just found out. But I was driven to come here too. Do I have a part? Who's left that I could have been? Or am I just a regular Earther tagging along for the ride?'

'The Pilgrim thought you looked familiar,' Jann reminded him.

'Really?' said Elaine, looking more closely at Patrick. 'What did he say exactly?'

'Just that,' Patrick said. 'I resemble someone he once knew, but he couldn't quite place me.'

Elaine sat forward and stared at him from several angles.

'I think I see what he means,' she said at length.

coastal region of utperi'tuk
23rd day of ter'bakamasa, 966

Elaine dismounted from Jaranyla, the chestnut mare

who had become her favourite of all the kudai in the King's stable over the months of her stay at Court. The final few hundred metres of her journey to the coast had to be negotiated on foot, the path to the sea being too steep and rock-strewn for a kudo's hooves to negotiate.

'There, there, Jara,' she crooned to the beast, stroking her strong neck and letting the reins fall to the grass. 'The grazing is sweet here. Rest. Wait for me my friend, I shan't be gone long.'

The sun rode high in the sky as she started down the rocky track, casting an annoying short shadow in front of her and making it harder to choose her footings. After a few minutes she entered a cleft in the rock. Once her eyes adjusted to the relative gloom of the gully, she found the going easier.

As she continued her descent towards the ocean she considered anew the Pilgrim's confirmation that her erstwhile travelling companion Jann Argent was the Gatekeeper. She recognised him at the spaceport, but having only recently recovered her memories had not trusted her judgement until someone else had corroborated his identity.

'This is incredible!' she had exclaimed, back in her chambers when the two men finished relating the tale of their journey. 'It means three of the original participants in the portal ceremony, or their descendants, have returned to Berikatanya.'

'On the same ship, from the same place,' said Jann, scratching his head. 'What are the chances?'

'I'm not sure chance has anything to do with it,' Patrick said. 'It's as if you were all drawn here. But I felt compelled to come too, and I don't have any connection to Berikatanya in general, or the ceremony in particular. Do I?'

'Do you feel any Elemental affinity?' Elaine asked.

'Not really,' Patrick shrugged. 'Would I know?'

'Yes. Even if you didn't know for certain, like I did,

247

you'd experience the pull of the power.'

'And you have no memory loss,' Jann added, 'so I'd say it's unlikely.'

'So we still need to find the Water Wizard and the Earth Elemental,' Elaine mused.

'Were they all definitely caught in the vortex?' Jann asked. 'The scrolls I read suggested all four of the Elementals were sucked out, but from the description I think it's at least possible the portal closed before the Water Wizard translated.'

'He took liquid form as soon as the danger became clear,' Elaine said. 'If any part of him remained behind when the vortex collapsed he would have been able to keep his essence here. But no-one has seen him since that day, and water spells have suffered a degradation in their power exactly the same as every other Element.'

'Where would he be, assuming he's still here?' Patrick asked.

'Somewhere he would be hidden from any chance of being seen,' said Jann.

'Not only that,' Elaine had said, 'but to explain the weakening of Water magic his hideout must be considerably further away than any Berikatanyans have travelled.'

To Elaine, that meant only one place. She emerged from the shaded tunnel, where the path ended in a narrow ledge running the length of the cliff, two thirds of its height from the summit. Below this the sea swelled and crashed, filling the air with heavy spray. From time to time a strong wave forced up a column of white water which cascaded over the rocks, drenching the ledge and rendering it dangerously slick.

Elaine watched the wild ocean for several minutes, allowing its smell, sound and heaving motion to summon her memories of the Water Wizard—her counterpoint in the balance of forces. She called to him, first with her mind and then out loud, shouting over the noise of the sea.

'Show yourself Wizard, if you are here! Did you fall with the rest of us, or are you hiding in your watery hole? It is I, Bakara, Fire Witch of Berikatanya, who summons you! Come to me now! Rise up from the surf and stand with me. We have need of you!'

Another gout of spray shot from the rock face below. Elaine believed for an instant her summons had succeeded, but when the jet broke against the cliff and subsided again she remained standing alone on the slippery platform.

'Where are you, Wizard of the Water?' she demanded. 'What have you been doing all these years while we were lost to memory and time? Snatched from our world to a distant place. Are you there still, or are you here? You may have been lost like us, but you can be found again! Hear me!'

She stood drenched and shivering, staring with rising anger at the implacable ocean, which continued to ignore her rants.

'Damn you Lautan!' she cried, invoking the Water Wizard's Elemental name at last. 'If you can hear me, why will you not answer?'

The unheeding waves swelled and roiled at her feet, the sound of their crashing echoing around the rocky inlet, the spray soaking her clothes until they hung on her like a shroud. Of the Water Wizard, there remained no sign.

'He won't come,' said a voice behind her.

coastal region of utperi'tuk
23rd day of ter'bakamasa, 966

Elaine spun around to discover who had uttered the words. The Queen's Piper stepped from the cleft.

'What are you doing here?' she asked.

The Piper moved into the sun, his habitual purple costume seeming to coalesce from the shadows, instantly recognisable.

'I could ask you the same question,' he replied. 'A strange place to find the Elemental of Fire. Such a vast volume of water could quench your flame for good, witch.'

Elaine's eyes widened, their orange flecks flashing.

'You think so?' she said, raising one hand. 'Shall I test your theory?'

The Piper shrugged.

'If you are attempting to summon Water, then a display of Fire power would be counterproductive in the extreme.'

'So, if you stood hidden in the dark of the rocks long enough to overhear my summons you do not need to ask my reasons for being here, Piper. My question, however, remains unanswered.'

'I was curious.'

'About what?'

'About whether you would succeed in your quest to find Lautan.'

'Which begs the question how you found out about it in the first place!' she snapped. 'Only two others knew of my journey here. We have told no-one else.'

'But others have heard, nonetheless. It is said there are no secrets in the Court of the Blood King.'

'Nor in the Black Queen's Palace, it seems. How do whispers from the one find the ears of the other, I wonder?'

'Those who wish to hear have only to listen,' the Piper said, his obtuse manner of speaking beginning to annoy Elaine.

'And why would you wish to hear anything I have to say?'

'Have you forgotten I was there that day too?' the Piper asked, stepping back to avoid the spray from another powerful geyser as it spewed from below. 'It was I who led the choir. I who saw you all disappear through the vortex. Or so I thought. The possibility that one of the four had remained here all along intrigued me. I wished to see whether or not you would be able to summon the Water Wizard from his hiding place, if indeed he has one.'

Elaine shivered again.

'Well, as you have seen, I was not able.'

She turned her back on the ocean and began to make her way up the rocky path, uncomfortable to have admitted her failure out loud. She was keen to rejoin Jaranyla and return to Court. A flickering glow of yellow flame surrounded her as she walked, limning the edges of her topaz-studded bangles. Summoned to dry her sodden clothing and restore her body's warmth, it had the added benefit of providing a little illumination for the walk. If her mind had not been preoccupied with her conversations with Jann and Patrick she might have thought to do something similar on the way down.

The Piper's footsteps followed behind her, crunching arythmically on the gravel as he stumbled on the uneven ground. His reasons for following her to the sea seemed rather inconsequential to her.

'There is more to this than you're telling me,' Elaine said over her shoulder. 'You wouldn't come all this way merely to see for yourself. If the Wizard had returned you would have heard about it soon enough.'

'There are rumours,' he replied. 'Of another ceremony. I needed to know.'

Elaine emerged onto the knoll where Jaranyla stood waiting. The mare snickered in recognition at her approach, stropping a hoof against the grass. She stroked the kudo's neck as the full implications of the Piper's words crystallised in her mind.

'What in the palace of the immortal flame are you talking about?' she demanded.

blood king's court, dormitory wing
22nd day of ter'bakamasa, 966

Jann Argent woke in the dark. He lay still while the

sleepy fog cleared from his head, trying to work out what
had woken him. He had been dreaming, but his waking
mind chased away the details of the dream before he could
hold on to them. In moments the elusive images were
completely lost.

Heavy drops of the malamajan rains beat an alien
rhythm against his window. Through the frame of his bed
he felt a strange vibration. As his senses sharpened he
realised the movement matched the tempo of the grinding
noise he first heard on his arrival back at Court. The sound
had become so commonplace, pulsing and scraping away
in the background, he was no longer conscious of it.
Though his ears had ceased to register it, his body was not
fooled. Now, freshly sensitised to the grating tone, he
heard it anew.

Jann sat up. Where did it come from? What was
causing it? Whatever the source, it had been going on since
before his return. Some manufacturing process? It
reminded him of the noise a millstone would make, but he
could think of no reason a miller would be working at this
late hour, even if one inhabited the Court. Elaine had not
yet returned from the coast and Patrick had been called
away to attend a meeting with some of the King's musical
advisors. It was up to him to discover the source of the
peculiar sound.

He dressed in the dark and cracked open his door. The
corridors of the guest wing were not patrolled, but with no
plausible explanation for why he was exploring the Court
in the middle of the night, he did not want to be seen. The
passageway outside his quarters was empty of guards or
courtiers keeping late hours. Jann crept out of his room
and closed the door behind him.

He turned his head left and right, trying to get a bearing
for the sound. Being transmitted through the stone walls
and floor, it seemed to be coming from everywhere at
once. He took a few paces, hoping to detect a change in
volume.

He struck lucky. By the time he reached the end of the corridor the grinding had become louder. Two or three passageways further on, with the noise now considerably more distinct, he arrived at an unlit part of the Court. Taking a torch from the wall Jann pressed on. He came to a narrow stone staircase, one of many servants' routes leading to the crypt levels of the keep which Jann had used in the past. His blood ran cold. The grinding noise drifting up from below had been supplemented by the sound of faint screams.

Foetid darkness shrouded the stairwell. Dousing his torch he started down, feeling his way. At first, pale moonlight filtered in through the slim window slits, but as he descended further the light dimmed even as the sounds of grinding and screaming swelled. By the time he reached the lowest level of the catacombs he no longer needed any help detecting the source of the noises. A solid iron door stood ajar at the end of the corridor. Beyond, a dull red glow illuminated another set of stairs leading downwards. Wooden steps this time, their treads dusty and rotten, handrails loosely attached to the rough stone walls upon which drops of moisture glistened in the vermilion light.

Jann started down this second staircase, testing his weight on each tread as he went. Any creaks would be drowned out by the screaming, which now filled the air, but he did not trust the stairs to hold him. At the bottom, a floor of packed earth led away around a corner. The passage afforded no alcoves or hiding places. Anyone exiting this dark crypt would walk straight into him. He pressed on until he came to the top of another stone staircase carved into the wall of a colossal cavern. Two enormous fires, one at each end, lit the great chamber beneath. Jann ducked down under a parapet overlooking the vast open space. The scraping of a giant grinding wheel was almost deafening now, punctuated by those terrifying screams. He risked a look to the floor below and choked back a rising gout of vomit at the sight.

A line of prisoners, each roped to the one behind, stood sobbing on a gantry leading to the centre of a massive circle of unpolished red granite. Naked, and covered in bruises, they were guarded by men in a uniform Jann had not previously encountered, either in person or in any of the scrolls and parchments he had seen in the Keeper's lair.

The guards wore masks of red leather covering their faces, with short breeches stitched together from pieces of the same material. Beaten copper plates protected their upper body, front and back, held by red leather straps. Each guard carried a short sword, with which they urged the line of prisoners forward and severed the rope connecting the leading unfortunate when he or she reached the end of the gantry before being forced, screaming, into the maw of the great grinding wheel.

From under the wheel a sickly stream of fresh blood poured out into a long trough carved in the red granite floor of the cavern. As Jann continued to stare, horrified, at the grisly scene beneath him, the surface of the blood swelled and burst, resolving into the figure of a man who stood, naked and dripping in the crimson gore. The firelight flickered and danced on the glistening ooze as it dribbled from his chin and outstretched hands. It was impossible to make out the man's identity until he spoke. With mounting horror Jann recognised the voice of the King, his title now a grim reality.

'Aarrgh!' the King roared, his guttural cry bouncing from the cave walls above the sound of the grinding wheel and the screams of the doomed prisoners. 'The Bloodpower is mine once more!'

Chapter 16

Jann ran down another dark stone passageway, impelled by the horrors he had encountered in the crypt. The vision of its grisly grinding stones still burned in his mind, the smell of fresh blood stung his nostrils. His ears rang with the screams of the victims and the sickly gurgle of the ichor oozing from the millstone's spout.

Jann's dread redoubled as he glanced behind him, a sudden increase in the nauseating sound of the gory tide drawing his attention. And it was a tide. A crimson bore, following him down the passage. Chasing him. Lapping at the stone walls and surging along the dusty floor, picking up anything in its path and carrying it forward on an oily red wave. The stench was appalling. Jann retched as he ran, stumbling and careering off the walls, careless of the cuts and bruises, wanting only to escape the gruesome torrent of blood that continued to rise, getting nearer with his every faltering step.

In his desperation, Jann ducked into a side corridor. Too late, he realised his mistake. The passage led downwards, and the swirling current of gore now blocked its entrance. He ran on, hoping to find another way out. He stumbled into a second cavern, lit once again by twin fires. This chamber, already almost full of blood streaming from an unseen source, contained a quadrangle of blue stone at its centre. For the moment the block remained above the shining vermilion lake although the level rose by the minute. It lapped at the edges, slicking them with gore. Three figures stood on the platform, the two nearest the edge screaming their defiance at the approaching tide.

Jann recognised them immediately. Claire and Elaine. Why did they not use their powers? Jann watched, unable to help, as a wave of blood overwhelmed the women, dragging them from the rock.

A lone figure remained, keeping to the middle of the stone dais away from the treacherous slippery rim. The man waved and called to him.

'Jann! Help me!'

Patrick! He ducked and dodged to avoid two shining steel blades, which reflected the firelight and the gory pool so they appeared already to be covered in blood. They swung perpendicular to each other only a few centimetres above the surface of the rock. One bore an intricate design in black and white, the other shaped like a child's drawing of a cloud, inverted.

Jann cast about for anything to help bridge the gap between him and his companion, but there was nothing. A repulsive gurgling sound belched from the passage behind him.

'I can't reach you!' he yelled to Patrick, sweat dripping down his face as he leaned over the parapet.

'Look out!' he shouted again as the swinging blades converged, their differing oscillations having put them on a collision course. At the last moment Patrick dived out of the way, rolled to the edge of the podium and slipped soundlessly into the lake of blood. The pendulums smashed into each other in a shower of sparks that blazed brighter and brighter like the heart of a furnace.

A solar furnace, shining in through the window of Jann's room as he sat up in bed, screaming and drenched with sweat.

The dream faded. His fourth since he had discovered the Blood King's macabre secret less than a week ago. His friends had chosen a poor time to leave him facing such a horrifying development alone, but there was no-one else in the entire Court with whom he could share his revelation. He poured himself a glass of water from the pitcher beside his bed, downed it in one draught, and wished desperately that Elaine would hurry back from her search for the Water Wizard.

coastal region of utperi'tuk
23rd day of ter'bakamasa, 966

Steam rose in the cool air of late morning as Elaine's clothes dried under the influence of her power. Her black mood was not evaporating so easily. Instead it condensed into a dangerous knot of anger that threatened to kindle a separate fire of its own.

'Come on!' she demanded. 'What do you mean by rumours of another ceremony? You can't be serious.'

'Just that,' the Piper replied. 'Rumours.'

'It would be madness!'

Elaine took a step towards him.

'Have you the slightest clue how it feels to wake up from a four-year-long dream with no idea where your home is or whether you'll ever be able to get back there?'

'It was pure luck that we—'

In the instant of speaking it occurred to Elaine that the Piper may not be aware how many of the original group had returned. If he was party to rumours and allied to those who listened behind walls, it would be unwise to reveal too much until she could more clearly determine his allegiances and plans.

'—I managed to find my way back at all. That the vortex took me to a world with the technology to travel across the void between the two. One close enough to Berikatanya to return while my contemporaries are still alive.

'Did we all traverse to the same place? I don't know. Where did the others go? And how far away in time? I don't know that either. They may all be dead. They may have been thrown back hundreds of years. Lived out their lives uselessly on other planets, never remembering who they are or, worse, recovering their memories but having no means of returning.'

Elaine's eyes flashed at the Piper, who stood blank faced, apparently unable to comprehend the depth of her rage.

'Another ceremony?' she repeated. 'If anyone believes me willing to risk being cast to the other side of the galaxy—for a second time—just because the Blood King's yellow peril thinks it would be a jolly jape to try again, they do not know me very well!'

'I had no idea,' the Piper murmured, his face a mask of shock.

'No. That about sums up the whole escapade,' Elaine said, shaking her head. 'No idea. I don't believe any of the Elementals really understood why we undertook the ceremony. We certainly did not know it would result in the vortex. Did you? Did anyone?'

Elaine turned her back on the Piper, unable to stomach his blank stare any longer. She adjusted Jaranyla's bridle and checked the cinch.

'I—'

'No,' Elaine said, ignoring the Piper. 'Not "no idea". *Bad* idea is more accurate. The ceremony was a bad idea, and the vortex was a disaster. I'll never take part in another, even if he banishes me from Court. Some things are not worth the risk.'

She turned to face the Piper once again and was surprised to find his eyes brimming with tears.

coastal region of utperi'tuk
23rd day of ter'bakamasa, 966

The Piper dashed the moisture from his eyes, his face reddening.

'The King knew,' he said.

Elaine let Jaranyla's reins drop from her hands.

'That, at least, does not surprise me,' she said, peering at him. 'Did you know?'

His watery eyes widened.

'No! I don't think anyone else did. Not at the time.'

'But others know now.'

'I discovered the truth later.'

'How?'

'I... have my sources.'

The Piper shivered. Whether from embarrassment, dismay, or because he was still a little damp from the spray and the sun had passed beyond the cliff, leaving him in a chill shadow, Elaine could not tell.

'I can't believe the Jester didn't know,' Elaine said with a disdainful expression. 'He only leaves the King's side to take a shit.'

The Piper shrugged.

'I only know it was the King who uncovered the original texts. They contained the details—the lore on how to conduct the ceremony,' he said. 'What music was needed, the roles of the Elementals, Gatekeeper and Juggler.

'And the outcome,' he added.

'I don't understand,' Elaine said, not taking her eyes off the Piper. 'Why would the King want to open a vortex to another world? Did he know where it would lead? How powerful it would be?'

The Piper shrugged once more.

'If he did, then he never shared the knowledge with anyone. At least, as far as I can tell. But he knew. That much is certain. Maybe he sought some advantage in the latest of his interminable wars.'

'*His* wars? Your allegiances are showing, Piper,' Elaine snapped. 'Both royal Houses are as bad as each other, and as chief advisor to the Black Palace, you are as bad as either. If one of them didn't start a war the other would. Thus it has been for centuries and well you know it.'

'That may be the popular myth,' the Piper retorted, 'but it's not true. At least, not any longer. Not with this Queen.'

'I would expect you to defend her.'

'Or her advisers,' the Piper added, ignoring Elaine's disdain. 'We seek always to protect. The royal strategies are uniformly defensive. She will attack only when provoked.

And behind the scenes we labour to forge bonds between the two Houses, or between their peoples anyway. To demonstrate the futility of further conflict that disrupts lives and destroys estates. There is little stomach for war in Kertonia.'

'And you would have me believe you are one of those working for peace?' Elaine asked with a wry grin. 'A pacifist in purple, rather than a vindictive viper in vaudeville violet?'

The Piper shivered again. He moved to stand in the last remaining pool of sunlight. His kudo, a grey stallion with a white tail, looked up from cropping the sweet grass of the clearing. Satisfied it was not yet time to leave, the animal bent his head to his task once more.

'I am a musician, not a warrior,' the Piper said. 'A seeker after beauty and creativity. Is it so surprising I hate this ancient feuding and its attendant destruction? I have never understood the Elementals' involvement. If I can set myself against it, why can't you?'

Elaine bridled at the implied suggestion of her complicity in one-sided warmongering. She took a breath, the warm musky scent of Jaranyla calming her anger. She stroked the kudo's neck.

'The Elementals' collaboration is necessary,' she muttered. 'There must be balance.'

'Ah yes. Te'banga. Your trump card.'

'Do not mock that which you cannot understand!' Elaine snapped. 'We have saved many thousands of lives over the centuries. Do you honestly believe those battles would have proceeded better without our influence? No. They would have lasted longer, been bloodier, and resulted in far more destruction.'

The Piper did not react, but crossed the clearing to check his mount's leathers. Satisfied that all was in order, he climbed into the saddle.

'We should go,' he said. 'This discussion has no resolution. We are wasting time.'

His pragmatic tone surprised Elaine. She took hold of her reins once again. There was more to this Piper than she had thought. He was right about one thing. Now was not the time, or indeed place, for debate. With Jaranyla's traces gathered in her hands she mounted her gentle mare. The kudo snickered her approval to be leaving the bleak and chilly glade.

'We can ride and talk I suppose,' Elaine said. 'If what you say is true, there remains the vital matter of what we can do to prevent the King following through with his plans to re-open the vortex.'

She nudged Jaranyla into a walk. The Piper fell in behind her on the narrow path.

forest clearance project
26th day of ter'bakamasa, 966

Terry stopped off at his garden on the way back to camp. His outburst, and the ensuing damage to his lovingly tended plot, had been preying on his mind. He had not visited it since the incident, now more than a week ago. With an embarrassment that was almost physically painful, it reminded him of the psychological nexus he had experienced back on Earth, when he trampled the young bloom. In a way, that event had brought him ninety-seven light years, to a horticultural project on a distant world that felt like home. And yet in this special place, in a fit of rage, he had caused even more destruction. Unforgivable.

The damaged plants at the edge of the bed still stood in their broken ranks, mute witnesses to his thoughtlessness, their severed stems grey and lifeless. He knelt beside them, picking up pieces of limp duntang that lay where they had fallen, and yearning to take back his impetuous swing of the hoe. What could he do? Time could not be reversed, and a mutilated shoot would remain mutilated.

His fingers tingled as he held the greenery. He plunged his spade-like hands into the earth to relieve the feeling, to soothe his tired bones and muscles with the cool refreshing feel of the soil. As it had done many times before, the earth sparkled at his touch. How? In the late afternoon, the sun had already sunk below the tree line and the malamajan clouds had started to gather. There were no rays of light to catch the soil's moisture. The vitality was in the earth itself, beneath Terry's hands.

He looked up. There *was* light. Not in the sky above, but deep within his mind. With the speed of a glacier slipping unnoticed over an ancient rockbed, the door in Terry's mind swung open revealing that summerland he had long dreamt of and always forgotten on waking. The land of his youth. This land. Berikatanya. An involuntary sob choked in his throat as he forced his hands deeper into the earth. With almost imperceptible slowness, the shreds of vegetation knitted themselves back together in front of his face. The restored duntang lifted their heads, springing up to catch the last feeble fingers of daylight.

*

'You should wash. Or sit downwind any way.'

Umtanesh grinned at Terry as he took a seat on the log beside him, still breathing heavily after completing his trek.

'Very funny,' Terry said once he recovered enough breath to speak. 'That climb out of Happy Valley always gets me in a sweat. By the time I've walked all the way back to camp I'm too damn tired to shower.'

'Downwind it is then,' Umtanesh said, still grinning. 'Or go throw yourself in river.'

'The river's at the bottom of the valley! That's twice the walk I've just done, plus more sweating on the way back.'

'Was easier when we have only small plot near to camp,' Pattana said, taking the last space on the log.

He lifted a steaming sunyok to his mouth.

'Stew taste funny tonight.'

'OK, OK, I'll get a wash,' Terry said, standing and groaning at the ache in his legs. 'Make sure you leave me some.'

When he returned wearing a fresh shirt and carrying a battered tin bowl brim full of the succulent meal, the others were discussing war.

'There is no way Queen will allow these attacks to continue,' Umtanesh said as Terry retook his seat. 'They already throw a dozen families out of homes and start build fences around water.'

'It not usually escalate again this soon after big battle.'

'Battle? Excuse for a fight that burned self out in flash of witch's fire? That nearly ten months ago.'

'Yes, and it burned out because of Batugan machine.' said Pattana. 'Nothing to do with witch.'

'I will bet she be keeping some new spells down inside her underwear for second try.'

'There's going to be another engagement?' Terry asked, swallowing a mouthful of stew.

The others shrugged, almost in unison. No-one spoke for several minutes, each waiting for another to voice what they were all thinking.

'Nothing for sure,' said Pattana at length. 'I don't know how they work this things out. Plotting and planning, war games. And... what the word? Issat?'

He looked at Umtanesh for help.

'Strategy,' said Umtanesh.

'Right. Strategy. But you be sure it not carry on like this much longer. No way. Queen already lose too much ground.'

'Too much face,' added Umtanesh, nodding.

'And she been training new Sakti Udara up. One who arrived with you Terry.'

'Training her up?'

'Elemental School. Mage learning. It good to have power from you blood and everything, but you must learn for use it. That Claire not making any beginner's mistakes next time, and that the truth.'

'But you don't know when this is going to happen?' Terry asked.

'Nobody does. Least, not outside inner rooms at Court and Palace. Simple men like us never told.'

'We don't get much news out here, that's true,' Terry nodded.

'Being out in country have nothing to do with it,' said Pattana, wiping the last of his stew from the bowl with a finger.

'It doesn't help!' Umtanesh said.

'Maybe not, but my cousin Utanna work with Palace guard. Even he don't know anything.'

'It be a big one though, this time,' said Umtanesh. 'All the tension that built up before, that didn't go nowhere when battle fizzled out. It all still there, wrapped up inside everyone. And now it burning hotter because of land grabs. Don't nothing make a man want to pick up a weapon more than seeing wife and kids put out of home.'

They fell silent once again. Terry thought about Claire, facing the prospect of another confrontation.

'Guys?'

Nembaka, who had as usual served himself last and was only now making his way to sit with the group, stood at the other side of the campsite, a steaming dinner bowl in his hands. Between them, an adult kuclar faced Nembaka. The fur standing up along its back could not hide the animal's extreme emaciation. It sniffed the air, growling.

'Guys?' Nembaka said again, his voice quaking.

Terry stood up. Pattana glanced at him, his eyes wide with fear.

'Careful Terry,' he breathed. 'Kuclar not usually dangerous, but this one starving. Be more desperate than normal.'

Terry inched away from their log bench until he stood in a clear spot of ground. He closed his eyes, conjuring a mental image of sunlight through open doors. Without being entirely sure of what he was doing, he fell forward onto the grass, slapping both hands suddenly and forcefully against the hard earth.

The kuclar span around at the sound but as it turned several square metres of ground fell away beneath it, pitching the animal into a deep pit, its sides as sheer as if they had been sliced with a scythe. Regaining his feet, Terry walked to the edge and stared down at the kuclar. One front leg was bent beneath it at an unnatural angle. A small trickle of blood oozed from between its jaws. It did not move.

As one the Berikatanyans dropped to their knees and bowed to Terry.

utperi'tuk trail
23rd day of ter'bakamasa, 966

'I don't believe the King can succeed in any attempt to recreate the vortex,' Elaine said, glancing over her shoulder to make sure the Piper rode near enough to hear.

They had left the chill of the gully behind them as the last golden rays of daylight dipped below the crest of the hill, but emerged into the warmth of the late afternoon sun once again on attaining the summit. Now, even this waned into early evening. Elaine drew her cloak more closely around her against the increasing cold. Neither of them had spoken since beginning their return journey, despite agreeing they could talk and ride at the same time. Several minutes more passed without the Piper reacting to her words.

'The ceremony requires all of the Elementals,' Elaine continued, in the absence of any response from her companion. 'We have no idea where Petani might be, and I could not rouse Lautan from his watery lair. Even supposing he has taken to the ocean.'

The Piper spurred his grey stallion to catch up with her until they were riding side by side.

'Yet two Elementals have returned,' he said. 'Is there not still a balance between Fire and Air?'

'Now it is you who are making assumptions,' Elaine

said, her nostrils flaring.

She gripped Jaranyla's reins, her knuckles white.

'I have learned the truth of it at last. I would never take part in the ceremony.'

'But with Air power he still may be able to—'

'I do not know the girl very well,' Elaine said, 'but I can certainly persuade her to side with me, given what I have uncovered. In any case, it is doubtful the portal could be opened with two Elements contributing. It will assuredly fail if there is only one.'

'The King may have an alternative source of power,' the Piper replied. 'One to supplement the forces of the Elements. To take the place of the absent energies and bring the ceremony to a successful conclusion.'

Elaine's eyes flashed.

'There is no power able to "supplement" that of an Elemental! What nonsense is this you are talking?'

'There have been other rumours from the Court,' the Piper replied, returning to his irritating evasive pattern of speech. He rode on for several moments, saying nothing more.

'Well?' cried Elaine, unable to contain herself any longer. 'What rumours? What powers? What do you mean?'

'The Blood King has returned to his heritage.'

The chill that now coursed through Elaine's body was no longer caused by lack of warmth from the fading sun. Her mind reeled. She gripped Jaranyla's saddle to prevent herself falling from her mount.

'It cannot be true!'

'My sources are very well connected.'

'It is madness!'

'Nevertheless. The King's distant forebears, their ancient and distasteful practices, have provided a means by which he can avoid any reliance on the Elementals to achieve his ends. He has unearthed the blood rituals for which he is named.'

'They were destroyed.'

'Apparently not. Not destroyed. Hidden, only. He has found them. Read them. And, if what I have heard is true, he has put them into practice. Blood runs once more in the deepest reaches of the Court. And the power it gives him is more than enough to reopen the portal.'

Chapter 17

The flaming torch held high above his head offered no assistance in navigating the complex maze of tunnels. Patrick Glass had been scrabbling around in the catacombs for an hour. He would soon have to admit to being lost. Had these people never heard of signposts? He had once scoffed at the detailed directions and department markers in his local hospital back in New York. What he would give for similar help here now.

A shadow of movement and a murmur of voices from beyond the next corner attracted his attention. He peered past the stone pillar.

'Jann! Thank God!'

Jann Argent stood engaged in muted conversation with another Court guard, whom Patrick recognised as a colonist from the Valiant.

'Patrick! When did you get back? And what are you doing down here?' Jann said. 'Are you lost?'

'Not now,' Patrick grinned. 'But it was close.'

'Are you looking for something?'

'Yeah. You. I need your help.'

'Well, you found me. And I could use your help too.'

Jann dismissed the guard.

'My help?' asked Patrick.

'Yes, but we can't talk about it down here. Too many corners.'

Jann looked over his shoulder.

'Too many echoes. Anyway, you were first. What can I do for you?'

'You remember the King asking me to lead the orchestra in some kind of ceremony, back before our expedition to the Valley?'

'I do.'

Patrick set his torch in an empty sconce and rubbed his aching shoulder.

'Well apparently I have to wear a proper costume.'

'Ah. Right. I *can* help you there. You need the Keeper.'

'What's that?'

'Not what. Who. The Keeper of the Keys. But keys aren't the only thing he keeps. He has a rack of costumes going back to the dawn of time. He's bound to have something suitable.'

Jann set off in the direction Patrick had come from, taking a different turn after a few metres. He kept to tunnels already lit with torches but even so each junction offered multiple choices. Within minutes Patrick was lost again, knowing neither where he was, or how to find his way back to their starting point.

'Slow down,' he said, panting.

'Nearly there!' Jann replied.

Moments later they rounded a corner into a wider area of tunnel, the intersection of six other corridors and passageways. Between the two largest of the seven openings stood a squat wooden door, polished to a silky patina and bearing scratches and dents from the knocks of many visitors.

Jann rapped on the old wood.

A hacking cough could be heard in the room beyond. The door creaked open to reveal a wizened face peering from the hazy room.

'Yes?'

'King wants my friend Patrick to be dressed as the orchestra leader.'

The Keeper stood in the doorway, blinking and scratching his head. Patrick began to think he was either deaf or addled.

'Ceremonial?' he asked eventually.

'Yes,' replied Jann.

The old man nodded.

'Come in, come in,' he beckoned to them, swinging the

door open wider.

Inside his chamber a fire burned in the grate, sending plumes of grey smoke into the room. It had been burning for some time, as a dense fug rolled and billowed in the space above Patrick's head.

The Keeper's leathery old fingers walked a shelf of massive hide-bound tomes while he muttered their titles. Reaching the required volume, he hefted it out from its place and dropped it onto a table. A cloud of dust took off to join the smoke at ceiling level.

'Should find what we need in here,' observed the sage, opening the cover and leafing to the middle of the book.

Jann and Patrick peered over his shoulder. The Keeper continued flipping through the yellowed pages, pausing to recite each title as he went.

'Moon Day ceremonial dress,' he declared, reading the Old Istanian text with practised ease. 'Palace Guard...'

Flip, flip, flip.

'So many ranks! Forest Ranger, Opening of the Royal Court.'

Flip, flip.

Patrick's attention began to wander. His finger traced a complex pattern of nested circles into the remaining dust on the Keeper's desk.

'Ah! Here we are! Orchestra Leader.'

He moved a candle carefully over the page, peering at it with his one good eye.

'Yes. I remember. I'm sure I have one over here.'

Jann returned the candle to its original position while the Keeper shuffled off to the other side of the room, muttering to himself. He opened a closet door and began rummaging through his extensive collection of rich tunics, coats and uniforms that hung in a bewildering multitude of colours and cloths.

Patrick remained beside the desk.

'Is he always this slow?' he whispered.

Jann flashed him an annoyed look.

'He might be old, but he's the only one who knows this stuff, and he's been a great help to me. Just have some patience!'

Jann moved to help the Keeper hold the heavy costumes out of the way so he could search those hanging at the back. Patrick picked up the candle and amused himself by dripping molten wax into his circular pattern, filling the depressions. The Keeper hobbled back with a robe over his arm.

'I think this one will—' he began, before his gaze fell on the results of Patrick's drippings.

'Careful there! What do you think you're doing? You'll damage my scroll!'

The old man snatched the candle from Patrick's hand and thrust it back into its candlestick. He glared at Patrick, looked again at the wax pattern and staggered back, the ceremonial garment slipping from his arm to land on the floor. The Keeper seized the candle once again and bent over the drying wax, tracing the pattern with shaking fingers as if to confirm what his eyes were seeing.

'How do you know this pattern?' he murmured, his gaze never leaving the desktop.

'I... I've always known it,' Patrick said, feeling the colour rise in his cheeks.

The Keeper stared at Patrick. Ignoring the fallen costume, he lifted the smallest bunch of keys from its hook above his desk, limped across to the other side of his room and unlocked a tall blackwood cabinet. Stretching up to reach to the back of the topmost shelf he retrieved a small shining object, locked the doors again and returned to the two men waiting beside his desk. He held up his hand and dropped a silver pendant to dangle above the desktop on its fine cable chain.

The pendant spun, catching the flickering light from the candles. The pattern it bore, enamelled onto the silver in glossy black and white, exactly duplicated the wax circles on the desk beneath it.

'I...' Patrick began. 'How is this possible? Where is that necklace from?'

'I retrieved it from the Valley of the Cataclysm shortly after the vortex closed,' said the Keeper. 'It fell from the neck of the Pattern Juggler as he was sucked into the void.'

Patrick looked at each of them, his face as pale as the white sections of the Pattern Juggler's device.

Jann stroked the front of his tunic.

'I've seen you doodle this pattern before, Patrick,' he said. 'How long have you been doing that?'

'Since I was a child. My father used to draw it for me. He taught me to copy it. I remember how pleased he was the first time I drew it exactly right. One of the only times he ever gave me any encouragement.'

The Keeper's eyes widened. He peered even more closely at Patrick, holding up his candle and looking first at Patrick's face, then the pendant, the desk, and back to Patrick.

'Remarkable,' he said at length, setting his candle down again, his hand trembling.

Wax splashed onto the pages of the old book.

'I thought I saw a slight resemblance,' he said, placing his hand on the page to quieten its tremors. 'But I never believed it would be possible.'

Jann retrieved the fallen robe from the floor of the chamber and dusted it off, his face a mask.

'I think we're going to need a different costume,' he said.

coastal region of utperi'tuk
23rd day of ter'bakamasa, 966

'It has been centuries since that fell power was used!' Elaine exclaimed, wheeling Jaranyla around to face the Piper. 'How are we to fight something we know nothing of?'

'Not nothing,' the thin man replied.

Elaine frowned, but the Piper continued, abandoning his habit of speaking in riddles.

'A few of my contacts have gained access to the ancient records. The text is arcane in the extreme. Hard to decipher and even harder to understand, but it seems likely the Blood rituals do not convey any power of their own.'

'Then what is their effect? They are still powerful enough to elicit horror whenever they are mentioned. There must be something to them, if the mere mention can cause such fear after all this time.'

'Indeed. They are a coercive force. Use of the Bloodpower allows control over whatever other magic is present, even against the will of its wielder.'

'Like the skill of the Pattern Juggler you mean?'

'In a way, although the Juggler can only operate on power already manifest, and only with the compliance of the provider of that power.'

'So how is Bloodpower different?'

'A user of Bloodpower does not require compliance, or for an Elemental to have called up their magic. They need only be present.'

Elaine shivered.

'By the palace of the immortal flame! He can suck the mastery of Fire from my mind even if I do not wish it?'

'Exactly. If you or the girl are present, the King will be able to wield Fire and Air through the auspices of Bloodpower. It is not clear whether you would even need to be conscious.'

'Then I must warn Claire,' Elaine said, spurring Jaranyla back once again in the direction of the Black Queen's Palace. 'Both of us must stay out of the Valley until we can find a way to combat this base magic.'

black queen's palace
26th day of ter'bakamasa, 966

Claire Yamani stood perfectly still, her eyes closed,

while her maid put the finishing touches to her ceremonial Elemental robes of power.

Her maid! Even now Claire had trouble accepting the idea that her position commanded servants, though she'd learned to summon the force of the wind with a single thought. Graduating from the Elementary Academy with the highest mark in recorded history, having mastered her gifts in time to avoid destroying the remaining buildings, still seemed a dream. So far she'd not woken up, despite pinching herself several times.

'There,' said Sangella stepping back from her task. 'You can open your eyes now, Kema'satu.'

Claire hardly recognised the woman who stood in the mirror in front of her. Her ash-blonde hair, newly washed and crimped, cascaded over the shoulders of a floor length gown of pure silk. Only it wasn't called silk here, she reminded herself. In Kertonian, it was satran. She twisted from side to side, checking all angles. Sunlight from her open window reflected off the folds and pleats of the gown, shimmering on the azure cloth as if the gown itself was the sky and had captured the sun in its threads.

'You look beautiful Kema'satu,' Sangella whispered, her eyes sparkling. She blushed.

Beautiful was a word Claire had never thought to hear applied to her. She smiled, a little embarrassed, thanking the maid both for her compliment and the excellent work on her gown and hair.

Outside in the Palace courtyard the ceremonial guests and performers had assembled ready to leave for the Valley of the Cataclysm. Whatever the King had written in his missive must have been very persuasive. One final visit to a place which wrought such ruin on so many lives, a ceremony that led to Claire spending most of her young life on a world those on Berikatanya couldn't possibly imagine.

Although sunny, the day was also blustery, wind sighing and rustling in the forest beyond the Palace walls. Claire stood on the threshold, inside the huge main door, until the Queen caught her eye. Seated on her black kudo, she offered Claire a half smile.

'It may be customary to keep a suitor waiting my dear,' she said, barely loud enough to be heard, 'but the same cannot be said of your Queen.'

Claire stepped out, blushing. A muted cheer rippled around the entourage, accompanied by a few gasps of "Sakti Udara". Whether because this was the first time any of them had seen her in full Air Mage regalia, or at the way the winds appeared to avoid her, Claire couldn't tell. She hadn't registered the presence of the breeze, yet her powers were now so instinctive she'd bent the air currents around her as she walked to Pembwana without even thinking about it. Not a single hair was disturbed as she took Pembwana's reins from the ostler's hand, thanked him, and mounted her steed.

'Apologies my Queen,' she murmured. 'The sight of so many awaiting me—'

'The Air Mage has no need of apology,' the Queen said, smiling more broadly. 'We are only teasing you. Come, it is late. If the King's reasons for calling us once more to the Valley are other than those he has shared with us, we would do well to arrive before him. We must leave.'

She urged Pembrang forward, leading the way through the Palace gates onto the blackstone grit road that cut a path over the greenery, skirted the forest, and disappeared up the nearest hill in the direction of the Valley. The day was warm despite the breeze and spirits were high among the travellers. A piper struck up a jolly tune. Claire glanced behind, expecting to see the familiar purple garb and unusual instrument of the Queen's chief advisor and choirmaster. She was surprised to discover that one of the passengers from the Valiant provided the travelling accompaniment. He played confidently without holding the reins, his mottled stallion content to follow the group unprompted by bit or bridle.

A few of the entourage recognised the song and joined in at the first chorus. After a short while they crested the nearest hill and the Palace disappeared behind them. From the tower the Queen's pennant waved a last goodbye in the stiffening breeze as it dropped out of sight.

black queen's palace
26th day of ter'bakamasa, 966

Elaine was relieved to see the Black Queen's pennant still flying as she approached from the West. She had made it in time! It had been many years since the Palace enjoyed the presence of the Fire Witch of Berikatanya, but Elaine welcomed the sight of the gleaming towers of obsidian and black granite. It being almost noon the Palace cast no shadow, but its atramentous walls seemed to absorb the daylight, sending an involuntary shiver along Elaine's spine. There was no danger here, surely?

Close to exhaustion, Jaranyla understood the urgency of the journey. Sensing their destination was near, she responded to Elaine's request for a final burst of speed. Kudo and rider galloped through the open Palace gate. Elaine reined her steed to a halt. There had been no signs of occupation, other than the pennant, since her first sight of the Palace.

'Hello!' she called. 'Does the Black Palace no longer deign to welcome its guests?'

Her words echoed from the ebon walls. There came no reply. Jaranyla's panting breath steamed in the chill of the shadowed courtyard, joining the flume rising from her quivering, hot flanks. Elaine dismounted, running to the stables to fetch a blanket and water for the exhausted animal. As she approached the stable door it creaked open, the wizened face of an old ostler appearing in the gap.

'Who is it?' he said before his rheumy gaze focused on Elaine. His eyes widened in shocked recognition.

'A thousand pardons Kema'satu,' he said with a low

bow. 'We were not expecting anyone.'

'My kudo requires attention,' Elaine snapped. 'We have had a long and arduous ride.'

The ostler's gaze flicked to the steaming beast and back to Elaine.

'Of course, of course. At once Kema'satu.'

He pulled the nearest blanket from a hook beside the door and hurried across the courtyard to cover Jaranyla. Once her quivering had subsided, he led her over to a trough and pumped water for her to drink.

'You'll—'

'I will see the mare is fed Kema'satu.'

Sure that Jaranyla's immediate needs would be met, Elaine strode into the main tower. At first glance it, too, was deserted. Her mental map of the Palace resurfacing with every turn and hall, she headed for the throne room, certain someone would be there at least.

The doors, when she reached the heart of the Palace, were shut, without even a guardsman to ensure their security. A side door opened and closed behind her and a young scullery maid hurried past carrying a tray laden with the remains of breakfast.

'Where is everyone?' Elaine demanded, almost causing the girl to drop her tray. 'I must speak with Cl— with the Air Mage at once!'

The young girl shuffled from foot to foot.

'Why, they are all gone mistress. Since early this morning.'

'Gone? Gone where?'

'To the Valley. For the ceremony.'

The black walls of the anteroom closed in on Elaine, her hands flying to her head in shock. The girl took a frightened step backward.

'So sorry mistress. Is there anything I can do?'

Elaine took a deep breath.

'No. Thank you. I must catch up with them, or there will be nothing anyone can do!'

The girl frowned, but thought better of seeking any explanation for Elaine's riddle. She bobbed a quick curtsey and scuttled off. Elaine returned to the courtyard where the old ostler stretched a large towel over a line to dry, having at that moment completed his rubbing down of Jaranyla. Elaine's kudo stood beside the stable door, chewing at a bale of jojo grass. She stroked the animal's flanks and began to check the saddle and traces.

'Begging your pardon Kema'satu but yon kudo won't be fit for riding until the morrow.'

'Tomorrow?' Elaine snapped.

The ostler twitched the blanket, his eyes betraying his fear of Elaine.

'That's ridiculous!' she continued. 'I—'

'She's fair exhausted,' he interrupted.

The man's expression telegraphed his conflicting emotions. Elaine had a fearsome reputation, yet he was clearly concerned for the animal's welfare.

'Don't think she'd last more'n a few hundred metres if you was to take her out now.'

'Damn it!'

He took a step back, cringing as if he feared her fire would consume him at any moment.

'Forgive me Kema'satu—I can see as it's important to you, but wherever it is you have to go, you can't do it on this beast. Not today. Not unless you want her dying underneath you.'

Elaine's eyes flashed, her fiery temper on the verge of boiling over. Something in the old ostler's face penetrated her red mist. She bit down on the bitter disappointment, letting out a long sigh.

'No. No, forgive me. You're right. She must rest. It's a two-day ride from here to the Valley. I still have time to catch up with them. See she's well fed and watered, and given the most comfortable stable.'

The ostler nodded, visibly relieved.

'That I will mistress,' he said. 'She's a lovely girl.'

Elaine stalked out through the Palace gates, unsure of her control over her temper and not wishing to frighten the old man any further. To her right a grassy slope ran down towards the forest, from which a handful of renegade trees had escaped and congregated to form a small glade on the near bank of the river, opposite the main part of the wood. Dappled shade beneath the trees looked cool, calming and appealing. Elaine walked down the slope and through the grove to the water's edge. The river ran past, gurgling, its song amplified by the canopy of leaves above.

She sat down, resting her back against the last tree and watching the running waters. Her mind raced faster than the river, calculating the likely point at which the Queen's entourage would stop and how early she needed to leave the next day to be able to catch them before they broke camp. She could not wait too long. Could not risk them entering the Valley itself before she overtook them. Who knew what fell power the King might bring to bear once Claire came within range?

The sound of the river drew her back from her reverie. Louder and more urgent noises had replaced its earlier tinkling song. The water, which had been slipping past with its usual glassy sheen when she sat down, now roiled and foamed. The river began to rise up the bank. Flecks of foam, thrown from the boiling surface, spattered her face and legs.

She scrambled to her feet, startled, as a column of bubbling white water rose from the river like an angry spectre.

Chapter 18

The foaming water continued to rise until it towered over Elaine's head. Droplets of spume splashed against her face, cold after the heat of the noonday sun. The river beneath the frothing pillar roiled and churned. Elaine watched, transfixed by the apparition, while the seething top of the column resolved itself into a beard, above which a watery maw opened wide.

'Bakara!' the mouth bubbled, using Elaine's Elemental name. 'I have come!'

The effervescence subsided as the water congealed into the form of a man, who stepped dripping onto the bank of the river in front of Elaine.

'Lautan, at last!' Elaine said, giving him a short bow. 'Why did you not come to me at the coast when I summoned you?'

The Water Wizard's eyes remained unfocused for a moment of inward concentration. The final few drips and rivulets of water disappeared as if his robes were made of blotting paper. Once he had solidified, Lautan returned her bow.

'My apologies Bakara,' he said, his voice deeper and richer now he had resumed corporeal form, although still retaining a slight phlegmy quality. 'Even the Water Wizard of Berikatanya cannot travel through the ocean at the speed of sound. I came as soon as I could, but I was uncounted leagues distant when I heard your summons. I have spent many years in the Kemudi Dalam Trench, where the seas are pure and deep, and the strongest currents bring news from all corners of civilisation. By the time I arrived at Utperi'Tuk, you had already left.'

He flashed her a wry smile.

'As I recall, patience was never your principal virtue,'

he added. 'But I am here now. How may I be of service?'

'How did you escape when the vortex snatched the rest of us into the void?'

A shadow passed over Lautan's face. For a moment, Elaine thought she could see a ripple in the man's cheek.

'By the skin of the great serpent Utan Besh,' he replied, his eyes seeming to sink further into his head. 'The vortex took the spray I had sent up, but I sensed the danger in time. I was able to draw the essence of myself back from the edge of the vortex and anchor it among the rocks of the Valley floor. The surface there is fragmented as I am sure you remember. Once I had spread out into the spaces between the boulders and pebbles, the pull of the abyss was insufficient to raise me a second time, although it was a near thing.'

'We were not so lucky,' Elaine said, eyeing the Wizard.

'No,' he said with a nod. 'So I saw. Where did you go?'

'All of us were flung an unimaginable distance across the cosmos. To a planet the inhabitants call Earth. But we were separated. Pulled apart in time. The Gatekeeper spent twice as long on Earth as I did. The Air Mage and his consort even longer. I would estimate double the time again, judging from the age of their daughter.'

'Sakti has a daughter?'

'Yes. She is here. And she is Sakti Udara now.'

The Wizard sat down on a large rock embedded in the riverbank.

'What of Petani? How did Earth fare in the maelstrom? And the Juggler? Is there word of him?'

'Of those two, I have no knowledge,' Elaine said, taking a seat on the rock beside the Wizard. 'We might guess that they were taken to the same place, but as to when? Who knows? For the most part it was pure chance those of us who have returned found passage at all.'

'Passage?'

'We journeyed in a ship the people of Earth built to cross the void between stars.'

The Wizard rubbed his eyes.

'Such wonders,' he muttered, shaking his head.

Elaine raised an eyebrow.

'Their magic is only in their technology,' she said, flicking her hand in a dismissive gesture. 'They have no powers such as ours. But we could sit here until the moons rise and I would still not have told you half the tale. It must keep for another day. For now, haste is needed to prevent a second cataclysm.'

The Wizard's eyebrows disappeared into his shock of grey hair.

'Whatever do you mean? There is to be a ceremony?'

Elaine filled in the blanks for the Wizard while the sun bid farewell to noon and the dappled shade crawled across the surface of the rock on which they sat.

'What can I do?' asked the Wizard once Elaine's account was complete.

'When Jaranyla is rested I shall ride after the Queen's party and stop Claire entering the Valley,' she said. 'Hopefully that will put paid to the mad King's plan. But we must also pass the message to the Gatekeeper. Jann Argent will be travelling with the King. You must stop him. Surely without a Gatekeeper the portal cannot be opened?'

'Is he still to be found at the Court?'

'We have no way of knowing. You'll have to search the path between Court and Valley until you find him.'

'And one more thing,' Elaine added. 'Those who travelled with us from Earth do not know me as Bakara. I'm certain Claire has never heard the name, and it may not be in the memories Jann Argent has managed to recover. If he is to believe the message comes from me, you must refer to me as Elaine Chandler.'

'Very well Elaine Chandler,' the Wizard replied solemnly, his voice beginning to bubble again as his form dissolved before her eyes. 'It shall be done.'

The last remaining vestiges of his body disappeared as

Lautan collapsed over the rock, his water running to join with the river below. Within moments no trace remained, the rock as dry as if it had sat in the full sun all day.

blood king's court
27th day of ter'bakamasa, 966

'I'm just relieved to finally be able to tell someone about it,' Jann said, leading his kudo from the barbican. 'Keeping it to myself was driving me crazy, but I had no idea who to trust.'

'There was no mention of Bloodpower in any of the scrolls you read?' Patrick asked, following Jann through the gate with his own mount.

'None. That's why I didn't ask the Keeper.'

'Even the idea of it is horrific, but your description...'

'...didn't come close to the reality.'

They took the path down to a brook that fed both the Court moat and the nearby lake.

'So you're not fronting the orchestra now?' Jann asked, changing the subject.

Patrick shook his head.

'Once the King learned who my father was, he insisted I take his place in the centre. You know what he's like when things are going his way. It was all "Capital, Glass, Capital! The Juggler is a vital player!". He's found someone else to handle the music. Didn't seem to think it was all that important any more. I don't understand him, to be honest. It was only two days ago he told me what a crucial role the orchestra leader is. Demanded I get kitted out for it.'

'The privileges of power—changing your mind and having everyone bow and scrape to fulfil the new plan. Still, if you hadn't come for that costume you may never have learned your true heritage.'

The King had left for the Valley earlier that morning. Patrick's kudo had thrown a shoe and Jann had remained behind so they could travel together. The delay did not sit well: they needed to start on their journey.

'My memory of the actual ceremony is still pretty hazy,' Jann continued. 'I can remember the Juggler being there in the centre of the quad, and the scrolls talk of him coercing the Elemental powers to form the vortex, but that's as much as I know.'

'Well you know more than me. At least you've read the transcripts. I have absolutely no clue what I'm supposed to do. The King was adamant that the power of the Juggler is an innate part of who you are. It's passed down through the generations. Apparently I'll know what to do when the time comes.'

They reached the water, leading their kudai to the bank.

'I guess the same is true of me,' Jann said, reaching into his saddle pack for a flask. 'This Gatekeeper thing is a closed book to me too. So far.'

He bent to fill the flask just as their two steeds wheeled away from the riverbank, each whinnying in fright as the surface began to boil. A moment later the figure of a robed and bearded man strode dripping onto the grass, the water drying the instant he set foot on land.

'Jann Argent,' the man intoned in a rich, deep voice. 'I bring a message from Bak—from the Fire Witch Elaine Chandler.'

'Wha...?' said Jann, stepping back in alarm.

Patrick struggled to calm the kudai, both spooked by the appearance of the old man.

'Who are you? And how—'

'I am the Water Wizard of Berikatanya,' said the man. 'Known among the Elementals as Lautan. I recognise you, Gatekeeper Jann Argent, though it is long since I last saw you.'

'Forgive me,' said Jann, recovering his composure. 'Although I am beginning to remember events, those who played a part in those events are often still lost to me. What message do you bring from Elaine?'

'The Witch explained how your memories were affected by the vortex,' Lautan said. 'Her message is that the Blood King intends to reopen the portal.'

'Portal?' said Jann. 'The King has already left for the Valley, but only to hold a memorial of the ceremony. We were about to follow him ourselves, Patrick and I, now that his mount has been shod.'

Patrick stepped out from behind the kudai, who had calmed down after their fright and were cropping the grass while keeping one eye on the Wizard.

'Juggler!' exclaimed the Wizard. 'I recognise you also, although unlike your companion you have changed a great deal since we stood together in the Valley.'

'You must be talking about my father,' Patrick said, touching his shirt beneath which his father's pendant hung.

'Ah yes, that would explain it,' the Wizard said, nodding. 'The resemblance is marked.'

He turned back to Jann.

'I am afraid there can be no doubt, Jann Argent. The Witch is concerned that the Blood King's true intent is to re-open the vortex. She has rather... personal reasons for preventing it. She has declared she will refuse to perform in the ceremony. She is on her way to persuade Sakti Udara—the Air Mage—to do the same.'

'The King expects us to take part also,' Patrick said, 'in our original roles. Even though neither of us is entirely clear what they are.'

'They would have come back to you,' said the Wizard. 'Such power as you wield is not easily put aside. But if the Witch is to be believed then you too must not partake.'

'The two of us will not be able to stop the King on our own,' said Jann, 'but if it is Elaine's wish to prevent the ceremony, we will do what we can.'

'There is more,' the Wizard said, stroking his beard. 'It may not be enough simply to stand by. The Witch believes the King intends to use Bloodpower.'

'She knows about that?' asked Jann in surprise.

'You know of it also?' said the Wizard, his eyes also wide with amazement. 'What is the extent of your knowledge?'

'I have none, beyond the fact of its existence,' Jann said. 'I've seen it being created, that's all.'

The Wizard laid a hand on Jann's shoulder.

'You have my sympathies young Gatekeeper,' he rumbled. 'If the stories tell even half the tale, that must have been a harrowing sight.'

'I'm still having nightmares about it,' Jann said. 'Did Elaine say how the Bloodpower would be used?'

'Supposition only,' replied the Wizard, 'but it is important for all the Elementals to remain at a distance from the King's attempt. It may be possible for him to coerce our powers even if we are not wielding them ourselves.'

'Then we should stay here,' said Patrick, 'if it is more dangerous to be in the Valley.'

'Unless the Bloodpower's reach is more extensive than Elaine expects,' Jann said. 'In which case it makes more sense to be there, where we can do something. Make an impact. React to events.

'There is another reason,' he added. 'None of us has yet discovered the whereabouts of the Earth Elemental. If he is here, and hears of the attempt, he will surely head for the Valley. We should be there to warn him of the danger.'

'You speak wisely Gatekeeper,' the Wizard said, his blue eyes sparkling. 'You should leave now.'

He turned to Patrick, an intense look on his face.

'You must make haste,' he said. 'You will find time is of the essence.

'And with that in mind, I can travel to the Valley more efficiently by river, so I will take my leave of you.'

They bowed, but the Wizard had already begun to dissolve. Within seconds he had flowed back into the river and was gone.

foothills of borok duset
27th day of ter'bakamasa, 966

A bustle of excitement spread through the Black Queen's entourage as the catering staff packed up the breakfast wagon and the order came to break camp. Claire left the complicated task of striking her tent to her aides. She needed to find the Queen. This second day of their journey was the final leg; they should reach the fabled Valley of the Cataclysm early in the afternoon.

The grass was still wet from the overnight malamajan, but the morning mist had almost burned away by the time Claire reached the Queen's tent. The Queen stood outside surveying the preparations for leaving and consulting with Hodak Negel. Her black bird, tethered to a travelling stand, regarded Claire with its piercing cobalt-blue eyes as she approached.

'Good morning my dear,' the Queen said, smiling. 'I trust you slept well?'

'Very well thank you your Majesty. How long before we arrive at the Valley?'

The Queen looked to the hodak for an answer.

'Good day to you Sakti,' said Negel with a slight bow. 'Provided we can be on the road within the hour, we should reach the entrance to the Valley soon after midday.'

A small tingle of anticipation ran through the back of Claire's head. She clapped her hands.

'Cool!' she exclaimed.

The Queen looked puzzled. She glanced at the blue sky and the remaining mist.

'I think the day will in fact be rather warm,' she said.

Claire hid her amusement while Negel excused himself to oversee the last of the preparations for the journey. A cloud passed over the sun as a breath of gentle breeze stirred Claire's hair, carrying a strand across her eyes that she tucked behind her ear with a practised gesture.

'Are you alright my dear?' asked the Queen. 'I have

learned to associate sudden changes in the wind with your mood swings.'

The unexpected chill of the hidden sun elicited a shiver. The Queen was unusually perceptive.

'I'm still worried about the ceremony,' Claire said. 'I don't really understand what it is I have to do.'

The Queen smiled.

'Come,' she said, setting off in the direction of the rudimentary corral where their kudai had spent the night. 'Walk with me. We can talk and ride.'

Seeing the Queen abandon her tent, several aides set to work to take down the sumptuous structure and pack it away.

'As I may have mentioned before,' she began, 'this will not be a full ceremony. We would not in any case be able to re-open the portal even if anyone was foolish enough to consider it. In the absence of the Earth Elemental and the Water Wizard the magic would be incomplete. It simply would not work.

'No, with only you and the Fire Witch in attendance we will just be creating a few fireworks to herald another attempt at détente between our two lands. It is the symbolism that is important in this case.'

'Why did anyone think it was a good idea the first time round?' asked Claire, coming to the nub of what had been bothering her for months. 'From what I've learned through conversations and the small amount of reading I've been able to do, the original ceremony was a disaster. It almost killed Elaine and my parents.'

'And several others too,' the Queen nodded as they neared the corral.

Two of the Queen's guard brought Pembwana and the Queen's kudo Pembrang out of the enclosure as they approached. The animals snickered in recognition.

'What you have to understand my dear,' the Queen continued, vaulting into Pembrang's saddle and taking the reins from the guard, 'is that Kertonia and Istania have been feuding for centuries, but in the years before the Cataclysm the situation had deteriorated to a dreadful low. After much desperate correspondence and many late nights of diplomacy, our two houses negotiated a treaty. The ceremony, which is the embodiment of an ancient ritual uncovered by the King's ancestors, was intended to be a celebration of the end of fighting.

'Of course, the Valley has not always been known as the Valley of the Cataclysm. Before the ritual it was a verdant place, but also one of the few natural harbours on Berikatanya. Both sides had aspirations to engage in voyages of discovery and possibly even trade if we were lucky enough to find other races in our world across the Lum-segar. Until the ritual, the Valley had been one of the chief reasons for warring between the Houses. Both wanted it for themselves.

'Although it happened many years ago when I was still a young woman, I have vivid memories of the excitement. We intended the ceremony to mark the beginning of a new era of peace, with a more equitable division of resources, sharing of prime land—like the Valley—and a total cessation of the violence. We were all sick of it by then. The ritual—in its original form—required all four Elementals to be present. Most people saw that in itself as a tangible and powerful symbol of unity. The first time they had ever acted in concert.'

Claire had mounted Pembwana while the Queen spoke. She fell in behind Pembrang on the narrow part of the path out of the dell in which they had camped. Once the track widened and they were again riding abreast the Queen continued with her story.

'I expect you're wondering what went wrong?'

'I was about to ask.'

'In truth I don't believe anyone really knows, although many theories were explored in the years following. Some believed it inevitable since the Elementals had never worked together before. Hindsight, as the Batu'n say, is a wonderful thing. Others blamed the lack of practice. Unlike the magic you have been using up to now, especially in school, we had no opportunity for a dry run. A few scholars suggested they could have prevented the vortex if they had been granted access to the scrolls. Professional jealousy in my view, and with considerable hubris too, since none of them had asked to work with the texts before the Cataclysm, or even demonstrated particular accomplishment with high magic. It may have been all of those, or any combination, or something that remains unknown to us all.'

'What had the others—those not expecting a vortex—believed would happen?'

The Queen adopted a puzzled frown for several minutes. At length she let out a heavy sigh.

'Do you know my dear, I can't honestly tell you. I half remember my father, before he died, reminiscing about how beautiful the Valley had been in his own youth. When it became one of our main battlefields, the lush landscape was soon reduced to a barren and blasted rock pile. I believe some expected the ritual to renew it, so it would serve as a permanent and ongoing symbol of unity and cooperation.'

Claire and the Queen had been riding at the front of the entourage, with only a few scouts ahead of them. They now crested the rise. Although still two hours or more away at the pace they were travelling, the Valley came into view, its dark and barren rocks a scar on the landscape which leeched the power from any light falling on it. Close to the Valley entrance the air rippled with what Claire took to be heat haze.

'Back then, each House had significant permanent encampments on either side of the Valley. As I said, it was a prime location to start the seagoing explorations both our peoples wished to undertake. We fought over access to the coast for decades. Those large camps had no other purpose than to prosecute the war.'

'Couldn't you have agreed to share it?'

'A wise question, my dear. Today we know that would have been the better approach, but you must understand our history. Any peace we have ever engineered has proved an uneasy one, riven with outbreaks of incursion, pillage and land grabbing. This time may be no different but—call me naïve—I believe we have to make the attempt. Even so, it's one thing for the Queen to declare peace. Quite another to enforce it against the will of the people. Antipathy between Kertonian and Istanian is bone-deep. Planted in the fertile soil of distrust and watered by the blood of our forefathers for generations past. It is not easily cut down.'

'So what felled the tree in the end?'

The Queen laughed.

'I don't think we've managed to bring it down yet my dear,' she declared, her eyes shining. 'A light pruning perhaps. In the end we came to our senses. Called a halt to the fighting and took stock. The Valley was a wasteland by then. Stark evidence of the effects of our constant warfare. We decided we'd had enough. When the King revealed the ritual, said it would regenerate the Valley and herald a new era of peace between our peoples, there was a general yearning for it to be true.'

They started their descent. The sight of the ocean shimmering in the distance reminded Claire of her second question.

'Have there been any other attempts at the ceremony?' Claire asked. 'To get it right I mean?'

They rode on for several minutes, the path becoming steeper and rockier, before the Queen replied.

'The rite is complicated. We have never again assembled all the components for a repeat of the full ceremony. Even if we were to suggest it, I don't think there is the will. We did hold a small memorial, on the twentieth anniversary of the Cataclysm. In honour of the lost Elementals.'

'Were the original problems resolved that time?'

'It wasn't a true repeat—more of a reduced version with a limited attendance. I don't know what we were expecting, but nothing happened. And it didn't satisfy our deep grief at the loss of our most powerful Mages. We never performed the rite again.

'Until now,' the Queen added, staring ahead at the approaching entrance to the Valley.

The rippling effect Claire had spied from the top of the hill now hung in the air in front of them. Close up, she could see it wasn't heat haze, or indeed anything natural.

'What is that?' Claire asked, pointing at the seething curtain of distortion standing between them and the Valley.

The Queen flashed her a dark look.

'I said the ceremony was supposed to renew the Valley,' she said. 'The result was not what most of us expected, or wanted.'

They stopped a little way away from the barrier. Pembwana tossed her head, whinnying with fear. Claire soothed her.

'This... effect,' she said. 'This is a legacy of the ritual?'

'Yes,' the Queen replied. 'Here on Berikatanya we had no way of knowing what happened to those who were lost to the vortex. What its effects may have been on them. But the ritual also affected the land on this side. The changes are restricted to the Valley. This curtain of strangeness, with its endlessly eddying air, marks the limit of their influence.'

'Influence? You mean the portal is still active?'

'Not active in the sense of being a gateway, no. But whatever it did to the Elementals who fell through, has also had an effect here.'

'What kind of effect?'

'Time passes more slowly on the other side of the barrier,' the Queen said, shifting in her saddle. 'I do not understand such things, but it is true nevertheless. Those who remained in the twin camps after the Cataclysm soon noticed the traders they dealt with from outside the Valley had grown much older between visits than they should have. Young people visiting relatives in other parts of the country, or serving apprenticeships, returned to find their parents unchanged, while they had aged considerably.'

'So what did they do?'

'When they learned what it meant to live in the Valley of the Cataclysm, they abandoned the encampments. The era of peace was upon us. No-one knew how brief it would turn out to be. Ideas of sea-going adventure were shelved in favour of rebuilding our fractured society, so there was no reason to stay. Once the camps had been struck and the wilderness had re-established its hold on the land, nothing remained to mark where they stood.'

'And we're going in there? Through the curtain?'

'We are.'

lem tantaran
29th day of ter'bakamasa, 966

Patrick Glass raced across the open countryside astride his kudo Jarapera. In front of him, Jann Argent lay almost flat against his mount's back, urging the foam flecked animal to even greater speed now that they had left the foothills of Tubelak'Dun behind them. Patrick's breathing felt ragged in his chest. Above the thundering of the hooves he could not hear whether Jann fared any better, but the heaving of his shoulders and the sweat stains covering the back of his shirt suggested he too was exhausted. They could not possibly cover the whole distance to the Valley at this pace.

'Jann!' Patrick gasped. 'Wait. Slow down!'

His voice almost inaudible, Jann's words flew back over his shoulder, each punctuated with a breath.

'No time! Must reach Valley!'

'We'll kill the kudai at this rate!' Patrick yelled. 'We

have to rest for a while!'

They approached a small copse, one of many dotting the route between the Court and the Valley, each one different in both shape and its mix of trees and bushes. Patrick recognised this particular one. They had camped here on their first sojourn to meet the pilgrim. It had water, and plenty of shade. A good place to rest the animals and themselves.

'Here!' Patrick shouted, slowing his mount to a canter. 'I'm stopping here.'

Jann galloped on, but after a few hundred metres, noticing Patrick was no longer behind him, he wheeled his kudo around and trotted back to where Patrick waited, his face a mask of anger.

'What are you doing? There's no time to lose!'

'We'll lose all of our time if the kudai die under our arses,' Patrick said. 'It's obvious we can't go the whole way without rest. We know this place. It's as good as any, and better than most.'

Jann wiped the sweat from his brow, still creased into a deep frown.

'Ach!' he exclaimed, sliding from his saddle and leading his foam-flecked kudo Perak into the shade.

Patrick dismounted and followed. Once beneath the canopy of the copse they rubbed the kudai down, led them to the water, and sat beside each other on a fallen tree while their animals quenched their thirst. To one side of the log a small spring fed the pool. Patrick filled his flask.

'I've been trying to figure out what the Wizard meant,' he said, taking a long drink from his flask before filling it once again.

'Which part?'

'The bit about time being of the essence.'

'Should have thought that was obvious,' Jann said, passing his own flask over to be filled. 'It means we need to get there as soon as we can. It means we shouldn't be wasting time here.'

Patrick ignored the jibe.

'No, there was more to it than that. You didn't see the look he gave me when he said it. His comment was intended for me personally, but I can't work out what he was getting at.'

'Well look, can you think about it while we ride? The kudai have stopped sweating.'

'Yeah but they're still knackered,' Patrick said. 'Another couple of hours won't make any difference.'

'Have you forgotten the vortex effect in the Valley?' Jann asked, replacing his water flask in a saddle pouch. 'Once the King's company passes through the ripple curtain they'll be working on Valley time.'

Patrick jumped to his feet.

'That's it!' he cried, an enormous smile creasing his face. 'You can relax Jann. We have as much time as we need, pretty much.'

'What are you talking about?'

'That was a timely reminder on your part,' said Patrick, laughing at his own joke. 'Right now the time dilation effect in the Valley is working in our favour. Everything beyond the distortion operates more slowly than outside. Remember we thought we'd only been with the pilgrim for a couple of days? When we returned to Court nine months had passed.'

'So...'

'So once the King, or the Queen, passes into the Valley they slow down, relative to us.'

He completed a quick mental calculation.

'Every hour out on this side is less than a minute in the Valley. Even if we camped here for the whole night, they will only have travelled another few hundred metres. Like I said, relax.'

*

They resumed their journey the next morning. Jann had taken more persuasion than Patrick expected. For some reason he seemed incapable of getting his head around the time dilation effect. Jann had only been exposed to Earth culture for eight years, and all of that on the prison moon, whereas Patrick had watched science fiction his whole life. He was thoroughly acquainted with paradoxes, parallel time lines and retrocausality. In the end he had convinced Jann it would be OK for them to take a proper rest before continuing.

After Patrick's explanation, the journey on the second day proceeded at a more sedate pace. They arrived at the Valley entrance around midday. In front of them, the air shimmered under the influence of the portal effect. Patrick reined Jarapera to a stop, but Jann continued.

'Wait,' Patrick said.

'What for?' asked Jann, slowing Perak to a walk. 'We're nearly there.'

'I've been thinking some more about this time stuff.'

'Not that again! Enough already! I understand. At least, as much as I need to. Come on! Let's go.'

'No, we can't. Not yet. Once we're through the curtain, it starts to operate against us.'

'Why? When we're on the other side, we'll be travelling at the same rate as everyone else in the Valley. At least, I think that's what you said. So OK we may need to pick up the pace a bit to catch them, but they shouldn't be that far ahead.'

'No. The problem isn't catching up. It's what happens on this side. Once we pass the curtain we'll be in the same position as they are now. Anyone following us will easily catch us.'

'Who's coming after us? The King is already on the other side. The Queen too, for all we know. Even if she isn't it won't make any difference once she arrives.'

'Maybe not, but it may give us problems on the way out.'

'How?'

'We don't know what will happen in the Valley. Can we stop the ceremony? Stop the King? What then? What if we need to leave the Valley in a hurry?'

Patrick jumped down from Jarapera and began to pace up and down, thoughts piling in on each other. He put his hands to his head, struggling to contain them.

'Argh! No, better, say one of the others tried to escape and we needed to catch them.'

'What? Who?'

'It doesn't matter. Like I said we don't know what will happen. But if someone manages to get out of the Valley when we're trying to stop them, once they leave through this curtain of time, we won't have a hope of catching them. Do you see?'

Jann had brought Perak to a standstill. He frowned.

'Not really.'

'It's the same effect in reverse!' Patrick said, fighting down his exasperation. 'Right now we're on Berikatanyan time. Call it fast time. They—whoever's inside—are experiencing Valley time. Slow time. If we were on the inside travelling out, chasing someone, then once they come through they would switch to fast time and we would still be going slow. They'd leave us standing.'

Jann dismounted and walked back towards Patrick.

'OK. Yes, I see what you're saying. But what can we do about it?'

'I think this is what the Wizard was trying to tell me. That there *is* something I can do about it. Something in the Juggler's portfolio that will allow me to change it.'

'But you don't know how to use any power you might have. You've already admitted that.'

'I know! But I have to work it out! It's important.'

'The Keeper told us the Juggler can only deal with forces the other Elementals create. How can you do anything when there aren't any Elementals here?'

'Maybe the portal effect is enough? It's like a residue of the vortex. Elemental power created it in the first place. Maybe I could manipulate it if I could work out what to do.'

Jann sat down on the grass, pulled out a stalk and sucked on it.

'Well, like you said, we don't have to hurry. Not where we're standing right now. Take your time.'

Patrick joined him. Perak snickered, walked over to stand by Jarapera and began to chomp at the greenery. A pair of large insects buzzed past, servicing the flowers. After a while, Jann pulled the chewed grass stalk from his mouth.

'Your Dad was the original Juggler, yes?' he asked.

'Apparently.'

'And the ability passes from father to son?'

'So they say.'

'So there must be some trait—something you have in common with your father—that lets you do whatever it is you can do.'

'I guess. But that's not going to help us much. I never really knew my father, remember?'

'Hmm. OK. But if we're to have any hope of working it out, we have to assume it's noticeable. Something unusual that you can do, or you've always been good at.'

'Well don't go looking for anything heroic. That's not me. I was always the shy kid, remember? I've only ever been really good at one thing. Designing stuff. Drawing. That's why I went into graphics.'

'Doesn't really strike me as an ability that would help you meld magical powers or bend them to your will.'

'It doesn't sound powerful, but there is a kind of magic in drawing. In artistic endeavour in general. Creating something where there was nothing before. Nothing except a few art supplies.

'In fact,' Patrick went on, following his train of thought with a gleam in his eyes, 'you might say there's a direct parallel between my day job and what the Pattern Juggler does. Both start with raw materials—me with pen, or pastels, and paper, and the Juggler with Elemental forces—'

Jann laughed.

'Not much difference is there? The unfettered Elemental power of the Fire Witch on one side and a crayon on the other. You couldn't imagine two things more alike!'

He laughed again. Patrick gave him a shove and he fell on his back in the grass, still laughing.

'Scoff all you like, on a fundamental level it's the same thing. Whatever material you're using, both end up with something else. Something created from the stuff you started with.'

Jann recovered his composure and sat up.

'OK, OK, point taken. So when you were starting out on a new project, what process did you go through? How did you start to conceive the finished article?'

'I didn't really have a process. It just came naturally.'

Jann's stared at Patrick open-mouthed.

'I think you might be on to something after all. Sorry for mocking. I'm guessing you've not thought any artistic thoughts since we got here?'

Patrick shrugged.

'No. Not really had the need. Or the inclination.'

'Do it now.'

'Do what?'

'Imagine tearing down that rippling curtain thing over there. Think about it as if you were contemplating a drawing. No! Wait! Assume you're creating a new version of the Valley without the time dilation effect in it.'

'That's a tough one,' Patrick said, scratching his head. 'I don't know how to destroy a time dilation effect.'

'You don't have to know,' Jann replied. 'You didn't always know exactly how a drawing would turn out did you? Didn't stop you making a start with it.'

Patrick jumped to his feet, staring at the undulating curtain of air. He began to imagine how the scene would change if the ripples were not there. He reached beneath his shirt and pulled out his father's pendant, rubbing his thumbs over the patterned surface. After a while, the nub of an idea came to him. From somewhere deep in the kernel of his creative self, in a kind of mental "hub" that up to now he had not consciously been aware of, an image formed. The sight of the Valley as it had been before the vortex. Whether it was an accurate depiction he could not tell, but the detail was incredibly fine.

'Wow,' he said.

'What?' said Jann, turning to stare in the same direction. 'I can't see anything.'

'I can,' said Patrick.

This was the place. The place he never knew was inside him, but which he recognised now as the source of all his best work. It had always been there. But on Earth all it could give him were drawings. Here on Berikatanya, where magic still lived, it gave him access to the Pattern Juggler's powers. His by birthright, power enough to do anything his imagination could conceive.

He lifted a hand, reaching out towards the rippling air, his palm turned up to the sun. In a single gesture, with his image held firmly in mind, he gripped the curtain and pulled.

valley of the cataclysm
30th day of ter'bakamasa, 966

'It's Utamasa here!' exclaimed Claire as she emerged from the curtain into the Valley.

The Queen, who'd ridden through the barrier in front of Claire, turned with a smile.

'The seasons wax and wane at a different rate on this side,' she said. 'One never knows what one will find on stepping through the veil.'

She faced ahead once again and stared down the Valley. Claire followed her gaze. Grassy hillocks with small clumps of trees dotted here and there gave way to a more barren and rocky landscape as the land dipped towards the ocean, the grey surface of the granite relieved by colourful mosses and outcrops of hardy flowering plants, purple, pink and vibrant blue.

'I'd forgotten how beautiful it can be here,' the Queen said, urging Pembrang forward.

One by one the entourage traversed the occultation, a quiet murmur of surprise passing along their ranks as each member noticed the change in season, or expressed delight at the view.

In the cleft between the two cliffs that defined the east and west sides of the Valley, Claire caught a glimpse of the ocean. A sea breeze whipped the tops of small waves into white spray. Even at this distance she thought she could smell the salt in the air.

The Queen led the assembly along the rocky path. They passed a line of shadow cast by the eastern hillside when a strange noise from the direction of the Valley entrance drew Claire's attention.

'What was that?' she called, nudging Pembwana to face back up the trail.

The sound had at first reminded her of someone tearing a sheet of wet paper, the hard edge of the ripping noise softened and deepened by the presence of moisture. Now it had changed to a low rumble. The clamour was approaching rapidly. The Queen rode up.

'I don't know my dear,' she said, steering Pembrang to a stop beside Claire, 'but it sounds to be heading this way.'

As they watched, a dark cloud appeared at the top of the rise they'd recently left, rolling towards them. As it descended the hill, Claire could see it wasn't a cloud. It was a line of destruction, crawling along the ground at a frightful pace, kicking up billows of dust in its wake. Claire's stomach flipped. Her immediate reaction was to run from the approaching menace, but almost instantly she realised she'd never outpace it. Pembwana reared at the sight but Claire controlled the animal with a word. The rapidly moving brume scoured across the landscape.

Where it had passed, grasses turned brown, withered and died on the spot. Trees collapsed in on themselves, their leaves shredded to dust, their trunks sagging with rot as they fell to the ground.

The wave of ruination roared past the entourage, laying waste to all living things except the Queen's party. Within seconds all that remained of the once beautiful scene was a dust bowl and a few petrified shards of tree trunk, sticking up out of the dirt like faceless guardians of the past.

valley of the cataclysm
30th day of ter'bakamasa, 966

'Whoa!' shouted Jann.

A layer of fine powder settled on the now barren landscape in front of him.

'Did you expect that?'

Patrick trembled, his face white.

'Not exactly. Although I can understand why it's happened.'

'Oh?'

'Yeah. Think about it. The Valley has existed at a different rate of time for several decades since the original Cataclysm. A slower rate. I just took away whatever was causing that.'

'So what time is it on now?'

'The same as us. As the rest of Berikatanya. What you could now call normal time.'

'Where did everything go?'

'Anything that was alive here before, well, effectively it was born, or germinated, or grew years ago. Because the Valley had been left so far behind in time, there is nothing left here, apart from the rocks, that could survive catching up with the present. As far as living things inside the curtain were concerned, "normal time" is sixty years into the future. Or as near as makes no difference.'

Jann shook his head.

'Too much for me. But it's done now. Let's get going.'

They persuaded their nervous kudai to step onto the dust-covered ground of the Valley. Once the animals had satisfied themselves that the earth was still solid they seemed to settle. The two men proceeded down into the Valley at a gentle trot. Jann reached inside his tunic and pulled out the Gatekeeper's amulet he had been wearing since being reunited with his few belongings at the space port. If ever there was a day to make a stand, this was it.

After an hour or so they reached the pilgrim's shack in sombre mood. Soft grey clouds, unmoving in the stillness of the morning, occluded the sky above them. There was no sign of the old man, but the dilapidated hut, perched on its outcrop of rock, gave them a good view of the Valley below. They could not see the granite quadrangle, the floor of the Valley being hidden beneath a thick layer of morning mist that roiled and bubbled. It was like looking into a black cauldron.

Jann's head ached. The scene was so familiar, but there were pieces missing, both in the tableau he could see and from his memory. Opposite them, atop the western hill, the Black Queen had already adopted her position for the ceremony. Dressed in her full black regalia and sat upon an impressive ebony stallion she looked to Jann like a shadow queen. An afterimage of a kudo and rider left behind after the real thing had departed, or perhaps a herald from the underworld sent ahead to presage the arrival of the living counterpart.

'Where is the Air Mage?' Patrick asked.

He was right. There was no sign of Claire. Jann would have expected her to stay with the Queen. He scanned the scene for any hint of her. As he did so a shaft of sunlight broke through the cloud cover, illuminating the willowy figure of the new Air Mage as she stepped out from behind the Queen's mount. Dressed in ceremonial costume, she stretched out her arms to begin conjuring her winds.

'She's there,' Jann said, pointing. 'Looks like she's going to try to clear this mist.'

A spark of reflection flashed from the black diamond set into the Queen's obsidian head band, blinding Jann for an instant. A sharp stabbing pain lanced through his mind and he collapsed to his knees on the rocky ledge.

'Argh!'

'What is it? What's wrong?' Patrick cried, crouching down beside Jann and laying a hand on his shoulder. 'Are you OK?'

Jann looked up into the other man's eyes.

'I should be down there. On the quad. And so should you. I remember it now. I remember it all.'

Patrick stood.

'That's great Jann. But you also need to remember we're here to stop the ceremony, not take part in it.'

Jann rubbed his eyes. He stared down into the Valley again, shaking his head.

'Yes. Yes, of course. Sorry. Just... it all came flooding back.'

At the foot of the rebuilt alabaster bell tower which stood at the northernmost end of the Valley, a group of women stood huddled together. Jann recognised some of them from Court. Their husbands had all been lost to the vortex on the day he had been sucked through with Patrick's father. Whatever fate had befallen them he did not know, but the intervening decades had not dulled the pain for the widows. Revisiting the scene of their loss had stirred up the old feelings. The women were supporting each other but all were visibly distraught. The sound of their sobbing could be heard even from this distance.

By contrast a peal of laughter reached them from the eastern hill. A richly clad group of three men stood near the Queen's kudo. Something had amused them. As Jann watched one of the men slapped a second on the back while the third bent double, mirth catching in his throat and making him cough.

As yet, there was no sign of the Blood King. Jann knew it was only a matter of time.

'Come on,' he said to Patrick. 'We have to stop Claire.'

'Wait!' called Patrick as Jann spurred Perak down the hill. 'Look!'

He followed the line of Patrick's pointing finger. Already halfway down the hill in front of them, Elaine's chestnut mare Jaranyla picked her way along the granite path, the Fire Witch's mane of red hair a glowing beacon against the unremitting grey and black of the hillside. Beyond the two cliffs, where the sea glistened and sparkled as the sunlight flashed between clouds, a boiling column of water had risen up, rolling towards the coast at speed.

Chapter 19

Jann watched in awe as Claire, no longer the plain girl from the Valiant, summoned her powers. Radiating confidence and inner strength she raised her arms and closed her eyes in concentration. The beginnings of a circling current of air teased her long, ash-blonde hair from her shoulders. Impelled by the Elemental's will, the gyrating wind strengthened. It caught the mist lying in the Valley and siphoned it from the quadrangle, sending it spiralling upward like the ghost of a tornado.

'We must catch up with Elaine!' Jann said, digging his heels into Perak's sides. 'Come on!'

He took off down the rock-strewn trail. Ahead of him on the same path, Elaine was already almost halfway to the Valley floor a hundred metres below. Unusually for such an accomplished rider she made hard going of the loose stone track. Jann pushed his kudo to reckless haste, heedless of the danger. Shards skittered and danced beneath Perak's hooves, others flew past his head, dislodged by Patrick who kept pace with him a few strides behind. Within moments, they had almost caught the Fire Witch.

'Elaine!'

Jann's voice echoed across the granite landscape.

'Wait!'

Elaine turned in her saddle to stare back up the trail, the whites of her eyes flashing in the gloom. She reined Jaranyla to a stop.

'How long have you known about the Bloodpower?' Jann yelled.

The Fire Witch waited while he closed the gap between them.

'About the concept or about the King having dusted it

off again?'

'Does it matter? Apparently we shouldn't even be here!'

'Someone had to tell Claire.'

'Someone might have told *me!*' Jann said. 'Maybe I could have avoided a week of nightmares!'

Elaine sighed, turning to look across the Valley.

'Yes. I suppose you're right. I didn't learn the King's intent until after I'd left. All I could do was send word with Lautan. I wasn't sure how much you'd remembered. All Elementals know about the Bloodpower. I assumed you would too. Centuries have passed since it was last used. Elemental power is vastly superior—there was never any need to resurrect it. My outburst at Court may have prompted the King to seek other alternatives, since he remains determined to go ahead with this mad attempt.'

A bell chimed from the alabaster tower, its flat, broken note rebounding from the Valley around them. In response to the tone, an orchestra struck up. Jann recognised the music.

'Is this the ceremonial music? The lullabies?'

'Yes, but that's a full orchestra. Last time we had only the Piper.'

'Where is he?' asked Patrick.

'I haven't seen him,' Elaine replied. 'He told me he would let the Queen know of our change of plan.'

'He won't have done that if he's not here,' Jann observed drily. 'So we still need to reach Claire.'

He swung Perak back along the path.

'Wait,' said Patrick, staring ahead. 'Look.'

On the path below them, a small contingent of the Blood Watch were approaching from the Valley floor. On the narrow trail, the three friends had no way of avoiding the red riders.

valley of the cataclysm
30th day of ter'bakamasa, 966

'That could've been better,' said Claire turning to the Black Queen as her ghostly tornado dissipated.

'It was perfectly fine my dear,' replied the Queen. 'You worry too much. All you need is a little more confidence. Your skill is outstanding, especially when one considers the short time you have had to develop it.'

'So you think I'll be OK.'

The Queen smiled, staring across the Valley at the movements of the King's troops on the opposite hill.

'I am sure you will be a lot better than "OK" dear. Such a strange expression.'

She stood in her saddle the better to see further down the hillside, where a small group of riders huddled together on the narrow path.

'I see your friend the Fire Witch has arrived, along with the Gatekeeper and... can it be? One of their party is wearing the costume of the Pattern Juggler! I cannot think who they have found to fulfil that role, but I suggest you take up your position dear, I believe the ceremony will be commencing forthwith.'

Claire shivered. She still didn't trust herself to handle such a monumental task. What if everyone disappeared again like last time? It would be a painful irony to be returned to Earth after all they'd been through. She followed the Queen's gaze across the Valley. A small squad of guards approached Elaine and the others.

'Who are those riders?' Claire asked the Queen.

'They belong to the Blood Watch my dear. The King's most able guardsmen.'

'What are the King's men doing?'

'I'm not certain,' she replied. 'It is most peculiar, but they appear to be trying to prevent the three of them taking their places on the quadrangle.'

She raised a hand to shield her eyes from the sun.

'I think you should go down anyway Claire,' she said. 'Even the Blood Watch won't be able to stand in the way of the Fire Witch of Berikatanya for long!'

*

Jann had no time to react to the guardsmen before Elaine confronted them.

'Let us pass!' she ordered. 'We have important business with the Air Mage!'

The leader, wearing the uniform of a Pena-lipan or Watch Commander, fidgeted in his saddle.

'Begging your pardon ma'am,' he began.

'I am not your "ma'am"!' Elaine spat. 'It is inconceivable that you do not know who I am, but perhaps a demonstration—'

The guardsman held up his hand.

'That won't be necessary Tema'gana,' he said. 'But I am under direct orders from the King. All Elementals and other participants are to leave the Valley immediately.'

'That doesn't make any sense,' said Patrick. 'The King is here to perform the ceremony. We are a part of that.'

Patrick winked at Jann. It was clear what his friend was doing.

'Yes,' Jann added. 'That's right. We need to take our positions on the quadrangle. The music has already started.'

The other three guards had dismounted while they were speaking. Each now took hold of one set of reins.

'My men will lead you back to the top of the hill,' said the guardsman.

An unexpected breath of wind from the Valley caught Jann's attention. Claire had taken up her position in the Northwest corner of the quad and begun to summon her winds.

'Elaine!' he shouted.

The Witch had already grasped the situation. Yanking the reins from the soldier's hands she reared Jaranyla in front of the guardsman's kudo, forcing it back onto a hillock beside the trail. With a whoop, Elaine spurred Jaranyla down the path towards the Valley floor.

Taking advantage of the confusion, Jann kicked his guard in the chest and urged Perak to follow the Witch.

'Sorry!' he called over his shoulder at Patrick. With all three guards now restraining her, Jarapera remained immobilised on the hillside.

valley of the cataclysm
30th day of ter'bakamasa, 966

Jann reached the bottom of the hill side by side with Elaine. Together they raced across the cold stone, the clattering of hooves echoing around the Valley basin. Claire's freshening wind whipped at Jann's face and hair, sending a chill through him. The two kudai splashed through shallow sea water now covering the Valley floor, throwing up salty spray that slicked Jann's face. Whipped by the wind, the surface of the water churned and foamed, sending up great plumes of fog to replace that which Claire had recently blown away. Within seconds it had become so dense Jann could not make out Perak's head in front of him. Unable to see the path or avoid obstacles, the confused kudo slowed to a walk and soon stopped altogether.

'What do we do now?' he said to Elaine, though the gloom had rendered her invisible too. His voice echoed eerily.

'Claire!' she shouted from Jann's right. 'Stop! Whatever you're doing, stop! We have to talk!'

Before either of them could move, the fog began to coalesce, rising from the ground like some impossible grey magic carpet, gathering itself into a dark storm cloud. The eddying wind carried the nebulous vapour in a slow circle until it hovered above Claire's outstretched arms.

In the newly cleared air, Jann could see they had almost reached her. The quadrangle lay only a hundred metres in front of them. Elaine sat astride Jaranyla, unmoving, watching the cloud.

Claire opened her eyes.

'What about?' she asked.

A lightning bolt shot from the thundercloud, striking the rock beside Claire's foot. She jumped back with a shriek. The air current dropped.

'Lautan!' shouted Elaine, urging her mount forward. 'Enough!'

The storm cloud broke before they had crossed the short distance to the quad, raining down onto the polished granite surface and soaking Claire to the skin in an instant. The cloudburst resolved itself into the form of the Water Wizard.

'What kept you?' he bubbled as soon as he could speak.

Elaine leapt from her saddle. She reached Claire's side as Jann dismounted. The nascent Air Mage stared at the Water Wizard, shock and awe plain on her face.

'Elaine?' she said, not taking her eyes off the Wizard. 'Who is this? What's going on?'

'It's OK,' Elaine reassured her. 'He's a friend. He's like us. It's the Water Wizard. One of the other two Elementals I told you about. We're here to help.'

Claire shivered.

'With the ceremony?'

'No young lady, quite the opposite,' said the Wizard.

Jann climbed onto the quadrangle. As he approached the group, Elaine put her hand on Claire's shoulder.

'We had to stop you,' she said, wrinkling her nose at the feel of Claire's wet clothing. 'Lautan! Could you not have been more careful? She's soaking!'

The Fire Witch summoned her power. Within seconds Claire's robes were steaming. In another minute they had dried. A small wan smile creased the corners of her mouth.

'Thanks.'

'Did you know about this too?' Jann shouted across the remaining distance between them. 'How long have you known of the King's plan? '

Elaine's eyes flashed.

'I do not know the King's plan!' she said, rounding on Jann. 'He keeps his counsel to himself. Or at least, it doesn't travel far beyond the Jester. Do you think I am in league with him? With either of them?'

'No, I—'

'That I would risk being flung back to Earth? Or some other dark hole of the universe?'

'Of course not, I—'

'Then I suggest you mind your tongue, Gatekeeper.'

She spat his title like an insult, turning back to Claire. The young Air Mage stood transfixed, her gaze locked on the amulet hanging around Jann's neck.

'We must all leave,' Elaine said. 'There is no time to explain, but it is possible the King has—'

A fanfare of trumpets from the western hillside drowned out Elaine's words, followed by a choir of voices lifted in a regal incantation, heralding the arrival of the Blood King. Attracted by the noise, everyone standing on the quadrangle turned to watch. The King's banner appeared on the crest of the hill, fluttering atop a raised spear carried by the Jester on a roan kudo.

'We're too late!' cried Patrick.

A silver dapple kudo descended the eastern hill at speed. As the rider neared the granite slab Jann saw he wore the uniform of the Queen's guard.

'We must go!' insisted Elaine. 'Once the King begins the Bloodcurse we are all lost!'

The Black guard reined to a halt beside the quadrangle.

'The Queen wishes to know why the Elementals have not taken their positions,' he said. 'The ceremony is about to commence.'

Elaine rounded on the rider.

'Has her Majesty not spoken with the Piper?'

He looked momentarily confused.

'The Piper has not yet arrived,' he said. 'We are waiting

on him to start the recital.'

Elaine let out a loud sigh.

'Thank Baka! We have some respite if she was expecting him to lead the choir.'

'Has he been delayed?' asked the Wizard.

'If I'm right he won't be coming at all,' replied Elaine.

The black rider's mount shied, disturbed by another fanfare from the top of the eastern hill. As one, the group turned again to watch. With the sun behind him glistening from his red coronet the King appeared, smiling broadly, his rust-red kudo Anak'Adah tossing his head and stamping on the rocks in front of him.

In the alabaster tower three bells began to ring, heralding the start of the ceremony.

valley of the cataclysm
30th day of ter'bakamasa, 966

As the sound of the trumpets died away and the initial peal of bells concluded, a heavy silence fell across the plain. Claire shivered. Elaine's fire had dried her clothes and warmed her skin but she nursed a bone-deep chill she could neither explain nor alleviate. It made her feel weak and helpless, especially in the company of this new Elemental who had such easy command of his powers, while she still fought to master hers.

Amid the confusion of the last few minutes, one image remained fixed in Claire's mind. Jann Argent wore the amulet her father had given to her in her life-saving dream aboard the Valiant. Dad had said it would show her the way, and it had. No matter what anyone said, Queen or Piper or anyone, she knew Jann and Elaine were right. She was determined they should stick together, whatever happened.

Spectators from both houses now covered the two hillsides, members of the guards in King's and Queen's liveries moving among them. An expectant hush lay over the crowds. Not a single cough disturbed the silence as they waited for the ceremony to unfold.

From the path at the foot of the King's hill, three shrouded figures approached the quadrangle. It seemed to Claire, at this distance, that each wore a strange headpiece. A deep red cowl rising at the front into a thin spike that bobbed and swayed as the mysterious figures walked. As they emerged from the shadow of the hill Claire saw the cowls were not part of the costumes at all. Each one trailed a crimson thread that rose through the air to the summit of the hill, where the King sat on Anak'Adah. He held the threads in his hand like mystical leashes attached to macabre pets.

'What is this?' she asked of no-one in particular. 'Those cords? Those people?'

'From the colour I'd say it was Bloodpower,' said Elaine, 'but I've never seen it used. I don't know what these cloaked golems are, but they're giving me the creeps.'

'It appears they intend to take our places.' said Lautan.

Two of the figures had already taken up positions on the opposite side of the quadrangle. The third approached their group, moving towards Claire who still stood on the Northwest corner—the one designated for the Air Mage. As the mannequin drew near, the thread of Bloodpower connecting it to the King thickened and began to hum. The silent figure lifted back the hood that had hidden its face.

'It's me!' Claire cried in alarm. 'It's meant to be me!'

Now revealed, the figure's features were indistinct, like a shop window dummy or an unfinished head at a waxwork museum. The skin glowed red under the crackling skein of Bloodpower, but even though rudely made the golem was clearly intended to represent Claire.

'They're clones!' said the Wizard. 'I could not understand why there were only three, but they are clones. Copies of we three Elementals. Among us only Petani is missing, and there is no Bloodpower counterpart for

Earth.'

'So that's how the King intends to open the portal!' cried Elaine. 'He doesn't need us at all, except to provide the template for these unnatural duplicates!'

'We have to stop them,' Jann said. 'Elaine?'

Elaine closed her eyes, shutting out the image of the cloned Elementals to concentrate on wielding her power. A moment later she gestured at the clone which now stood on her corner. A tongue of incandescent fire leapt from her hand across the smooth granite surface of the quadrangle towards the figure. It was met by a matching bolt from the hand of the clone, the two flaming jets crashing together in the middle of the plate and bursting in a coruscating explosion of sparks.

'Argh!' cried Elaine, falling to her knees.

'Elaine!' Jann called, rushing to her side and lifting her up.

Horrified by the counter-attack, Claire summoned the wind. Her own duplicate had now approached to within a few metres. She couldn't let it reach its intended position. Fighting down her fear to allow her Elemental energy to flow, she sent a pulse of air shooting towards the hooded figure, intending to knock it from the granite ledge. But she wasn't quick enough. Even before the energy had left her body, the Air clone, with a gesture unfamiliar to Claire, conjured a strong updraft which easily deflected her own attack.

The clone's use of Air power diminished Claire. She felt her energy draining away. She fell to the cold stone with an anguished gasp, half fainting from the sudden exhaustion.

'It's no use!' Elaine said, passing a hand over her face. 'It has all my lore and experience.'

'Mine also,' cried Lautan.

'My clone controls more power than I know how to wield,' Claire sobbed. 'It's like it knows the innermost core of me even I cannot access. And its presence diminishes what little power I have.'

'Yes,' said Elaine. 'Never before has there been more than one Elemental for each discipline. I feel almost schizophrenic, as if I were in two places at once. I have no control over what the clone is doing, but I am constantly aware of it. I'm an observer inside the clone as well as a participant in my own mind.'

'You sum up the situation accurately Bakara,' said the Wizard. 'I have the same thoughts regarding my own clone. My powers are rent in twain. But what are we to do about it? It seems these clones also share the connection with our minds. The two attacks we have attempted have been expected and countered with unnatural haste.'

The arrival of the men of the Blood Watch, who had made their way to the quadrangle with Patrick in tow, pre-empted any answer Elaine may have made.

'Will you now come with us Bakara?' the leader asked. 'Now it is plain your actions are in vain?'

The Elementals looked at each other. In the end Jann spoke for them all.

'We may as well go,' he said. 'We need to regroup. Analyse what we've learned and think of an alternative approach.'

'We do not want any trouble with the exalted ones,' the Pena-lipan added, 'but the King has informed us that if needs be he will instruct the Rohantu to use their powers to persuade your compliance.'

'Rohantu?' asked Claire.

'These beings you see on the quadrangle,' the Pena-lipan explained. 'They are the Rohantu.'

As the commander finished speaking the bells in the alabaster tower began to chime once more.

'Come on,' said Elaine. 'It looks like we don't have much choice.'

Those with kudai mounted up. Lautan chose to summon a standing wave of water beneath his feet and ride on it behind the animals, much to their dismay.

'My memory may not be what it was,' Jann said as they rode from the Valley, 'but this whole ceremony seems much more haphazard than when we were involved. Everything is happening in the wrong order. It's all mixed up.'

'I had the same thought, Gatekeeper,' intoned Lautan from atop his wave.

'And how does the King expect to complete the incantations with only three Elementals?' asked Claire.

valley of the cataclysm
30th day of ter'bakamasa, 966

The strange counterpointed melody of the three lullabies swelled as the orchestra hit its stride, still apparently without a leader. Music boomed out over the Valley and rebounded from the rock faces to set up ever more complex harmonics. The voices of the choir lifted in response to the richness of the music, the whole choral work punctuated by the pealing of the three bells which acted as both back beat and metronome for the increasingly convoluted sound.

Jann looked back towards the Valley floor. The three Rohantu had now reached their allotted corners and were beginning to compel the Elements into action. A circulating wind had picked up dust and small shards of rock that still littered the Valley and teased them into a vortex shape. Elaine's counterpart juggled two large balls of fire in preparation for the magma phase of the enchantment and the Water clone was working to create a shallow moat around his position ready for the final dousing. As yet, without an Earth clone, there was not enough loose stone for the magic to work. Jann had another idea.

'They have no Patrick,' he said.

'What's that you say Gatekeeper?' asked Lautan, a deep gurgle in his throat.

'How are they going to direct the Elements?' Jann went on. 'There is no Pattern Juggler.'

'Yes there is,' said Patrick. 'At least, I am feeling the same schizoid delusions Elaine described. He's here somewhere, he just hasn't stepped onto the quad yet.'

'Yes he has,' said Claire, pointing. 'There.'

They followed Claire's outstretched finger and saw a fourth figure striding to the centre of the granite slab. No thread of Bloodpower connected this golem to the King. Instead it appeared to draw strength from the Elemental clones who surrounded it on three sides.

'Can you use their Elements Pat?' Jann asked. 'Before your counterpart is in place? Can you turn their powers against them?'

'I can try,' said Patrick, reining Jarapera to a standstill and dismounting.

He stood beside his mount, his eyes closed in concentration. Jann looked from his friend to the tableau below and back again, unable to discern any change.

'Are you doing it?'

'Give me chance!' Patrick said, raising his hands to his head. 'I've only done this once before.'

Elaine glared at Jann. He decided against further comment. Down below, a thin skein of flame began to leave one of the orbs in front of the cloned Fire Witch. It knitted itself into a small fireball and shot across the granite towards the new player.

The ersatz Juggler did not react until the fiery bolt had approached to within a few metres. Making a circular gesture with his left arm and a snapped flick of his wrist in Patrick's direction, the red-robed figure sent a pulse of air back at Patrick, so strong it distorted the space through which it passed. The pulse passed over the fire bolt, extinguishing it instantly. Before any of the party could avoid it, the powerful air blast lifted Patrick from his feet and crashed him against the rock face behind. He collapsed to the ground, unconscious.

Jann leapt from his kudo.

'Patrick!' he shouted, kneeling down and lifting his friend's head from the stone.

'Is he OK?' asked Claire. 'Is he hurt?'

Jann checked Patrick over.

'There's no blood. I think he's just been knocked out.'

A low rumble from the landward side of the Valley attracted their attention. Rocks and gravel from the hill had been disturbed by what looked like a small earthquake. They rolled down in a landslide. The kudai shied at the sight, neighing and stamping their hooves on the rock, the whites of their eyes flashing. The King's guards fought to quieten them as a short, stocky figure appeared at the top of the disturbance, sliding down the moving earth as if he too were surfing a wave.

'It's Terry!' said Claire.

'No,' said Jann. 'It can't be.'

'I spent weeks working with him,' Claire insisted. 'I'd know that posture anywhere.'

A few moments later the cascading earth came to a stop. The man began walking towards them. Soil and dust fell from him as he approached until enough of his face had been revealed for Jann to recognise him.

'You're right, it is him!' he said.

'Which gives us all sorts of problems,' said Elaine. 'Look.'

Atop the hill, the King now held four glistening red threads. The new filament stretched to the Southeast corner of the quadrangle where a fourth clone materialised from the ground up, as if pure blood were being poured into a Terry-shaped mould.

'What in Utan's name?' shouted Lautan.

As soon as the arms were formed, even while the head was still taking shape, the copy of Terry raised its upturned hands and began to impel a circle of granite to crack away from the surface of the slab, following the ancient groove that had scarred the quadrangle since the first portal opened sixty years before. As if energised by the appearance of this new material, the Witch clone sent her fire balls into the air where they began to melt the rock into a circulating oval of magma that flew above their heads emitting plumes of smoke into the clear air.

In the space inside the spinning ellipse, the sky darkened. Occluded by the fell power of the ceremony, it could no longer be seen through the gap. The portal was opening once more.

'We're too late!' shouted Jann.

'You should have stayed away Terry,' Elaine said as the old gardener joined the group on the narrow path.

'Apparently, you can call me Petani,' he said, smiling. 'Although it still doesn't sound right to these old ears.'

'Do not lay all the blame at Petani's feet,' Lautan said. 'I did not think it would be possible to open the portal without a Gatekeeper, and the Blood King has yet to make a copy of you Jann Argent.'

Elaine rounded on the Water Wizard.

'Have you not considered that without a Gatekeeper the portal may be even more dangerous than before? When Jann was in place we were all dragged through. If there is no-one controlling the threshold what is to stop some nameless terror coming *in* from Baka knows where?'

Above their heads, in the blackening centre of the oval ring of fire, a few bright stars began to twinkle.

Chapter 20

'If you're going to do something Gatekeeper,' said Lautan, watching the developing vortex above their heads, 'now would be a good time.'

Jann eyed the portal with mounting dread. That part of his mind where the Gatekeeper's lore lived still remained locked to him. Was there anything he could do?

'This scene seems so familiar,' said Terry, 'in one way. And yet different.'

'You picked a bad day for storytelling, Gardener,' snapped Elaine. 'We may well be waking up on Earth again at any moment, mindless, unless we can think of a plan to stop these abominations from completing their work.'

'I'll tell him,' offered Claire.

She put her hand on Jann's arm.

'Try your best. I never believed I could do it when I started. If it's anything like Air power, it feels as if you have nothing until you start looking for it. But it is there, deep inside you. Reach for it. It's the only hope we have right now.'

She took Terry to one side and began bringing him up to speed with what they knew. On the Valley floor, the Witch clone had melted the flying rocks into a miasma of circling fire. The duplicate Wizard continued summoning his black pool of water on the granite surface which Patrick's double would soon deploy to quench the fire. In the sky above them more stars appeared as the portal hovered on the verge of existence, the reality between Berikatanya and the vortex now thin enough to see through.

'Now, Gatekeeper,' urged the Water Wizard.

Jann tried to quieten his mind. To access that

321

innermost part of his essence Claire had seemed so certain he could find. He had never been one for introspection, preferring action over deep thought. Yet now the future of all of his friends, those who had already traversed the portal once and those who had avoided it, or been born on the other side, may depend on his ability to unlock the power he supposedly possessed.

He looked up at the rapidly forming vortex. Tried to remember how it had appeared last time. He hoped the sight of the new anomaly would trigger a memory, just as the Valley scene had opened his mind to knowledge less than two hours ago. It did not. He closed his eyes on the spinning circle of fire, trying to replace the image in his mind with one from his memory. Perhaps the reality of the new vortex occluded the old. Still, he found nothing. Sweat stood out on his brow, a rivulet running from his temple catching reflections of fire from the orbiting miasma.

Without warning, his mind flipped, replacing the memory of the scene he had shut out moments before with something else. Not a memory. At least, not as far as he could tell. This was new. The same shape as the vortex, in the same position, but this new object lay in his mind like an obsidian slab, hovering in the air above them. He knew it was a gateway, although he could perceive no visible evidence. Its gatewayness communicated itself to him on some innate, inexplicable level. A tangible property so obvious as to be irrefutable. And yet, though he tried, he also knew—in the same visceral but unexplainable way—that he would be unable to open it, or see through it, let alone prevent anyone from traversing it in either direction. This new gateway was inherently different from the old. He could not have conveyed why, but it would remain closed to him until those who created it decided to open it.

Jann collapsed to his knees, weakened by the enormous mental effort.

'It's no use,' he said. 'I can't open it, or force it to

remain closed. It is beyond me.'

'You cannot access your powers, Gatekeeper?' asked Lautan, reaching out to help Jann to his feet.

'No, it's not that. I did find something. No idea if it's the whole thing, but I saw enough to show me I wouldn't be able to control it.'

'Then we are lost!' Elaine said.

'Not necessarily, my hot-headed young friend,' said Terry, who had completed his debrief with Claire and been listening to the exchange.

He nodded towards the King, still sat on Anak'Adah at the top of the western hill, his eyes closed as he concentrated to summon the extreme limits of his Bloodpower to complete the reopening of the portal. The lemon-clad figure of the Jester stood in front of the King on the precipice, waving his banner and grinning.

'The ceremony follows a prescribed sequence,' said Terry, measuring his words as if they were shovelfuls of earth. 'Each Elemental has a part to play.'

'Yes, yes, we know that Terry,' snapped Elaine. 'We have all been here before.'

Terry eyed the Witch calmly, a gentle smile creasing the corners of his mouth.

'Indeed we have young lady,' he said. 'And you will therefore, of course, remember that once each player has played the role ascribed to them, they have nothing further to do.'

He paused to allow his meaning to filter through.

'And?' said Elaine.

But Jann had seen where Terry's thoughts were leading.

'You mean, once the first Elemental—Claire's clone— has conjured the wind, then she will not need her powers again?'

'By thunder!' exclaimed Lautan. 'The second and third in sequence are also complete. If those clones are quiescent we may yet be able to counter them!'

Terry held up his hands.

323

'Not so fast! You have caught my drift but there is more to it. The cloned Air Mage is still active, keeping the circle of elements aloft. It is unlikely Claire will have full mastery of her powers. However, now the magma has been created, Elaine and I may be able to achieve something. Enough to allow Claire to contribute with what power she is able to conjure.'

'I do feel stronger, it's true,' said Elaine, her cheeks colouring in embarrassment at her earlier outburst. 'What did you have in mind Petani?'

'Whatever it is, make it quick,' said Jann, pointing into the Valley.

The black pool of water had grown ankle deep. The first fine droplets of spray were being lofted with a combination of Water and Air power. Scant minutes remained for the true Elementals to stop the ring from cracking.

'You are right, young Gatekeeper,' said Terry, turning back into the Valley. 'There is no time to explain my plan. Suffice to say the rocks of the Valley have spoken to me. This is not merely the best place for the portal ceremony. It is the only place. If we can stop it here, today, we will have stopped it for all time.'

He looked at Elaine, Lautan and Claire in turn as he hurried past them.

'Follow my lead,' he called over his shoulder. 'You will know what to do.'

He moved with a speed Jann would never have thought him capable of. Within moments he had attained the Valley floor. He knelt, burying his hands into the soft earth beside the granite slab. Closing his eyes he gave a low roar. A rumbling sound from deep in his chest that reminded Jann of the earthquake they had seen a few minutes before. But where that earlier disturbance had loosened material from the hillside, this time Terry directed his Elemental Earth power down, to the bedrock beneath the Valley.

Seconds later the earth answered his call. The ground trembled and shook as several columns of rock, each as thick as a man's waist, rose like a giant crystal lattice. They grew taller, reaching toward the circle of fiery magma above, new shafts of solid substratum joining them until an earthen cage surrounded the quadrangle on all sides. Barely a hand's breadth separated each of its rocky bars.

'Bring fire, Witch!' Terry called, hardly sparing a breath for the cry to maintain his guttural roar, adding more earth and rock to the gigantic pillars he had created.

Once again, Jann's intuition leapt ahead of Elaine's response. Whether it was a latent Gatekeeper virtue or just a matter of him being on Terry's wavelength, he knew the Gardener's intent as clearly as if the man had given him a written plan.

'Melt it, Elaine!' he shouted. 'The whole pile!'

The Fire Witch did not need a second telling. She bent to her task with such ferocity that the rest of the group had to step back. The men of the Blood Watch, who had long since given up any hope of restraining the Elementals, turned tail, taking flight at this latest display of raw power.

White hot flame coalesced in the air in front of Elaine, flying towards Terry's columns of stone and engulfing them. The topaz stones in her golden bangles shone with a fire of their own while Elaine's torrent of flame continued to pour from the space before her, the Element conjured from nothing by the force of her will. In less than a minute the rock was glowing red hot. Steam escaped from between the shafts. Jann gave out a bark of laughter, forcing Elaine to open her eyes to see what had amused him.

'You've boiled their water!' he cheered. 'Don't stop! They'll never crack the sky now, but don't stop. I know what Terry's doing!'

Elaine shut her eyes once more, the white heat of her concentrated Elemental power soon turning the column to molten lava. It began to sag.

'Air Mage!' called Terry. 'Swiftly!'

'You need to keep it up Claire,' Jann shouted. 'Hold the magma up as long as you can!'

The top of the cage began to close as the molten shafts of stone bent and congealed. The last of the steam from the clones' water blew out through the cracks in the bars as the gaps closed, sealing the duplicate Elementals behind a wall of bubbling lava.

Claire reached out her hands towards the wall, executing a complicated helical gesture that Jann could not follow. Instantly a howling cyclone surrounded the molten rock, its enormous power sucking at the cage walls, twisting and extruding them upwards until the whole edifice filled the centre of the still circling magma.

With a gargantuan grunt Terry buried his arms into the Earth up to his elbows, roaring a slow, rumbling incantation at the dirt beneath his face. At his urging the column of molten rock drove upwards a further ten metres, lancing the ring of magma from the inside. Speared, the circle ground to a halt, settling atop the pillar like a troll queen's coronet.

'Lautan!' called Terry, sweat streaming down his face. 'Now!'

Jann turned to the Water Wizard but the old mage needed no explanation. With his arms upraised and a deep sonorous song that reminded Jann of rolling waves crashing against a rocky coastline, Lautan called up a tsunami from the nearby ocean. Several cubic kilometres of sea water, impelled by the Wizard's call, came funnelling along the Valley floor, breaking on the molten column and emitting vast gouts of steam that hissed and bubbled from the new rock face.

Jann realised they were in danger.

'Claire!' he shouted.

The combination of Claire's gale and Lautan's control over the water carried the enormous wave around the entire circumference of the glowing rock, but the hot, spitting steam was heading directly for the group, threatening to engulf them.

Alerted by Jann's cry, Claire saw the danger. Trusting that the cooling rock would stand up by itself, she executed another arcane gesture and sang a single keening note to deflect her wind along a path between the Elementals and the granite column. The shearing wind cut off the jets of steam with seconds to spare.

The top of the pillar, where the rock had not yet been quenched, bent inwards, severing the Bloodpower threads and sealing the clones inside the rocky cage. A bright ripple of redness raced back up the threads and exploded in the Blood King's hand, shredding the last remnants of the filaments and spattering him with blood. With a cry of immense pain he fell from Anak'Adah, the Bloodpower spent.

Lautan ceased his song. The waters subsided, bubbling and gurgling away into cracks in the Valley floor, or back to the ocean along the now engorged river. As if the heat had been washed from the air, a sudden chill fell over the Valley. Claire altered her melody to a soft lilt, summoning a gentle breeze to dispel the remaining steam. Before them, in the centre of the Valley, a new mountain stood. Fully one hundred metres high, with a thick granite ring encircling its top, the crowned pinnacle had closed the portal, permanently.

valley of the cataclysm
30th day of ter'bakamasa, 966

Patrick Glass opened his eyes. For a moment, he did not know where he was. True, he still lay beside the track halfway up one side of the Valley of the Cataclysm. He had a vague memory of landing here after being knocked from his kudo, but this place in which he had regained consciousness could not be the Valley. It had a mountain where the granite quadrangle should be.

He rubbed his face, willing himself awake. He heard voices from further down the path, beyond a small rise in the hillside.

'A fine monument to your work, Gardener.'

It was the Fire Witch.

'Our work, dear lady. Our work.'

That was Terry's voice! But he had not been here. Patrick shook his head in confusion, before recognising a third speaker.

'Indeed,' Lautan's deep bubbling laugh rolled over the hillock. 'We shall have to rename this Valley henceforth.'

This must be the Valley. Patrick rose, shaking, to his feet. He limped down the path, rubbing a painful bruise on his hip where he had landed.

'What the hell happened?' he asked. 'And when did you get here Terry?'

'Ah, my young friend,' said Terry. 'I am glad to see you're awake once more. You missed quite a spectacle, though I say so myself.'

'We made a mountain!' said Claire, beaming.

'And gave it a crown I see,' said Patrick, smiling back at her. 'Where did the clones go?'

The story of the last hour of the battle was soon told. Before it was done, a black rider approached from the Queen's hill. He waited in silence until the Elementals had finished talking.

'The Queen respectfully requests an audience with the masters of the Elements,' he said, as if reciting a well-prepared speech, 'and offers her sincere gratitude for their help in averting what she now understands could have been a most perilous crisis.'

Elaine looked up to where the Queen still sat unmoving on Pembrang, a splash of purple visible at her side.

'So the Piper finally made an appearance,' she said. 'Good of him to turn up.'

The rider reddened.

'Where is this audience to be held?' Elaine asked.

'If it please Kema'satu, the Queen has asked that you assemble at the entrance to the Valley.'

The kudai having returned to their riders once the terrifying spectacle had subsided, the group mounted up. Terry accepted Claire's offer of a seat behind her on Pembwana.

At the edge of the Valley, now marked with a ragged demarcation line where dead vegetation gave way to greenery instead of a rippling curtain of distorted air, the Black Queen sat waiting on Pembrang. The stallion's breath steamed in the chill that had fallen around the Valley in the wake of the latest cataclysm.

'Greetings exalted ones,' said the Queen, favouring Claire with a happy smile.

'Well done, my dear,' she continued. 'Well done all of you. When the Piper revealed the King's intent I believed we were all lost.'

Patrick looked around.

'Speaking of the King, where is he?' he asked.

If the Queen thought anything of the impudence of being asked a direct question, she did not show it.

'He has of course to travel from the other side of the Valley,' the Queen replied. 'He will be here presently, I'm sure.'

'What did you wish to speak with us about, Majesty?' asked Elaine.

Patrick smiled.

'*Eager to get on with things as always,*' he thought.

'I have no wish to repeat myself,' said the Queen. 'We will await the Blood King.'

'I think he's coming now,' said Claire, looking back towards the Valley.

Sure enough, the King's banner was approaching. After a moment, the sound of his entourage making their way up the hill could be heard. Led by the Jester, the King's kudo, Anak'Adah, appeared over the rise. A murmur passed through the ranks of the Queen's forces as the King came into view, strapped onto a crude litter dragged behind the animal. The Jester guided Anak'Adah around until the stricken King faced the Queen.

'Hail, Ru'ita!' said the King, his hoarse voice barely audible over the noises of the throng.

Patrick had never heard the Queen addressed by her given name before. Judging from the faces of his companions none of them had even been aware she had one. The King's face looked waxen, except for a livid swollen bruise on his temple. His regal costume was torn in several places and soaked with blood. A light sheen of sweat still covered his cheeks and brow, the legacy of his exertions when using the Bloodpower.

'What is the purpose of this?' the King continued, a deep frown creasing his brow. 'My men are weary... and... in need of rest. We would return to Court with all haste. No... need to parlay with you so soon after the latest disaster that has befallen this forsaken place.'

'Befallen, Jadara?' the Queen replied, sitting up straighter in her saddle. 'A strange choice of word given it was your own actions which brought about this new cataclysm.'

A slight blush relieved the King's pallor. He passed a hand over his face, leaving behind an erubescent smudge.

'Had I known—' he began.

'You knew well enough!' snapped the Queen. 'But I have not called this summit to discuss the past! It is the future I am concerned with. Where do we go from here? My people have had enough of this endless bickering...'

A murmur of approval rippled through the Queen's ranks.

'...as, I'm sure, have yours.'

Many of the King's entourage looked embarrassed, avoiding the King's gaze as he scanned the faces of those closest to him. It was clear to Patrick that a majority of them agreed with the Queen but did not dare make any sign of assent.

'We have seen what the combined might of the Elementals can achieve,' the Queen went on, 'even in the face of the ancient and accursed Bloodpower.'

What little colour had returned to the King's cheeks drained away once again as the Queen named the nameless.

'And they too have no desire to remain in balanced servitude to a pair of warring potentates. For myself, I am willing to use the events we have just witnessed as a marker for the end of hostilities. Whatever agreement we may come to, however long the negotiations take, today must be the start of a new era of Berikatanyan peace and prosperity, such as we hoped for many years ago when we first stood on the two hills. An end to fear, war, and famine. What say you?'

The King held the Queen's gaze for several minutes, conflicting thoughts visible on his face. At length he let out a long sigh.

'I am no lover of war,' he said, avoiding the Queen's gaze, 'unlike some of my ancestors. Make your arrangements to negotiate. Start when you will. My advisors will attend in good faith.'

He paused, face contorted in pain.

'For now,' he added, wincing, 'all I wish is rest and some courtly refreshment. Let us depart this desolate place for our homes and lick our wounds for a while before beginning the long task of seeking a way out from under our mutually destructive histories.'

If this rather tepid response from the King disappointed the Queen she did not show it, but instead flashed him a wide smile.

'Very well. Let us depart,' she agreed. 'I shall send word as soon as my advisors are ready to begin.'

With that, she wheeled Pembrang about, turning her back on the King in what Patrick hoped was a conscious gesture of dismissal.

'Come!' she shouted to her throng. 'We leave for the Palace at once!'

A loud cheer rose up from the black mass as they set off. Patrick looked from one of his companions to another.

'What about us?' he asked. 'Where are we going?'

'You heard the Queen,' said Elaine. 'Although I had not thought of it until she voiced it, she speaks the truth. I have no desire to remain in service with that blood-letting bastard.'

'I think he can do without me in his Court guard,' said Jann.

'Come back with me,' Claire urged. 'The Queen would love to entertain you all at the Palace, I'm sure.'

'You will forgive me,' bubbled Lautan. 'After all these years I am unused to maintaining human form for long. It makes me ache for the ocean. I will see you all again ere long, but for now I must take to the waters once more and recover my strength.'

With that he dissolved into a short-lived fountain of clear water that drained away through the grass and down the hill in the direction of the Lum-segar Sea.

'For myself, I would love to see the Palace again,' said Jann, eliciting a beaming smile from the young Air Mage.

Patrick said nothing. From the body language of the group it seemed obvious Jann had spoken for them all. They turned their kudai north-east and rode after the Queen towards the Palace of Kertonia.

tunnels of the blood lake
2nd day of run'bakamasa, 966

A hubbub resounded in the smoky room, the clamour of multiple conversations bouncing from the old stone walls as if the chamber were filled with a hundred voices rather than two dozen. In front of each animated speaker a foaming flagon of ale sat on the heavy wooden table, its notches full of spilt brew giving further testament to the energy with which the denizens prosecuted their many points of view, reflected torchlight shining in the sweat of their faces.

'Order!' shouted the bearded man at the head of the table. 'Order! I cannot hear myself think!'

'We don't need to hear it' growled the man to his left. 'We can see the cogs going round.'

A roar of laughter greeted this weak joke, providing yet more evidence of the inebriated state of most of the attendees.

'Never mind "order",' shouted a second, 'where's the friggin' Piper?'

'Here,' said the Piper, already halfway down the stone staircase and unremarked before now on account of the heated debates that had filled the room.

'Mungo!' called the first man.

'About time!' said the second.

'Yes, well I make no apologies for lateness,' said the Piper, completing his descent. 'If you had seen what I have seen you would know I am lucky to be here at all.'

Ignoring the offer of a full tankard, he took a seat at the other end of the table from Beard. A hush descended as he took his seat, all eyes on him, their owners eager for news from the Valley.

'There is a new entente between the two Houses,' he began.

'A new what?' called a voice from the back of the room.

'Let him speak,' said Beard, holding up a hand. 'And get a dictionary.'

The Piper allowed the ripple of amusement to subside.

'A new accord,' he said. 'A new understanding. Or should I say, there soon will be. At the Queen's insistence, there are to be talks between the Houses with the aim of ushering in an era of peace.'

There was a moment's stunned silence while they

digested the information before the room erupted again in a cacophony of questions and expletives.

'My arse!'

'As if.'

'Who says?'

'I don't believe it!'

'What about the Elementals?'

Again the Piper allowed the melee to subside. After a few moments he held up his hands.

'Enough. Clearly our plan to evacuate the Elementals once more through the portal has been thwarted. The Bloodpower, at least under the control of the King, proved insufficient to withstand their onslaught. The fool controlled the blood clones well enough, but he failed to keep them busy. Once the real mages were able to recover use of their powers...'

His sentence hung in the air while its intent seeped into the minds of the attendees.

'What has been done with the blood clones now?'

'That, my friend, is a tale for another day and it will be long in the telling. For now, suffice to say they are... beyond reach. And though I understand little of its workings, I believe such Bloodpower as the King deployed to conjure them has gone with them to their stony grave.'

'Where is Jeruk? He must hear of this!'

'Jeruk has seen everything I have seen. He was also present later when the Queen made her request, and the King acceded. I am sure he will reveal his interpretation of events and his future plans for us all once he arrives.'

'He is coming?'

'No!' said a loud voice from the top of the stairs. 'He is here!'

All eyes turned to the staircase, from the top of which there shone a pale golden light: the reflection of a dozen flaming torches from the bright yellow costume of Jeruk Nipis as he descended the stone stairs into the meeting room of the Puppeteers.

'Welcome, leader,' said Beard, getting up from his seat and bowing low. 'I defer to you.'

He backed away from the Jester and took a seat further down the table, displacing one of the others. The Jester circumnavigated the table, regarding each of the Puppeteers with an angry expression, until he came to a stop at the head of the table. He leant on the ancient wood, staring at the wet, empty space where Beard's ale flagon had stood.

'We will all need clear heads if we are to deal with the situation that now faces us,' he said.

He took his seat, looking across the table at the Piper.

'How much have you told them?'

'Only that the Queen is arranging talks,' the Piper replied. 'To end the war.'

The Jester barked a sarcastic laugh.

'To end the war! Yes, peace between the Houses. A laudable aim. Or should that be laughable?'

A subdued and nervous murmur of laughter passed around the room.

'Well that bitch can parlay all she likes,' the Jester went on. 'Our plans to cast the hated Elementals from our world once and for all may have been thwarted this time, but that has only strengthened my resolve. Our work has only just begun.'

'What can we do Jeruk?' asked Beard. 'We have no power to stand against the Elements.'

His words were greeted with a murmur of assent.

'Darik speaks the truth Jeruk,' said another. 'Even the Bloodpower was not enough to overthrow the Elements.'

The storm on the Jester's face broke.

'There is power,' he murmured, a silence falling over the assembly as everyone strained to hear his words.

'We must seek it out,' he went on. 'The power of legend and myth. Did you think we would just sit back and accept that nothing has changed? What are we doing here? Our aim is unchanged. This is a minor setback. We will find a way to prevail. Over the Elementals. Over the Blood King. And most of all over that black bitch in her Palace. We are the rightful rulers of this world and we will take it back, even if we have to work with the arriviste Batu'n to do it.'

'That power you speak of,' said the Piper. 'How can you be certain it exists?'

The Jester stared hard across the table at the Piper.

'Do not doubt me, Mungo,' he said. Several of those seated close to the Jester paled at the chill in his words.

'I have not spent these long years listening to the drivel that pours from the mad King's mouth and giving him every sensible thought he has ever laid claim to, only to have power snatched from my grasp at the final hour! There must be a way to rid ourselves of these insects. And we will find it.'

palace of the black queen
3rd day of run'bakamasa, 966

A bright shaft of morning sunlight cut across Claire Yamani's pillow and into her waking dream. She'd been walking arm in arm with Jann Argent along a beach of crystal white sand, the azure breakers crashing beside them and a group of pale blue gulls calling in a clear sky. She stretched beneath the heavy quilt, rose from her bed, and walked to the window.

In the courtyard outside, the artisans and domestics had already started their daily tasks, preparing breakfast or packing their carts for market. The sun burned in a sky almost as blue as the one in her dream. She smiled at the lack of even the gentlest of breezes on this fine day. The time was long gone when she'd been unable to control her powers. Locals still teased her about the months of windy days they'd suffered, but now she'd learned mastery of her talent and could legitimately call herself the Air Mage. The Berikatanyan weather had resumed its normal pattern and summer was upon them.

In the days following the events in the Valley, which Kertonians had started to refer to as the Clone Rout, the Palace thrummed with new hope. Ordinary folk, gentry and warriors alike welcomed the forthcoming mediation talks. Since Elaine and Terry had forsaken the King's service, Claire had enjoyed the company of the other Elementals. Even the mysterious Lautan had visited once, rising unannounced from the Palace moat late one evening and drenching the three of them as they sat on a low wall sharing their stories of the Clone Rout. Claire smiled again at the memory of Elaine's mock outrage that she'd had to dry them out yet again, but they'd all been so happy to see the Water Wizard again no-one could stay cross for long.

The large stable door on the other side of the courtyard opened. Perak stepped out onto the cobbles, led by Jann Argent.

'*If he's going for a ride,*' Claire thought, '*maybe I can go with him. We may yet have chance for my dream walk along the beach.*'

She snatched up a wrap to cover her nightdress and rushed downstairs.

'Good morning!' she called as she ran into the yard, but although Perak still stood beside the stable door, Jann had disappeared.

He emerged moments later from a store-room, carrying an enormous back pack. Claire stopped, her dream memory of a romantic beach walk forgotten.

'Going somewhere?' she asked.

Jann shielded his eyes from the glare of the low morning sun.

'Yes,' he said, 'but I wouldn't have left without saying goodbye.'

'Goodbye?' said Claire, crossing the courtyard at a slow walk. 'Where are you going? How long for?'

He laughed.

'Always so many questions!'

He swung his pack from his back and began fixing it

behind his saddle. Perak snorted, as if eager to be going.

'I can't really answer them Claire,' he said, avoiding her gaze. 'Oh, it's not a secret,' he went on as she began to protest. 'I can't tell you because I don't know. Either where I'm going or for how long.'

'But—'

'I was useless at the Valley. You were all brilliant, but I... I could feel that there was something I should be doing. Something I *could* do, if only I'd been able to work out how. I thought I'd recovered all my memories, but...'

He shrugged.

'There's still so much missing. I have to find it.'

'And you think it's out there?' Claire asked, waving her hand at the Palace gates.

Jann smiled.

'Maybe not. But it's not here. There are too many distractions. I need to get away. I need time to—'

'Find yourself?' said Claire, hating the petulance in her voice but unable to prevent it. Her dream was receding again like it always did.

'Find who I really am on this world,' he said. 'I'm not a Court guard. That was only ever temporary, and if the Queen gets her way there'll be no need for guards anyway. Except maybe for ceremonials, and I've had enough of them. I'm not a prisoner, and I'm not "the Gatekeeper"— whatever that means. So what am I?'

'My friend?'

Jann finished strapping his pack. He pulled Claire into a tight hug.

'Of course. I'll always be that. But I can't stay here right now. You do understand?'

Claire couldn't answer right away. She didn't trust her voice. She distracted herself with stroking Perak's strong neck, breathing in the dusty scent of the kudo and blinking back a sudden tear.

'Yes,' she said at length. 'What kind of a friend would I be if I tried to stop you?'

He smiled again, checked Perak's traces, and climbed into the saddle.

'I will be back,' he said. 'Eventually.'

'Do the others...?'

'I said my goodbyes last night,' he said, 'after you'd retired. You're the last one. I was about to come and find you when you found me instead.'

'Can I ride with you for a while?'

'Best not,' he said. 'I'm heading north over Temmok'Dun. To whatever is there.'

'Temmok'Dun? The Wall of the World?'

Claire shivered. The morning no longer felt so warm.

'Yes. I'll need to make good time over the mountains. I have no idea if I'll reach a decent camping spot before nightfall.'

Claire stroked Perak one last time.

'Bye beautiful,' she whispered in his ear. The kudo lifted his head and snickered.

'Bye then,' she said to Jann.

'See you soon, Sakti,' he smiled, turning Perak's head and spurring him forward into a gallop.

Claire followed them to the Palace gate. She watched as kudo and rider travelled down the stony path, heading West towards the river crossing. A broad savannah lay between the river and the foothills of Temmok'Dun. She watched until she could no longer make out even the dust thrown up by Perak's hooves, and she continued to gaze at the speck of rock they had ridden over until a cloud passed over the face of the sun and another cold shiver ran through her blood.

...oooOooo...

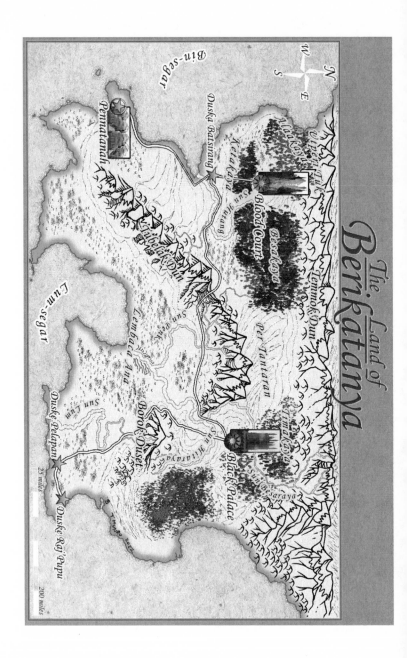

Glossary

Air Mage
The Elemental who controls Air

Airena
A combat arena on the prison moon of Phobos whose atmosphere is held in place by a hemispherical field arc and within which gravity is reduced to half Earth-normal

Alaakaya
Forest behind the Court ("Medium wood")

Albert Yamani
Claire Yamani's father

Anak'Adah
The Red King's kudo – rust-red stallion

Baka
The god of the Fire Element

Bakamasa
"Fire season" – the Berikatanyan equivalent of Summer

Bakara
Elemental name for the Fire Witch

Barawa fish
A blue fish, considered a delicacy

Batugan
Of, or pertaining to, the Batu'n

Batu'n
Berikatanyan term for Earth people (both languages)

Berikatanya
Local name for the colonised planet, home to the Elementals & Princips

Besakaya
Berikatanyan forest, part of which is undergoing the Forest Clearance Project ("Great wood")

Bin-segar
Wild Sea

Black Queen
Unofficial title of the ruler of Kertonia

Borok Duset
Eastern Mountain ("Devil's Boil")

Bumerang
A Berikatanyan fruit, red in colour and similar to an apple

Buwangah
Cloud fruit wine

Car'Alam
Berikatanyan term for the Ceremony that led to the opening of the vortex

Celapi
Berikatanyan musical instrument similar to a guitar

Cellbike
Delivery vehicle for participants in the Tournament on the

prison moon of Phobos

Claire Yamani
Daughter of Albert and Nyna Yamani who makes the journey to Perse aboard the Valiant

Court
Home of the King of Istania

Dauntless
Prism ship – intended to be the last ship to make the journey to Perse – under construction at the time of this story

David Garcia
Team leader of the forest clearance project

Dunela
Berikatanyan vegetable

Duntang
Berikatanyan equivalent of a potato

Elaine Chandler
Fire poi artiste with Miles Miller's Marvellous Manifestations travelling circus who later makes the journey to Perse aboard the Valiant

Elemental
A supreme mage who can control a single Element. Leader of the corresponding Guild

Endeavour
Prism ship – the first to make the journey to Perse

Endurance
Prism ship – intended to be the third to make the journey to Perse, but destroyed by a failure of its Prism drive

Felice Waters
Senior officer at the Earther planetary immigration station at Pennatanah Bay

Fire Witch
The Elemental who controls Fire

Ghantu
Berikatanyan bird that lives in woodlands. Known for its screeching call

Gravnull
A technology that nullifies gravity, allowing vessels equipped with it to hover. Used in planetary flight, not for space travel

Guild
An assembly of Mages

Hodak
A rank in the Queen's forces

Infradone
Drug invented by Torsten Vogler

Intrepid
Prism ship – the second to make the journey to Perse

Istania
Local name for the Red King's realm

Jambala
Berikatanyan fruit, often juiced to make a refreshing drink

Jann Argent
Phobos inmate who later makes the journey to Perse aboard the Valiant

Jaranyla
The name of Elaine's kudo – chestnut mare ("Horse of the Flame")

Jarapera
The name of Patrick Glass's kudo ("Horse of the Artisan")

Jester
Principal advisor to the Red King

Jojo grass
Tall Berikatanyan grass often dried and fed to animals

Juggler
See Pattern Juggler

Kaytam
Black wood native to Berikatanya

Kedu-Bul
Smaller of the two moons of Berikatanya

Keeper of the Keys
Custodian of the Court keys, and ceremonial costumes

Kema'katan
The "power pulse" air spell

Kemasara
a generic honorific title conferred out of respect (in Istania). Literally "eminence"

Kema'satu
An honorific title conferred on Elementals out of respect (in Kertonia), literally translated as "force of nature"

Kertonia
Local name for the Black Queen's realm

Ketakaya
Forest between Penatannah and the King's Court ("Small wood")

Ketiga Batu
Berikatanyan term for Earth (both languages)

Kinchu
Small Berikatanyan herbivore similar to a rabbit

Kuclar
Big cat, native to Berikatanya, that habitually lives in forested areas

Kudo (pl: kudai)
Berikatanyan word for horse (in both Istanian and Kertonian)

Lautan
Elemental name for the Water Wizard

Lem Tantaran
Valley Plain

Lembaca Ana
Berikatanyan name for the Valley of the Cataclysm. Location of the original Car'Alam ceremony which opened the vortex.

Looper Feldsen
Phobos inmate who opposes Jann Argent in his final attempt at the Tournament

Lum-segar
The ocean at the mouth of the Valley ("Mud Sea")

Malamajan
The rain that habitually falls on Berikatanya once the sun has fully set ("Night rain")

Mizar
One of the major rivers of Berikatanya. It rises in the foothills of Tubelak'Dun and flows through the forest of Besakaya before reaching the western coast.

Negel
Rider who accompanies Claire to the Palace

Nembaka
One of the Berikatanyan natives working on the forest clearance project

Nerka jugu
Berikatanyan expletive (literally "hell's teeth")

Nyna Yamani
Claire Yamani's mother

Pac Sau'dib
Claire's tutor

Palace
Home of the Queen of Kertonia

Parapekotik
Court musicians' town

Patrick Glass
Graphic designer who later makes the journey to Perse aboard the Valiant and befriends Jann Argent

Pattana
One of the Berikatanyan natives working on the forest clearance project

Pattern Juggler
Controller of Elemental forces during the Car'Alam ceremony. Capable of directing forces to achieve particular aims, but not of generating those forces in the first place

Pembrang
The name of Black Queen's kudo – black stallion ("Black Rider")

Pembwana
The name of Claire's kudo – black mare ("Bearer of the Wind")

Pena-lipan
A rank in the Red King's forces

Pennatanah
Earther Landing point (Land of the newcomer)

Pennatanah Bay
Landing site for the colony program

Per Tantaran
The battle plain on the border of Kertonia and Istania

Pera-Bul
Larger of the two moons of Berikatanya

Perak
The name of Jann Argent's kudo – silver stallion

Perse
The colony planet first targeted by humanity

Petani
Elemental name for the controller of Earth power

Pilgrim
Character who inhabits the Valley of the Cataclysm

Piper
Principal advisor to the Black Queen

Princips
Generic term for senior courtiers / landowners / Blood King & Black Queen

Prism drive
See Wormwood star drive

Prism ship
Colony ships powered by the Wormwood "Prism" drive

Pun'Akarnya
The New Mountain

Racun
A poison secreted by the glands of several Berikatanyan animals

Rebusang
The meat stew eaten at the forest clearance

Red King
Unofficial title of the ruler of Istania. Also "Blood" King

Remalan
Months

Rohantu
The blood clones. Literally "soul phantom"

Sakti Udara
Elemental name for Air Mage

Sana
The god of the Air Element

Sanamasa
"Air season" – the Berikatanyan equivalent of Winter

Sangella
Claire's maidservant

Seba-tepak
A rank in the Red King's forces

Sickmoss
A variety of Berikatanyan moss that induces violent and immediate nausea on contact

Suhiri
The Berikatanyans name for mages who are not Elementals

Su'matra
Berikatanyan name for the people

Sunyok
A Berikatanyan eating tool

Tana
The god of the Earth Element

Tanamasa
"Earth season" – the Berikatanyan equivalent of Autumn

Te'banga
The agreement between Elementals whereby they divide their loyalties and efforts evenly between the ruling houses

Tema'gana
Istanian equivalent of Kema'satu

Temmok'Dun
Northern Mountains ("Wall of the World")

Tepak
A rank in the King's honour guard. Equivalent to an army captain.

Terry Spate
Horticulturalist and gardener who later makes the journey to Perse aboard the Valiant and befriends Claire Yamani

Torsten Vogler
Phobos inmate who defeats Jann Argent during his second attempt at the Tournament

Tournament
A knockout combat competition held regularly on the prison moon of Phobos whose eventual winner is released. Inmates are allowed three attempts.

Trapweed
A rapidly growing form of plant life, similar to bindweed but much stronger and faster growing. It reacts to any movement by wrapping itself around the unwary intruder.

Tuakara
Fire Witch at the time the Te'banga was first agreed. Distant ancestor of the current Fire Witch

Tubelak'Dun
Western Mountains ("Spine of the World")

Umtanesh
One of the Berikatanyan natives working on the forest clearance project

Utamasa
"Water season" – the Berikatanyan equivalent of Spring

Utan
The god of the Water Element

Utperi'Tuk
Coastal region where the Fire Witch attempts to summon the Water Wizard ("Sea Nymph's Cove")

Valiant
Prism ship – the third to make the journey to Perse

Valley of the Cataclysm
see Lembaca Ana

Water Wizard
The Elemental who controls Water

Wormwood star drive
Propulsion system for the colony ships which reaches near-light speed. Known colloquially as the "Prism" drive since it focuses energy through a series of extremely dense prisms.

Berikatanyan Calendar

Although the day length on Berikatanya is virtually the same as on Earth, the planet orbits farther out, making the year much longer. Seasons are named for the four main Elemental gods:

God	Season name	Earth equivalent
Water	Utamasa	Spring
Fire	Bakamasa	Summer
Earth	Tanamasa	Autumn
Air	Sanamasa	Winter

Each season is divided into four periods of thirty days, which may be thought of as equivalent to Earth months. Indeed the concept of month has, over the time since the first Prism ship, transferred into Berikatanyan culture especially in the centres of civilisation.

The periods are named for their position in the season:

Period	Name	Derivation
1	Far	The "dawn" of the season
2	Ter	The "rising" of the season
3	Run	The "falling" of the season
4	Sen	The "dusk" of the season

So the first month of Spring would be Far'Utamasa and the third month of Autumn would be Run'Tanamasa. Here's a handy look-up table:

Season Period:	Far	Ter	Run	Sen
Utamasa	1	2	3	4
Bakamasa	5	6	7	8
Tanamasa	9	10	11	12
Sanamasa	13	14	15	16

ABOUT THE AUTHOR

Since the first time a story of his made the rest of the English class screw up their faces in horror and disgust, John Beresford wanted nothing more than to write. He was 12. Later that year he came second in a sponsored writing competition with a short story about how the Sphinx is really a quiescent guardian against alien invaders. He won £10. That was big bucks in 1968.

For more than three decades, real life stepped in between him and his writing. During a 35+ year career in computing he wrote dozens of design documents, created and delivered presentations to audiences from 1,000 technical experts to a handful of board members, interviewed innumerable technical candidates and taught core skills and development subjects to many younger colleagues through both formal courses and ad-hoc coaching.

But all that was really just a way to hone skills that might be useful as a writer. And, of course, to pay the bills and support the family. A man's gotta do...

In 2001 John woke up to the passage of time and decided to get serious about writing before it was too late. His first novel – War of Nutrition – took 7 years of spare time to write and after a series of rejections from traditional publishers was self-published for Kindle in 2012.

Since beginning that first novel, John has also created work as a songwriter, screenwriter, freelance TV reviewer and playwright.

Gatekeeper is John's second novel. Now retired from the computing industry, he writes full time, and is working on a second trilogy set on Berikatanya.

Connect with John online:
Facebook: https://www.facebook.com/garretguy
Twitter: https://twitter.com/#!/garretguy
Web site: http://www.johnberesford.com/

Manufactured by Amazon.ca
Acheson, AB

13583612R00210